Toledot

Toledot

Post-Self book II

Madison Scott-Clary

Also by Madison Scott-Clary

Arcana — A Tarot Anthology, ed.

Rum and Coke — Three Short Stories from a Furry Convention

Eigengrau — Poems 2015-2020

ally

Post-Self
I. *Qoheleth*
II. *Toledot*
III. *Nevi'im*

Sawtooth
Restless Town
A Wildness of the Heart

Learn more at *makyo.ink/publications*

ISBN: 978-1-948743-23-5

Toledot

Cover © Iris Jay, 2021 — irisjay.net

First Edition, 2021. All rights reserved.

This book uses the fonts Gentium Book Basic, Gotu and Linux Biolinum O and was typeset with X$\exists$LATEX.

Content Warning: themes of suicide, manipulation, and abuse.

Esau said, "I am about to die; of what use is a birthright to me?"
Jacob said, "Swear to me first."
So he swore to him, and sold his birthright to Jacob.

— Genesis 25:32-33

Part I

Departure

Ioan Bălan—2325

The first thing that Ioan did when ey arrived before that low-slung house, there among countless acres of rolling buffalo grass, was laugh.

The prairie was as ey remembered. Grass tickled at eir lower calves even through the socks and slacks; clouds threatened rain as they always did; wind tugged at eir hair in all the very same ways it first had however many years ago now—was it really twenty? And yet the house! Banners were hung about in deepest black, streamers running from pole to pole in a welcoming path, guiding visitors. The house itself was lit about with flames of all sizes: tea-lights scattered among the dandelions, elaborate candelabras set upon tables, braziers set upon tripods, wall sconces set beneath the cantilevered roof. A glow painting the grass beside the house suggested a bonfire out back.

And there, the largest banner of them all, draped from that roof, shouted in stately capitals: "HAPPY DEATH DAY".

Still shaking eir head, ey walked up along the streamer-lined path up toward the house. When the threshold was crossed, a chime sounded from within.

Ioan need not have looked hard for Dear; the fox was already sprinting around the corner of the house. Foxes, ey realized, for as it ran, it forked off copies of itself of all sorts: that iridescent fennec ey remembered, yes, but also scampering foxes no larger than a double-handful, a few grinning copies of the Michelle

Hadje of its past, and even a shoulder-high lumbering beast with eyes that crackled with a light of their own.

Dear—the real Dear—was easy to pick out, for it was dressed in mourners' garb. A black suit, almost-but-not-quite masculine, with its eyes hidden by a gauzy black, almost-but-not-quite feminine veil.

One by one, the various forks quit, and Dear, Also, The Tree That Was Felled skidded to an unceremonious stop in front of the historian.

"Ioan! Mx. Ioan Bălan! It has been too long! I have missed you." The fox held out a paw.

Ioan bypassed this and went straight for the hug. "Dear, this is patently ridiculous."

The laughter against eir ear was giddy as the hug was returned. *"I hold no patent on the ridiculous. It is precisely as ridiculous as it needs to be. Come! Come around back. You are early, and that is perfectly fine, but folks will want to say hi."*

Following after the fox and laughing at the way the occasional non-anthropomorphized fennec would blip into being, scamper into the grass with a (frankly rather horrifying) screech, and then disappear, Ioan tried to chat with Dear.

The fox was short on speech after the greeting, eventually hushing em. *"We'll all talk together."*

"Ioan! Goodness!"

Ey smiled. "Codrin, you're looking well."

What similarities the two had borne early on had since started to blur. Codrin had started out, as a matter of absent-mindedness, an identical copy of Ioan. While Dear could fork out all the unexpected shapes it wanted, Ioan had never mastered the art. Time changes much, however, and eir up-tree fork had deviated in style from Ioan's stolid adherence to form. Codrin's hair had long-since grown past Ioan's tousled look, and the curls ey hated so much adopted as an integral part of em. Eir face, too, had changed, adopting a femininity that suited eir features. The warm-colored sarong and tunic ey had last seen em in, however, had been replaced with clothes as funereal as Dear's.

Matching, Ioan realized. They were a triad now, Codrin, Dear, and Dear's partner, and ey supposed there was no reason that the three of them shouldn't match on their so-called death day.

There were hugs all around, and Ioan hid eir secret smile at the uncanny act of embracing one's own fork, however far they had diverged.

"How are you three? Excited?"

"Nervous is more like it." Dear's partner laughed. "At least, I am. I can't speak for Codrin, but Dear hasn't shut up about this for months."

The fox looked quite proud of itself. *"Guilty."*

Ioan looked to Codrin, who shrugged. "I play the moderate, as always. I'm nervous and excited in equal parts. The nervousness comes from the irreversibility, and the excitement from the inevitability."

"Ey has a way with words, as always. I have been unable to be nervous, even about the irreversibility."

"A new project, then?" Ioan guessed.

It smiled wryly. *"You know me well. Yes, I cannot seem to think of anything else. Fewer things in life than we imagine are truly irreversible. Time is the one that everyone thinks of, and whenever they name some other process in life that seems irreversible, it really boils down to the ways in which it is bound by time. Breathing? Digestion? Aging? Death? All time-bound aspects that only bear the semblance of irreversibility.*

"And yet we have short-circuited so much of that here. We have found ways to take time and set aside some of the constraints that it puts on those processes. Breathing, digestion, and aging are all optional, and death, as we must know, is something that must be chosen. Even then, a true death remains elusive. Perhaps we quit and merge down tree, but is that death? Perhaps all of our instances quit, but even this lacks some of the savor that a true death contains."

"You're declaiming again."

Dear stuck its tongue out at its partner, a gesture that bordered on cute on that vulpine face.

Its partner laughed. "It took you a surprisingly short time."

"It has already been established that I am excited. Permit me this." After a pause, it continued. *"Now, however, we have been permitted the wonder and curiosity that drives so many images of the afterlife. Now, we get as close as ever to knowing that an afterlife exists, and ghosts will speak to us from beyond the heavens."*

"For a time," Codrin said.

"For a time, and even that carries with it the irreversibility of time."

The ideas touched on some subconscious musing that Ioan had carried with emself ever since the choice to remain had been made, and the group settled into a silence broken only by the crackling of logs on the bonfire. Ey didn't know what the others were thinking, there in the flickering light, but for em, the weight of that decision settled at last on em, and eir thoughts scattered before the implications.

Ey had made eir own irreversible choice, and while ey knew that ey could technically reverse it up until that final point of no return later this evening, ey knew that ey would not.

"Ioan?"

Ey realized that the triad were staring at them. Ey shook eir head to dispel the rumination. "Sorry. Yes?"

"Where is May Then My Name?" Dear's partner asked.

"Here."

Four heads turned to watch the skunk, similar to Dear in so many ways but for species, pad around the corner. She smiled apologetically and bowed. "Sorry I am late."

Dear brightened and bounced up to the skunk, part of its own clade, and once she stood straight again, hugged her. *"My dear, a pleasure as always."*

Ioan waited for Dear to release May Then My Name Die With Me before getting eir own hug. After, she looped her arm through eirs, letting em play the escort and settling into a familiar pattern of constant touch.

"Glad you could make it," Dear's partner said.

"I would not miss it for the world. Besides, I am one of the honored guests, right?"

Codrin smiled. "We've only invited honored guests."

"Of course! And here come more."

For the next hour, the chime of arrival was near constant as guest after guest arrived. Much of the Ode Clade showed, though Ioan noted that some of the more conservative members were absent, grudges remaining even to this day. Michelle Hadje herself, the root instance, was notably absent, and a tug of still-unprocessed emotions pulled at the insides of eir chest.

Ioan had only met her once before, shortly before this whole plan had been set in motion. She was unfailingly kind, though if madness rode the whole of her clade, it seemed to affect her deeper than the rest. She was often taken by long silences, sometimes in the middle of sentences. During these, she lost coherence, her form rippling and changing, waves of skunk rolling down her form, followed by equally tumultuous waves of her human self. These spells would last anywhere from a few seconds to a few minutes, and even after they were quelled and the conversation resumed, afterimages of mephit muzzle and ears would ghost suddenly into place and just as quickly disappear.

After that visit, Ioan had asked Dear about them. Its features darkened and it had averted its gaze. *"We all have our ways of dealing with loss. She could seek change if she wanted, but...it is complicated."*

It was rare for the fox to leave a thought unfinished, but Ioan could not think of a way to ask it to continue.

While every guest was noteworthy in their own way, a few names stood out to em. Dear's sibling instance, Serene; Sustained And Sustaining, arrived, a deranged grin on her face as she ran directly at Dear and tackled it, the two foxes wrestling briefly on the ground before standing up and dusting themselves off again, both laughing.

"I cannot believe you are going to destroy this place, you asshole. I spent weeks on the grass alone!"

Dear grinned lopsidedly. *"It is not yours anymore, however, and I am a sucker for grand gestures."*

"Some gesture!"

"Asshole, remember?"

Serene had arrived with her and Dear's down-tree instance, That Which Lives Is Forever Praiseworthy. The entire clade, all one hundred of them, had each taken a line from a poem for their names, the shortest of which was What Right Have I, and the longest The Only Time I Know My True Name Is When I Dream, a jumble of syllables often shortened to just True Name. Both were present.

Ioan was surprised by a guest who arrived late in the evening when the champagne and wine were already flowing. Simien Fang, the head of an institute that both Dear and Ioan had worked for at times in the past, made his appearance in classic understated style. He was dressed in all black, but only when viewed head on. He had apparently made an agreement with Dear to allow the occupants of the sim's vision to be modified such that when viewed out of the corner of the eye, his outfit flashed in a whirlwind of phosphene colors. Not only that, but his normally calm features distorted into a devilish grin, no matter the expression seen directly.

The party rolled on inevitably. Good conversation, good wine, good food, good company.

And riding along with it, a sense of impending change, of anxiety and excitement in unequal measure.

A sudden peal of thunder, louder than any Ioan had ever heard, brought silence in its wake.

"It is time! It is time! Please gather around the fire!" Excitement filled Dear's voice, though Ioan thought ey could now detect a hint of nervousness that had not been there before. *"There is no time for speeches, there is no time for goodbyes! It is time!"*

The fox forked off several copies, all wide-eyed and feral-grinned, who helped to herd the hundred-and-change guests into a loose ring around the bonfire with shoves and snapping teeth before quitting.

Ioan and May Then My Name took up places about a third of the way around the fire from Dear and its partners, the better to see without flames in the way.

The triad stepped forward, and the circle closed behind them. Each forked in turn, the forks bowed, and disappeared.

The weight of inevitability began to crest as midnight reared its head.

The three within the circle began to sing.

> Should old acquaintance be forgot
> and never brought to mind?

Something about their posture forbid everyone else from joining in just yet. Their voices were raw, earnest all the same, carrying above the roar and crackle of the fire.

> Should old acquaintance be forgot
> and auld lang syne?

Ioan realized that ey was crying, that May Then My Name was crying, that many in the circle were crying, and when Dear raised its arms to the sky, all the gathered attendees around the fire began to sing as one.

> For auld lang syne, my dear,
> for auld lang syne.
> We'll take a cup of kindness yet,
> For auld lang–

Before the final note of the song could be sung, Dear gave a jaunty salute, bowed with a flourish, and quit along with its partner and Codrin Bălan.

With a deafening silence, the landscape around them immediately crumbled into voxels, those voxels joined together by powers of two, and with a soft chime, a descending minor triad, all the members of the party were shunted off to wherever they called home.

Ioan stumbled and fell to eir knees on the parquet of eir entryway, May Then My Name standing, defiant against the change in scenery, in air and light and gravity, beside em.

"What an asshole," she laughed.

Ioan and the skunk let the intoxication of the night cling to them a while longer while they sat on the balcony of Ioan's house, overlooking that perpetually lilac-scented yard, and talked. They talked of the party, of the modern house on the prairie, of Dear and the contradiction of formal intensity and playfulness that it seemed to embody, and then they talked of nothing at all as they sat in silence.

It did not seem time yet to snap sobriety into being.

It had taken Ioan several weeks to get used to the skunk's affectionate nature. When she first moved in as the intensity of the project began to ramp up, it had taken em by surprise. Even the act of her moving in was unexpected and new. Ey had needed to have a series of awkward conversations discussing boundaries and intentions.

Now, it had become comfortable and familiar. May Then My Name was as she should be and Ioan had grown to enjoy that.

As she slouched against eir side on that bench swing and ey settled eir arm around her, ey asked, "What's the story behind your fork? Or your stanza?"

"Mm?"

"Well, Dear said that it and Serene were forked when their down-tree instance wanted to explore an interest in instances and sims. Is there something like that which led to...to whatever your down-tree instance forking?" Ey supposed that, were ey sober, ey might have better luck dredging up the lines from the stanza. Something about true names and God.

May Then My Name shrugged, shoulder shifting against Ioan's side. "In the early days, I—Michelle, that is—did not have much direction to her forking. Forks were created at need essentially to handle the increased workload. The first ten were created all at once in a burst of activity so that she could take a break."

"Were the early days busy?"

"Very busy. We were one of the founders you know, and there were a lot of details that needed to be seen to before this place became what it is today."

Ioan nodded. "Dear said that Michelle had campaigned to include sensoria in the System."

"Yes, though that is something of an elision that has become shorthand for experiences rather than thoughts." Her voice was clear, though it still held the careful articulation of one who has realized that they are not sober. "We were not beings of pure thought, there were still experiences, but there was no guarantee that they would be shared. It was chaotic, as you might imagine from a set of unique individuals trying to dream the same dream.

"This was back in the early days, you understand, before the System had become a dumping ground for the world's excess population." She smiled, far off. "We were all starry-eyed dreamers, you know, and so were the engineers phys-side. Hard problems remain hard, however, and it kept getting deprioritized. Michelle and the rest of the founders provided arguments for the means by which we have consensual sensoria, as well as additional sensorium tools such as the messages."

Ioan relished the long-faded impulse to bristle at this. The Ode clade was notorious for their fondness for sensorium messages, those sensations and images that barged in on one's own senses. Ey still found them unnerving. Ey said, "Just how much of the early System did your clade influence?"

May Then My Name's laugh was quiet and muffled beside em. "I am sure we have lost track. The first lines of each stanza quickly picked up interests of their own—even then they were rarely in communication—and each picked up a project of their own, and whenever a new project would come along, they would have to generate enough reputation to fork again. Everything was much more expensive back then, and we would sometimes have to pool our resources."

"What was your stanza's project?"

She waved a paw vaguely. "We lost the idea that the whole stanza would be working on similar projects after a while, so they are not as tightly connected any more. Early forks were much more likely to share similar interests, if only because the individuation had not set in as strongly. The first line of mine, though, The Only Time I Know My True Name Is When I Dream—True Name, you met her briefly tonight—was heavy in the politics of the early System and its relations to phys-side."

Ioan blinked, startled. "I had no idea. I'm guessing that's back when it was a bigger deal?"

"Very much so, yes."

"I thought there wasn't much political interaction after Secession, though."

She shrugged noncommittally, then rested her head back on Ioan's shoulder. The alcohol of the night still dogged em.

"And the reason for your fork?"

"To feel."

"To feel?"

"To feel. True Name kept spinning off instances to work on such concrete things, I think she forgot how to feel. Emotions became distant out of habit. Touch became a distraction. I was to become her anchor. We would merge every few months after that, though it has been a long time since we last did so. She says that we will merge once this project is finished."

"You haven't diverged too far?" Ioan asked.

"She would like us not to," the skunk murmured. "That is why I am acting as coordinator. It is a familiar role."

Ioan nodded. "Close enough to politics, I suppose."

Another moment of silence. Ey permitted some of the drunkenness from the evening to drift away, allowing thoughts to come more clearly. May Then My Name relaxed further against eir side, and ey suspected she was not far away from sleep. Tomorrow, eir work would begin to pick up in earnest, so ey was tempted to let her sleep, but a question nagged at em.

"May?"

"I like it when you call me that," she mumbled.

"It's a good name." Ioan smiled. "I had a question, though. How much do you remember from back then?"

She sat bolt upright, wrenching at eir shoulder. "What did you say? Sorry."

Ey reclaimed eir arm, rubbing at the shoulder. "It's okay. How much do you remember from the early days of the System? Around the time you uploaded, I mean."

"You, my dear, are a fucking genius." She was on her feet within a second, pacing back and forth in front of the bench swing. She paused mid-pace to lean down and bump her nose against Ioan's forehead; her form of a kiss. "Fucking genius."

Given that she appeared to have sobered up, Ioan allowed emself to do the same. "What do you mean?" ey asked.

"I want to modify the project scope. Can I tell you a secret?" She was speaking quickly now.

"Yes, of course."

"I want to modify the project and add in an early history of the System, of Secession. Do you think you would be up for adding that in?"

Ioan frowned. "If can I fork for it, I suppose."

May Then My Name laughed. "You are talking to an Odist, of course you can fucking fork."

"Alright, alright. What's your secret, then?"

"I want to write an early history of the System to parallel the current. They are eerily similar, you know, but it has been two hundred years. We are well past history, and doubtless there are histories already written. I remember the secession, I remember uploading, I remember getting lost, I remember everything. Yes, I remember. Of course I do. All the great and terrible things that we did. We could write a history, but that is all already there. There are paper trails and journals and everything phys-side already knows about us, but–"

Ioan's eyes went wide as ey picked up on her idea. "You want to turn it into a story."

She clapped and bounced excitedly on her feet. "Yes! Yes, a mythology. I know I have mentioned them before, and we had talked about incorporating that aspect with Dear and Codrin. The history is important, and perhaps you can write that too, but now is not the time for *only* history. Now is the time for–"

"Stories."

In a decidedly Dear-like move, the skunk forked several times over, crowding the balcony before the bench swing with copies of herself, all of which had the same expression of glee. They quit quickly, and May Then My Name leaned forward to give Ioan a handful more of those nose-dot kisses. "You get it!"

"I worked with Dear, you nut. Of course I get stories." Ey laughed, reaching up to grab her around the waist and haul her back onto the swing beside em.

How different she was than Dear. Individuation is born in the decades and centuries, though. Ey would never have thought to be so physical with the fox, but as she laughed and slumped back against eir side, ey realized ey had long since fallen into the habit of physicality, of touch. Of, ey realized, feeling, just as she'd said.

Douglas Hadje—2325

When Douglas Hadje pressed his hands against the sides of the L₅ System, he always imagined that he could sense his aunt along with however many 'great's preceded that title, sense all of those years separating him from her, and he pressed his hands against the outside of the System every chance he could get. If he was sure that he was alone—and he often was—he would press his forehead to the glassy, diamondoid cylinder and wish, hope, dream that he could say even one word to her. His people, humanity, now nearly two centuries distant from the founding of the System, forever felt on the verge of true speciation, of mutual incomprehensibility, from those within. Did they still think the same? Did they still feel the same? Their hopes were doubtless different, but were their dreams?

But always his hands were separated from the structure by that thin layer of skinsuit, and always his helmet was in the way of the carbon shell, and always he was at least one reality away from them.

He would spend his five minutes there, connected and not by touch, thinking of this or that, thinking of nothing at all, and then he would climb away from the cylinder down the ladder, down the dozen or so meters to the ceiling of his home, climb through the airlock, and perhaps go lay down.

Others knew of this. They had to. All movement outside the habitat portion of the station was tightly controlled. Everything was on video, recorded directly from his eyes through his exo. All audio was recorded.

But he never spoke, and he always closed his eyes. For some unknown reason, he was permitted this small dalliance.

The System sat stationary at the Earth-Moon L_5 point, a stable orbit with relation to the earth and moon such that it only very rarely required any correction to its position. Once a day, as the point rotated beyond Earth from the point of view of the sun and more briefly by the moon, it fell into darkness, but other than that, it was bathed in sunlight unmoderated by atmosphere. It rotated at a stately pace in relation to the moon and Earth such that its vast solar collector was always pointed toward the sun.

The station itself comprised three main parts. At the core of the station was the diamondoid cylinder, fifty meters in diameter and five hundred meters in length. The solar collector was attached to the sunward end of the cylinder, spreading out in a series of one hundred sixty thousand replaceable panels, one meter square each, held in a lattice of carbon fiber struts. Surrounding the cylinder was a torus, two hundred meters in diameter and as long as core cylinder itself, such that it was forever hidden from the sun by the solar collectors. Seventy-seven acres, of living space, working space, factories, and arable land, all lit by bundles of doped fiber optic cables which collected and distributed the light from space and cast it down from the ceiling. The entire contraption rotated nearly three times per minute, fast enough that they had an approximation of Earth's gravity.

That is where Douglas lived along with about twenty others.

To fund such a project, the torus had originally operated as a tourist destination. Many of the living spaces consisted of repurposed hotel rooms. It had long since ceased to serve in that capacity as humanity's curiosity for space dwindled and spaceflight from Earth once again began to rise in price.

To build such a project, the area had been cleared of much

of the Trojan asteroids that had collected there, either used for raw materials or slung out into space into eccentric orbits that would keep them from impacting Earth or winding up once again captured in the same Legrange point. Even still, one of the many jobs was to monitor the area for newly captured rocks and divert or collect them as needed. The material could be used for new solar panels, or perhaps the two five-thousand kilometer long launch arms sprouting on opposing sides of the torus, the Hall Effect Engines that kept the rotation of the station constant as the arms had been extruded from its surface, or of course the two new cylindrical launch vehicles at the tips of those arms that had, over the last two decades, been constructed as half-scale duplicates of the core.

Little of this mattered to Douglas.

He was, he was forever told, a people person. He was an administrator, a boss, a manager. It was his job to direct and guide and herd people into doing what was required for this twenty-year project. He was forever told that he had the empathy and skills to lead, though he forever doubted it.

He simply cared about this with a fervor that was dimmed only by the idea that, somewhere within the mirror-box that was the System cylinder, his distant ancestor dwelt.

Douglas was the launch director. He was the *director*. He was high enough on the food chain that he had ungated access to the textual communication line that connected the phys-side world to the sys-side world. He was the director, and he knew that, if he wished, all he need do was pull up the program, type up a letter, run it past security, click 'send', and Michelle, his generations-gone aunt, would somehow receive it.

And yet he never did.

He didn't know why. He asked himself again and again what it was that kept him from reaching out to her. Was it that speciation? Was it the confounding societal differences? Was it that unfathomable distance between the physical and the dream? He did not know, he did not know.

Instead, he worked. He oversaw the construction of the Launch Vehicle Systems, those two smaller cylinders that would be, in a few days, released from either end of the launch arms at incredible tangential velocity. He worked with the sys-side launch coordinator to ensure that everything was working appropriately, that the micro-Ansible connection between the main System and the launch vessels was appropriately transferring entire identities.

Who this coordinator was, this confusingly-named May Then My Name Die With Me, he had no idea.

He needn't even message Michelle directly. He had May Then My Name Die With Me, perhaps she would know her. He could ask her. She could mediate.

And still, he never did.

Director Hadje,

The launch is tomorrow and communications are looking good. A status report will follow, but before I get to that, I would like to open a dialog with you surrounding topics beyond the launch itself. Please ensure that this is both acceptable by the hierarchy of superiors that doubtless read our communications and yourself, as they are of a somewhat more personal nature. As my role of launch coordinator slowly dwindles, I have been asked by both my clade and a historian sys-side to collect information through extant lines of communication, a sort of oral history of the events leading up to, surrounding, and immediately after the launch.

Thank you,

May Then My Name Die With Me of the Ode Clade

2325-01-20—systime 201+20 1303

Status Report

- **Micro-Ansible transmission:**

    - *Outbound functionality:* five-by-five (go)
    - *Inbound functionality:* five-by-five (go)

- **Transmission status:**

    - *Personalities transferred:* 2,593,190,433 / 100% (go)
    - *Individuals by clade transferred:* 1,123,384,222 / 100% (go)
    - *Personalities remaining to be transferred:* 0 / 0% (go)
    - *Individuals by clade remaining to be transferred:* 0 / 0% (go)
    - *Personalities transferred leaving no immediate forks (pct):* 3.8%
    - *Individuals by clade transferred leaving no immediate forks (pct):* 0.00000018%
    - *Social makeup of transfers:* 84% dispersionista / 10% tracker / 6% tasker
    - *Social makeup of L_5 System:* 23% dispersionista / 38% tracker / 39% tasker
    - *Transfers irrevocably lost:* 8 (go)

- **System status:**

    - Castor:

        * *Stability:* 100% (go)
        * *Clock offset:* 0ns (go)
        * *Clock skew:* 0ns/ns (go)
        * *Clock jitter:* 0ns/ns/ns (go)
        * *Entanglement:* 100% (go)
        * *Fork reliability:* 17 nines (go)
        * *Merge reliability:* 23 nines (go)

- Pollux:

  * *Stability:* 100% (go)
  * *Clock offset:* 0ns (go)
  * *Clock skew:* 0ns/ns (go)
  * *Clock jitter:* 0ns/ns/ns (go)
  * *Entanglement:* 100% (go)
  * *Fork reliability:* 18 nines (go)
  * *Merge reliability:* 21 nines (go)

• **Disposition:** go for launch

Notes: the level of transfers irrevocably lost is disappointing but cannot be helped. Still, it is far below the loss from the Earth-L_5 Ansible, which, as a matter of course, implies the loss of a clade rather than a personality. One clade was lost irrevocably, but, at the risk of sounding crass, they knew they were signing up for this, and it is always a risk for taskers. That one loss represents 0.005% of the total transfer loss, and is vanishingly small in the grand scheme of things, though I am sure it is of no consolation to their friends. Congratulations, as always, for another step closer to launch.

Attachment: history questionnaire #1

As mentioned, I am working with a historian—or rather, three forks of the same historian—to compile a history of the launch. Due to a certain incorrigible tricksiness, this will take the form of a mythology; something romantic to be passed down through the years. To this end, data collection is ramping up in the form of countless interviews. I have, of course, all the status reports a girl could ever want for the basic facts, all of the trials and tribulations over the last two decades, but that is only a small portion of a mythology. Should you and your superiors agree, I would like to begin the process of collecting testimonies from those phys-side.

Concrete questions

- How long have you been working as phys-side launch director?
- What is involved with your role as phys-side launch director?
- How long have you been working with the System phys-side?
- What led you to pursue a career working with the System?
- What led you to remain phys-side rather than uploading, yourself? Will you upload in the future? Why or why not?
- What led you to pursue your position as launch director rather than remaining in your previous position?
- Please provide a biography of yourself to whatever level of detail you feel comfortable.
- Please provide a physical description of yourself to whatever level of detail you feel comfortable.
- Do you have any hobbies?

On the System

- How do you feel about what you know of the founding of the System?
- If you were suddenly removed from your position as director, what would you choose to do as a career in its stead?
- If you were suddenly removed from your location in the extra-System station and returned to Earth, how would you feel and what would you expect?
- If the System shut down and all personalities irrevocably lost, how would you feel?

Gestalt

- If you were told that, one year from now, you would die painlessly, what would you do? Would this change if you knew that your death would be painful? Would this change, in either case, if your death was seven days from now?
- If everyone but you disappeared, what would you do?
- How do you feel about being alone for extended periods of time?
- Do you remember your dreams?

On history

- How long wilt Thou forget me, O Lord? Forever? How long wilt Thou hide Thy face from me?
- When you become intoxicated—whether via substance use or some natural process, such as sleep deprivation—which of the following applies to you?

  1. Ape drunk: he leaps and sings and hollers and danceth for the heavens.
  2. Lion drunk: he flings the pots about the house, calls his hostess whore, breaks the glass windows with his dagger, and is apt to quarrel with any man that speaks to him.
  3. Swine drunk: heavy, lumpish, and sleepy, and cries for a little more drink and a few more clothes.
  4. Sheep drunk: wise in his own conceit when he cannot bring forth a right word.
  5. Maudlin drunk: when a fellow will weep for kindness in the midst of his ale and kiss you, saying, "By God, Captain, I love thee; go thy ways, thou dost not think so often of me as I do of thee. If I would, if it pleased God, I could not love thee so well as I do."—and then puts his finger in his eye and cries.
  6. Martin drunk: when a man is drunk and drinks himself sober ere he stir.

7. Goat drunk: when in his drunkenness, he hath no mind but on lechery.
8. Fox drunk: when he is crafty drunk as many of the Dutchmen be.

- While walking along in desert sand, you suddenly look down and see a tortoise crawling toward you. You reach down and flip it over onto its back. The tortoise lies there, its belly baking in the hot sun, beating its legs, trying to turn itself over, but it cannot do so without your help. You are not helping. Why?

- Two by two, two by two, and twice more. We always think in binaries, in black and white. We remember history two by two. We consider the present two by two. We think of the future twice over, and twice again. I have looked back on history and seen ceaseless progress or steps backward. I look back a hundred years and see illness and failure, and I look at today and see _____?

- Oh, but to whom do I speak these words?
To whom do I plead my case?
From whence do I call out?
What right have I?
No ranks of angels will answer to dreamers,
No unknowable spaces echo my words.
Before whom do I kneel, contrite?
Behind whom do I await my judgment?
Beside whom do I face death?
And why wait I for an answer?

Please take your time, and remember that the launch takes precedence over your answers.

In friendship,

May Then My Name Die With Me of the Ode Clade

May Then My Name Die With Me,

Thank you for the updated status report. I am looking forward to the launch, and will provide you the best textual description that I am able as it happens from phys-side. I will attempt to provide real-time updates, though the exigencies of the situation will take precedence. Congratulations on making it this far, and thank you for all of your help. Status report follows.

While we were largely baffled by the nature of your questions, the launch commission and myself have accepted the task of aiding you and your companion in your history/mythology project. Answers(?) will follow in a separate message.

Thank you,

Douglas Hadje, MSf, PhD
Launch director

2325-01-20—systime 201+20 1515

Digital signatures:

- Douglas Hadje
- Launch commission:
    - de
    - Jonathan Finnes
    - Thomas Nash
    - Woo Hye-won
    - Hasnaa

Status Report

- **Station-side status:**
    - *Systems check:* Complete (go)
    - *Staff:* 100% (go)

- *Gravity compensation:* 100% (go)
- *Tiedowns:* 100% (go)
- *Expected rotational impact:* Nominal (go)
- *Rotational compensation engines:* Nominal (go)
- *Power storage:* 98% (go)
- *Power consumption:* 86% (go)
- *Panel efficiency:* 5 nines (go)

- **Launch arm status:**

  - Castor:
    * *Launch strut integrity:* 100% (go)
    * *Launch arm integrity:* 100% (go)
    * *Launch arm path:* Clear (go)
    * *Launch arm cameras:* 100% (go)
    * *Launch vehicle path:* Clear to 1.8AU, 5 nines confidence (go)
    * *Capacitor charge:* 6 nines, on track to 100% (go)
    * *Speed:* 100% (go)
    * *Expected acceleration:* Nominal (go)
    * *Expected jerk:* Nominal (go)
  - Pollux:
    * *Launch strut integrity:* 100% (go)
    * *Launch arm integrity:* 100% (go)
    * *Launch arm path:* Clear (go)
    * *Launch arm cameras:* 100% (go)
    * *Launch vehicle path:* Clear to 1.2AU, 5 nines confidence (go)
    * *Capacitor charge:* 6 nines, on track to 100% (go)
    * *Speed:* 100% (go)
    * *Expected acceleration:* Nominal (go)
    * *Expected jerk:* Nominal (go)

- **Launch vehicle status:**

  - Castor:

    * *System surface integrity:* 100% (go)
    * *System interior integrity:* 100% (go)
    * *Sabot integrity:* 100% (go)
    * *Sabot ejection system:* Tests pass (go)
    * *RTG power rate:* Steady (go)
    * *RTG temperature:* Nominal (go)
    * *RTG pre-launch heat sink:* Nominal (go)
    * *RTG post-launch heat-sink:* Tests pass (go)
    * *RTG post-launch heat-sink deployment mechanism:* Tests pass (go)
    * *Solar sail integrity:* 100% (go)
    * *Solar sail deployment mechanism:* Tests pass (go)
    * *Solar panel integrity:* 100% (go)
    * *Solar panel deployment/retraction mechanism:* Tests pass (go)
    * *Attitude jet functionality:* 100% (go)
    * *Raw material capacity:* 100% (go)
    * *Raw material manipulator functionality:* 100% (go)
    * *Raw material manufactory functionality:* 100% (go)
    * *Dreamer Module functionality:* 100% (go)

  - Pollux:

    * *System surface integrity:* 100% (go)
    * *System interior integrity:* 100% (go)
    * *Sabot integrity:* 100% (go)
    * *Sabot ejection system:* Tests pass (go)
    * *RTG power rate:* Steady (go)
    * *RTG temperature:* Nominal (go)
    * *RTG pre-launch heat sink:* Nominal (go)
    * *RTG post-launch heat-sink:* Tests pass (go)
    * *RTG post-launch heat-sink deployment mechanism:* Tests pass (go)
    * *Solar sail integrity:* 100% (go)

* *Solar sail deployment mechanism:* Tests pass (go)
* *Solar panel integrity:* 100% (go)
* *Solar panel deployment/retraction mechanism:* Tests pass (go)
* *Attitude jet functionality:* 100% (go)
* *Raw material capacity:* 100% (go)
* *Raw material manipulator functionality:* 100% (go)
* *Raw material manufactory functionality:* 100% (go)
* *Dreamer Module functionality:* 100% (go)

- **Disposition:** go for launch

  Notes: We are 1% away from desired power consumption reduction on the station. While this is within tolerances, we are expecting that, with the shutdown of the glass furnace at 2330, we will hit our mark of 15% station-wide power reduction. Congratulations!

Message stream

Phys-side: The launch vehicles in their sabots are settled into their creches and the doors are shut. Everyone's excited, but I'm pleased at the calm efficiency of the control tower I'm in (Pollux). We are 1deg offset spinward from the launch arm, so we should be able to see the launch well enough, but the arm appears to disappear into nothingness "below" us after about 100m, so the show won't be great past then. We'll all be watching the cameras. Even those won't be very exciting, given the speed the LVs will be going. Models suggest that we might feel a jerk and fluctuation in gravity, that will be quickly compensated by the engines.

Phys-side: Given your apparent interest in the subjective aspects of the launch, I have to say that I wish there was a big red button I could hit to trigger the launch. Wouldn't that be satisfying? I picture it like one of the keyboards, where there's some sort of spring in there, and a satisfying click as the button snaps down that last bit and makes some physical electric contact. Everything's done on a timer, however, and the chances of any manual intervention being required are essentially zero. Everyone in the tower here is in place to take in data and give reports. I didn't receive permission to pass those on directly, however, so you're left with them being filtered through yours truly.

Phys-side: One minute.

Phys-side: Thirty seconds.

Phys-side: Ten seconds. Godspeed.

Sys-side: Godspeed, you dumb bastards.

Phys-side: 3

Phys-side: 1

Phys-side: Launch looks good.

Phys-side: Watching the struts flex and jolt with the release of mass is quite beautiful.

Phys-side: They weren't kidding about the jerk. Two of them, actually, as the engines fired a half second after the jerk reached the torus. We've got two injuries down here—bumps and bruises. Reports from the torus indicate that damage was minimal. Some sloshing from the hydroponics, but that's easy to clean up. One of the furnaces will need some care. Worst bit of damage, however, is that the solar array suffered a cascading failure: one panel broke loose and tumbled end-over-end across a few hundred others. Power's still nominal, though. We'll get it fixed.

Phys-side: Did you feel anything up there?

Sys-side: Har har. No, nothing up here. I, like you, wish that we had, though. If there had been some sudden jolt or a flicker of the lights, I think that perhaps this launch would have felt more real. I suspect that my cocladist, Dear, Also, The Tree That Was Felled, would have simulated an earthquake at the exact moment of launch, destroying its home in the process, but alas, it was one of those hopeless romantics who transferred entirely to the LVs without leaving a fork. I will have Ioan (my pet historian) ask it if it did so from the LVs. I would not be surprised.

Phys-side: Your clade sounds fascinating. I don't understand a single bit of it.

Sys-side: I will tell you a story one day.

Sys-side: How do you feel with 20 years of work gone in an instant?

Phys-side: I'm still processing that. Numb? Giddy? Can I be both at the same time?

Sys-side: I see no reason why not. Why numb? Why giddy?

Phys-side: Numb because there was nothing to see. Not even a flash. The LVs were here, and then they were gone. I'll never see them again. Giddy because it worked. Telemetry is good, speed is nominal, entanglement is nominal, radio communication is nominal, though the rate at which message times are increasing is surprising, though I knew that this would happen. How neat is that?

Sys-side: Very neat. I feel much the same. I feel numb for the reason I mentioned above. They were here, and then they were gone, and there was no feedback from the action. We are still talking despite this. This is where the numb and the giddy cross, as, in some ways, it feels as though they never left (modulo the fact that Dear would almost certainly rather talk via sensorium messages rather than text), but Codrin (Dear's pet historian) is much suited to words. Giddy, though, because this remains exciting for all of us, both here and on the LVs. Already they diverge, already they are no longer the ones who left here, already they are no longer us.

Phys-side: That's not something I can picture, but I'll trust you on that.

Sys-side: Different worlds, different problems. I must see to Ioan and to writing. Douglas, congratulations once more, and I will stay in contact regarding the LVs and my research.

Phys-side: Thank you for all your hard work, May Then My Name Die With Me.

Sys-side: You may call me May Then My Name, now that the hard work is over.

Phys-side: Thanks! Be well.

Sys-side: You too.

Michelle Hadje/Sasha—2306

Come to me.

Come alone.

That was all that the message had said.

Michelle had long considered this moment, and just as long considered what she might say. She was of two minds. She was of two minds.

The part of her that desired knowledge, that craved a reason in all things, that part of her felt compelled to give an explanation. It felt the need to rationalize and understand and comprehend, and it craved the knowledge that others also understood.

That part was Sasha.

That had felt inverted to her, at first. Was not Michelle the rational one? She was the one who had maintained her ties to her body. She was the one who remembered all of the *things*, all of the *actions* of her past. She was the one who wanted to fork and keep all of those memories.

But instead it was Sasha who felt incomplete, unwhole, when her reasons were unspoken. Eventually her gestalt came to the awareness that this was because Sasha was the one who felt, just as Michelle was the one who remembered, and thus she was also the part that desired compassion above all things. She wanted to explain herself so that others would not be left hurt. She was the one who decided, in the end, not to fork, to fix, to repair. Those memories that mattered—really, truly mattered—all of her instances already shared.

Michelle did not want to tell anyone.

She was of two minds/she was of two minds.

So she edited and rewrote and pared her message down. Thousands of words. Hundreds of words. Ninety-nine words. Ten words. Two commands. A duality like her.

Come to me.

There had been a date, a time, an address. *Come to me,* she thought/she thought. *Come to us.*

Come hear. Come learn. Come understand. Or don't, but come all the same, that we might hear, learn, understand.

She was of two minds/she was of two minds.

Come alone.

She had met their friends and lovers and hidden, forbidden selves. She had met their scribes and their amanuenses and their biographer-historians.

Come alone, she thought/she thought. *I only want you. I only want us. I only want me.*

And she knew they would. She knew they would. She knew they would come and they would do so without hesitation, for a request from the root instance was a thing that had never happened before, and it bore more weight than any possible life event or schedule could ever hope to. She knew they would come because she would be there/she would be there.

She was of two minds.

And so on the allotted day and at the allotted time and in the allotted place, they came. They appeared one by one in that field of grass, that field of dandelions. They came and they stood and they waited. Some of them chatted amiably. Some of them were crying, and she knew which was which because she also felt amiable/she also was crying.

They came to her/they came to her.

They came alone.

One hundred and one of her stood in that meadow. Qoheleth was gone, but there were two of her/there were two of her, and the number was still as it should be.

No, not as it should be. Not as it ought to be. There ought to be only one hundred of her there without Qoheleth, but she was of two minds/she was of two minds.

She smiled to them/she smiled to them, and that was enough to bring them to silence. Those who had felt their amicability frowned now, picking up on the sudden anxiety of the meadow, of that green grass yellowed by dandelions.

"I am of two minds," she said/she said. Waves of Sasha/waves of Michelle rippled across her form, two identities washed through her mind, and she quelled the urge to vomit. "We are of two minds. We do not want to do this, and there is nothing more in life that we desire than to do this. There is too much in me. There is too much *of* me."

There were more crying eyes in the crowd now, and she was crying/she was crying.

Her voice wavered, but she asked all the same. "Please fork. Please fork and merge down-tree."

In less than five seconds, the number of copies of her had doubled, and some inner part of her/some inner part of her smiled, sensing now that doubling that she felt as a core part of her being expressed in all those versions of herself that had grown these last nearly two centuries.

"Since then—'tis Centuries—and yet Feels shorter than the Day—" she thought/she murmured, words borne of a thought/of a memory. A few of the clade who could hear her weak voice joined. "I first surmised the Horses' Heads Were toward Eternity —"

Many were sitting now, some were pulling at tufts of grass, stalks of dandelions, anything to ground themselves.

"I just want...we just want to experience...a little more," she choked out. "Can you give us that?"

The reasons for the forks became clear, now, and over the next hour—for some had diverged so far that a great amount of effort was required to reconcile conflicts—they began to merge their outermost instances down-tree, down-tree, down toward the root. Many looked shell-shocked as years and decades and centuries of memories poured into them, and then were passed on down. Many looked as mad as she felt.

She held up her hand when the mergers had completed down to the doubled-versions of the nine first lines and one second line (for Qoheleth had been a first, Michelle remembered/Sasha remembered) standing before her.

"We have a task for each of you who will remain. One last task." And she walked down the line/she walked down the line, leaning close to whisper into each of their ears, whether they were skunk or human or something new and different, what she wanted them to accomplish, whether it be vague or specific.

"Now," she said.

Of the twenty before her, ten merged into her, one by one.

"Oh," she said/she said. "Oh."

She was laughing/she was crying/she was furious/she was in love/she was knowledgeable/she was a being of emotions/she was an ascetic/she was opulent.

She was.

She was of two minds.

She was of ten minds.

She was of ninety-nine minds.

She was of a thousand times a thousand minds as more memories than any one individual was ever meant to have poured into her and through her and consumed her. She cherished them one by one by one by one by one...

"Oh," she said, feeling more singular than she had in two hundred years.

And then she quit.

Yared Zerezghi—2125

Although Yared Zerezghi was treated with the deference that was afforded to those who had attained such feats as he had, he was also regarded with the wary eyes due to anyone who might be considered hero and villain both.

At least, he realized, until he had made it to the airport. No one wanted to be there. No one wanted to sit through that liminal process. Everyone wanted to be where they were going, not sitting in uncomfortable chairs surrounded by people they were studiously trying to ignore.

The last flight to Yakutsk was dull, but it was that singular type of dullness that allows anxiety to build and grow. He stared out the windows at first, watching the cities and towns that built up around the transit hubs, and then, when all was replaced with desert or windswept grass or bare mountains or burnt husks of forests, he would stare instead at the pages of his book. He could not get the symbols on the pages to line up into words and sentences, but it was better than looking out at the world he was leaving.

The book remained unread when he finally landed in Yakutsk and, as he was about to pack it into the small plastic bag that was his only luggage, he thought better of it and shrugged, handing it to the passenger next to him.

"Want a book?"

She frowned. "Are you...just giving me your book?"

He turned it so that she could see the cover. It was something on politics. Pop drivel, mostly. "I guess I am, yeah."

"Why?"

"I won't need it."

A look of understanding bloomed on her face and her expression shifted from confusion to a cautious smile. "No, I suppose you won't. Well, thank you. I'll give it to the library if I don't wind up reading it."

Yared nodded and gave a gesture of thanks. It was only after the conversation was over that he felt a hotness in his cheeks. He had been lucky that the woman spoke English so well. She was very white, and while that might not mean anything, he *was* flying into the Sino-Russian Bloc, and she could just as well not have been a native speaker.

The act of landing, of deplaning and customs, was as dull and rote as he expected it to be, and yet some protective action of his mind had buried that overwhelming anxiety under a blanket of numbness, which had soon spread to encompass all of his feelings and emotions.

The stop through customs was met with another wide-eyed expression.

"You are the first that I have met," the agent said.

"Oh?"

"The first of the ones heading to the System."

Yared nodded.

"I think that I will see many more the longer I work here." The agent stamped his passport with an expert twist of the wrist, adding a smear to the ink which added a layer of authenticity. It would be all but impossible to mimic that smear. She handed his passport back with a sly smile and a tap to her temple, "I do not think I will go. I am terrified enough of my own head."

Yared could only smile back and move on through the line.

He was met at baggage claim by a slight man who took him by the hand and led him out into the heat of the afternoon. He was shunted into the air-conditioned back of a black car—so many memories of weeks and months ago beneath that blanket of numbness—which took him to an unassuming office complex.

Unassuming from the outside, at least. Inside, he was met with white tile and calm, efficient staff who swished on the floor with white, paper booties.

He was directed to a waiting room where he was instructed to disrobe and push his arms through the sleeves of a paper gown. He was even provided with his own booties.

"You have fasted?"

"Yes?"

"Forty-eight hours?"

"More like seventy-two."

The nurse looked up from her tablet and gave him a kind smile. "Are you nervous?"

"I...don't know." He looked down at his hands. They were perfectly still for the first time in three days. "I was. I don't know what I am now."

She nodded and swiped something on the tablet before clipping it to a bandoleer of various medical goodies strapped across her front. "If you would like medication for your anxiety now, I can provide. Your procedure is in ten minutes, however—you understand the rush—so if you can wait that long, you will shortly not feel a thing."

Her English had the same clipped, stilted accent of the man who had driven him to the medical center, of the customs agent, of all of the flight agents. He wondered briefly if it was some S-R Bloc accent, or if the overwhelming numbness had distorted all he heard.

"Please, Mr. Zerezghi. If you would lay down here. I will place an IV, and we will get you to the surgery immediately. You understand, yes? We are on a schedule, yes?"

He nodded and did as he was told. The numbness, he realized, had extended to the physical as well, as he didn't notice the needle in the back of his hand until the nurse clipped a line to it.

The surgery was...well, Yared was something not quite awake, not quite asleep for most of it, but what he did remember was that it was in all ways unpleasant. The noises that drifted in and out of his awareness, the last remaining scent, the last remaining taste, both of some nickel-plated sourness that he could not place. The last remaining sight of just light, just light.

And then a stretching. A stretching up of his arms while his feet remained anchored, there on that bed. He stretched up tall, kilometers up, light years. So tall that he began to thin out, tapering in the middle until he thought that he would snap...

Whether there was any discontinuity or not, he did not know. He was simply...there. Simply standing in a cube of grey walls, grey ceiling, grey floor. It was lit by lights that seemed to come from everywhere and nowhere, and the lack of a shadow was disturbing in a way that he could not place.

A soft, familiar voice spoke to him, then. Or did not come to him. He did not hear it through his ears, but it was there, nonetheless, through something more and less than hearing. "Yared. Can you speak?"

He opened his mouth and exhaled in a gasp. His throat worked at least, though everything was...different. So different.

Remembering—somehow—how to move, he tilted his head forward to look down at himself. Naked, but sharp and clear. He lifted his hands to look at them, seeing the same dark skin, the same well-trimmed fingernails.

But no contacts. None of those silvery pads on his fingers. He rubbed his thumb over the spots where they had once been, then reached his other hand up to touch at the back of his neck where the long-familiar exocortex implant was missing. Smooth, soft skin, with only what hair and blemishes he remembered from this afternoon, from so long ago.

He took another breath, and let it out in a long *aaah*, then another and said, "Yes, I think so."

"Fantastic," came the voice once more.

"Is that...are you True Name?"

A soft chuckle, and then, "Yes, it is me. Or a portion of me, at least. You are still in the upload clinic's system, which cannot easily fit two."

"So, not in the System yet."

"No, but the transfer is nearly complete. You will not remember this encounter, I am afraid, but you will have new ones." The voice sounded as though it was smiling. "So very many new ones. I am just happy to see you move and hear you speak, as it means that the same will be true sys-side."

Yared frowned. "I will...not remember?"

"This instance is in a temporary location for the purpose of testing, so eventually, you will either quit or be halted, yes."

"But then I'll be in the System?"

There was a pause, and then a laugh. "You already are. The upload has complete, and I—the real True Name—am speaking with you."

"But I will die here?"

"Not die, no. You will quit. You are already living on."

The words made him tremble. They were so final, which jarred against a tone of comfort, of reassurance. "I don't know if I'm ready for that."

The voice still sounded like it was smiling. "There is little I can do to reassure you, so, tough shit. You are already on the other side."

And with that, Yared Zerezghi ceased to be.

"Yared. Can you speak?"

He blinked open his eyes, confronted with a shape of black and white, then shouted and fell backwards.

The shape that stood before him, laughed and leaned down to offer a hand. "I will take that as a yes. I am True Name. Do you remember me?"

He stared up at the shape, something half human and half animal, a tapering snout and white-striped black fur. Feminine form. Soft tail. Friendly eyes.

"True...Name? The Only...The Only Time..."

"The Only Time I Know My True Name Is When I Dream, yes." It– she was smiling, though Yared was not sure how he knew that. She wiggled the fingers of her offered hand—paw? Paw—and said, "Come on, let us get you up."

Yared still did not accept the offer, looking around himself instead. He sat atop a small hill in a grass field, dotted liberally with dandelions. The sky was cloudless and blue above him. The sun stood on high.

He shook his head, marveling at the sudden change from cold clinic and unpleasant sensations to so prosaic a landscape, then took the paw at last, letting himself be helped to his feet.

"There you go," True Name said. "How do you feel?"

"Um."

"Naked, perhaps?"

He looked down at himself and started back from the animal. "Uh...yes. How do I..."

"Picture yourself clothed how you wish. Your favorite outfit, perhaps. Picture that, and then want it. Want to be clothed."

Squinting his eyes shut, Yared did his best to think his clothes into being. He heard a laugh from True Name.

"Relax. Breathe in, and then when you breathe out, think of that outfit and say to yourself, 'gosh, I wish that I was wearing that right now!', and then smile."

"Smile?"

"That part is not necessary, but I find that it helps with the newly arrived."

Breathe in.

Breathe out. "I would like to be wearing that nice thawb I got to try on."

Smile.

And then he was. He felt the fabric hanging comfortably

from his shoulders. It was not sudden or slow, he did not feel the transition, he just was simply wearing the garment as if he always had been.

"There, see? It will become second nature, and you will not need to smile or speak out loud."

Yared nodded. Breathed in, breathed out, and then the fabric had two gold brocade stripes heading down from the shoulders to the hem.

"Excellent!" The skunk—as he now remembered her to be—clapped her paws. "I figured you would be a fast learner after so long."

"Where are we?"

"We are in a private sim. Usually, new arrivals show up in a gridded gray box, and then a guide will arrive and show them basically what I showed you, but you are something of a celebrity, at least among the circles that I run in, and so I pulled some strings with the Council of Eight."

He nodded absentmindedly, reached down, and plucked at a dandelion. It felt real enough. Finally, he said, "You are not exactly how I pictured you. I've seen pictures of Michelle."

"What were you picturing?"

"I don't know." He frowned. "I guess I never really internalized the whole 'skunk' thing."

True Name smiled and shrugged. "I look like this. Rather like my av back in the 'net. I can look-" There was suddenly a short woman standing beside the skunk. The resemblance was clearly there in the shape of the profile and the way she moved, but for the fact that she looked like the photos Yared had seen. The human spoke. "-like this, but that is not my preferred mode."

And then she was gone, with just the skunk standing before him.

"What was that?"

"I forked. I created a new instance of myself from that moment. I just let it slip back into that other form I remember."

"You can do that?"

She laughed. "I can, though it does cost some reputation if the fork lasts longer than five minutes."

"And then it just...went away?"

"She quit, yes."

"And I can do this, too?"

Before she could respond, Yared breathed in, and then two of him breathed out. He let out a shout of laughter.

True Name looked startled, then clapped her paws once more. "Well done! Usually it takes new arrivals a few days to get to that point. Now, one of you—you have not experienced too much that is different from each other, so it doesn't matter which—one of you think, 'okay, I am ready to quit'."

"And what will happen then?"

"Then? Nothing. That instance will stop. If you quit-" she pointed at the newer of the two Yareds "-then you-" and then at the first "-will have the option of merging the fork's memories back in."

"Will I feel anything? Is it like dying?"

"No, Yared. It is fine. The experiences simply stop." She smiled wryly, adding, "We still have not answered the question of an afterlife, but we are told from outside that System capacity increases when an instance frees up space."

He frowned, but gestured to the newer fork, who backed away a step and crouched. "If you promise it's not like dying. I can't...I can't have gotten this far just to die."

"I have never died, so I cannot promise, but when I just forked and then merged, the memories that I received did not include anything that felt like death. They just stop."

Yared's fork—he realized he knew it as Yared Zerezghi#323a998a, though not how—slowly straightened up, closed his eyes, and breathed out.

Then disappeared.

There was a sudden, demanding pressure on Yared, as though a memory of something important was *right there*, and all he needed to do was remember it.

So he did. He remembered the suddenness of the beginning of existence. He remembered the sight of himself. He remembered the different angle that he had seen True Name from, so incongruous with where he was standing now. The conversation, the shock of being informed that he should quit, the fear, the determination. And then the memories just ended.

"See? There is nothing after."

He tilted his head, trying to remember anything past that point, but there was nothing else to grasp. "Not really, but I suppose I'll get used to it."

"You do not need to fork if you do not want to. And you will learn how to control the merger over time, and only remember certain parts. You will learn. But come, secession and launch are only a few minutes away. Think to yourself, 'I want to be at Josephine's#aaca9bb9.' You will also get used to remembering those letters and num–"

Yared's eyes took a moment to adjust to the dim, steamy light of a restaurant. It was chilly outside, but delightfully warm inside, where silver and red stools lined a bar and the sizzle of eggs could be heard from a griddle. There were a few dozen people inside, including a gaggle of other skunks and women that looked eerily like True Name and Michelle.

True Name appeared beside him, laughing. "That was fast. I know that I should not be surprised at the quickness with which you are picking this up, but I am."

The skunk padded over to a corner booth where seven others waited. Three well-dressed individuals, a dirty pile of rags that may have contained a human, a nondescript face that he couldn't seem to focus on, another animal of some sort that reminded Yared of a ferret he had seen once, and a perpetually smiling man with artfully tousled hair.

Both of them slid into the booth, and as they did so, the noise of the restaurant dimmed almost to inaudibility.

"Uh, hi."

"Mr. Zerezghi, a pleasure!" The tousled man reached out his

hand and Yared shook it on instinct. "Jonas. Happy to meet face to face at last."

Yared straightened up. "Jonas? Really? Nice to meet you as well. Is this...are you the Council of eight?"

True Name nodded. "That is us, yep. Michelle could not be here tonight, so I am here in her stead."

"You meet at a diner?"

"We meet all over," Jonas said. "There is no headquarters, *per se*. We just find interesting places and meet there."

"Wherever's most boring." The nondescript person shrugged.

A mug of coffee was placed before him and Yared lifted it automatically for a sip. He wasn't sure why this surprised him, but he figured he had a lot to learn.

"You're the last one," rasped the pile of rags. "The last arrival before secession. You didn't want to be the first one after? It's your big deal, right?"

"No. I don't know why. I suppose just in case something goes wrong with the launch."

"Nothing will go wrong. There is a backup facility, anyway," the ferret-shaped one said. "Debarre, by the way. Nice to meet you."

The rest of the council introduced themselves.

"So, how long until secession takes effect?" True Name asked.

One of the well-dressed women tilted her head, then smiled. "Ten seconds."

Yared set his coffee down quickly as the table began a countdown. He looked around and then realized everyone was counting down. Shouting the numbers. Grinning and laughing and clapping.

By the time they hit four, Yared was counting along with them.

"Three!" he shouted.

This is what it was all for, he thought. *Sitting in a diner, drinking terrible coffee, and meeting friends.*

"Two!"

I dreamed for so long, and I get here minutes before it all happens at once. This is what it was for.

"One!"

It was all for these smiling faces and complete and total freedom.

Everyone began cheering at once. The windows lit up with a fireworks display. True Name stopped clapping in order to hug him around the shoulders, and after a moment's hesitation, he returned the gesture.

"This is why you wanted to be the last one, is it not?" she murmured in his ear just loud enough for him to hear. "You greedy son of a bitch. You just wanted to be the last one to join the party."

He laughed. "You know, I think you may be right."

Part II

Progression

Codrin Bălan#Castor—2325

After their 'deaths', such as they were, Dear cackled madly and ran about the still roaring bonfire, prancing and leaping, forking dozens of copies as it went. Its sim had been set up in the Launch Systems, both Castor and Pollux, precisely as it had in the L5 System, down to all of the decorations and flames. As soon as they had transferred themselves over to those Systems— something which they had been told would take several minutes across the micro-Ansibles connecting the three systems, but which was as subjectively instantaneous as any normal transit— they were alone. The crowd was gone, the singing was gone, and any chance of reversibility had gone with them. There was no way that Codrin or Dear or Dear's partner could ever go back. The transit was one-way. *"There is no going and there is no back,"* Dear had been saying for months now.

"It is done! It is done!" the fox hollered. *"It is done and those poor saps did not even get to finish their song! Oh, to see their faces! Crumbling sim, friends forever cut off!"*

Dear's partner also laughed, hopping to their feet and chasing after the fox in a drunken dash, leaving Codrin to sit and smile and watch and think.

There was no more Codrin in the L5 System. Ey was only here. Ey couldn't remember being there, for were the sims not the same? And if ey had never been there, had ey ever really existed there? Ey was only memories, and perhaps that is all ey had ever been. Navel gazing and existential crises mixed with the glee of having actually *done* something. No longer just the passive amanuensis, but now the active participant.

Or, well, nearly so, for it was Dear who talked em into this, as it was so good at doing.

When Dear and its partner finally collapsed into a laughing heap amid the dandelions and shortgrass, Codrin stood, raised eir hands to the fire-dimmed sky, and addressed fox and human and flames. "Hwæt! We great three have made it! We have made it to safety and sanctuary!"

Dear rolled up and immediately focused on Codrin with a singular intensity that ey had seen countless times before and yet never gotten used to.

"We three, the heroes, the shield-bearers of Elf Hive had long since sought the beast. It lived in the caves, they said. It dwelt in the fields and disguised itself as tall grass, ready to ensnare the traveler. It was as large as a mountain and crouched beside the valley, unseen, traversed, summited, and still it claimed lives in its hunger. Who knows the truth, now, but us three? None who met its gaze had ever lived to tell the tale, and none now will ever hear, for we are the only ones who have seen it face to face and lived, and yet we escaped only by jumping from the world up to the heavens.

"We sought it by night until we realized that it was not there–"

"*We sought it!*" Dear shouted, hoisting a tankard that had appeared in its paw.

"We sought it by day, supposing that that is where it must be hiding–"

"*Sought but did not find!*"

"We looked to the morning, supposing that it might dwell between the two, but morning is the time of creation! The beast of destruction cannot live there. And so we sought in the evening gloaming and there we found the slavering teeth–"

"The jaws that bite, the claws that catch." Dear's partner chimed in, lifting their own tankard.

"And we braved them. We braved, but though we tried, we could not best them. There was no fight to be had–"

"No swords could cut it!"

"No spears could pierce it!"

"–and all we could do was hold off its attack to run away until true darkness fell and we could finally rest. The next morning we would take off running, and hope to gain some distance, but always the beast was there, ready and waiting–"

"Ready to pounce!"

"So we grew weary, for nothing we did could not be undone by the beast. It *did* dwell in the grass! It *did* live in caves! It *was* the mountain! It was all these things and more."

"So much more, yes."

"So, the best that we could do," Codrin said with an air of finality. "Was to leave behind the earth, the realm of the physical, to leap up and up–"

"Up and up!"

"Up and up!"

"–and ascend directly to the heavens to live as gods!"

The three of them all lifted their newly created tankards high, spilling spruce beer and laughing as they shouted, "Hail! Hail!" before drinking deep.

"You, my dear, are quite drunk," Dear's parter said, grinning.

Codrin giggled. "That I am!"

"But that was delightful! Much better than signing a waver that we might be lost and then waiting for the appointed time." Dear paused, tilted its head, and adopted a sly grin that surely meant trouble. *"But I do not think that that is* actually *what happened, for when God hath ordained a creature to die in a particular place, He causeth that creature's wants to direct it to that place."*

Codrin sat down on the ground as the other two had and awaited Dear's version of the events.

"I knew that because from the moment that God opened up the heavens and reached down to touch me on my crown and opened my third eye-" It forked into a version of itself which had such a feature. *"-that I was to seek far and wide for those who saw the world as I did and guide them into a fullness of being that no one had ever seen before right up until that ordained moment of my death.*

"In short, I began a cult."

Its partner laughed. "You might well have, given the chance."

"Shush, you. I began it in all good intentions. I had seen the truth as revealed to me by God itself—for is not God made in the image of me?—and certainly the best that I could do to help my fellow man was to lead them to the truth. The truth is beautiful and cruel. We are not meant to own a thing! We are meant only to suffer, and by suffering, be purified, and by being purified, ascend from this mortal plane through the cosmic vibrations to something akin to ecstasy!

"Power, as the tired saying goes, corrupts, and I bore power. Eventually, I attained absolute power, at least among my followers. I was their prophet, was I not? We were not meant to own a thing, yes, but as the ephemeral physical items passed through our lives, I sampled the greatest among them. The truth may be cruel and we are meant to suffer, but is not even the highest pleasure a form of suffering of its own? Orgasm is called the little death, is it not?"

Both of the fox's partners laughed.

"And so I took what I wanted and did it all in the name of suffering and poverty. I believed it as hard as the rest of my followers, though. There was no cynicism, back then, down in the physical plane, where all is tainted by evil. I was a prophet and the prophecy applied to me, as well.

"There was no hope of a grand death, I knew that. I knew that I would die in the agony of flames-" It gestured at the bonfire still roaring. *"-and I knew when, so I was expecting the hammering on my door and the shattering of its hinges. I was expecting my team of tame Judases to come crashing into my meditation chamber. My followers! Some of the greatest and best among them! They all came for me, and I*

let them in full knowledge haul me to my feet by my very scruff—grab me there and I go limp as a kitten!"

Both of the audience members grinned at this. Both knew it to be true.

"I let them drag me to my pyre, my last great possession, my last great suffering, and I wept with joy at the beautiful, terrifying, and irreversible agony of that final moment. Even my screams contained ecstasy!

"The cosmic vibrations welled up within my heart and my mind and my soul and my body and when there was nothing left of me but ash, I found myself here, surrounded by love and peace and all that I could possibly desire!"

With that, it bowed dramatically and sat back down amid the applause.

When both Codrin and Dear had stared at their partner for a long few seconds, they finally held up their hands and surrendered to the pressure. "Fine, fine, but I'm not the storyteller that you two are, so you'll have to forgive my tale."

"Pish and also tosh, my love. I look forward to it."

"You are also very drunk, fox."

"But of course!"

They clambered to their feet and stretched their arms upward, then nodded. "Alright. My appearance here began shortly after Dear's. Its gift of prophecy was accurate more often than not, and, at first, it was humbler than any single one of us could possibly hope to be.

"That, you see, was the secret to its power. It was not simply that it would think of others any time a choice was presented between itself and them, though that was surely true, but that it seemed to exist without ego. Completely without. It would forget to eat. It would forget to drink. It would even, though I am happy to count this as a rarity, forget to breathe. Why would it? In its mind, the self was non-existent, and by that point, breathing had come under its own control, such was its mastery of self, and if it was always focused on the betterment of others, it could neglect itself. I wouldn't be surprised if its heart would forget to beat some day.

"This is the source of the passion in its followers. When one sees that total reduction of the self in the service of others, that does not inspire greed in nearly as many people that you might suspect. Instead, they are unable to help themselves before that one. It's almost impossible to resist the paradoxical allure of one such as that, and perhaps some more primal need draws one to try and equal that nadir."

For as much as they had downplayed their ability, Codrin was pleasantly surprised at the fluidity of their telling, and ey sat as rapt as Dear.

"I had a gift of prophecy, myself, though I had not understood it until joining this cult – and yes, it was a cult. It was during a nine-day fast and I had been meditating for at least thirty six hours straight, and in that, I received word from God in the form of a vision: our dear leader's death, it cackling in the flames, and I saw the reason why.

"It was after that that I started to notice it, the slow regrowth of its ego. It started with little things, at first, a morsel of that required food more than the rest of us received, or an extra smile of particular friendship between it and one of the others.

"I kept this to myself, at first, but eventually it began to grate on me more than I cared to admit. The strange thing about anger, though, is that it has the roots in the self, and so I felt that it was keeping me anchored where I made no further progress on my journey to utter selflessness.

"So I did what any other acolyte would do and began to talk with the others in secret. I was not the only one, it turned out, though I was the only one who had seen the inevitable conclusion. When I mentioned this to my co-conspirators, though, they immediately grew wide-eyed and listened to what I had to say. I didn't put the pieces together at the moment, but soon enough I began to feel the subtle nudges toward assuming the role of prophet.

"I don't know who began the mob. Was it Aya? I think it was Aya. I think it was her who began the chant and then began the roar. It was her who battered down Dear's door and dragged it, strangely limp, strangely smiling, out to the bonfire, and it was her who threw it on, for it had become a slight creature long ago."

"It was! Aya, that bitch."

"And then, of course, it was her who grabbed my hand and thrust it up into the air, proclaiming me as the next prophet. It was unanimous. I was to be the one in charge.

"And you can surely guess my fate. You can surely see that it had come much sooner too, as all of those little luxuries that Dear had accumulated were now mine, and I succumbed as I knew I must to temptation.

"Weird though. They skipped the fire and went straight to beheading!" They finished with a bow and sat down grinning at the hearty applause. Both Dear and Codrin leaned in to give them a kiss on the cheek.

There was silence for a while as the three of them sat and drank their ale and looked at the fire or looked at each other or looked at nothing. Perhaps they left to walk the prairie. Perhaps they huddled by the fire in shared warmth. Who knows? It did not matter in that moment. They were home, and they were together.

I was only later, when Dear and Codrin had curled together in bed—Dear's partner having fallen asleep on the couch—that the fox elbowed Codrin in the side, and ey could hear the grin in its voice. *"Beowulf? You are such a nerd."*

Codrin laughed and buried eir face in the fox's scruff. "Did you doubt that I knew of Beowulf?"

"Oh! I did not doubt, but the fact that you pulled that out to start a story time makes me giddy. How long had you been planning on doing that?"

"It wasn't planned. It just struck me in the spur of the moment."

"I knew there was a reason I loved you."

Codrin poked a finger against the fox's stomach, getting a yip in return. "Did you doubt that, too?"

"It is always nice to have confirmation."

"Happy to oblige."

There was silence for a bit. Codrin began to nod off.

"Codrin?"

"Mm?"

"When you write back to Ioan and May Then My Name, will you send those stories instead of what our actual reasons were?"

"Don't they already know those?"

"The surface ones, yes. Not the emotional ones, though. Not the ones from the heart. Not the drive to get out, get away."

Codrin nodded, silent.

"If you can do me a favor, Codrin, can you send only the ones from tonight?"

"You don't want them to know the real ones?"

"No."

The finality of the word brooked no argument, and Codrin left it at that. "I'll get them sent over in the morning."

"Thank you." Even the fox sounded on the edge of sleep. *"I think May Then My Name will enjoy that too. She is probably already poisoning Ioan with talk of myths and legends, if I know her."*

"Ey'll rise to the occasion, I'm sure. That's as much up eir alley as history is."

"You two do make good storytellers."

"Well, your clade does seem to attract quite a few stories."

Dear laughed and wriggled itself closer against Codrin leaving space for its partner when they would inevitably crawl back to a real bed.

"Do you think the Codrin on Pollux did the same?" Dear mumbled.

Ey was awake only enough to say, "I hope so."

Michelle Hadje—2124

Michelle Hadje mastered the urge to vomit.

She knew that could change this. Change all of these things from so many dreams that pressed in against her. She knew that she could will them away, or perhaps spring for a fork that would simply...not have them. She had enough reputation, by now, to fork a dozen times over. Some perks came with being on the council, after all.

But she hadn't, and she was not quite sure why.

At one point, she had entertained the idea that it was out of a need to keep some part of herself tied to the her of eight years ago, the panicked and wild-eyed woman who had scrimped and saved all that she could to get a one-way ticket into the System. Perhaps she needed to keep some tenuous connection to the Michelle left so changed by getting lost that year on year become madness on madness.

But that wasn't quite it. Perhaps, instead, she felt as though she wasn't worth it. She hadn't been able to save her friends, not in the end, and it was only by dint of luck that she managed to survive the years after that terrible day her mind was wrapped in on itself, squeezed, stretched, knotted, and all her thoughts and all her dreams were mirrored back upon her. Perhaps she deserved these bouts of lingering disconnection, depression, dissociation, derealization, depersonalizeation.

That wasn't it either, though. She may sometimes feel the

weight of responsibility, but thoughts as gloomy as that came only when she was feeling particularly peaky.

Lately, her best guess as to why she kept this madness draped around her was the slew of memories of RJ that hit her at unexpected intervals. She could feel em, sometimes, as a ghost, perhaps, or a wish, a dream, but then that feeling would disappear and she'd be left with despair and the urge to vomit and the flickering of herself.

Michelle.

Sasha.

Michelle.

Sasha.

That last hypothesis encompassed much of the previous two, and would explain why the looming tenth anniversary of the founding of the System seemed to make it all the worse. Ten years since the founding, eleven years since RJ disappeared, giving emself up to the act of creation.

Ah well. She had lingered long enough outside the coffee shop, so she swallowed down her rising gorge and mastered a few waves of shifting form, skunk fur and human flesh fighting for dominance. The human form won today: round of face rather than mephit snout; curly, black hair rather than thick black fur. It would do. She would be Michelle for the meeting.

The Council of Eight, for all its high status and demand, met in incognito in unassuming, downtempo sims rather than some conference room or grand palace. The eight of them would trickle into the sim over the course of a few hours, set up camp on a hilltop or in a cafe, enjoy the ambiance, and then set up a cone of silence to discuss business. They had been noticed once or twice, but never hounded and certainly not attacked.

Debarre and user11824 were there already, slouching before their coffees in comfortable silence. Both looked up and waved to her when she entered, so she requested a mocha and joined them around the table.

"Hey Sa–er, Michelle. Hows tricks?" Debarre asked.

"Tricksy, as usual." She smiled wanly. "How about you two?"

user11824 shrugged. His features were nondescript to the point where Michelle doubted that he even needed to work at being incognito. Eyes simply slid over him without pausing. "Bored. Boring. Bored."

"How are you bored? There's always too much to do." Laughter came from behind her, followed by a friendly touch to the shoulder. Jonas, on the other hand, was perilously handsome, well past the point of standing out, and friendly with a casual ease that left all feeling envious.

"Yeah. Boring shit."

Jonas slid into the seat next to Michelle, coffee in hand. There were a few minutes amiable chatter as the other four octarchs trickled in: two well-dressed women, one well-dressed man, and one slouching form of indeterminate gender (and occasionally species) that looked more like a discarded pile of rags than anything.

Michelle blinked, and a cone of silence spread around the table. The proprietor raised an eyebrow, but made no other move to acknowledge it.

"So," she began, rubbing her hands over her face. "I know we just had a meeting, so I am sorry for stealing you all again, but I have a thing to ask of you all. A question, for sure, but it may morph into a favor, depending on the answer."

"Boring one?" user11824 asked.

Michelle forced a tired chuckle and wobbled one of her hands over the table. "Maybe. Probably. Most things are boring to you."

He rolled his eyes. More chuckles around the table.

Swallowing down another wave of Sasha washing across her body, she continued. "I would like to create ten forks to delegate responsibility. Would that be okay?"

Jonas frowned. "That'd be pretty expensive."

"Would it be worth the expenditure?" the pile of rags rasped.

Michelle quelled the instinct to shrug again, nodding instead. "I think it would be. Just temporarily. At least for the next year or so. I will shift my role to a more managerial one, acting as consensus builder for my clade. I would not gain any more say in votes."

"Would you take on additional responsibility, too?"

"I can. I am always happy to do my share of the work, and if that share increases ten-fold while I shift to a consensus point, I will be okay with that."

Debarre gave a lopsided smile. "If it's simply about more hands on the ground, I see no problem with it. It's your reputation to spend, and..." He hesitated, smile fading to a more serious expression, continuing, "And if it helps you out, then it's probably for the best. I'm sorry Michelle, but you look like hell."

She forced herself to keep tears out of her voice. "I feel like hell, if I am honest. I will ensure none of the forks have...all this."

Nods around the table. A woman from the well-dressed trio spoke up. "I'm comfortable answering your question with a 'yes'."

They went around the table, and none of the others challenged the first vote. Michelle slouched in relief, letting her control slacken and her form blur for a few moments.

"Does that answer mean that you have a favor to ask?"

She nodded to Debarre. "A two-part favor. I would like some help delegating to my forks, if we even have ten things that need doing, and then I would like a week off."

Jonas laughed. "You're allowed a vacation, Michelle. Go for it. I'm sure we can all find something for your new clade. The Hadje Clade?"

"The Ode Clade."

Debarre stiffened in his seat, frowned. Michelle did her best to maintain her tired mien, keeping her gaze on Jonas.

"No clue what that means, but hey, Michelle-slash-Sasha of the Ode Clade it is."

"Do we applaud? Is this exciting?" user11824 asked. He

looked honestly befuddled, and Michelle admitted that she could use a life so bound by boredom that excitement could go unnoticed.

"It's exciting for me. I get to sleep in."

Laughter around the table.

The pile of rags shifted, rasping its words. "Are we comfortable with this as a general rule? Perhaps we would all benefit from a fork here and there to help us out."

"Can we come up with a mechanism for tracking hands on the ground, as you so eloquently put it?"

Michelle nodded eagerly to the sharp dressed man. "Please. It is not my intention to take more work just so we can do more things my way."

"And we'll have to be careful not to overextend our reach. There being only the eight of us kind of limits our capabilities by necessity."

"We can be open about it, set limits for ourselves. Maybe no more than ten per council member."

"It might be handy to fork further for personal reasons down the line," Michelle said, carefully avoiding Debarre's gaze. "I can think of a hundred things I would like to do."

The weasel's frown deepened.

"Sounds fair enough. I figure we've all got personal lives outside this," one of the women said.

"Yeah, boring ones."

"You're such a drag. Take up fishing or something. Then you can be bored with purpose."

"I've got a stack and a half of trashy novels to plow through."

"There's some changes I've been meaning to make. Maybe I can even figure out how to make it like a real demolition process, too. Putting a sledgehammer through drywall? Exquisite. Simply exquisite."

The chatter continued around the table. Michelle focused on her mocha, studiously avoiding Debarre's searching gaze.

The cone of silence was dropped, and council members left at their own pace until only Michelle, Jonas, and Debarre left.

"So, what's the deal with the clade name? And why are you two being so weird around each other?" Jonas asked.

There was a moment's silence, then Debarre murmured, "You tell him."

"A friend of mine—of ours—wrote this poem, an ode, and I was thinking that I would name the instances after lines from it. A hundred lines, ten stanzas. That gives me ten first lines to start with, and I can go from there."

Jonas shrugged. "Well, fair enough, if strange. You didn't answer why you two got all weird, though."

"Complicated stuff. Both Michelle and–"

"We were both among the lost," she interrupted, shooting Debarre a warning glance.

Jonas held his hands up to forestall further conversation. "This is between you two. You can share what you want when you've got it sorted out."

Debarre nodded sullenly. Michelle looked down at her hands.

"While we're on complicated subjects, I have an admission to make." Jonas looked sheepish. "I have a small clade of my own on the side. All for personal stuff, of course, nothing tied to the Council."

Debarre tilted his head, then laughed. It was an earnest laugh, full-throated, and Michelle realized that Jonas had said precisely the right thing to cut through the tension.

"Do you have some equally stupid clade name?" Michelle said, grinning.

"Oh, just the Jonas Clade. I'm going to keep forking as long as I have reputation, I figure, so we've been naming ourselves with syllables. There's plenty enough of those. I'll stay Jonas Prime, but there's already a Ku, Ar, and Re Jonas."

"Fucking nerd."

Jonas batted his eyes at Debarre. "Thank you. I try."

After a bit more chatter, Debarre made his goodbyes and left the sim.

Michelle and Jonas tacitly agreed to go for a walk down the street. The sim was of a comfortable, small town plaza, so it was a pleasant enough walk. They made their way to a central fountain and, while Jonas sat on the rim and watched, Michelle dumped hunk after hunk of reputation to create her ten forks. They alternated between looking like Michelle and looking like Sasha. Each introduced herself in turn.

"I Am At A Loss For Images In This End Of Days of the Ode Clade."

"Life Breeds Life But Death Must Now Be Chosen."

"Oh, But To Whom Do I Speak These Words."

And on down the list of first lines. Eventually, a crowd of eleven stood near the fountain, in front of a bemused Jonas.

"So, what next?"

"What is next is that I get assignments from the Council and then take a fucking vacation. I plan on sleeping for at least three days straight."

Jonas laughed. "I wholeheartedly endorse this course of action. One of you want to take on an assignment today?"

After a short conversation, one of the skunks stepped forward. "Sure. What kind of assignment?"

"Which one are you again?"

"The Only Time I Know My True Name Is When I Dream."

Jonas winced. "Got something shorter I can call you? Even if only in informal settings?"

She laughed. "Oh, sure. Let us go with 'True Name'."

"Much better! Alright, your assignment is to work with me on the individual rights conversation."

"Is that heating up?"

"Yeah, there's some real grade-A stupidity going on out there." Jonas paused to wave to the rest of the Ode Clade, which left the sim *en masse*. "Lots of this and that about how software can't be an individual blah blah blah. One particularly vile shithead suggested that if we wanted to be treated as individuals, we would need to contribute to society as equals with those still in the embodied world. He suggested we could split the System and dump individuals into flight computers and software rigs and other expert systems to run those so that they wouldn't have to keep designing them."

True Name frowned. "What a dick. Is that kind of opinion common out there? I am still coming off the mountain of work that was the reputation market."

"Not so common now, but those voices are getting louder by the week."

"Damn."

"Damn indeed. Thankfully, those aren't the only voices. The DDR still has a good number of folks who remember the lost and just how fucked up it was for whole-ass people to be dumped into nothingness, and that sounds awfully similar to becoming a glorified flight sim."

"But that is on the DDR. Do we get votes? Do we even have access?"

"We do not, no. All we can do is read the forums. What we do have is the ability to communicate."

"Influence, you mean."

Jonas smiled, nodded. "Influence."

"I did pretty well in debate class."

"Good, we'll have need of that. And you can write, too. Your proposals are a thing of beauty."

"Oh? A joy for ever? Their loveliness increases?"

Jonas looked blank.

True Name laughed. "Never mind. Let us go change some minds."

Yared Zerezghi—2124

When one is uploaded, the only thing that is left behind is the body, and that in pieces. It is an uncomfortable, perhaps gruesome fact of the process, but unavoidable. The intellect, the emotions, and all that makes a person an individual are sent to that building (or compound, we don't know what it looks like) in the Sino-Russian Bloc and then they become a part of the System. We do not see what they see, and cannot, but we do talk to them. They are quite the talkative bunch, and they describe all sorts of wonders. The System is much like our sims but far, far more real. Realer than we could ever imagine. It is, I'm told, quite literally a dream world.

All of this—the chatter from the System, the continuity of lives from here to there, the vibrancy of the place—points to a collection of real, actual people. They may not have the bodies, but they are no less real, living, feeling, laughing, crying, joyful beings, and they deserve the recognition of their reality, their individuality.

I hear many arguments against their individual rights:

"Because we cannot interbreed with them, they are a different species, and thus are not guaranteed the same rights."

This is a crass and ridiculous idea. Of *course* we cannot interbreed, The chances of us interbreeding with a moth are more likely, as at least a moth has a body! However, if we see that their lives in the System are continuous progressions from the lives they lived here and they had inalienable rights here, then there must also be continuity of rights. Whether or not we can interbreed is nothing but a distraction.

"They should have to pay for the power requirements for running their system."

This argument carries weight when it is viewed from a strictly logical point of view. Running the System *does* cost money, and even if they have little need for money in there as they go about their day-to-day lives, perhaps they can to find a way to help subsidize that ability. I can think of a dozen ways off the top of my head even while writing this.

However, for the argument to be used as a reason that they must not have individual rights—those of freedom, happiness, and access to necessities—borders on the incomprehensible. When an individual is out of a job outside of the System, we do not simply strip away their rights on the spot! We must have the correct conversation, here, and this is just muddying the waters

"If they are essentially expert systems running on a computer, they should be treated as such and used to run expert systems out here."

This is it, here. This is the worst of almost all of the myriad arguments that I've heard. This is the pillar of cynicism that everyone's inner sociopath leans against. This is the bit of us that says: if I cannot see it, it isn't worth the scantest thought. This is the bit that says: every individual must serve a tangible use in the world in order to exist. This is the bit that says: they deserve this because I am also a cog in this horrendous machine.

Humanity is, as ever, a race of cynics-at-heart, yet this approaches such a low as to turn the stomach. You would afford dogs and cats greater rights than those who we know for a fact can think and talk and feel and know. We know this because they *are* us.

Without compromising their identity, I can say that I have received a letter from two representatives of the Council of Eight, the leadership within the System, and on this we agree. They are alive, and because they are alive, they deserve the rights guaranteed those who are alive. They are individual, and so those rights must be individual. They can feel happiness, they know what it means to be free, and they are completely dependent on this one necessity, and so those rights afforded us must be granted them.

One of these representatives with whom I have been speaking is one of the lost. I know that the collective conscious moves quickly, and it's a lot to ask it to keep in mind a single incident from nigh on twelve years ago, but they are important. They were among the lost, those unlucky few trapped within their own minds and exocortices by the whims of tyranny, and when they were returned to our shared existence from their solipsistic one, they were among the voices campaigning for change from the very political systems who failed them and many others. As one of the lost, their experiences were integral to the creation of the System, and have been a part of it from the inside for almost a decade.

Their memories are real.

Their life is real.

Vote for the granting of rights. Vote yes on *referendum 10b30188.*

Yared Zerezghi (NEAC)

Yared submitted the post to the DDR forums and swiped his way out of the whole damn trash fire, feeling for that cool air on the back of his neck, backing out of his rig fast enough that he teetered on his chair.

Every time he had to write something about this, every time he had to force himself to reiterate the arguments of others, it made him angry. Irrationally so.

He slung his bag over his shoulder, donned his cap, and stomped out of his apartment. He needed away from computers after something like that.

Sunlight assailed him on the street. The view was as bright as ever, the weather as oppressively hot as always. He swayed for a moment as he struggled to acclimate, and once he was able, continued to stomp his way down the street to the coffee shop on the corner.

He could let his anger cool, but it felt too good to nurse it just a little while longer.

His usual low stool was free, so he claimed that and sat to watch as the coffee was roasted, ground, boiled, strained, poured. Despite the urge to stoke that fury further, the meditative aspect of watching the coffee being prepared, the smell of it and the small cakes of himbasha, calmed him quickly.

He was partway through his second cup and nibbling on his second slice of the sweet cardamom bread when another man sat down next to him. This would not normally be cause for concern, except for the fact that the man was wearing a suit. A *black* suit. This was not just incongruous, it was alarming in a place where the sun shone so hot.

Yared looked around, then spotted the black car parked down the cross street. Obviously that must have a cushy, air-conditioned interior, which would at least make the choice of clothing tolerable.

He nodded to the man, who nodded back, ordered three coffees, and waited.

Yared finished his coffee and reached out his hand to grip the contacts to pay for his coffee, but the man gently pressed his arm down.

"Please, allow me to purchase your coffee and food. Do you like the himbasha here?"

Frowning, he nodded. "It's quite good. May I ask why you're paying for me?"

"My passenger would like to meet with you," the man said, nodding over toward the car. "The coffees are for the three of us."

"With me?"

"Yes, Mr. Zerezghi."

Yared reached once more for the contacts to pay, hoping he could simply walk away from the situation, which was quickly moving from alarming to frightening, but his arm was once more gently pushed away. Instead, the man reached forward and let his implants connect with the contacts, the touch completing the payment.

"I think I should leave, sir."

"Please, stay. It is cool in the car, and we only wish to talk."

"About what?"

The coffee was poured into paper cups and the himbasha was slid into a paper packet.

"Please, Mr. Zerezghi, this way."

Yared remained seated. "You haven't answered my question, sir. About what?"

By way of answer, the man smiled, not unkindly, and said, "My passenger has read your post from this morning and was most impressed. Please, you may stand outside the car if that would make you feel better."

Still frowning, Yared stood, nodded to the woman who had prepared the coffee and let the man in black lead him to the car.

The man set the tray of coffees on the roof of the car, removed one and set a slice of himbasha on it, before opening the back door and handing the tray and other slices to the person inside.

So incongruous was the context that Yared did not recognize him at first. The man was dressed much as he was, in loose white pants and a white shirt, but the clothing was much finer, with an elaborately embroidered neckline on the shirt, and spotless pants where his own were dusty and overdue for a wash.

Still, the face was unmistakable. "Councilor Demma?" he asked, voice small.

"Mr. Zerezghi! The very one. Please! Come in and sit with me, and we can drink our coffees. They smell delightful."

Yared stood at the door a moment longer, feeling the cool air against his face. His mind had gone blank. Any thought of the coffee, of the message earlier, was gone, and all he could think was, *What in the world does Yosef Demma want with me?*

A gentle hand on his shoulder from the driver urged Yared into the back of the car where he took a seat opposite Councilor Demma, who handed him his coffee and offered him the bag of himbasha, which he declined.

"I suppose you've already eaten plenty, hmm? It does smell delicious. I rather like it when they put orange in it as well as the spices." He broke off a corner of the bread and set the rest aside. "I will get straight to business, Mr. Zerezghi, as I know that this is rather unexpected for you. We have been keeping tabs of your posts on the topic of individual rights on the DDR forums. Your voice is one of the loudest, most consistent, and most eloquent out of the whole system, and would like to work with you on those."

Yared coughed on a swallow of coffee. "You have been...watching me?"

Councilor Demma laughed and waved his hand, chewing on his sweet bread. After swallowing, he said, "Do not worry, Yared. The NEAC Council is a political body, the DDR is a political entity, so of course we monitor the forums. We are monitoring everybody, not monitoring you specifically. Except, of course, in as much as you are a part of that everybody."

"But you came for me, sir."

"That we did. Your posts have attracted our attention. They are quite well written, very well researched, and the information you have by virtue of your relationship with your two companions is invaluable. We—that is, the interests in the council that I represent on this topic—feel that you would be a useful aid in reaching our goals."

"And what goals are those?"

Councilor Demma smiled in a way that did not exactly instill confidence. "Individual rights and autonomy of the System."

Yared blinked, frowned, and took the few seconds offered by a sip of his coffee to work up the courage to ask, "Autonomy?"

"We are like you, Yared. We desire that the uploaded individuals maintain individual rights. Our dreams are perhaps a little bigger, is all. You fight for their rights, but we fight for their independence."

"How can they be independent. Aren't they a part of the S-R Bloc? Those who upload have to get a visa, even if only for a few hours, before they join the System."

"Yes, but it is dual citizenship!" the councilor said, stabbing his finger toward Yared. "They remain citizens of the Western Fed or of the Northeast African Coalition or wherever they are from. They essentially only have a visa for the S-R Bloc. If they are our citizens, they must still have the rights we grant them. That is your argument, yes?"

Yared nodded numbly.

"We, like you, wish to protect those rights, but we want to grant them even more. We want to grant them their independence."

The import of Councilor Demma's request struck him like a blow to the stomach. "You...you want to help them secede?"

The man across from him smiled and finished his coffee, setting it aside before taking another bite of the himbasha. "This is quite good, Mr. Zerezghi. I will have to remember this place."

Yared frowned at the non sequitur.

"This is not something that they have in the System. They do not have delicious coffee and delicious desserts. Neither do they have hamburgers or Sichuan noodles. They have none of the same stuff as us, as crude or as plain or as beautiful as it may be. They don't have the same stuff that makes our societies what they are. They have their own society-stuff. They have their own world and their own customs.

"Have you heard about the way that they can make copies of themselves and become two individuals? It is fascinating to me. They call those collections of individuals clades, because they can form a branching tree of personalities. Wonderful! Can you imagine the culture that must spring up around that? Are clades families? Do they fight like siblings? Culture has sprung up around our coffee, our himbasha, our *stuff*, and it certainly does not involve these clades of theirs."

The councilor was intensely charismatic. The argument made sense, too, and a part of him was ready to dive in head-first if it would accomplish his goals. The rest of him prevailed, though, and he asked, "But where do I come into this?"

"Excellent question." That disconcerting smile again. "All we would like you to do is continue on your campaign for individual rights now. However, we would like to suggest some small changes to your arguments, just little nudges here and there. They will not start right away, but soon, we would like you to shift the language you use. We have confidence that individual rights will be granted, but we want the way primed for what comes after."

"Confidence?"

The councilor tapped his temple. "We keep an eye on the forums, remember? We keep our finger on the pulse of the DDR. I also have the interests that I represent, and I have confidence in them."

"You just want me to campaign as I usually do, but subtly suggest that the System should secede?"

"Ideas grow organically, Mr. Zerezghi, but they all start from a seed. You are ideally placed to be that seed, both for the DDR and for the Council of Eight."

Yared sat up straighter. "Oh, so not just the DDR, but also the System?"

Councilor Demma nodded, still smiling. "There is nothing you need to do yet, but let us meet up for coffee again, yes? Perhaps here, again, in two days time? I would love to make these chats over coffee a regular part of our schedules."

"Can I take those two days to think on it?"

That smile faltered only briefly but was quickly replaced. "Of course, Yared, I understand that this is a large request to make of you. All the same, I do hope that you will agree to join us. Much is resting on this venture."

At some unseen signal, the car door was opened from the outside. The meeting, it seemed, was at an end, and he was back on the street, back in the brightness and heat, watching the car disappear around a corner.

Douglas Hadje—2325

May Then My Name,

As promised, I'm returning to the questions you asked. The launch went well, we had our party, and now my plate is mostly clear. I have a bit of work to do with the launch arms, but responsibility has shifted over to the flight coordinator.

I suspect that you are still interested in the subjective view of things. It's a little weird, not having so much to do all the time. I tried to sleep in this morning, but wasn't able to. Who knows, maybe I'll relax over time, or find something else to fill my days. Take up knitting. Something.

Anyway, to your questions. These were all very strange and cryptic, but in the spirit of building your mythology, I'll try to answer them in earnest. If you need clarifications, I'll be here.

> How long have you been working as phys-side launch director?

From the very beginning. I was a senior System manager before that, and submitted my resume to the launch commission on a whim. It was a bit of a shock when they picked me, if I'm honest. I suspect it was the name. It'd look good to people such as yourself.

> What is involved with your role as phys-side launch director?

As mentioned, very little now. Previously, though, I was the one who had to keep everything in his head. Those directly under me would supervise things such as the micro-Ansibles or launch timing or the HE engines, and I just pulled all that together and kept everyone moving at about the same pace so that nothing was rushed and no one was left behind. In short, I was a manager.

> How long have you been working with the System phys-side?

As long as I've been working. My first job back in 2294 was as an Ansible tech in a clinic.

> What led you to pursue a career working with the System?

I've always had a fascination with the System and just how different it was from life on Earth. I had considered uploading as soon as I hit the majority but something kept me out here, I guess. I think it was just that the whole idea was so beautifully audacious that I just wanted to keep it up and running smoothly.

> What led you to remain phys-side rather than uploading, yourself? Will you upload in the future? Why or why not?

I think I answered the first part up above, but I will add to it that there is some aspect of fear that kept me from doing so. Or, maybe not fear, but intimidation, if that makes sense? I felt like I would be outclassed there. I would be able to rub elbows with people from 210 years ago! It makes me feel small.

Will I upload? I think so. I think when everything is finished out here and I can comfortably leave my position and say that I did a good job, I'll head back planet-side, go on a week-long bender, and then go to an upload clinic when I'm still hung over. I've done a lot out here. I've given decades of my life to the System, and I think it would be a fine place to retire.

There is one other thing, and I hesitate to mention it because I'm not sure if it would be uncouth, but doubtless you recognize my name. My great-great-something aunt was Michelle Hadje, who was formative to the creation of the System itself, was one of the earliest uploads, one of what I think are called the 'founders'. I want to meet her.

I know that I could just message her. I *want* to just message her! Something keeps me from doing so, though. I feel weird about it, or intimidated, rather in the same way that I feel intimidated about uploading. She's family, but so distant as to be a total stranger; she's more than two hundred years old; she's been essentially silent from phys-side for most of that time as far as I can tell, so I don't even know if she's still alive. Some day I'll work up the courage to talk to her, but I'm not sure if that will be before or after I upload.

> What led you to pursue your position as launch director rather than remaining in your previous position?

Like I said, I just submitted my resume on a whim, and before that, I was just managing station-side Ansible stuff. The next step up the ladder shouldn't have been launch director, but, like I said, here we are. The launch program totally captivated me. I was part of a messaging campaign to get it approved, and took part in as many debates as I could from out here. I desperately wanted it to happen, though I knew there was little chance of me actually getting to work on it. I was surprised and elated to get the chance.

> Please provide a biography of yourself to whatever level of detail you feel comfortable.

I was born Douglas Fredrick Hadje-Simon on April 9th, 2278 in Saskatoon to the last in a long line of Uranium miners. I got my implants along with the rest of my class at age five, and quickly took to the 'net. I spent as much time as I could in there, as did (and still do) most folks. I don't know when you uploaded, but most of Earth is not a pleasant place anymore, so the net is where one goes for literally anything but living in a shithole on a giant rock that is also a shithole, if you'll forgive the language.

Like I said, I took a job working on Ansible stuff as soon as I could. I'll admit that this was a selfish act. I was hoping that I would eventually wind up station-side to get away from the mess down there. I don't regret it. I don't miss my family. I don't miss my friends. I don't miss home. This is home now, as much as anything. I will do my best to either upload or die up here rather than go back. I'll work myself to the bone if I have to.

I moved up through the ranks quickly enough and, first chance I got, I headed up with a few other techs on a ship headed to some mining site on the Moon. I spent probably five minutes on the Moon before the other techs and I headed out to the station. I started out as a senior station-side Ansible tech and made my way up to lead before making it to launch director. You know the rest.

> Please provide a physical description of yourself to whatever level of detail you feel comfortable.

I'm nothing special, I think? Average height (I've heard that shifts over time? I'm 190cm), average weight, brown eyes, brown hair from my dad, curls from my mom. I have no idea whether I'm attractive or ugly, and honestly haven't thought about it until this question. I don't even know what to write here, I guess. My body's just a tool and vehicle to get me from place to place.

> Do you have any hobbies?

I still tool around on the 'net (though since there's more than a second's latency to Earth one way, it's mostly entertainment sims rather than chat), and for the mandatory exercise, I like running well enough. We're not allowed to cook up here, but I remember being fond of that back planet-side.

This is super embarrassing, and just between you and me. I'd prefer you not tell anyone about this, and please, please don't tell Ms. Hadje. One of my hobbies is picking up any EVA task I can get just so I can go touch the System itself. Hardly anyone's seen it, but it's beautiful. It's coated in an inch or two of manufactured diamond, and the inside is a glittery mix of gold on black that seems to go on forever.

On these EVAs, I'll go touch the System and imagine that I can feel family in there.

I don't know if it counts as a hobby, but it's important to me, and it isn't work.

> How do you feel about what you know of the founding of the System?

I don't know what I feel. You have to understand that it's been existence for more than four times as long as I've been alive. I know some of the big highlights, I suppose. It was invented some time in the 2110s, and seceded in 2125. It used to be super expensive to get to, then in the 2170s when things started getting really bad, several governments started offering incentives to upload. It turned into a weird combination of a brain drain and a dumping ground for the poor. There were a few periods where one government or another would outlaw uploading, but it would never last. It was this huge allure to us, like some sort of perfect utopia. Some folks hated it. Some still do. There were even sabotage attempts on the launch.

I don't know, though. It's almost getting to mythical status out here, so maybe your work is coming at the right time.

> If you were suddenly removed from your position as director, what would you choose to do as a career in its stead?

You sent me this before launch, and it means less now, so I'll answer how I would have felt at the time. I think I would have gone crazy and thrown myself out the airlock. I'm really not kidding about how much this means to me.

> If you were suddenly removed from your location in the extrasystem L_5 station and returned to Earth, how would you feel and what would you expect?

See above. I'd rather die than leave the station.

> If the System shut down and all personalities irrevocably lost, how would you feel?

See above.

> If you were told that, one year from now, you would die painlessly, what would you do? Would this change if you knew that your death would be painful? Would this change, in either case, if your death was seven days from now?

Obviously, if it's possible, I would just upload in all of these cases. If it was not possible for whatever reason, I'm not sure. I think I'd spend as much time as possible working with the System as closely as possible. If I had the choice to die, painlessly or in agony, while touching it, I think that I'd be happy. Or maybe not happy, but it would feel like a worthwhile death.

Maybe I'd finally screw up the courage to talk to Michelle.

> If everyone but you disappeared, what would you do?

Um...I don't know! Much of the uploading rig here is automated, though I know there are some buttons that need pressing and knobs that need twiddling. I'd probably spend every waking moment trying to automate it the rest of the way so that I could upload. If you mean the System too, well, see above.

How do you feel about being alone for extended periods of time?

This is a very rare occurrence. Earth is crowded. The shuttles are crowded. The station is less crowded, but it's also a place where one lives with a bunch of coworkers, so I'm usually not all that alone. The closest I get to being alone is sleeping or during EVAs. I spend most of that time dreaming, and I don't mind that at all.

Do you remember your dreams?

My dreams when I'm asleep? Rarely. They're usually confused images of long hallways or being super crowded in a small space. Waking dreams are much more pleasant.

How long wilt Thou forget me, O Lord? Forever? How long wilt Thou hide Thy face from me?

I have to say, I started talking with de, one of the launch commission members, and we agreed that your questions grew exponentially weird starting about here. I originally thought I'd answer each in some snarky way, but the more I thought about them, the more I realized what you're going for. In that vein, I'll try to answer each as best I can.

There are a good number of people who think that God/god(s) forgot about Earth. There have always been doomsayers and end-of-the-world-ites, but they have seen a huge uptick in my life alone. I think this last century has been defined by coming to terms with how fucked up everything is. And it's not that we don't blame ourselves. Many of us do! But many of those same people tack it on God, too. "God is disappointed with us and that's why everything's terrible" or whatever.

Me? I'm not so sure. I was raised thinking much of that, but I also feel like I left those feelings in the shuttle station back planet-side. I don't think about God much anymore. Maybe that's part of the problem: when we forget about God, we get complacent and then get into trouble, and suddenly he's much more relevant again. Who knows. Life up here is easy. I work, I get tired, I rest, I eat well, I get to do the thing I love most of all. Did I forget God back on Earth? Did I leave him there when I came here? Is there room for God in space? Do you have God in the System, and is that God the same one we talk about physside?

Maybe I can't answer the question without asking a bunch more because God and I forgot each other.

> When you become intoxicated—whether via substance use or some natural process, such as sleep deprivation—which of the following applies to you?

I laughed at this one. Where did you find this? I dug but couldn't find the source. I know that the previous one is a Psalm of some sort.

There are very few chances to get intoxicated here on the station. I had a glass of champagne after launch, and it was the first drink I had had in at least a decade, if not longer. You spend that long away from alcohol, and you lose essentially all of your tolerance, so I'm ashamed to say that, while I did feel drunk, I basically stumbled off to bed and slept.

However, you talk about other intoxications. I am no stranger to insomnia, and you're right that there is a sort of intoxication to that. I tend to get goofy and laugh a lot at the stupidest things when I've not slept for a day or two. I will laugh and laugh at the smallest thing, and then the laughter will fade and I'll sigh and say, "I'm so tired." And then I'll do the whole thing all over again. I think that might be kind of like Ape Drunk?

One thing this reminded me of, though, was of when I had just turned twenty and got incredibly sick. I had a very high fever, and when it was at its worst, I felt as though I was being offered a chance to peek behind a curtain, or at least see the shadows moving around backstage beneath the hem of it. I felt that I was granted a glimpse of some thinner reality that sat just behind our own. I was writhing in my bed, unable to hold still, with my back arching and my tongue sticking out, and yet there was this sense of the numinous and a short wave of ecstasy, and I felt pleasantly drunk. I don't know what "when a man is drunk and drinks himself sober ere he stir" means. Does it apply to functional alcholism? Even if it does, it feels like that moment. When I was in fever, I burned all the brighter before I got better, and in that moment, I saw the most clearly.

> While walking along in desert sand, you suddenly look down and see a tortoise crawling toward you. You reach down and flip it over onto its back. The tortoise lies there, its belly baking in the hot sun, beating its legs, trying to turn itself over, but it cannot do so without your help. You are not helping. Why?

I don't know. I don't know why I flipped it, and I don't know why I'm not helping it, but I see myself there, watching it flail around, and I'm sobbing. I'm sobbing because for some reason, I'm not flipping it over and I wish against everything that I could give it relief. I feel guilt and shame in equal measure, and I watch myself beat my fists against my thighs, trying to force myself to do the thing, do the thing, just *do the thing*.

This is a truly nightmarish question, May Then My Name.

> Two by two, two by two, and twice more. We always think in binaries, in black and white. We remember history two by two. We consider the present two by two. We think of the future twice over, and twice again. I have looked back on history and seen ceaseless progress or steps backward. I look back a hundred years and see illness and failure, and I look at today and see _____?

I recognize this! We read it in class. I know that the next words are "twice that and more", but I don't think that's quite what you're getting at.

I look back a hundred years and see illness and failure, and I look at today and see twice that and more *below*, but up above, as it were, I see only the clean purity of space and the steady brightness of stars. If I literally look up, beyond the walls and hull, there is the System, and while I probably hold overly optimistic ideas of what goes on inside, I don't think you have illness and failure to nearly the same extent as we do phys-side. I doubt it's a utopia, but I would be hard pressed to imagine it as any worse than outside.

> Oh, but to whom do I speak these words?
> To whom do I plead my case?

I am writing this to you, but if I have to plead my case to anyone, it's to myself. I have to make my case to myself that I am worth enough to upload, that I can bring *something* to the System, that I would be welcomed there. I'm a very harsh judge, though, and it's taking a lot of work to convince myself of that.

> From whence do I call out?

Close. So close. I call out to myself from within myself. I call out to the System through a few inches of diamondoid coating and the fabric of my EVA suit.

> What right have I?
> No ranks of angels will answer to dreamers,
> No unknowable spaces echo my words.

This is the crux of the problem, isn't it? I am convinced, on some level, that I don't have the right to want this thing. Immortality is for the gods, and that's what you seem like to me. You seem like gods, and here I am, the mortal sweeping the floor of your altar. The candles are out, the celebrants are gone, no ranks of angles will answer to a dreamer like me, and as always, sound does not travel in space.

Before whom do I kneel, contrite?

That part of me that says, "No, you are not a god." And when I beg his pardon, he laughs and says, "No amount of contrition will get you into a place separated from you by an impossibly large gap. Only death will get there, and you are not worth that."

Behind whom do I await my judgment?

I wait behind that part of me which desperately hopes that you think kindly of me, that you accept me. You, May Then My Name, as well as Michelle Hadje and the whole of the System. If that part of me is allowed in, then maybe I will be seen as worthy, too.

Beside whom do I face death?

There is no one beside me. I have few attachments here, and what professional contacts I do have with whom I've fostered a friendship have no plans to upload. It's just me before the System, waiting for death and hoping it's enough.

And why wait I for an answer?

Please answer, May Then My Name. I wait because I have to know that there is something beyond this. I went into this questionnaire with an open mind, and now I'm having a hard time continuing because I just want to curl up in my bed and cry because these last questions have stripped me of any pretense that I had about my desires and what's keeping me from them. I don't recognize where you got them from, but they have me truly unsettled. They sound almost like your name, and if you are a part of these questions, then please answer.

Ioan Bălan—2325

There was a rhythm to research, Ioan had found. The ideas and information did not always flow smoothly; sometimes, ey would go days without breaking through the current blockage, or perhaps ey would rush forward in leaps and bounds, the periods of sleep and waking growing longer and longer until ey was out of sync with the world around em.

But despite these peaks and troughs, there was a rhythm. Ey would find a pace at which the project would bloom, fits and starts or a smooth progression, and would slowly be able to predict the ways in which it would move.

There had been work before the launch, but the way in which it shifted after Dear's Death Day had knocked Ioan into enough of a different mindset that this felt like a new project. Ey supposed that it had to do with the sudden cessation of sensorium messages from Dear. That the fox was now restricted to text only must've been a shock to its system, and when eir thoughts would drift away from the task at hand of collating histories, ey would picture it sitting at a desk scribbling away, frustration on its features and agitation in its tail.

Then again, ey thought. *It still has plenty of company to pester up there.*

"Woolgathering?"

Ey snapped back to attention and smiled sheepishly at May Then My Name where she had parked herself on the other side of the room. "Yeah, I guess. I get in the zone and then an idea gets away from me and I forget to keep working."

She nodded. "Well, come here, then. Let us plan instead of read or write or whatever it is you are doing over there."

"Woolgathering, apparently," ey mumbled, but gathered up a notebook and a pen to go plop down next to the skunk all the same.

When May had moved in with Ioan the year before the launch, she had quickly requested several changes to the house. A desk for her to work at as well as a private room—a cube with all grey walls—in which to do whatever it was that she did when composing her mythos. She had also requested a few items that would work with her physiology. A stool for the desk that would let her tail drape down and curl around her feet, that sort of thing

She had declined, however, another room or bed, which had initially staggered em.

"Are you going back home to sleep?" ey had asked. "I thought you were moving in here."

She had laughed and poked em in the stomach with a finger. "You have a bed, Ioan, yes? It fits two, yes? If not, just make it fit two."

Ey had formed few attachments over the years, and certainly none which included sleeping in the same bed as someone. Eir confusion must have shown on eir face, as May had rolled her eyes and laughed.

"I do not mean anything untoward by it," she had said.

Ey had struggled to speak with a mouth suddenly dry. "If you say so. I just haven't slept in the same bed with someone...uh, ever, I guess."

Her eyes had widened and she tilted her head. "Really? Never?"

Ey had shook eir head.

"Well, I would still prefer to share your bed with you, it is just the way I work. I do not sleep well alone. But if you feel uncomfortable, I will be fine with another bed like yours."

So now ey slept beside a skunk. She had also requested a few beanbags that she could curl on, more comfortable than a couch for one with an outsized tail. Each of these was larger than Ioan had felt was strictly necessary, and it had required that ey expand the bounds of the rooms to fit them, but ey had quickly gotten used to them, as ey could stretch out on them just as well as May. They were a little too amorphous to sleep on, but still plenty comfortable.

Ey sunk into a slouch on one next to the skunk, feeling the way it molded around em. Ey knew well enough by now to lift up the arm on the side where the skunk was curled, and she predictably scootched up by eir side to rest her head against eir chest at the shoulder, arm around eir middle. Ey let eir arm drop again, curling it around her shoulders.

"Alright, planning," ey said, reaching eir free right arm down beside the beanbag for the lap desk which had proved so useful for times such as these. "What should we plan?"

"How about your forks?"

"Right, yes. Do you think I should have one for both Castor and Pollux? And I'll probably need one for history, judging by what you've told me already."

She nodded, the fur of an ear-tip tickling at eir neck. "Start with one each. You can always cut down from there if it is unnecessary, or use them only as needed. If that first message from Codrin on Castor is anything to go by, better safe than sorry. Monsters and cults! It is all very like Dear. I bet it put Codrin up to it, what with me doing the myth bits."

"Ey's been infected by Dear's weirdness."

"It is an Odist thing. You will catch it, too, from me." She laughed.

"I don't doubt I will. I'm thinking the triad on Pollux fell asleep instead. They're already diverging." Ey started a diagram on the page. "So that's three. Would it be four Ioans Bălan total, then, with me to collate the information?"

"Probably for the best, yes."

"This down-tree instance to collate, two for the LVs, one for early System history–"

"I will fork for that as well."

"More Mays?" Ioan laughed.

She poked the tip of her tongue out of her muzzle. "Are you complaining?"

"No, no, I'm sure it'll be fine. That's three forks. A fourth as needed for interviews for those who stayed behind." Ey tapped eir pen against eir lower lip. "How often should we merge?"

"I would suggest once a day to start with, perhaps an hour before you—your #Tracker instance—plan on stopping work for the day. You can use that hour to do your collating. You are less used to frivolous forking than the Odists, and much as I might enjoy multiple Ioans to canoodle with, I would prefer that you not get overwhelmed."

Ey laughed and shook eir head, jotting down notes on the paper as ey talked. "You're probably right. Besides, I'd have to make the house even bigger to have enough bedrooms."

She tightened her arm around eir middle and shrugged. "Or the bed, but there will be only one of you. I may keep a fork or two around working on other tasks, but they can shift schedules if you would prefer not to have multiple mes crowding in on you at night."

Ioan brushed the fingers on eir left hand through the soft fur on the skunk's arm. "I'd prefer that, if that's okay. I'm only just getting used to sleeping next to one you."

Tilting her muzzle up, she dotted her nose against the underside of eir chin. "For which I am grateful! I struggle to be around people without being close to them. Thank you for indulging me."

"Of course," ey mumbled, feeling the skunk's snout lingering beneath eir chin. "It's just new to me. Unexpected."

"Why?"

Ioan frowned and set the lap desk and notes aside, opting

instead to brush eir fingers along her arm. This conversation had slid off course, and ey knew that it was hopeless to get it back. Once May began to talk about feelings, all was lost. It was evening, anyhow, and a good time to set work aside.

"I suppose it just never occurred to me," ey said. "Forming attachments that would lead to something like...whatever this is has never really been a need of mine, so it just never happened."

The skunk nodded against eir chest, and ey could sense a frown on her muzzle. "That is so counter to the way I function that I cannot even picture it. I am a being of attachments. I think we all are, just to greater or lesser extent."

"I guess. I'm not a total recluse. I like interacting with others."

"Just not beyond a certain point."

Ey hesitated, then said, "It'd probably be more accurate to say that it's never happened before. I enjoy it now, it just didn't even really cross my mind until recently."

"When you had someone addicted to close attachments move in with you?"

"A bit before, perhaps, probably when working on *On the Perils of Memory*, what with all that went into that Qoheleth business, though I couldn't put my finger on it at the time. That's where Codrin came from, after all."

May slipped her arm from beneath eir hand so that she could lace her fingers with eirs. "That makes sense. Do you understand it better now?"

"A bit, though I suspect I have a long ways to go yet," ey said, squeezing her fingers between eir own. "Why are we talking about this, by the way?"

She laughed. "We are part of this story, too."

"Does that mean we're going to figure in your mythology, too?"

"Oh, of course! The archivist of tales and eir lover, the painter of myths!"

Ioan laughed. "Lover? Really?"

"It makes for good reading," she said, poking her nose up at eir chin again. "Though I would not turn it down."

Ioan tensed. Ey could feel eir cheeks burning. "Uh...there's another conversation I've never had to have before."

"We will have it another time," the skunk murmured. "Your heart is racing and making my pillow uncomfortable."

Ey forced a laugh. "What is it with you Odists? Are you all this good at turning everything on its head? Dear and Codrin, and now–"

"You and me?" May giggled.

"I was going to say, "And now you're pushing me in weird directions." I wasn't expecting Codrin to find emself in a triad, if I'm honest."

"You, my dear, lack a certain self-awareness for someone who spends all eir time up in eir head."

"Thanks, I think." Ioan shifted to the side enough to look down at the skunk. "How do you mean, though?"

She laughed and licked em on eir chin. It was an odd sensation. "It is not surprising at all, knowing Dear. For as inventive and high-minded it is, it has a pattern of conforming itself to a situation such that those around it *want* to get close to it, and it does so in such a way that they think they want to be close of their own volition. It tailors its charisma to fit."

"Are you saying it's manipulative?"

"Oh, no. Not really, at least. I do not think it knows that it is doing that. It also lacks that self-awareness. It is more like..." She trailed off, visibly searching for the words. "It is like it knows what feels good but not why, so it has developed mechanisms to ensure that those good things happen more frequently."

"More like a self-reinforcing behavior, I guess?"

She nodded.

"I suppose that makes sense, then." A silence fell during which Ioan thought about what self-reinforcing social behaviors ey had. "I like to work. It's a really fulfilling feeling. So I work. I try hard to do a good job, and when I do, it leads to more work. I developed a way to keep myself interested."

"A coping mechanism for the terminally immortal."

Ioan laughed. " 'Terminally immortal'? How does that even work?"

"I do not know. You are the word nerd, here."

"The archivist of tales, you mean."

She laughed. "Of course. And eir pet mythologist."

"Oh, now it's 'pet'?"

"I am still trying on labels. I am the one who has to write that sort of stuff, after all."

Ey lay back against the beanbag and May made herself comfortable against em once more.

More woolgathering. That's what the evening called for, more than work. More woolgathering for the both of them.

Lovers? Ey let a tape run forward in eir mind. Ey watched the friendship ey had formed with May progress into some form of romantic relationship. How would it start? Would it start with em making a formal decision to let that happen? Or would it happen by accident? Would ey some day wake up and realize, *Holy shit, I think we're dating. Are we dating? I think we are.*

And ey set a different tape to playing. A tape wherein ey set firmer boundaries, prohibited the friendship from progressing further than it already had. Or, worse—strange to already be placing value judgements!—a world in which ey pushed the skunk away, backed off from the physical affection, from the talk that bordered on flirty, from even the hypocorism 'May'. If ey let that tape play beyond that point, ey knew ey would find all of the ways in which that would hurt May and how, knowing her, seeing her express that pain would hurt em in turn.

How do they do this? ey thought. *How do the Odists just worm their way into your life and make themselves comfortable, letting you think it was your idea? That's what she'd said, and now I'm in exactly the same position as Codrin twenty years ago.*

"It is not intentional, Ioan, I promise. Not wholly."

Ey jolted, blinking rapidly as her words registered. "Wait, what? What isn't?"

"Getting close. Wearing down your inhibitions. What we were talking about before."

"You reading my mind?"

She shook her head and ey could hear the smile in her voice. "You mumble when you think really hard."

"Shit, right. Sorry. I trust you on that. I'm not upset or anything, I like, uh...this, and don't have any plans from rolling that back. You mentioned a pattern, though, and got me thinking about it."

"This is what I like about you, Ioan. What the whole clade likes about you, if history is anything to go by. You spend enough time up in your head that you start thinking about what you are thinking about and putting words to what you are feeling. You get surprised, and then you think about your surprise and break it down to make meaning of it. What you lack in self-awareness you make up in easy self-analysis."

"Feels like overanalysis, sometimes."

"Mm, probably is, and sometimes I wish you would come back down out of your head to be present. But it is the same as we are prone to overdoing whatever it is that we are specialists in. Dear goes hard on instance art, I go hard on feeling."

"What are you feeling about..." Ey forced himself to push away encroaching work-thoughts. Ey had been about to say *about this whole venture*, but instead went with, "About this?"

"Now?" She squeezed eir fingers in her own before disentangling them to tap at eir nose. "I am feeling comfortable with you, and I am feeling happy about that. I am feeling like asking you to cook something because I am starving or asking you if you'd like to go to bed because I am tired or asking you to get back to work so that I can do the same."

"That's a lot of feelings at once," ey said, grinning.

"Like I said, we overdo it."

"Well," ey said, focusing enough to fork off two more Ioans, which ey tagged #Castor and #Pollux.

"I'll finish up work," #Castor said.

"And I'll cook dinner," #Pollux said.

"And we can head to bed after we eat."

May's laugh was bright as she clapped her paws. "Well played." She slid off the beanbag and stood. She forked another May to go help #Pollux cook before stretching and offering a paw to Ioan to help em stand.

"What?" Ey took the paw and let her help lever em out of the beanbag. She kept the grip on eir hand after. "Bed now? Instead of eating?"

"Excuse me. We are adults in this house, Mx. Ioan Bălan, and adults eat at the fucking table and not on a pouf."

Yared Zerezghi—2124

The discussion of speciation continues, I see.

And you know what? You all begin to convince me of this fact. If you have been following the System feeds, you will have doubtless seen the ways in which the System differs from life phys-side in levels so completely fundamental that they strain the imagination. We (by virtue of the fact that you are even reading this) have all used the 'net. To greater or lesser extents, we have all felt the ways in which it is different than 'real life'. I myself have often found the ways in which tactility differs here from out in the world: there is touch, yes, and there is something akin to the sensation of hot and cold (thermoception, the dictionary tells me), and it obviously could not function without a fairly accurate simulacrum of proprioception. If you don't know where you end and the rest of the sim begins, it is nigh useless as a shared space.

But touch? Touch is subtly different in so many ways. I remarked on this to a friend who is far, far more into the tech side than I am, and he immediately mentioned that he had felt similar. The reason, he explained, is that no matter how hard the implants try, they can only approximate the sensation of touch. Hearing? Fine. We have decoded the phenomenon of sound well enough that we are able to toss that sense in there just fine. Smell? Well, that's a bit more difficult, as I've read that there is some funny quantum aspects to that sensation. In the end, however, it is just a matter of simulating chemical interactions well enough.

Touch is so inexact, though. For each person it is different, and for each location on the body, the reaction is different. If you touch me on the shoulder, I might turn around to look at you. If you stick your finger in my ear (please don't) I will likely react much more violently. However, if I stick my finger in my ear, it elicits no such reaction, and can even feel pleasant.

Those in the System talk of such varied experiences, but when I brought this up over the chat-line with some friends that I've made over there (I've been asked to withhold their names), they seemed more confused than anything, and had me try in several ways to describe this difference in touch, the way I sometimes fail to sense a touch, or the way I sometimes feel a strong, sudden pressure (for who has not accidentally stubbed a toe?) with about the same level of intensity of brushing my fingers over a surface.

They said that there is no such issue within there. The dreaming brain is far more capable of coming up with the sensation of touch than the limited version we find in our implants.

An example: One of these friends is a furry, which means that her form (what we might think of as an avatar) comes with all the accoutrements that that entails. She has fur, whiskers, and a tail. Those may come with some expanded sensations via implants, but in there, in the dream, her body knows how they work. She can wag her tail (if that's a thing that her species does, I don't know the specifics), can feel the ways in which the teeth of a comb move through her fur, can lick her chops, and has even told me that she enjoys having her ears petted. None of these, she told me, were things that she found possible via the 'net.

This is a complete and total fundamental difference between us phys-side and those who live sys-side.

And what a small one, too! Consider the larger ones:

- *Forking:* Those who upload can create copies of themselves. Complete and total copies that live and experience completely separate lives. Not only that, but when a fork wants (*if* a fork wants!) it can merge back with the original copy or persona or whatever you want to call it, and then that persona has the memories of *both* copies. This beggars the imagination: we simply have no way to *actually* understand this, bound as we are by those pesky laws of physics.

- *Reputation markets:* Well, I say we're bound by the laws of physics, but on a subtler level, they are as well. The System only has so much capacity (though it is growing every few months), so in order to limit this potentially boundless expansion, there needs to be some factor which places limits on them, whether it's strictly for keeping bad actors at bay or simply to conserve space for new arrivals. But of what use is money to them? They don't *need* to eat. They don't *need* to pay for travel.

There is nothing for them to buy except this capacity to create, which means there is no money changing hands. Instead, they have decided on a currency of reputation. The more you do and interact and contribute, whether it is from being on the Council of Eight or simply having a really good conversation with a friend, you accrue reputation, and it is through this mechanism that one pays for expansion. Create more? Interact more? Gain the *ability* to create more, the *ability* to interact more.

- *Creative potential:* This is what happens when you combine the first point with the second. Say you are a mathematician. It can be frustrating to work on a complex problem one step at a time, and managing a team comes with its own problems. What if you had more brain power to throw at the problem, and that brain power had *exactly the same knowledge* going into it? Obviously, there are plenty more situations that require collaboration with other unique individuals, but this alone makes it worthwhile. Already, there have been great contributions to the fields of math, theoretical physics, literature, and sociology/psychology. Hell, some of these are already being used to earn money which is being put to use in the day-to-day demands of the System. For them, though, this is the basis of an economy that cherishes such pursuits. Already, we are seeing more individuals in those fields uploading than any other.

When I think about all of these facts, I have to admit, I think that you may be right on the question of speciation. It is not just that we cannot interbreed with them, for that is a question of biology, and one party lacks that aspect. It is not just that they are not of human stock, for that is demonstrably not the case. But it does come down to a complete and fundamental change in the very fabric of being.

The term "post-human" has been thrown around plenty, of course. It mostly fits, too, but I would argue that it also implies some remnant of humanity other than those within the System have (the creation of new, unique post-humans springs to mind). They are something *more*. They are something *different*. They are exohumans, perhaps. Postbiological. The language fails.

They are uploads, and we are not.

I stand by my firm argument against so many tired and played ones that I have seen. They are beings. A new species, perhaps, but we afford rights to *beings*. We afford rights to *individuals*. That they can fork presents new problems, but what has ever stood between humanity and a solution but staunch conservatism?

Vote for the granting of rights. Vote yes on *referendum 10b30188*

Yared Zerezghi (NEAC)

As soon as he received confirmation that his post was visible on the DDR forums, Yared backed out from his rig and headed for the door, stretching a crick out of his spine as he went.

This had become routine. The action of posting a particularly frustrating essay to the forums had often been followed by going out for coffee, but now, as soon as he posted, he knew that Councilor Demma would arrive for a debriefing. This had turned into coffee together every two days. Yared would always go to the shop at the end of his street and wait for Demma's tireless driver to show up, buy three coffees and three pieces of himbasha, and lead him to the car. Sometimes, they drove out past the edge of the city to the fields of low-moisture corn and beans. Sometimes, they drove into the city center by Government House and circled the perimeter.

Or, as today, they simply sat in Demma's car, sipping on coffees and nibbling sweet bread while they talked.

"Mr. Zerezghi," the well-dressed driver said, enough acknowledgement for the day.

The owner of the coffee shop had already made their order as soon as Yared showed his face, so they collected their tray of drinks and food and walked through the late morning heat to the black car that stood idly by.

As always, it took Yared a moment to acclimatize to the blast of conditioned air that greeted him when he slipped into the car, so Yosef Demma sipped his coffee and waited until Yared could speak once more.

"Mr. Zerezghi, a pleasure to see you as always. How are you? Have you had a good day?"

"Yes, Councilor," Yared said, sipping at his coffee to stave off the chill of the air. "I trust that you have as well?"

"Quite good, quite good."

The formalities, those were also rote by now.

"We have read your post. It is quite the well written essay."

Yared nodded. "Thank you, sir."

The councilor leaned back against his seat, switching his coffee for a slice of the himbasha. "You know, originally, my constituents and I were nervous about the idea of letting you craft your own posts. Many thought it unwise to let you choose your own words, thinking it best that we write your arguments for you and have you simply post them. I disagreed, as I think that something of your style would be lost in the process. You rely on a lot of imagery and word choices that are good at swaying readers, and I think this isn't necessarily a thing that my speech writers would be able to accomplish. You have recently changed their minds."

"I'm happy to hear that. I like to think I'm a good writer."

"You are, you are," Demma nodded. "But it is always good to see that working to your advantage. To our advantage."

Yared suppressed a smile.

"We are also pleased to see the way in which you incorporated our suggestion."

"I'm glad to hear. I was worried, I'll admit. It's not that I don't agree with the speciation argument, I just had originally worried that it was distracting from the topic at hand."

"Of course, Yared. You have your own reasons to argue for individual rights, and we do want to respect those. You must understand, however, that we have the benefit of a team of analysts on our side, and they have determined that, from the Direct Democracy angle, this is the most efficient way forward specifically for the secession movement."

Leaning back into his seat and holding his empty coffee cup in his hands to leach the last bits of warmth from it, Yared sighed. "Of course. And as I mentioned, I'm not necessarily against the arguments you suggested."

The note had come late the night before, delivered via courier, along with an apology that he had been given so little time to work it into his next post. *Begin to agree with speciation*, it had read, and a tang of distaste tickled at his senses. *Not quickly, just hint that you're being swayed. Say you're starting to be convinced, but that this only strengthens your arguments.*

Demma reached out a hand for Yared's cup, as he always did, and crumpled it together with his to dispose of in a waste basket hidden in the back of one of the seats of the car. "Mr. Zerezghi," he said, bowing slightly in his seat. "Thank you once more. I won't take up any more of your time. You should have your next suggestion in the next day or two."

Yared returned the bow and, as if that were the command

he was waiting for, the driver opened the door to let him out into the growing heat of the day. He swayed once more at the shock of the temperature difference.

"Yared," the driver said, nodding, then slid back into the driver's seat of the car.

Once he could walk again without stumbling, he made his way back to his room and out of the sun. It was air conditioned, yes, but the unit in the wall had seen better days. *Much* better days.

A sudden wave of exhaustion crashed over him, but all the same, he settled back into the chair before his rig and delved in once more.

A message was already waiting for him at his desk, so, in the sim, he sat down before it, smiling inwardly at the oddly duplicated action.

> **Jonas Prime:** Yared! Beautifully done. Ping when you're back around.

He swiped a keyboard into view and instructed his desk to do just that.

> **Jonas:** Welcome back. How goes?
>
> **Yared Zerezghi:** Well enough. Hot as ever. Thanks, by the way. Think the post will help?

Inwardly, he fretted, worrying that his counterparts in the System had picked up on the slow change in direction over the last few posts.

> **The Only Time I Know My True Name Is When I Dream:** Probably! I am pleased that you enjoyed my description of brushing and petting.
>
> **Yared:** I felt it got the point across quite nicely.
>
> **True Name:** That it did.

Jonas: We've been tracking the speciation argument, as far as we can see, and it's an interesting idea. I go back and forth on it. Sometimes, it feels like a distinction without a difference, and sometimes, phys-side ideas just leave me completely baffled. I've forgotten how strange the System sounded when I was outside of it.

True Name: Yes. It is a good talking point, but also a line that you should walk carefully. I worry that it will lead the discussion back to the "sub-human" arguments that pop up here and there.

His heart dropped. So they had picked up on the change.

Yared: I'm worried about that as well. Still, when I've argued on the forums in the past, I've found that building a strong argument and then slipping a little bit of empathy for the other side nudges them to do the same.

A lie, but hopefully a helpful one.

True Name: I had not thought of that, but I was never big into the DDR. Calling it both "Direct Democracy" and a "Representative" made it sound disingenuous.

Jonas: I mean, it makes sense. If they start feeling our empathy in the equation, maybe they'll start feeling empathy towards us.

Yared: That's the hope! Some of these people though...

Jonas: Numbskulls.

True Name: Dipshits.

Yared: Both accurate.

True Name: Just do not generate too much empathy in them. I do not want them latching onto anything to use against you.

True Name: Against us, in the end.

Yared: Of course! I'll keep monitoring the forums and chatter, and it looks like some governments are waking up to it.

True Name: Whoopee.

Jonas: I'll have you know that she just rolled her eyes at me.

True Name: Jerk.

Yared: Haha. Still, I think it'll help. It means that this is is going to be taken into consideration and not just turn into a DDR-only referendum. If we get them discussing it, then we have a smaller target to influence. DDR votes carry less weight when gov'ts weigh in. They read the forums as much as any DDR junkie, so the arguments can sometimes carry more weight.

True Name: As much as it pains me to admit, you have a point.

Jonas: When you get a chance, you and I can go into it more in depth, Yared.

Yared: Have some thoughts?

Jonas: I was a politician phys-side, so, yeah.

True Name: WHAT

True Name: You are kidding.

Jonas: I'll have you know that she just punched me in the shoulder.

True Name: And I will do it again. Fucking gross.

Jonas: I'll have you know that she did, indeed, do it again.

Yared laughed. He was pleased to see them in good spirits.

Yared: Don't beat him up too bad, True Name. He probably does have some good info, even if it is a few years old.

True Name: ...

True Name: I GUESS

True Name—2124

The next meeting spot for the Council of Eight was in a rooftop bar. However, given that that rooftop bar was in the midst of a block of apartment buildings and vertical malls that had built with shared walls, such that there was a cubic half-mile of stair-climbing, elevator rides—down as well as up—and trestles that bridged buildings of lower height than higher ones, it was more adventure getting to the venue than the meeting itself promised.

Still, The Only Time I Know My True Name Is When I Dream climbed.

The apartment buildings ranged from serviceable to gutted, and more than one time, she had to step carefully through a path covered in rubble. She could not decipher whether this was due to abandoned renovations, some unknown battle, or the simple degradations of time.

The malls offered different dichotomies. Some of them were sparkling new with speakers that whispered to her in Mandarin and lights that shouted in her face, while others played placid muzak through halls lit only by emergency lights, darkened storefronts yawning onto scuffed and over-waxed parquet floors.

She wondered who it was that had owned this sim, what collective it was that had decided to mash all the best and worst multiple clashing centuries worth of Kowloon Walled City and

111

the North American Central Corridor.

And then, the rooftop bar. Despite no vehicle entrance to the complex, this was situated on the top level of what appeared to be a car park straight out of a mid-western American airport, complete with one or two of those vehicles that seemed perpetually parked, ones that had lingered for months or years, accruing a parking debt of thousands, tens of thousands of dollars.

The bar itself was a pop-up affair, with walls and ceiling of corrugated plastic held together with rivets and tape, a bartop that was a few two-by-eights set across a trestle, fronted with further corrugated plastic to keep the patrons from kicking fridges or sinks out of alignment.

The drinks: early 2100s hipster bullshit, all intensely sweet or riddled with smoke-scented fizzy water or long strips of seaweed or clams within the ice cubes, steadily making the drink more and more savory over time.

True Name found it all confusing and jarring.

She liked it immediately.

Debarre was already at one of the tables—similarly cobbled together—sipping something that seemed to be all foam. He waved to her as she entered, and she waved back, heading to the bar to pick up one of those seaweed concoctions before joining him.

"That looks fucking gross, Sasha."

She laughed and shrugged. "I am True Name, but yes, it really does. If we are going to meet in a place that gives me a headache to walk through, it is probably best that I get something with...protein? Is that how this works?"

"Uh, sorry. Yeah. True Name." The weasel splayed his ears and averted his eyes. "Can we talk about that sometime?"

"Yes, but probably as Michelle, if that is okay."

"Why?"

"She is...closer to it than I am."

Debarre gripped his glass more tightly and twisted sideways to swing his leg over the bench and straddle it. "Yeah, I don't get it. Before everyone else gets here, can you at least give me a sentence or two?"

"When she forked, when I...became me, she decided not to fork that part of her that suffers, if that is the right word." True Name frowned. "Already we are drifting further apart. The species remains, the appearance and the speech patterns remain, the *mind* remains, but not that part of her that is so split. I am me, I am templated off of Sasha, because being both Michelle and Sasha at the same time was no longer tolerable."

He shrugged, still staring down into his drink. "I can't speak to that, I guess. But why Aw–"

True Name slammed her glass down on the table a bit harder than intended, some of the drink spilling over her paw. "Do not say that fucking name."

The weasel jumped at the sudden intensity, and when he recovered, he finally met her gaze. His expression softened from fear and anger to a tired bleakness. That moment drew out for a long few seconds of quiet and seething sadness. He reached for a napkin from the dispenser at the end of the table and handed it to her. "Here."

She hesitated, mastered a surge of unnamed emotion, and accepted the napkin to wipe the sticky drink from her paw and then, on realizing that she was crying, the tears from her face. "Sorry, I am just..."

"We'll talk." He reached over and gave her dry paw a squeeze in his own. "Michelle and I will. There's something I'm missing here is all, and I want to figure out why more than what."

True Name hid her muzzle in her drink and pretended to take a sip until she was sure she wouldn't slur her words when she spoke. "Thank you. She is open to messages still, I will let you two work it out. For now, I need to focus on the meeting. Jonas and Zeke are here."

Looking over his shoulder, Debarre nodded and turned to sit on the bench to face her again, leaving room for the other two.

Jonas settled next to True Name so that they could give their speech together when the time came, and Zeke, that shifting bundle of rags and grime slid onto the bench beside Debarre.

"Good afternoon," the almost-face within the bundle rasped.

Jonas grinned. "It's morning, isn't it?"

A pseudopod that may have been a hand waved the comment away. "Time has lost all meaning. I seem to have forgotten how to sleep, these days."

"You need a vacation like Michelle."

There was a low rattle from the rags, and True Name imagined that must be Zeke's laughter. "Don't tempt me. I don't have the funds to fork, so you'd be down to seven."

"Why *did* you make it so expensive?" Jonas elbowed True Name in the side.

She held up her paws defensively and laughed. "I did not. The price is tied to System capacity."

"The laws of physics were a mistake and reputation is a lie."

"It is the best limiting factor that we have that is not a complete fabrication, at the moment."

"I rather miss coins."

"My dad used to collect coins, you know."

And so on, until the table was full and the cone of silence fell.

"Sasha? Uh...True Name. Jonas?" one of the well-dressed triad asked.

"Right," Jonas said, setting his drink down. "The bill. Things are progressing slowly, as they always do, but it sounds like they might start picking up steam shortly. Our main contact on the DDR side, one Yared Zerezghi based out of the Northeast African Coalition, says that some of the governments are starting to take interest in the bill, which could work to our advantage. Having it just be a direct vote would mean that we would have far, far more representatives to convince, since that'd mean essentially everyone on the DDR. The more governments in play, the more the role of the DDR shrinks."

"How does that even begin to help? Aren't they super stodgy?" Debarre asked.

"They can be," Jonas hedged. "But if we can form contacts with each of them, we can argue our case directly. Yared might be the one to give us a good in for the NEAC, and I still have some Western Fed contacts."

"Anyone for the S-R Bloc or anywhere in SEAPAC? Middle east? India?"

The trio of suits raised their hands. "S-R Bloc. We don't know any of the oligarchs directly, but we had some big money interests of our own."

"Israel," Zeke said, then laughed at the awkward silence that followed. The trio frowned. "Sorry, nothing to be done there."

"And SEAPAC?"

user11824 shrugged. "I was a nobody, but I was a Maori nobody."

"You had enough to upload. That has to count for something, doesn't it?"

He shrugged again.

"We will take all the help we can get," True Name said. "Even from nobodies."

"Alright, I'll poke mom."

Zeke nodded to True Name. "What's your take on the situation?"

She stirred her drink to buy herself some time to think. "I think it is leaning our way. One of the big arguments remains speciation, but Yared's turning that into a pro-rights argument instead of a neutral- or anti-rights one. His voice is getting louder, too. It sounds like he is getting a lot more upvotes on his posts than before."

"That's good."

True Name nodded. "I think so. He is not the biggest voice on the issue yet, but it sounds like he is probably in the top three."

"You said he's NEAC, right?"

"Yeah, Addis Ababa," Jonas said. "Not exactly the seat of power, but I guess not everything has to be Cairo. Sounds like we have a good mix, at least. No one from South America?"

Everyone shook their heads.

"I suppose that's alright. They're a big enough voice in Western Fed, but they're still in the shadow government side of things. They don't even have the shadow minister of System affairs."

"Who does?"

"Lithuania."

One of the suits laughed, and Debarre looked blank.

"Politics," Jonas said, grinning lopsidedly.

"If you say so."

After a moment's silence, Zeke rasped, "So what are our next steps?"

"Let's all talk to our respective interests—Zeke too—and we'll meet again soon. True Name and I will keep working with Yared and guide as best we can from our side. Speaking of, though, any thoughts on the speciation topic?"

Six sets of eyes flitted between Debarre and True Name, between weasel and skunk, then the whole council laughed.

"I don't give a shit," user11824 said. "But if your Yared guy can twist that argument against the opposition, then that's just one more tool, isn't it?"

"We aren't seeing that," the man in the suit spoke up. "Two thirds of our power structure still think child restrictions are a good enough idea that those laws have bled into Russia. I'm pretty sure they see speciation as a positive. What better way to help in population control?"

One of his companions shrugged, "I wouldn't be surprised if they started putting limitations on uploading by gender, but that is a separate topic."

"Zeke?"

The pile of rags shifted in a shrug.

"Debarre? True Name? Anything you can leverage?"

The weasel laughed. "I mean, if you want to point to us as an example to push that along, and Yared's tack seems to be working, go for it."

"Alright. It's something you can suggest to your respective interests if you think it'll help. We'll reevaluate next meeting. Anything else on the agenda?"

Everyone shook their heads, then lifted their glasses to a toast. The cone of silence dropped.

"Well, then, you are all free to stick around or go if you want," True Name said. "I am going to stay and get well and truly plastered."

Codrin Bălan#Pollux—2325

Interview with Dear, Also, The Tree That Was Felled#Pollux
On the reasons for vesting entirely in the launch
Codrin Bălan#Pollux
Systime: 201+25 1014

Codrin Bălan#Pollux: Before we get into the heavy stuff, how are you feeling?

Dear, Also, The Tree That Was Felled#Pollux: [laughter] You are going to have to be more specific, my dear. Do you mean my general disposition?

Codrin: Yes. I just want to see how you're feeling before all these discussions, then afterwards, I'll ask the same thing and we can see how the topic influences you.

Dear: Clever, clever. Well, I am feeling fine. It has been a good day, and it was a good night last night. For the record, I hosted a get-together of those interested in instance-art, so it was bound to tickle my fancy.

Codrin: Good. Have you noticed any difference in that realm of late?

Dear: No.

Codrin: Alr–

Dear: I take that back. Sorry for interrupting. I take that back. I have noticed that about the same number of people showed up to the gathering as used to on the old System.

Codrin: How do you mean?

Dear: Well, only a portion of us transferred, yes? I would have thought that this would have lowered the attendance at such events. I have also noticed, in looking around, that the majority of our fellow travellers are dispersionistas.

Codrin: I know that May Then My Name has some stats on that. It might be interesting to see.

Dear: [nodding] That would be interesting, yes. You had a goal for this interview, though, so shall we get to that?

Codrin: Yes, might as well. I am curious, first, why you decided to travel on the launch. Was there anything in particular that drew you to the idea?

Dear: Other than the fact that I am a hopeless romantic? [laughter] There were a few. I am a hopeless romantic, yes, and—I will not actually be able to see them—I want to see the stars. I want to be one of the lucky few, or few billion, who get to travel between them. Another is that, when one is functionally immortal, boredom is a very real problem. I do not like being bored, and after something like two hundred years sys-side, I was getting perilously close.

Codrin: So it's a sense of adventure?

Dear: I suppose, though that brings to mind something more active than this is, to me. I hear adventure and I think sneaking behind enemy lines or guns at dawn. It is a desire for the new and interesting. Not just that there be new and interesting things going on around me, but that those new and interesting things change me in some deep way. I like stasis even less than boredom, and uploads are at risk of falling into patterns familiar enough to be considered stasis.

Codrin: Is there an aspect of being the first to do something involved?

Dear: Perhaps. I am not against being something other than the first, but I do like it when I am.

Codrin: Did you have other reasons for transferring?

Dear: A few, though they are less easily put to words. If you remember the Qoheleth business, there is some of that involved. I have been unable to forget what he said, and beyond the very literal sense that it was couched in. If we are doomed to forever remember everything, then the only way— or perhaps one of the only ways—to relegate something completely to memory is through inaccessibility. If I– if all instances of Dear, Also, The Tree That Was Felled were to quit, then there would be no more objective instance of myself for others to remember.

Codrin: I would prefer that you not.

Dear: [laughter] I have no plans on it. If exploring this strange mystery were a project, then I would not be served by not being around to complete it. The launch gives me a chance to do that very thing.

Codrin: Perhaps you could say that you would go from being someone who is remembered to someone who is missed? Does that sound like a fair assessment?

Dear: [excited] Yes. Yes! That is it precisely. If we are doomed to forever remember everything, then the closest we can get to being forgotten is to turn memory into longing.

Codrin: You mentioned a few more reasons. Do you have others?

Dear: Even less easily put to words. I like the idea of relativity. The faster we go, the more our perception of time will drift. I like the idea of the ever-increasing transmission times. Already, we are losing seconds and minutes to distance. I am interested to see what will happen to the population of a System that will no longer be receiving new uploads. Will we relax the taboos on finding ways to merge separate personalities into children? That would mean that we would be even closer to a new species, as the tired rationalizations go. Would the taboo of incest remain, and we will continue to frown on generating new minds from in-clade personalities? There are many questions to ask during this journey.

Codrin: And we will have time to do so.

Dear: [laughter] Yes, we will.

Codrin: Can you speak to your decision to invest your instance solely into the launches? You left no immediate forks back on the L_5 System, correct?

Dear: [tense, sober] Correct, I left no forks behind. I have two main reasons for doing so, one more personal than the other.

Codrin: Perhaps we can stick to the less personal one for now.

Dear: I will tell you both, as long as I am able to add one condition.

Codrin: Of course. I'll honor that as best I'm able, and if I'm not able to, we can pass on that reason.

Dear: Thank you, dear. You may transfer this interview in its entirety, but you and Ioan may not use the second reason in your histories. May Then My Name Die With Me may use it in her mythology, as long as it is not associated with my name or clade.

Codrin: Certainly. I can honor that. Would you like me to get confirmation from Ioan?

Dear: [laughter] You are not so different from em yet. I trust that if you agree that ey will as well. Though Ioan, when you read this, please imagine a sly smirk or quippy saying or well-placed 'fuck' when I see your face fall at the request that your history be incomplete.

Codrin: [laughter] Even I'm feeling disappointed now.

Dear: You historians, tsk. Anyhow, the first, less personal reason is this: I mentioned that it would be interesting to explore what it means to be missed as an analog to forgetting. I want someone to miss me.

Codrin: Do you worry that you won't be missed, on some level?

Dear: [long pause] I am not comfortable answering that question.

Codrin: I understand. Let me ask this instead-

Dear: I have changed my mind, but Codrin, I love you dearly, but fuck you for making me cry.

Codrin: I'm sorry, Dear. Do you want to stop?

Dear: No, no. That is my choice usage of 'fuck' for the interview. [laughter, short break in interview] Okay. Early on in the System, some wag, when pressed to build a library, uploaded every single book they could get their hands on, legally or otherwise, into the perisystem architecture, going all the way back to the Epic of Gilgamesh. When I was forked and still trying to figure out ways to play with instances, I went on a tear of reading biographical works, going through dozens of books at a time, hunting for little moments that could be used, somehow, in an exhibition.

Dear: I came across a book of essays from goodness knows how long ago, and I was so taken aback by one part in particular that I snipped it out and stored it in an exo. Ah, let me find the correct part [pause] Okay. "Should you happen to be possessed of a certain verbal acuity coupled with a relentless, hair-trigger humor and surface cheer spackling over a chronic melancholia and loneliness— a grotesquely caricatured version of your deepest self, which you trot out at the slightest provocation to endearing and glib comic effect, thus rendering you the kind of fellow who is beloved by all yet loved by none, all of it to distract, however fleetingly, from the cold and dead-faced truth that with each passing year you face the unavoidable certainty of a solitary future in which you will perish one day".

Dear: I worry sometimes that, as a public personality, first as Michelle Hadje, then as an Odist, and now as an artist with an ebullient personality and the aforementioned "verbal acuity coupled with a relentless, hair-trigger humor and surface cheer" *et cetera, et cetera,* that I... [pause] Okay. [pause] Okay.

I sometimes worry that I, as those things, fall into the category of "beloved by all yet loved by none".

Codrin: *I* love you, Dear.

Dear: [waving paw, tears] This was not supposed to be the personal part of the interview. Codrin, Ioan, please just say that I want someone to miss me, that I want to haunt the L$_5$ System as some quiet ghost who communicates in words from light-years away and memories that you will never forget. I want to haunt you because that is one thing I cannot do without merging into oblivion. I want to be missed.

Codrin: Perhaps here is a good place to stop.

Dear: The second reason is short.

Codrin: Okay.

Dear: And this is for the myth only.

Codrin: Right.

Dear: I want to die.

Codrin: Dear, I–

Dear: I am sorry, my dear. I should have prefaced that. I want to die eventually. I do not want to quit, I do not want to be killed. But you must understand, by the whims of gravity, both Castor and Pollux will eventually be captured by a sun or a black hole or whatever the fuck is out there, and they will be destroyed. And even if not, the power source will die, or the factories will not be able to manufacture replacements or some other technobabble bullshit. There is no suicide in me, nor any desire to be murdered, but I want to experience– Ah, Codrin, I am sorry. I love you. I am so sorry. I will stop.

Codrin: Let's go inside, please.

Transcript ends, no closing remarks

Codrin Bălan#Castor—2325

The sim in which Dear's house squatted low, that short-grass prairie filled with buffalo grass and dotted with yucca and hardy dandelions, ran to the horizons in ceaseless waves, and often, when eir mind was too tangled up in itself to get anything done, Codrin would hunt those horizons.

When ey had first moved in years ago, ey had asked Dear what else was on the prairie, and it had laughed. *"I do not know."*

"Did Serene not leave you a map?"

It shook its head again and had repeated. *"I do not know. She does not know. It is just a prairie that never ends. You can walk as far as you want and there will always be more prairie before you. There are no mountains on the horizon, there are no rivers or creeks, and while there are a few rock outcroppings, they are largely uninspiring."*

"So, just an empty prairie?"

"You say 'just', but Serene assures me that it is more complicated than that. The prairie is generated out to the horizon, and as long as you walk, it will continue to be generated out to the horizon. Only the places that we have seen are locked down, as it were, and remain after we have left."

"That sounds like it would just continue generating prairie."

It had shrugged at that. *"All I have seen is prairie, and I have walked for days out there. Serene is no less a trickster than I, however, and I would not be surprised if there is something out there, perhaps triggered by a mood or a word."*

And so when eir mind was too tangled up in itself to get anything done, Codrin would walk and walk and walk, always with the idea at the back of eir mind that perhaps ey would stumble across a creek or a cave that ey could bring Dear out to see.

The endless prairie also provided an outlet to seek solitude. Moving in with Dear and its partner had been decided on a whim, originally as a way to complete the project ey had undertaken, and then when their relationship began to encompass em as well, ey had found emself suddenly surrounded by those other than emself.

This had had its ups and downs. Ey did not realize that a not insubstantial portion of what ey had previously labeled boredom or listlessness had been loneliness. That feeling of becoming a part of something that required emotional investment and paid back emotional dividends had fulfilled em in a way that ey had not expected. Ey had talked about this with Ioan a year or so after ey had noticed it, and eir down-tree instance had agreed far more readily than ey had expected, saying that the Ode clade project had led to something of a sea change within em, and then reminded Codrin that ey had merged before moving in with Dear and had both perspectives within em now, solitary and social.

However, it had meant that that part of em which was built up of things solitary now required conscious intervention to satisfy. Ioan had needed to seek out the social, and now Codrin needed to seek out the solitary.

Ey needed to be away from Dear.

It wasn't that the fox was hurting em. It was a delightful partner, kind and considerate, and it knew how to apologize when it had made a misstep. It wasn't even particularly loud, as its partner had long ago kicked it out of the house for working on anything that would be noisy.

It was just a lot.

The first time that Codrin had stepped away from the house when Dear was being a lot, the fox had gone into a small sulk, sending Codrin a curt apology via sensorium message and not responding when Codrin said that ey'd be back in a bit. They had soothed ruffled fur over dinner. Now, when Codrin stepped out to take a break from a very intense fennec, ey would leave with a reassurance and still take comfort in the loneliness of the prairie.

Dear had been a lot today. Codrin had suggested that they do an interview together after Ioan had sent both launches—Castor and Pollux—a note asking that Codrin include the trio's reasons for leaving as well as those ey would be interviewing.

"We already told em that our fireside stories would be the only reasons we would send."

"Well, yes," Codrin said. "But from the sound of it, the Pollux launch didn't do fireside stories."

"Then why not send that request only to Pollux?"

"There was more to the message than that, Dear. Maybe ey just wrote the same thing for both launches and sent it in one go."

The fox had stared down into eir wide mug of coffee, a series of emotions crossing its face, before nodding. *"Yes, of course. I apologize, Codrin. I have been thinking about those stories since launch night, and the more I do, the less I want the actual reasons to wind up in some history book."*

Codrin had laughed, sipping eir own coffee. "I understand the impulse, believe me. I'm not even sure *I* know your reasons."

"That is by design, Codrin."

Ey could not place why that had bugged em so at the moment, but as it continued to snowball in eir mind over the next hour, picking up emotions as it went until it was an outsized lump tumbling around within em, ey had walked over to where the fox was blocking out stage diagrams of some sort, kissed it between the ears, and said that ey would be back soon.

During eir previous expeditions, ey had begun placing cairns at regularly spaced intervals with rocks pointing directions where ey had split off this way or that, so as ey walked from cairn to cairn, looking for new ways to explore, ey thought about the conversation.

"That was such a dramatic thing to say," ey said, sorting through eir reasoning aloud. "If it simply didn't want to talk about it, it would equivocate or tell me to fuck off. So why be so obviously sly about it?"

The rocks did not reply. Ey set down another marker stone atop the cairn and walked off into the grass perpendicular from eir trail.

"If it had told me to fuck off, I would've just written that in a note back to Ioan, and we would've had our private laugh about it. If it had equivocated, it knows that I probably would have kicked it way down the priority list and likely not bugged it again. Was it something about the stories themselves?"

The grass did not answer, only rustled and tugged at the hem of eir sarong.

"It prides itself on being deliberate, and it *knows* that I know that, so why did it say that in particular? Am I supposed to ask it? Am I supposed to feel curious or chagrined or envious?"

The wind only murmured to em.

Ey walked out into the grass and focused on letting the litany of questions go, counting eir steps up to one hundred, where ey paused to build a new cairn out of flat clods of dirt and stones dug up from between the tussocks of grass. The sensation of the dirt gritting against eir palms, of the way it got trapped beneath eir fingernails, anchored em to a moment in time, rather than spinning off into abstract thought.

"I won't push it. Not yet," ey murmured to the pile when it had reached above the thin stalks of grass. "But that does sound like an invitation, doesn't it? *That is by design.* Like an invitation to play, or tease the reasons out of it."

Ey frowned and pushed emself up to standing again. "Or maybe not."

As ey continued to walk out into the prairie, a small portion of eir mind kept an eye out for a break in the scenery, anything other than that endless, rolling sea of grass.

The rest of eir mind, though, continued to prowl through conversations that ey had had with Dear over the last few years as the prospect of the launch became more and more real. The fox had often talked about irreversibility, about how some things that one thought of as irreversible weren't. It had talked about having a drive to leave, and how there were some decisions that came from the head and some that came from the heart, but never what drove that drive, those decisions.

"Does it feel guilt? Or regret or something?"

Ey held onto that thought as ey walked another hundred paces to where ey would plant the next cairn. Soon enough, however many decades or centuries in the future, the prairie would be dotted with regularly spaced piles of rocks and dirt for miles spreading out from the house, and they would become as much a regular part of the landscape as the prairie itself, rather than this new thing that Codrin had introduced.

As ey worked, digging up rocks and roots, ey tried to think of what all Dear might have to feel guilty about or regret over. Ey knew that that experience with Qoheleth had come with some regret. It had mentioned more than once while Codrin worked on the story that had come out of that experience that it wished it had pushed harder to learn more before trying to pull the whole clade together.

But it had stopped talking about regrets once the project had been completed. It had been happy with that, and it had giggled and clapped its paws at the spike in reputation it had gained the newly-formed Bălan clade.

"See what a corrupting influence I have had on you?" it had said.

"I'm a ways off from having a clade listing like you, Dear." Ey had pulled up the reputation listing for Dear, and then for the entirety of the Ode clade, and they had both marveled at the numbers.

"Well, okay, yes. But still! The Bălan clade! How delightful!"

Was it something to do with the clade? The Odists had been

around long enough—what had Dear said? After Secession? 2130 something? Still almost two centuries—that there was certainly enmity between the various factions, perhaps there was some regret there.

Ey sat before the cairn so that it came up to eye level, and watched the long, slow sunset begin.

Perhaps it was regret or guilt, perhaps not. The fox had attacked the idea of leaving, of truly leaving the L₅ System and leaving no fork behind, with a ferocity that even Dear's partner admitted was somewhat unusual, as though it had *needed* to leave, to escape something.

And then it's story, building an ascetic cult until it had been killed by its followers. Did some of that ring true to the fox? Did it feel that it had a cult following? Did it feel as though there were some risk of being destroyed by the thing that it had built up? Did it feel like an ascetic who had taken too many liberties?

"I'm overthinking this," ey mumbled.

All the same, eir frustration had burned itself out, and all that remained was exhaustion and worry. Ey would forever worry about Dear, seeing how brightly the fox flared, that some of the madness that it had said plagued the Odists, whether from age or from something before uploading, surely dwelt within it as well.

As the sky purpled, Codrin sighed and stood up once more, stretching and beginning the long walk home. Ey could just arrive there, but the walk felt necessary to process so many strangely-shaped thoughts.

Dear and its partner were waiting to greet em when ey returned home, each with a kiss in turn. The sun had slid fully below the endlessly distant horizon, and while ey had spent full nights out in the prairie twice during these excursions, those had been preceded by arguments (both of which had been fallout from eir newness to the concept of relationships), and since this one had not, the two had started to get concerned.

"Dinner's ready whenever you are."

Ey perked up and nodded, "Very ready. Sorry for staying out so long."

Dear shook its head. *"I was worried, but I always worry. Did you sort out whatever needed sorting out?"*

"Mm, halfway, perhaps?" Ey nodded toward the table, where the settings had been placed. Ey smelled the tang of sauerkraut, the smokiness of paprika. "Shall we?"

"Thank fuck. If you had insisted on keeping us out here to talk our ears off, I would have filed a petition to have you censured."

"Dear," its partner said. "Don't be a shit."

Codrin laughed. "No, no. It's okay. I'm doing fine. Dear's alright."

"Mx. Codrin Bălan!" the fox growled, stamping its foot. *"I have just been called a shit, do not take this moment from me."*

"Alright, you little shit. Have your moment at the table."

It looked proud, bowing extravagantly and leading them into the dining room, where they dined on székely gúlyas and spätzel and chatted amiably about only the small things.

Dear, having clearly waited until the food had disappeared, finally spoke in a tone that told Codrin that it had been scripting the line since ey had returned home. *"Now, will you tell us why you went for your walkabout? Was it just for alone-time, or did it have to do with where our conversation ended this morning? I have thought myself in circles about that, but want to hear your take before I burden you with mine."*

"Alright." Codrin stalled for time by pouring emself some wine, trying to decide where to begin. "I can accept that you have your reasons for leaving the System behind. I think all three of us do. I would like to know why, but at your own pace. I had a thought out there, though. When did you say Michelle uploaded?"

The fox very carefully set its wine glass down. Codrin noticed that it's paw had begun to shake. *"Did you go looking?"* it asked.

Ey blinked, startled at the change of its demeanor. "No. You said the 2130s, and I had no reason to doubt you. Should I have?"

"No, of course not."

Its partner had a strange look on their face, somewhere between anxiety and dread.

"Isn't that what you said?"

"Yes, it was. It was. That was after the Secession, but early enough to be plausibly within the realm of 'founders' as I had said." It cleared its throat, composed itself. *"You may add this to your histories, but I would like the chance to read over what you write before you commit it."*

Codrin shrugged, nodded. "If it's a story about you, I don't see a reason why not."

"Thank you, dear. But no, I uploaded in 2117. I—Michelle—was one of the Council of Eight."

Ey coughed on eir next sip of wine. "What? You were? Uh...holy shit." Ey looked to it's partner. "You knew this? I don't mean that in an accusatory way, sorry. I'm just a little shocked. More than a little."

"Yes. I left it up to Dear to tell you. It's always been tight-lipped about that."

"It is there for anyone to look up, but most who look it up do not seem to care very much, or find it simply a curiosity." It hesitated, then added, *"It is also particularly difficult to look up for reasons that I will not go into now."*

"So you were there for Secession? For the L5 launch?"

"Not this instance, but yes. Did you read up on the lost for your publication?" It shook its head. *"You must have, yes, I remember. Do you remember Debarre?"*

Codrin nodded dumbly.

"We pooled our money and uploaded together. He was also on the Council." Dear sighed and rotated its wine glass anxiously on the tabletop. *"Michelle soon became unable to participate in the council— you saw her before she...before she quit—so she forked the first ten lines, dumping much of her reputation into the process, and talked the*

council into letting them sit in her place."

"So it became the Council of Eighteen? Er...Seventeen? I'm realizing how little I know about the Council."

"No, no. Not at first, at least. The deal she struck with the other members of the Council was that her responsibility would be split evenly among the ten. At first, The Only Time I Know My True Name Is When I Dream was the only one to sit council, then as her responsibilities to the secession process began to grow, more of Michelle's ongoing projects were given to further first lines."

"You said not at first. Did she—the Odists—wound up with more than an equal share of responsibility?"

Dear nodded. *"It was slow and subtle, and, initially, unintentional. She was-"*

" 'Initially'?"

It sighed. *"This is the part that keeps me tight-lipped."*

Codrin nodded for it to continue.

"She was the origin of a lot of projects, you must understand. She helped Ezekiel, one of the other council members, implement the idea of forking. She and Debarre helped implement the reputation market to limit that, given the technical limitations of the early System."

"And Secession?"

"Her and Jonas, yes."

"Secession was initially the idea of one of the phys-side campaigners," its partner said. "Initially they were campaigning for individual rights, and that debate intensified when news of forking reached the outside world."

"Yes. There were some truly ugly suggestions from phys-side. Mostly on the DDR. Did that still exist when you uploaded?"

Codrin shook eir head. "At least, I don't know the acronym."

"It stood for Direct Democracy Representative. It was a silly idea to allow for members of the public to have direct debates and to vote on referenda." Dear's expression soured. *"A terrible idea, I should say. It is what lead to the lost debacle, and we learned nothing from it. It was still heavily used during Secession, and the debates surrounding individual rights on the DDR were heated. Some wanted to treat it—*

the System, that is—as essentially an employer, having those who up-loaded be treated as employees who must work to earn their place. This, I think, stemmed from the fact that many who uploaded were middle or upper middle class. The wealthy remained, preferring to keep their wealth, and the lower classes could not afford it.

"Some who uploaded agreed, at least after a fashion. They sus-pected that they would be brains-in-a-jar who would be able to devote themselves entirely to their science or art. Those phys-side wished to use uploads to drive factories or fly planes or what have you. Menial labor. Capitalism is ever the opportunist, and we were seen as tools, as was any employee."

"That sounds disgusting." Ey thought a moment, then shook eir head. "Or impossible."

"Capitalism was never one to let impossibility stand in its way," Dear's partner laughed.

"Yes, well, there were at least still those phys-side who wished to help. Dreamers to the last." It smiled fondly, lifting its glass to swirl the wine within. "Many of them uploaded. You have doubtless talked to a few without knowing. I don't know if Yared—he was our biggest champion—decided on joining the Launch. Perhaps he did. If he did not, I will nudge Ioan to him if May Then My Name does not do so first. If he did, you may yet meet him."

"Dear," Codrin began, softening eir tone. "You don't have to answer this, but do you have regrets about this period in your life?"

This time, the exaggerated care when setting down its glass was missing, as it nearly slammed it on the table. "I will not an-swer that."

"Dear," its partner murmured.

It was nearly a minute before it mastered its anger. "No, I will not answer. Not now, at least."

"Sorry, Dear."

"It is not on you, my dear. I am...ashamed. Many of the first lines...well, no. I will not elaborate now." It grinned wickedly at Codrin. *"You will doubtless tease it out of me, bit by bit, you tenacious fuck."*

Ey relaxed, nodding. "You know me well."

"I do, at that."

They sat in silence, drinking their wine.

"I am ashamed." Dear said, voice far off, distant. *"Yes. I am ashamed."*

Codrin let the rest of the evening drift into quiet. Dear remained thoughtful, even as the three of them decided on bed, but it didn't seem time for prodding. It was simply time for being. For enjoying each other's company.

The questions would wait. It was time to just be.

Douglas Hadje—2325

May Then My Name,

Thank you for writing back. I was not expecting to get so emotional from your questions. They struck a nerve, and I'm still not sure why. I sent my answers and then went to lay down and do exactly as I said: curl up and cry.

Then I sobered up, such as it were, and immediately regretted it. I feel like I was too emotional, too caught up in the moment. Too personal, maybe? You and I have had a very professional relationship, and I am grateful for that, because we did just launch two interstellar probes full of a few billion souls. I feel like my answers were maybe too familiar.

Your reply put much of that anxiety to rest, for which I am also grateful. I will answer your next batch of questions momentarily, but I want to address some points from your letter leading up to those, first.

Of course I will write back! I have no intention of stopping. Ioan and I will continue to bombard you with questions until either you tell us to stop or we come out with our history and mythography—and even then, do not count on it. Also, please feel free to ask us your own questions. Not only will we enjoy answering them, but they will continue to help us build our picture of you which will help us put your answers in context.

Oh, don't worry! I will have plenty of questions for you. If I'm going to upload in the future, I'd also like to know more about how things are sys-side. I mostly only contact you (and I guess Ioan through you? Hi Ioan!) so it all sounds very surreal.

> I do remember the name Michelle Hadje. She was one the founders as you mention, but more, she was the source of (or at least involved with) many of the ideas that drive the System to this day. She helped with consensual sensoria, for instance, as well as the reputation market that we use in lieu of currency in order to regulate forking in the early days. Unfortunately, Michelle herself does not remain in the System as of a bit under twenty years ago, so I will not be able to put you in touch with her, and should you choose to upload in the future, you will not be able to meet her face to face. I am sorry for your loss.

Thank you so much for letting me know. I'm saddened by this, but strangely calm as well. That I will never get to meet her comes with grief, but that I now at least know something of her (even if it's of her end), a portion of my curiosity has been sated.

I say a portion, though; did you ever meet her? You say she was formative for a lot of the System's tech; does everyone know that about her? Is she famous? If you did know her, what was she like? You say that Ioan's a historian, perhaps ey knows?

I know her end, but I remain hungry for any information that you can give on her life.

> You mention having little to do. Do you know when you might upload? Failing that, might you ask the Launch commission if you can add real-time communication with us to your list of duties? It would

be convenient to have someone on the station to talk to so that we are not limited by the transmission time planet-side.

I asked, and they said yes. Though again, they were largely baffled by the request. They have suggested that I keep communication as the last priority on my list of duties, which, sure. I'll send a message when I'm able to talk, if you're amenable. Will they wake you if you're asleep? (Do you sleep? I realize I don't even know.)

> You say that you consider your body a 'tool and vehicle to get you from place to place'. I would like you to know that, upon reading that I ran to show Ioan your response and laugh in eir face for being almost exactly like you in this respect.

I am not sure whether to thank you or be offended, but since Ioan sounds very interesting, I'll go with the former. Everything is so much bigger than I am, I sometimes wonder why I ought to worry about my body at all. Perhaps this is an artifact of an unpleasant upbringing and a long series of very intellectual jobs, and perhaps it's just foreshadowing me uploading.

Ioan, if you're reading this, maybe you can explain this to May Then My Name, if you haven't already!

Before I get to answering questions, here are a list of mine not already included above:

- What does your day-to-day life look like?
- What did you do before uploading?
- Where were you before uploading? If it's not insensitive to ask, do you have an accent while speaking? I've noticed a few habits you have when writing, so it got me thinking English might not be your first language.

- I sort of asked in my previous email, but I worry that I overstepped my bounds by asking when you uploaded. Is that a sensitive topic?
- Where does your name come from? Does it come from that snippet you sent to me?
- On that note, do forks generally keep the same name (you mentioned three copies of Ioan, for instance), or is it common to change names for different forks?
- In the status reports you sent for the launches, you mention dispersionistas, trackers, and taskers, and in the final one, you mention that investing fully in the launch was a danger for taskers. By this, and from some surface-level research, I infer that these describe habits of forking. I'd like to hear your take on it, though. What habit do you have? Is this something people even talk about? Argue or fight about? Is it insensitive for me to ask? If so, apologies!

These questions are for Ioan, if ey's up for answering them:

- What does being a historian on the System look like? I keep imagining that you live in a sort of repository of all knowledge anyway and can just look up whatever you want. Is that true?
- What are some things that you enjoy researching/writing about?
- Is there a university up there where people study? What other occupations are there?
- Were you a historian before you uploaded?
- I asked May Then My Name above; if you're comfortable answering, what habit of forking do you have?

And now, for the answers to your questions.

If you are willing, tell me more about your child-
hood (where you were born, what your parents
were like, what your schooling was like, etc).

As mentioned before, Earth was a shithole, so while I'm happy
to talk about it, don't expect me to be kind or friendly about it.
I was born in Saskatoon which, as a city, had gone through
the usual cycles of boom and bust. In 2278, it was heading down
from a boom cycle when the second great uraninite vein had
been depleted. It was one of those times where everyone starts
to realize that there's not going to be another that they can just
drill their way towards, and by then, even the tailings had been
refined as much as they could conceivably be.

When a city goes downhill like that, there really isn't any
drastic change. It's all little things. The mine stops hiring. The
trickle of new employees slows to a stop. When people move out
in search of work, their houses sit empty with 'For Lease' signs
for weeks, then months, then years. Your friends at school start
moving away. Your class size dwindles. Stores and restaurants
close.

It's not until something big happens that makes you lift your
head, look around, and realize, "Holy shit, this place is terrible."
In my case, it was when one of the two Ansible clinics closed. I
had long been a dreamer, but to have one of the outlets for that
dream disappear was my "Holy shit" moment. My parents had
been talking about the city dying, about having to drop break-
fast as an option in their restaurant except on Saturdays, cut
staff, all that stuff, but it had never really clicked for me what
that actually meant.

Saskatoon was such a brown place, too. Dust storms, summer droughts, wildfire smoke turning blue skies tan six months
out of the year. You grow up with that, you'd expect to be used
to it, but like I said, we spent as much time in-sim as possible
for lack of anything else to do, so we knew what it could be like

but wasn't. No reason to play out in the streets when there are AQI advisories. No reason to go shopping when you can't afford to buy anything, and all the toys you could possibly want are online.

I think that the Simon side of the family came with a heriditary pessimism that dogs our heels, so I suppose there may be a lot of that at work. My parents were pessimistic, so I was raised in that environment. Were others happy there? Maybe. Maybe they had taken it with them when the mine shut down. Maybe there were other places in the world with greater concentrations of happy people.

If so, I never saw them, unless they were online.

What is your earliest memory?

I had to give this one some thought. I was going to say that it would have to be prepping for implants. I got them the week before my first year of school started, and I remember there were two appointments leading up to the procedure. The first was more a meeting than anything. "Will he get the standard set?" "Yes." "Any health problems?" "No." "Great, we'll do a pre-op in a week."

But I don't think that was quite it. Before then, I remember my dad playing with me where we would sit on the floor, legs spread out, and roll a racquetball ball back and forth between us. He laughed like a loon whenever the ball would go wide and I would have to get up and go run after it, but, on thinking back, he always made sure that those were in the minority, and that once I started to get frustrated, he'd stop and go back to just talking about animals or food or whatever.

Tell me more about Earth. We can get the facts from broadcasts and information requests, but I want to see it through your eyes and feel it through your hands.

There's only so many times I can call it a shithole, I guess.

South of the 50th parallel or so, most everyone lives belowground and works above ground. We went on a few trips out east to visit the Hadjes and I always got a kick out of it for the first few days, running through tunnels ahead of the family, looking up at the balconies, all that sort of thing. Eventually, though, I'd grow tired of life in a linear strip, with nothing further away than a few hundred yards to focus on.

Lets see, what else.

There's two main governmental powers, loosely dividing the planet into the Northwest and Southeast hemispheres, plus a couple dozen smaller jurisdictions that will come and go every decade or so. We talked about various wars, uprisings, troubles, etc in the past, but there weren't really any when I was down there other than the occasional saber rattle. The two blocks were basically trade divisions centering on the Atlantic and Pacific. Overland trade is pretty rare and mostly automated, but still runs the risk of breakdowns, etc. Easier to do things by sea, I guess.

The ultimate cynicism of capitalism remains, though we were taught that it ebbs and flows. When I was down there, it was on its way out of a trough, where social services were being cut back, wage gaps increasing, etc etc. Rich folks lived at the poles, poor near the equator. Rich folks ate meat, poor folks ate tofu and tempeh. That sort of thing.

The 'net was also starting to undergo a boom of advertising as I was leaving (as mentioned, the station still has some connectivity, but it's rarely worth interacting via sims due to the lag), perhaps to make up for the lack of offline ad venues. I remember coming home and diving in and daydreaming through half an hour of trailers and interactives and the like, then just getting into trouble wherever I could.

I wish I could tell you more, but I either blocked out the rest or didn't pay attention in class.

> If you could go back anywhere in history and change any one thing, what would it be?

Shit. Um...I guess in light of your last letter, I'd stop whatever made Michelle leave or quit or die or whatever happened to her? I don't think I'd want to have uploaded sooner. I'm proud of what I did for the launch. Doesn't change the fact that I'd love to have met her.

Is that weird? I'm starting to feel like it's weird.

> If you could go back in time and tell yourself any one thing, what would it be?

Of all the things that I have groused about already, I don't actually have any one thing that needs changing. I don't wish I'd uploaded sooner. I don't wish I'd left sooner. I don't have any regrets about the way I got here. Maybe go back and kick my ass and tell myself to talk to Michelle sooner? It's starting to sound like an unhealthy fixation at this point, and I'm kind of wondering if it is, to some extent.

> You are given three wishes, with three restrictions: they must have plausible deniability (that is, be explained by luck, natural causes, etc.; no changing people's memories!); they must provide a benefit, rather than a detriment; they must not involve singular personal benefit for you or any one individual. What are they?

Throwing me the hard ones, huh? This is probably the one I spent the longest on.

I'm going to assume by plausible deniability, that rules out changing anything about the past.

First, I'd wish there to be some technological breakthrough that would make it easier to communicate with the System. Text is fine and good for those who live up in their heads, but I think that one thing that keeps a lot of people away from uploading is the mystery of what's up there. They hear that life is better, but hearing is not seeing. They hear that they'd be functionally immortal, but hearing is not proof. If we had a way of seeing what day-to-day life was like in the society, we'd feel less of a taboo of making our way there.

Second, I'd wish that whenever a nuke or bioweapon was launched, there'd be some plausible failure in it. A firing mechanism doesn't work. A worker comes to work hungover and snips the wrong wire during a fix. That sort of thing. I said saber rattling, and that mostly comes down to a slow, quiet arms race, and even if the chances of anything *actually* happening are very low, I have an intense paranoia of that kind of widespread death and destruction.

Third, I'd wish for some sort of astronomical event that would kick interest in space down there back into gear. It's weird, because I realize that this is contrary to the first wish, since folks zooming out into space is kind of the opposite of folks uploading. Still, everyone's got their heads down. There's some threshold level of hardship that makes folks turn to survival rather than out to the stars, and I think it's higher than one would expect. A rogue asteroid? Some crazy discovery on the moon? Hell, aliens? Anything grander than keeping a job or a house or just plain staying cool.

> Do you have any romantic attachments? I am assuming no by your previous message. Have you in the past? Will you in the future?

This next batch of questions was irksome. They're incredibly personal, and while I vowed to try to keep an open mind and be approachable about any subject you'd ask about, I'm frustrated with how much I didn't want to answer some of these. Oh well, no growth without pain, right?

No, I've never had any real attachments. I dated a few times back in school, but it was always one of those things that I did because it felt expected, rather than one I wanted to.

It's not for lack of desire, as I think that having someone meaningful in my life would be comforting and fulfilling, but it always came second-place to work or hobbies, so I'd spend those dates thinking about a project I was working on or dreaming about the stars or the System. Relationships are frowned upon on the station. Allowed, but closely monitored, with mandatory counseling, etc. That's too much time away from the other things in my life.

Will I have one in the future? If I remain phys-side, probably not, if I'm honest. The drive will still be there, but knowing myself, I'll work myself to death before I find the time for one. If I head sys-side, maybe I'll explore it. If that gives me the chance to deal with projects on the side, whether through greater free time or forking or whatever, then I don't see why that would stop me.

I'm not so lonely as to be hurting for one.

If yes, what do you look for in a partner?

I don't know, really. Similar interests, for sure. I'd like someone who is interested in the System as the wonder that it is, and I'm sure that those people exist even sys-side. I'd like someone who is comfortable with my general desire to focus on those interests. Not that they'd be second-seat, of course, just that I'm not going to be able to shut up about those things even at the best of times. If they share those interests, we can get all excited together.

I don't know that I have any real tastes in women (more my type than men, though I've known a few I could see myself spending that much time with). It's not some grand statement on, like, the inherent validity of all types of women, just that as mentioned, I spend most of my time up in my head, so that's lower on the priority list. I don't know. They ought to have a head, probably.

If no, explain why not.

N/A

When was the last time someone said 'I love you'? How did that feel?

Mom, the day I launched. It came with an implicit "...and I hate you for leaving me behind." I don't like talking about it, but I still hate her for that in turn. I don't do well with guilt.

What are your opinions on sex?

It seems fine? I don't know. I don't have much (or any) experience with it. Again, it's low enough on the priority list that I just forget that it's even a thing most of the time. I imagine it feels good, of course, and I can see how it'd deepen an emotional connection. Those are good things, so it's probably a good thing, too, but I can also see it being used as an emotional weapon because of that intimacy. It seems fine.

Have you had sex before?

No. It's been offered, but in such a strange manner that the woman I was with at the time used my missing those cues as reason for leaving me. My social awareness is minimal, though, so I don't really know what she expected. I was left mostly baffled after the whole relationship. It was my last before leaving for the station, and I haven't tried dating since for previously mentioned reasons.

Will you have sex (again) before you upload?

No, see above.

Do you masturbate?

I don't know how it works sys-side, but this is generally an insensitive thing to ask someone phys-side. I'll say yes and leave it at that.

Assuming you have one, where is your favorite place to be touched? Least favorite?

When I *was* dating, the type of physical contact I enjoyed most was having my hair played with. I assumed most others did as well, so I would often offer an equal exchange, brushing my girlfriends hair for them and letting them play with mine in turn. My favorite spot was probably at the back of my neck, which I suspect is due to some ancient inhibition against letting people touch dangerous spots on the body, so if you are intimate enough with someone to let them do that, they must be a safe person to be around.

No idea about least favorite. I guess I just don't have that much experience with being touched.

What is your favorite texture?

Fur, I think? Grandpa Hadje on the east coast had a cat, and one of my fondest memories from those trips was when she'd fall asleep on my lap or on my chest with me petting her. One of the girls I dated long-distance (I know that this makes it sound like I dated around a lot, but I only had three relationships: two local, and that long-distance one in the middle) had a feline av, and I was always happy when we would just relax in sim together and she'd let me pet her.

What is the greatest pain you have ever felt, physically, mentally, or emotionally?

I was knocked off the edge of the torus by someone (I mentioned sabotage attempts before, right?), and the tether caught me around the middle and swung me up against the side of the station pretty hard. I broke an arm and a collar bone in the process. That hurt like hell, but you mentioned mental pain too, and the same applied there. Seeing the stars reeling beneath me, seeing the station leave me behind, and seeing the core of the System racing away led to a fear that made my chest and stomach hurt so hard that I retched in my suit. I'm just thankful that the guy was tackled before he could cut my tether. He was sent back planet-side to be charged.

> If you could change any one thing about your body, what would it be?

I'd like to be less demanding, if I'm honest. Bodies are a lot of work to upkeep. Is that the case in the System? I've heard that a lot of bodily functions are optional, but not whether opting out of them was pleasant or not. My arm still hurts sometimes when I change gravities, and that reminds me of the fear of falling away from the torus, and if I could stop my arm from doing that, that would be nice.

———————

You asked me to react to the following lines without looking them up.

> Since then—'tis Centuries—and yet
> Feels shorter than the Day
> I first surmised the Horses' Heads
> Were toward Eternity —

This took a few readings before I was really able to understand it. It sounds like the middle of some longer work. I'm not totally sure what to make of it. Is it about immortality? I can see what it would be like to have to face down eternity, and assuming that by virtue of the horses heads pointing toward it, that one is inexorably carried into it yet never actually reaching it, you've got a sort of void you are constantly gazing into. It's terrifying and a little exhilarating.

> I was of three minds
> Like a tree
> In which there are three blackbirds.

This one felt impenetrable until I realized that it might be about forking. Is it a contemporary thing? I can see that being the three minds portion, and I can see the tree as a metaphor of the same root personality, but blackbirds haven't existed in any of the places I've lived for decades, so if there's specific symbolism behind that, I'm missing it.

Birds = flight and freedom, maybe? Black = death? Or maybe eternity? Three minds, each of which is bound up with those things? The freedom of eternity? I can see why this would appeal to one sys-side.

> She has but does not possess,
> acts but doesn't expect.
> When her work is done, she forgets it.
> That is why it lasts forever.

I've never heard it this way, but this is from the Tao Te Ching. Of those who are not focused on doom-saying, Taoism is popular planet-side, particularly among the 'net crowd, as a lot of people use it as a way to focus on letting go of the terrible things.

This is particularly interesting in the way that the System and the LVs are designed to last forever. "When her work is done, she forgets it" makes me think that those who helped build or worked on the System wind up forgetting about it when it *becomes* their life. "Has but does not possess/acts but does not expect" took more thought, but I can see it applying to the act of uploading, maybe. All those things you had, you never really possessed, as you leave them behind. Uploading itself is terrifying, in a way, as you can never go back and no version of you keeps living on phys-side. Maybe the only way you can get over that fear is to let go of expecting the procedure to succeed/fail. You need to leave behind your expectations, too.

> Flown to space by what callous earth destroyed,
> I chase the long-flying radio waves,
> and sift to find again your breathing voice
> Far away from grief and a potter's grave.

Does this have to do with the launch? It certainly feels like! It feels like how even now my mind is chasing those radio waves that are coming from the LVs, now so far out of reach for any one of us that we can barely comprehend. But still, we keep on searching for those voices that come back to us ever slower. Did someone on the LVs leave you behind? Someone you love? Family? One of your forks? Basically, someone whose voice you keep on searching for. Or maybe they were one of the eight irretrievably lost personalities?

"Far away from grief and a potter's grave" makes a lot of sense to me as someone who left Earth behind. I don't know what it was like when you uploaded, but I can see it as a way to dream of some place better.

> Time is a finger pointing at itself
> that it might give the world orders.
> The world is an audience before a stage
> where it watches the slow hours progress.
> And we are the motes in the stage-lights,
> Beholden to the heat of the lamps.

You never answered me about your name. This is another one of those snippets from the work you sent earlier, isn't it? It has the same feel as your name, so I can't help but wonder if that is related to you in some way.

There is something feverish about these words that I don't quite understand. I don't know what they mean, can't even begin to give you an interpretation, other than it makes it sound like that feeling of insignificance that comes with looking at the stars and being buffeted about by forces we can't understand.

I'm trying to hold back on replying to you in the same emotionally inundated state that I ended my last letter, so I'll just say that this left me feeling things that I can't even name. Loneliness? Insignificance? I don't know, even those don't feel right. Can you send me the whole work? I'll block out some time to cry over it or something.

Thank you as always, and I look forward to hearing from you soon.

Douglas Hadje, MSf, PhD
Launch director
Digital signatures:

- Douglas Hadje
- Launch commission:

  - de
  - Jonathan Finnes
  - Thomas Nash
  - Woo Hye-won
  - Hasnaa

Ioan Bălan—2325

May Then My Name Die With Me sat across from Ioan at their dining table, looking somewhat diminished.

"Are you comfortable with this?" Ioan asked.

"This feels unusually formal."

"Yes, well, I'd like to be able to see your expressions." Ey grinned. "Also, it's easier to write when I don't have a skunk hanging onto my arm."

She rolled her eyes, sighing dramatically. "I suppose. Ask away then, O archivist."

"I'm not–"

"I know, I know. Not an archivist. Grant me this whimsy."

"Alright." Ey tested the nib of eir pen on the corner of the page and then began to jot in eir comfortable shorthand. "Uncomfortable question first. When did you upload?"

May frowned down to the table, drawing lazy Lissajous curves on its surface. "I would have gone for the shit-sandwich approach. Do you promise to ask lighter questions after?"

Ioan laughed, nodded.

"Alright. Michelle uploaded in 2117. I know that Dear mentioned to you that she uploaded in the 2130s after Secession. This is a small lie it told to downplay our role in helping the System become what it is today. Michelle uploaded, burned through what energy she had on early projects, and then forked to let her clade take her place, opting for an early retirement, herself."

"Do you mean her work on sensoria?"

"That, and several other projects."

"Such as?"

"You will doubtless learn, Ioan, but not from me. It is not my story to tell."

Ey lifted eir pen from the page. "Can you tell me why? I can leave it out of the notes if you'd like."

"You may include this. I have distanced myself from much of that time out of shame. You know as well as I do that I cannot forget it, but I can at least think about it as little as possible." She smiled, abashed, then the smile grew sly. "I will not tell you who to ask about it, either. I have confidence that you will find out on your own, and I am curious to see how quickly."

Ey laughed. "Alright, if you won't talk about that, that's okay. It's enough that you mention it; I'll keep my eye out."

She reached out and took eir off-hand in her own, brushing thumbpad over eir knuckles. "Thank you, dear. Do you have a more pleasant question for me to answer?"

"Of course. Why did you stay behind."

At this, the skunk brightened considerably. "This is what I was expecting. I have a response prepared and everything."

"Dear always mentioned that it scripted its conversations, as well. Is that an Odist thing?"

"Perhaps! I do not doubt it, from that fox. It is always so dramatic." She retrieved her paw to fold it with the other before her. "Right. I remained behind because it tickled me to do so. Could I have invested in the Launch? Of course. However, it occurred to me early on, soon after you and I agreed to work on this project together, that acting as a fulcrum between the two LVs would not just keep my instance from infecting the responses that I received, but would allow me to play them against each other.

"Besides," she said, stabbing her pinky toward em. "There

is no Ioan on the Launches, and I am busy wrapping you around my little finger."

Ey laughed. "Well, keep up the good work, then."

"I could just as easily turn this question around on you, Mx. Ioan Bălan. Why did you not invest yourself in the Launch? We do not yet know Codrin's reasons, but why remain, yourself?"

"I'm not sure, honestly. I think what you say about not influencing the responses that we get fits me, too. I don't want Ioan's thoughts, I want those of the LVs unfiltered through my transmissions."

"But Codrin–"

"Has diverged significantly in the last two decades. I have no concerns about contamination. Ey is not me any longer."

She nodded approvingly. "Good. There may be hope for you yet."

"Wrapping me around your little finger, indeed." Ey finished eir current line of scratchy notes. "You say that it tickled you to remain behind. Can you talk more about that?"

"Of course. Many of the clade—many of the liberal side, at least—enjoy using our functional immortality as a plaything. If we are to live forever, then, it is worthwhile to find as many things to keep it interesting as we can along the way. It is interesting to me that I have acted in a very intentional way such that I will not get to experience our three societies begin to diverge that directly. There is no going back to change that, because there is no going and there is no back. It is already fun to see the differences between Castor and Pollux through the eyes of both Codrins, and to realize that the L_5 System contains neither, and then realize in a flash of insight that there is no May Then My Name Die With Me to witness directly. Do you experience the same?"

"Maybe a little bit," Ioan hedged. "But if what you tell me is true, I'm not nearly old enough yet to be so concerned in finding fun in the little nooks and crannies of experience."

"You are no fun," she whined. "But I see your point. You

also do not have the decades of split mind from before the beginning of the clade. You do not have the strange avenues of thought that preceded our creation. The Ioan of the 2230s or whenever it was that you uploaded had a baseline sanity that Michelle lacked."

"You don't seem insane."

She forked a version of herself atop the table lacking all human attributes that hissed at Ioan with foaming mouth. Ey startled back, and she laughed as the creature quit. "Do I not?"

Ey shook eir head. "Weird, perhaps, but your thoughts and actions are consistent with each other. You're an internally consistent individual."

"Yes, well, Michelle was not. She was a being of irreconcilable contradictions, and we are lucky that she did not pass that on to us when we came into existence."

"If she hadn't quit as she did, do you think that she would've remained on the System, invested entirely in the launches, or split between the two?"

May's features fell and she averted her eyes. "She could not do but what she did. You were not there at the end."

"Feel free to not answer, but can you tell me about that?"

"I will only say that she was ready, that, whether or not she had been planning that day from the very beginning, that was precisely the time that she was meant to die."

" 'Die'? Not quit?"

"In her mind, I think that it was death, yes. She quoted her—our—favorite line of poetry at us, and the death thoughts proceeded apace. We are no longer branches of a unified whole, but trees of our own." There was a long pause before she added, "I think that had been true perhaps from shortly after Secession, and that she was already dead, in her own way. Reality just caught up with her."

Ey nodded. Something in the skunk's expression told em that the topic was closed, that while she might answer another question, she would resent it. Instead, ey let a moment of quiet fall between them, a silent acknowledgement of that ending.

"You have another question. I can see it on your face."

"Perceptive, as always. Whenever you talk with Douglas, your cousin however many times removed, you always evade his questions about your name, and have yet to tell him about your origins, though I know that that would mean a lot to him. Why?"

Her laugh was musical and expression almost giddy. "We already talked about having fun, dear."

"Well, yes, but that was fun involving yourself. What's the origin of this fun involving someone else?"

"I have fun with you, you know that."

Ioan smirked, but waited for her to continue.

"Alright, have it your way. First of all, I am not Michelle, though I am of her. All the same, I am doing my best to build up the suspense with him. I know that it would mean a lot for him if I were to simply drop the bomb on him now—though I realize, having said that, that that is perhaps a poor choice of words, given his admitted fear. But how much more an impact it will have if I build it up like this! I cannot wait to see what emotions play across his face."

"'See'? You intend to wait until he uploads?"

"And why should I not? I know that he will."

"He always talks about it as a potential thing, though."

She grinned and shook her head. "He will. He has already made up his mind, he just does not realize it yet."

"How will you tell him, then?"

"I will continue to drop hints for another few months, and when he does—I think he will do it within the year—I will bring him home. There, we will talk, and you will observe as, over the course of a few minutes, I reveal the truth."

Ioan straightened up. "Me?"

"Of course. Can you think of a better myth? Can you think of a better story in history than of the man who brought the launches to fruition learning that he is talking to an instance of the very woman who helped bring Secession to fruition, the one who he has desired above all things to meet, who he thinks dead?"

"A little grandiose, don't you think?"

She stuck her tongue out at em, a strangely cute gesture on her features. "Is that not a requirement of myths? A myth that is not grandiose is just a story."

"You Odists do seem prone to grand gestures."

May preened.

Ioan set down eir pen and folded eir hands on the table. "Tell me a story, then."

"One for the history? One for you?"

Ey shrugged.

She thought for a moment, once more drawing designs on the table with a claw.

"Alright," she said, standing up. "Come with me, my dear."

Ioan stood to follow her as she padded from the common room to the balcony, then down the steps from there to the yard, a rectangle of grass hemmed in by a moat of mulch, a fence of lilac bushes making up the border. They were technically the end of eir sim, though between the leaves and trunks of the bushes, one would occasionally catch a glimpse of another yard, another house, a street beyond.

"Look," she said.

Ey looked at the yard, at the lilacs, even the patio and the sky.

"What do you see?"

"My yard. What am I supposed to see?"

"Look at the grass. What do you see?"

Ey focused on the green carpet of grass, then frowned as ey began to notice the two or three yellow flowers spotting the yard just barely visible. They sat only a few millimeters below the tops of the trimmed grass. "What are those?"

The skunk grinned at em toothily.

"May, what did you do?"

"I talked you into a small addition. That is what I did."

Ey knit eir brow. "Talked me into...how do you mean?"

"Do not worry, Ioan, you are the only one who has ACLs over your property. I do not. I just made a few suggestions, mostly when you were asleep—or at least very sleepy—or head-in-the-clouds at work."

"You're saying I made these?" ey asked, stepping out into the grass and bending down to inspect the flower, yellow, a myriad of petals, grand-toothed leaves radiating from the base.

"I am saying that *we* made these." She bent down beside em and plucked the flower from near the ground, lifting it with a dream-clouded smile. "I am saying that you trust me—*really* trust me—and that life in the System is more subtle than I think you know. You trust me. You let me into your life as a coworker, then cohabitant and cosleeper. You let me into your dreams, my dear, and your dreams influence this place as much as, if not more than, your waking mind."

That waking mind was now whirling with the ramifications of what she was saying. "I did this on your suggestion?"

She shook her head. "If you would like to think of it that way, yes, but I would prefer to say that we did this."

"Is this your story?"

"No. Sit down by me."

They both shifted to a cross-legged position before this brand new plant in the yard, both looking at the yellow flower May turned this way and that in her paw.

"This is a dandelion. It–"

A memory clicked into place for Ioan and ey laughed. "Oh! Of course! I've been here too long, haven't I? Here in the System, here in the house with its perfect yard. Almost ninety years now, I think. They were all over back phys-side, though."

May nodded and beckoned for em to continue.

"We didn't have a yard where I grew up. Just an apartment block facing the street, a strip of weeds between the building and sidewalk, and then between the sidewalk and road. At one time, I think that strip had contained grass and trees, but now it just contained a narrow path full of thistles and dandelions.

"I only ever saw lawns in movies or on the net. The world wasn't as bad back then as Douglas makes it sound now, but still, we weren't wealthy, and it was hard enough to ensure a steady supply of clean water for the residents, never mind grass like this. We were certainly not wealthy enough for that." Ey laughed. "Well, we were dirt poor, actually. Most of the weeds were green, leafy things with fuzzy green flowers that would turn into bundles of seeds, or spiky thistles with purple bulbs of flowers, but there were a few dandelions scattered about."

"No lilacs?"

"More stuff from media. I remember wishing I could grow some indoors because I thought they were small enough to be houseplants until I was corrected. I have no idea if these are accurate, but I remember loving the smell."

"They are spot on, Ioan."

Ey smiled.

"So you uploaded and made your sim like this?"

"Yeah. Sort of. It was inspired by some sim I frequented on the 'net, something a friend built. I found something close to it on the market, and when I had reputation enough, I dug the sim and grabbed that template, then spent a year rebuilding it as best I could remember. No dandelions."

She laughed, bumping her shoulder against eirs. "Of course. They are a weed, yes. Or often thought of as one. The leaves make a good salad, though, and I was told that you could dry, roast, and grind the roots to make a coffee substitute."

Ioan made a face. "I'd rather coffee."

"I have no idea if the substitute was any good, but I like coffee, too." She held the flower up to her snout and smelled long at it. "Me, though, I like the flowers. They are too complicated for their own good in this stage, are they not? Sure, they close up and then become the puffballs that spread them further and further, but here, they are almost platters of yellow."

Ey grinned as she held the flower in both paws like a tray carrying food.

"But that is not what I like about them. I am telling you, now that you are awake, the things that I whispered to you to bring about this story. The things I suggested, as you put it. What I love is their scent." She held it up for em to sniff. "They smell like muffins. How can anything that smells like muffins be bad? "

Ey breathed deep of that scent. There was, indeed, the scent of some baked sweet bread, but that was layered atop a vegetal scent. It was not unpleasant, but not precisely like a muffin. Ey decided not to share this opinion with May.

Instead, ey asked, "Is that your story, May?"

"Of course not. You told the story yourself. Young Ioan with eir indoor lilacs." She laughed, peeking up at em slyly. "Or perhaps we told the story. You asked, so I suggested, as you say, and you told the story."

Ioan frowned, then rolled eir eyes. "That's not what I asked, and you know it."

"Tough shit. It is our story now," she said. "Now, give me your hand."

Ey held eir hand out for her, then let her turn it over in her paws. Before ey could object, she flipped the flower over, pressed it firmly to eir skin, and rubbed it in a vigorous circle.

"There." She held eir hand up so that ey could see, looking proud.

On the back of eir hand, the skin shone a golden yellow in the circle where she had rubbed the flower.

Ey shoved her over onto the grass, laughing. "You nut."

She lay there among the grass, giggling helplessly. Among the grass where a brand new dandelion poked through the green in front of her snout. One that had not been there before.

Yared Zerezghi—2124

Mention how the System almost feels like its own nation, mention L5 but only in passing, the note read. *Expect agreement from a new faction. Act pleasantly surprised.*

As he had found himself doing increasingly often, Yared stepped out of his apartment to walk the town and draft his new post in his head. They used to flow so easily, when each one did not feel like some school assignment.

He walked out past the coffee shop, waving to the woman behind the counter, and shaking his head to an offer of coffee. He was already wired enough.

He kept on walking, instead, out and down the street past apartments, the store where he bought his food, apartments, the restaurant that he ate at once every other week, and yet more apartments. Out and out until he ran into that patch of scrub that somehow never got developed, then right and into where the scrub turned into scattered bushes, and then trees. There had been a fence, once, but all that remained were the posts.

He'd never bothered walking up here until he'd accepted the unnerving assignment to convince everyone to secede. Explicitly, to convince the DDR and various governments to allow it, but implicitly, he felt, to convince those he talked to on the System, as well. Convince True Name and Jonas to suggest it from the other side.

It had been unnerving at first, at least.

Why would he, a nobody who dumped all his free time into the 'net, into the DDR, be expected to make any change? He knew that, once a referendum was picked up by more than a couple of the various legislatures, it was hopeless to expect the DDR had any real impact. It became the joke that he was sure so many thought it was.

He had picked up the topic of the System's individual rights as his next pet topic, for even though he had felt little interest in the System or its labyrinthine technologies at the time, when the previous bill he had hyper-fixated on had failed on the floor, and after a night of far too much tej, he needed to set his mind on *something*.

He didn't know why he did this, why he felt the need to dive into politics. He was a no one in Addis Ababa, a city which paled in importance in the NEAC, a governing body that paled in comparison to the others in the world.

He had a data analysis job he could do from home reasonably well, and he didn't slack off while at work (though he did leave DDR alerts on in his field of view). He made enough of a living to stay in his apartment in an alright part of town. He was comfortable. He had no plans to upload.

Or hadn't previously. The more he learned, the more enticing it seemed.

It certainly seemed like an easier life than this, accepting messages from shadowy government agencies to try and influence what was supposed to be a direct means of being represented in the legislatures of the world. It was one thing to try to do so from one's own perspective, but to accept such influence, even if he was only paid in coffee and cake...

It had surprised him that he had even picked up the task at first. Secession seemed like such a strange thing to ask for. What did the NEAC—or any government, really—gain by having the System secede? What was the System doing that threatened them so much? There was the brain-drain that some feared, but this seemed to rely on some more basic instinct or need to have that which is different separated from that which was familiar.

He didn't know why he had picked up the task, but it was working, even on him. *Especially* on him. The idea of secession from a government's point of view was one that fit neatly into his worldview without him needing to change anything, and that was strange in and of itself.

The System probably should secede. At that point, uploading became a simple matter of emigration, one to a country that was guaranteed to grant you residency. Not only that, but, though the cost might be high and the move permanent, it offered a ready-made haven for refugees, whether from the increasingly hot climate or the countless little spats along disputed borders. Uploading was an option for those who had nowhere else to go, and one that offered them more freedom than any other country on earth.

And this new idea that had started showing up, first in his conversations with True Name and Jonas, and then on the DDR in general, of tacking the System onto one of the launches for the L_5 station construction. The timing—True Name and Jonas, then the DDR—made him wonder if the Council of Eight had its fingers in other pies, too.

He wasn't sure how to feel about this. What an opportunity that had presented itself! All those arguments about the resources the System used would be all but put to rest. The station would house it, the station's solar power source would power it, and the Station Hotel's revenue would fund it. It would be another part of the tourists' experience. There were already plans for a new transmission system that would be easy enough to build for uploads to make it from Earth to the System without having to fly to the station first.

It was all starting to feel like such a good idea, and some part of him felt embarrassed that Councilor Demma's bald-faced political machinations were working just as well on him as they promised to on the masses that filled the DDR forums.

He realized he'd been so lost in thought that the wooded grove had already spat him out the other side, back into heat and back into traffic.

"Well, shit," he mumbled, and began the long trek back to his apartment, polishing the draft of his post in his head.

I won't lie, I'm pleased to see this discussion take a turn to the positive. There are some great minds thinking and talking here. Here on the DDR forums, out on the 'net, and now out in the subcommittees that will feed into the legislatures of the world.

What heartens me more than that, however, is to see some names that I had previously seen arguing *against* independent rights now campaigning *for* them (or, at the very least, neutral in tone). This is how the DDR is meant to work: it's a forum for us, the rank and file of the nations of the world, to be able to participate in the legislative process that will bind us in more ways than of old. No more relying solely on representatives. No more collecting signatures for yet another petition that will fall on deaf ears. No more letter writing campaigns that doubtless fed countless shredders and trash folders.

To those arguing for independent rights, keep working hard, as there is still much to be done, but to those who are arguing against this referendum, I would like to address a few of those points that seem to keep cropping up:

The System has no meaningful way for us to control its goings on, and thus could be a good place for disaffected citizens to coordinate with phys-side agents on acts of terrorism.

This is one of those arguments that is difficult to refute because, on the surface, it is indeed a potential reason that one might upload.

That said, enough thought about how international terrorism works is enough to put this to bed as yet more FUD. First of all, it is the responsibility of each country to monitor their own citizens to within the limits of their national policies (and, let us not kid ourselves, well beyond). If a disaffected citizen is willing to engage in a terrorist act on their home soil, then it is the responsibility for the government to deal with that individual.

I will grant that this leaves the upload to contend with. There is no easy way to detect whether or not the System has punished them, and there's certainly no way for them to be extradited, should they be discovered.

Do not doubt your respective governments' abilities to track these actions, however. It is something of an open secret that they are always a decade ahead of us mere mortals when it comes to encryption, and thus cracking of those encryption methods used ten years prior. They'll be able to track communications from the System easily enough, just as they track any other form of text-based communication.

(And to my NEAC government handler who reads all of my posts, finger hovering above the big, red 'arrest' button: hello! I hope that you are well.)

Without clear news sources coming out of the System, there is no way for us to tell that the Council of Eight is effective at governing those sys-side.

Disregarding the Council of Eight's mandate to "guide but not govern", I'm curious, now! What would a "clear news source" would look like?

When one thinks about news sources here, one thinks of a stream of information about concrete events: what hurricane hit which part of North America; what stock jumped to what price; what the cricket scores are. These are all *things*. They all have to do with *stuff* or *places* or *money*.

Think of one thing that has made news recently that does not have to do with any of those things. I will preempt many of your examples:

- Legislation—that is, new laws to govern stuff, places, or money.
- Scientific advances—that is, new ways to work with stuff, places, or money (and before you suggest theoretical sciences, consider that those are future ways to work with stuff. Psychological breakthroughs? Better ways to keep us happy so that we can produce and consume more stuff).
- International relations—that is, which group people in which places have which stuff that which other group of people want.
- Technological breakthroughs—stuff.
- Exploration—places.
- Travel, entertainment, comedy—commodified experiences.

Here are some things that you might find in this theoretical news source that also appears in ours:

- Opinions
- Interpersonal relations
- Religion

When one is unbound by the constraints of stuff, places, or money, one finds that there is little news that is worth treating as news.

Doubtless they have news out there. I don't mean to imply otherwise. Of what worth would it be to us to know of a cult surrounding, say, some upload who has found a neat thing to do with forking? Of what use is the knowledge of what is the new, hottest sim? Which of us really, truly cares about their petty squabbles?

I would say that I do, but lets be honest, I can't even begin to understand those, but I can certainly respect their rights to have them.

Now, tell me what effective governance looks like in such a system. Resources are controlled through the reputation market. As far as I can tell, there is no murder, there are no wars, fights can be over in a blink if one of the parties just leaves, and the worst offense someone can commit is stalking, and even then, one can be bounced from a sim.

We come yet again to the idea of speciation. We are fundamentally different. Or, to use a metaphor from the first point, this is an entire *society*, human or otherwise, that is fundamentally different, as one might see with the vast gulf between customs in different areas of the world.

The L5 station has no obligation to host the System.

Correct, and yet they volunteered. This is a nonargument for a non-problem.

They are an international cooperative effort with business interests involved. The System is neither of those, true, but it is also not *not* those, either. A nation to cooperate? It is not a nation, but I believe

I've argued the point that, given fundamental differences, it might as well be. A business? It is not a business, but it does have employees and businesses associated with it, and it produces some delightful results in terms of the new ideas that constantly flow through the communications channels.

Friends, I struggle to see the merit of many of these arguments, and of the ones that do hold water, there are sensible compromises available. These people are *people,* and it has long been established that people deserve rights. They are a *culture,* and it has long been established that cultures deserve protection.

Vote for the granting of rights. Vote yes on *referendum 10b30188*

Yared Zerezghi (NEAC)

Codrin Bălan#Pollux—2325

Codrin and Dear walked, hand in paw, from cairn to cairn out through the prairie, tracing lines of exploration that Codrin had built over the years.

Ey had been surprised, at first, that Dear had agreed to this walk. The offer had been made on a whim: *I'm going to walk the prairie, do you want to come?*

And it had agreed, forking off an instance to continue its work in quiet while the down-tree fork tramped out into the fields. There was no storm today, hardly even any clouds, just a few patches of lazy shadow that drifted across the rolling landscape as their corresponding cumulus slid between sun and grass. It made for a pleasantly warm spring day with enough of a breeze to keep it from becoming outright muggy, and quiet enough that the occasional clattering of a startled grasshopper sounded clear.

Historian and fox walked, hand in paw, from cairn to cairn, saying little, but saying it kindly.

"Codrin," Dear asked as they passed another pile of rocks. *"Did you bring me out here to talk about the interview?"*

"That was on my list of things to talk about, but I also just wanted to spend time with you."

It squeezed eir hand in its paw and smiled. *"Thank you, my dear. It does mean a lot. Still, do tell me your thoughts on the interview."*

Codrin bent down to pluck a thin stem of grass as they walked, fiddling with it between nervous fingers, tapping the tip against eir chin. "I don't know. It was surprisingly painful for me. I think it was painful for us both, in our own ways. Still..."

"It still scared you?" Dear hazarded.

"I think so, yeah. I can understand the anxiety that one might not be missed after one leaves a place. Even in the face of knowledge that that's not true—Ioan will miss you, May Then My Name will miss you, just about everyone who showed up at the death day party will, too—it's hard to really internalize that others will still be thinking of you when you aren't there."

The fox frowned, but nodded to Codrin all the same.

"It was just hard to hear you say, "I want to die" so plainly."

It squeezed eir hand in its paw again, but remained silent.

"Especially after Michelle..."

Dear stopped suddenly, there by a cairn, leaving Codrin to keep walking until its paw tugged em to a stop in turn.

"Michelle made a difficult decision, but the right one," it said. "I remember that pain, the inability to be just one thing, to be an entire person. I remember how those waves of instability always made her—made me—so nauseous and being touched felt disgusting. It was lonely-making for someone who needed—deserved—love and affection. She made the right decision to choose her own end."

"And the decision to not fix the split-mindedness?"

It frowned down to the ground. "I do not know if that was the right decision."

Codrin turned to face the fox, taking its other paw in eir free hand. "Do you know why she made it, at least?"

"Yes. I think so. At least, I know why she made the decision two centuries ago. She felt that she was honoring the Name, that to get rid of that part of her that left her in that state after getting lost was to disrespect the referent of that name and all that they went through. She thought that, after seeing how her first forks were locked into singular aspects, she would lose that."

Dear looked off into the prairie, so Codrin took the opportunity to lean forward and kiss it's cheek. "It was difficult seeing her and then learning of her death, and given the associations that you have with her, I couldn't help but think that there might be some of that in you when you said you wanted to die."

"I know, and I apologize for that. It did not adequately express what that means to me, but was too sharp a phrase to turn down. I will be more careful with how I phrase these topics in the future."

"Thank you, Dear. I've been giving it some thought, and I think I understand what you're going for. I think we even talked about it after Qoheleth's meeting. You wanted to find a way to...end, I think you put it."

Dear grinned. It looked tired. *"That we did, yes. I will say that this is not the same idea, though it does come from the same roots. I was thinking then that there ought to be some way for one personality to lead to another, to be free of those memories, yet for someone new to live on. The core of that is still there, but I suppose what I want is to come by an earnest death. A real death. Natural causes, such as it were. I don't want to know when or how, but knowing that there is a limit to our immortality has become a comfort to me."*

Codrin disentangled eir hands from the fox's paws, opting instead to hug it around the middle. Dear reciprocated by looping its arms around eir shoulders.

"That's what I suspected you meant, yeah. I just didn't pick up on it at the time is all."

"Yes. Sorry, Codrin."

"It's okay, promise."

They stood for a while, there in the prairie, silent, thinking, until by some unspoken signal, they turned toward the side of the cairn that hadn't been explored and began walking.

"What is next on your list?"

"Hm? In terms of interviews and such?"

"Yes. Do you know where you will start looking?"

"I was thinking I'd start asking around our friends and see who invested totally up here and who didn't, then perhaps put out the question to a wider audience. That ought to get me a good amount of responses."

"*It is a bit of a shotgun approach, is it not?*"

Codrin laughed, shrugged, and knelt down to begin building the next pile of stones. "You got any better ideas, fox?"

It knelt beside them, digging up stones of its own and handing them to em. "*Of course I do. Do ask our friends, as I think they will have much to say, but also, while poking around, I saw that several of the founders have made the launch. I am not surprised that this is the case.*"

"Oh? That makes sense, I suppose" Ey plopped a root-tangled rock on top of the growing pile, laughing. "Something exciting after all those years, back to being at the heart of something important."

Dear splayed its ears. "*It is hard to let go of that desire, yes. A few of them are quite mad now, however.*"

"Mad how?"

"*All of the council, all of those who uploaded so early, were reasonable in their own ways, but some more logical than others. I sure as hell was not.*" It sat back on its heels and watched Codrin finish the cairn. "*After things with the council began to disintegrate and the meaning of being a founder grew all the more poignant with the explosive population growth, many got frustrated and left to get up to their own things. Many of us...lost track of each other after that, but I have seen many of their names here and there, and I know that several are on the launches as well as the System. They might have some interesting insights to give you.*"

"Interesting good? Interesting bad?" Ey laughed. "You can't call them mad and then just leave 'interesting' hanging in there."

"*Of course I can.*" It stood again, dusting off its legs. "*But I love you, so I will not. As far as I can tell, many initially picked up artistic endeavors of some sort or another, and almost to a one, they became interested in history and preservation. I am sure that you have read several of their works. For those who experienced such, much of the strain on their personalities began to show about twenty years ago.*"

"Twenty years ago, huh? Around the time of *On the Perils of Memory*? Or the launch?"

The fox only grinned.

"Well, I'll put them on the list, then. I'm curious to hear what a mad founder has to say about travelling however many kilometers a second through space. Anyone else?"

"I am sure there are more Odists on here who would be willing to talk. Some of them might even be interesting." It admired the waist-high cairn, smiling. *"If you want actually interesting perspectives, however, you cannot go wrong hunting down artists, though. They will always have something to say."*

True Name—2124

The Only Time I Know My True Name Is When I Dream met with Jonas at a sim of her choosing. They had tacitly agreed that they would switch sims every time they met, if possible, and alternate who chose which. It followed the general outline of how the council met, but, being just the two of them and learning where they would meet only minutes prior meant even less of a chance of being found out.

Found out from what or by whom, True Name had not yet divined. Perhaps it was just a good habit.

She felt constantly aware of who was around her. Not in the sense that she was being watched, though she certainly entertained that idea. It wasn't that she and Jonas might be discovered as members of the council and accosted. Nor was it that they were doing anything untoward. They were just getting together to do their jobs and do them to their full abilities.

Perhaps it had something to do with lingering anxiety left over from Michelle. Perhaps it was due to the tenuousness of her position on the council—not that they doubted her as a fork of Michelle, but she did sense some hesitancy surrounding allowing forked instances to sit while the root instance did not.

Maybe I have drifted too far, she often found herself thinking. *Maybe I am no longer Michelle enough to see things in the same way.*

So, she remained vigilant, regardless of whether or not she knew why, and kept as much as she could above-board with the council. Always at the forefront of her mind, she held her goal of ensuring the continuity of existence and continuity of growth of the System. That's what this all boiled down to, right?

Today, they met at a place of her choosing, and she had chosen the closest thing that she could find to the Crown Pub of old: a well-aged, British-style pub, complete with a few high-topped tables and the types of small beer that she had never quite grown to love, yet drank all the same.

Jonas blinked into the sim outside, so she was first alerted to his presence by a quiet ding from the bell above the door. She watched him step inside and look around with an appraising glance before spotting her and joining her at the two-top.

"Nice place. How's the beer?"

"Flat. Weak." She took a sip and shrugged. "Perfect for the setting, as far as I can tell."

"Better than clams frozen in ice cubes?"

She laughed. "Much. Want to get a drink and find a booth?"

"Sure. You find the booth, I'll get the drink, then we can talk."

The booth in the corner is where the sim diverged from the one she had known so well back on the net. Where those at the Crown had been high-walled, wood dividers reaching up to the ceiling even after the cushioned backs ended, these were low-backed and reminded her more of the types of padded benches one might find on the bus or train.

Ah well, they cannot all be perfect.

She waited until Jonas sat and she ribbed him good-naturedly about his choice of a fruity vodka drink before setting up the cone of silence.

"So," he said, offering her the neon-pink cherry out of his drink.

"So." She bit the cherry off the stem and chewed thoughtfully, the fruit sweet enough to make her sinuses burn. "Have you read Yared's recent post?"

He nodded.

"Thoughts?"

"It's written well enough. He's good at picking three points and tackling them. He's been focusing more on questions of government."

"And have you read between the lines?"

His face split into a grin. "I believe so."

"And?"

"No, no. I want to hear you say the words first."

She laughed and tossed the cherry stem at him. "Alright. Do you think that he is suggesting that we somehow become our own country?"

"I most definitely do." He sipped at his drink and leaned back against the back of the booth. "Secession isn't something that I'd considered with any seriousness before. Then again, it didn't really feel like it'd be necessary until all of this talk about rights, and even then, it didn't even feel worth considering from a feasibility standpoint until the L_5 team offered to bring the System with."

"Agreed, yes. I am happy to see that our friend has some subtlety."

"It wasn't *that* subtle."

"Well, no, but he at least refrained from mentioning secession or making any direct suggestions as to our independence from the S-R Bloc or dual citizenship. That must count for something."

"Of course. Though it does have me wondering. Do you think he's acting on his own volition?"

True Name tilted her head. "Are you suggesting that he is a front for some larger player?"

Jonas shrugged, finishing off his drink in one smooth swallow before setting the glass back down on the table. "Nothing so grand. I'm just wondering if he's being influenced by someone."

"What makes you say that?"

"The way the topics of his posts are drifting. It's not that one doesn't follow another, so much as there seems to be a trajectory in mind, with each getting closer to a specific goal."

She frowned. "Are you saying you have seen this coming?"

"No, no," he laughed, holding up his hands. "Just that, taking this new info into account, when I look back at the recent posts, I'm seeing a small pattern."

She drank in silence as she digested this. Yared seemed like an honest and earnest supporter, though certainly from the standpoint of a DDR junkie. He also seemed like a nobody. A nobody who was a reasonably good writer and loud on the 'net.

That combination probably made him a fairly attractive target to influence.

"Had you known this was coming," she began, lifting Jonas out of his own reverie. "What would you have thought? What would you have done?"

He raised his empty glass to her. "An astute question! I'll make a politician out of you yet."

She kicked his shin beneath the table, and he laughed.

"You're a bit late to be whining about that. You've been on the council longer than I have." Twirling his glass between his fingers, he said slowly, pacing his words with his thoughts. "What would I have thought? I would've thought much as I mentioned above. I would've considered it unnecessary, then infeasible. What would I have done, though? I think I would have used him in turn. Gently steering him away from the idea while trying to find out who was behind this shift, if anyone, and try to dig up dirt on them."

"I see. He does seem rather pliant. He would be a useful tool for us to wield, too."

"First the astute questions, now the cynicism! You're well on-ow!" He laughed, reaching beneath the table to rub at his shin. "It's a good idea, though. No matter what we decide, we can always push him a little this way or that to help us out. I still want to figure out who's behind him, though."

"I do too, since you brought it up. Do you have any hunches on who it might be?"

"He's NEAC, right? Probably one of his own council-members. No one too high up, but someone high enough that they can read the situation better. Likely someone from the ruling coalition, but not the head of the council. Probably a more senior position, too. The grandfatherly type, or at least avuncular."

True Name laughed. "Really?"

"Really. They're always the sly types you need to watch out for. Nothing they say is not a coldly calculated maneuver to get you to agree with them." He shook his head. "Even their wives—and they're almost always men—are probably married to them only because they told them that they loved them in *just* the right tone of voice to get them to say yes."

"Manipulative shitheads."

Jonas laughed. "Very. Probably Demma, or maybe Bahrey. Both fit the bill. They'll have all the plausible deniability in the world, too. Some underling did the actual work, while they sit back and get whatever it is that they want."

"So, tell me, O great political teacher, how do we find out which without asking?"

"Bring up something about the bill and pretend to be disheartened by it or like we don't understand it, ask him who would be the one to address it, now that it's reached their ears."

"Right. I was thinking we would ask him what government types are thinking about the launch, if anyone has been pushing against it or for it, who seems neutral, and then ask for names under the guise of doing research, see who he names first."

"There you go," Jonas said. "You'll run the risk of maybe getting more names than you were hoping for, but chances are, the first one that'll come to his mind is whoever's driving him."

True Name smiled, sipping the last of her warm, flat beer. She was pleased at just how much trust she was building with Jonas. Ask the questions you already know the answers to, look like you're thinking, then suggest something that's almost but not quite right.

She was nothing if not an actor.

"This secession angle, though. Do you think that would be worth pushing towards?" she asked.

"I'd like to steer a little closer to it, first, just to see what that'd look like. It'll require the launch amendment to pass, as I don't think System hardware can remain on Earth without someone getting upset at whoever's land it sits on. Once that's sorted out, though, and we have a better idea of what an independent System will look like, I say we push hard."

True Name nodded. "It sounds like there is no reason not to. If the System is to remain beholden to existing government influences, it will always be at risk of reinterpretation of those laws. We are uniquely positioned to be almost entirely impossible to invade as a sovereign kingdom, and we have enough support that there is low risk that we will be simply turned off. Too many people want to join. Too many still see utility for us. Too many dreamers."

"Listen to you, my dear!" Jonas laughed. "You sound like a dreamer, yourself."

"Perhaps." She grinned. "But also someone willing to devote myself—several of me—to getting what I want."

"Speaking of, what are the rest of you doing?"

"End Of Days says is working on remaining sensoria stuff, talking with the S-R trio to round out the proposal for sensorium messages. Praiseworthy is reading up on propaganda. Life Breeds Life is keeping an eye on how tasks are divided. Most everyone else is out and about, keeping a feel for the place, or making things."

"You and your names. What sorts of things are you making?"

"Writing. Performances. Friends."

"Hobbies?"

She nodded, tapping absentmindedly at the rim of her glass with a claw. "Minus the friends part, yes. I was a theatre teacher, phys-side. Need to have fun somehow." She could feel the conversation drifting into small-talk territory, and she wasn't yet ready to lose Jonas's attention. "You have your forks already, do you not? What are they working on?"

Jonas sat up, then slid out of the booth. "Come on, I'll show you."

True Name set her empty glass aside and slid out to follow him.

The next sim they traveled to was an apartment. Something high up, somewhere over a city she didn't recognize. It was well furnished and quite spacious, but could hardly be called upscale.

As soon as they arrived, two other members of the Jonas clade appeared from a door that appeared to lead to an office. There was no doubt about their identity as Jonases: they were identical.

"Skillfully done," she said, laughing. "Who was I speaking to today? Not Jonas Prime, I imagine."

The one who had brought her here laughed, shaking his head. "No, I'm Ar Jonas. What tipped you off?"

"If I had several identical copies of myself with the same common name, all forked from the same root instance, I would not send the root instance out to a meeting not at a place of my choosing."

One of the other Jonases nodded appreciatively. "Well spotted."

Ar Jonas disappeared from beside her and, with a blink, reappeared. "Merged with Prime," he explained. "I'll leave you two to talk."

He and the other Jonas left to go pick up where the work had been left off in the office, leaving Jonas Prime to guide her to the sofa.

"How often do you show up at council as Prime?" she asked, once they were seated.

"Used to be every time," he said. "Then one day, I nearly missed it as I was in the middle of a...discussion, so I sent Ar. I was nervous that someone would see through it, but no one did.

I tried to keep going myself for a while, but after there were no repercussions, I gave up on it, and alternate between the other six."

"Six?"

"Of course. Ar, Ku, and Re, as I mentioned, and now Ir, who forked from Ar and looks nothing like me, so he's got more latitude."

"And the other two?"

"Why would I tell you everything?" He laughed. "They're my instances, doing the things that I do, which should be enough."

"As they must. You have already told me more than you probably should have."

"I trust you'll keep quiet about it."

True Name grinned, putting her finger to her snout in the universal hush sign. "It is a neat enough trick. I think that the Ode clade already differs too much to send one of them in my place, so perhaps not for me."

"It's up to you, yeah." Jonas sat back against the couch, one arm draped casually along the back. "I honestly was surprised when no one noticed my reputation drop, but then I figured out that most people just look at the clade's reputation, rather than the instances. I have a feeling that'll change eventually, but for now, no one seems to pay all that much attention."

The skunk frowned, browsed the markets—something that felt more akin to remembering what the stats were, rather than looking anything up—and saw that, while she had less reputation than Michelle had before she forked, the clade had a good bit more, likely from what each of them were doing to build reputation. Jonas naming his clade after himself was a fairly savvy move, in the end. 'Ode' having no direct ties to Michelle it seems like something unrelated.

Ah well. I am still happy to have done it, she thought. *And perhaps we will find our own way to build reputation that does not involve a constant game of make believe.*

"Thank you again for your trust, Jonas," she said, standing.

Neither the booth nor the couch had been all that kind on her tail. "I am going to go do some digging in the recent news from the NEAC and wait for our dear Yared to get in touch with us again."

He nodded up to her. "Alright. I'll be in touch, I'm sure."

"And, Jonas?" A grin twisted the corner of her mouth. "Do not call me a fucking politician. I have an image to maintain."

He laughed and waved her away.

Douglas Hadje—2325

Douglas doffed his suit and packed into its carry bag, which had previously held his clothes.

Why did I do that?

He finished straightening his jumpsuit and began the slow walk back to his apartment. He ignored the colored strips on the wall that would guide him back the quick way, and instead walked anti-spinward, the long way around. This would take him through the manufacturing sector, but that was alright. It would be loud and there would be the quietly efficient drones carrying out all their little tasks, but it would give him more time to walk, more time to think.

Why the hell did I do that?

He wound his way through a few of the factories, from the glass furnace to the thick cylinder that housed the strut-works, a complex of sturdy supports and extrusion machinery that had grown the launch arm out of this side of the station. He brushed his hand along the smooth wall of the cylinder, before continuing to wind his way through the manufacturing wing.

The reasons eluded him. He didn't know why he did that. Why he kept doing that. Why would he run himself through this exercise time and again? Why would he grab his suit, dream up some small errand that warranted an EVA, and go out to touch the side of the System?

Why would he keep doing that to himself.

She was dead. Dead, or close enough to it. *Nowhere on the System.* That's what May Then My Name had said. This woman he had essentially no ties to other than a family name, this woman he'd never met, one who owed him nothing and to whom he only owed dreams.

She was dead and there was nothing he could do about it. No funeral, no memorial that he could reach. He wanted so badly to mourn this woman he'd never met and felt as though there were no possible way to do so without something to do. Something to say. Some cold stone to stand before or unfeeling metal plaque where grieving fingers could trace the letters of her name.

She was dead, and that shouldn't even matter to him.

That was the worst part, he'd decided: that his grief felt unwarranted. There was no connection between them other than the name, they'd never talked, and she likely didn't even know that her family had continued on after her through her brother, so what did he do to earn the right to mourn her? Doubtless she left loved ones behind on the System, too, people she'd known for more than two hundred years, lovers, enemies, colleagues and friends who respected her. *They* had the right to mourn.

He was just that weird guy who would take EVA walks from the narrow gap of the station to the System, press his hands and forehead to the glassy exterior, and dream that he was dreaming along with the billions who lived inside. No one inside knew of him other than the sys-side launch team, and no one actually knew him personally aside from May Then My Name and perhaps Ioan.

The manufacturing sector ran out beneath his feet, and he stepped from there to the spotless, black control center for the machinery. It had hardly been used since the development and construction of the strut-works. It had only really existed for the pleasure of the tourists who had made the station possible in the first place, for the walls of the control center were glass, letting tourists gawk at all of the machinery that went into running a station.

No tourists anymore. No gawking. The glass walls offered little to those who worked on the station other than a place to lounge and zone out, watching robots scurry to and fro.

He swiped his way out of the sector and passed from there to what had previously been a strip mall running most of the length of the ship. Shops had long ago been decommissioned and transitioned into various offices. This had been divvied up into threes, with one third being dedicated to running the station itself, one third to running the System, and one third to science and research, for those who were still able to make the long, expensive trip out to the moon and from the moon to the station, where they might do their concrete astrophysics or space-bound astronomy.

The mall opened up onto a promenade and park. The grass and gardens there remained meticulously well kept, doing their part along with the atmospheric regulation system to keep the air inside clean.

Gardens faded into low trees and greenhouses where most of the food for the station was grown. Potatoes, yams, soybeans, apples, millet, and the precious rotating crop of grains that blessed the station with the occasional bit of bread.

All was tended by automated systems, along with the help of a few botanist-nutritionists.

He walked through the sectors of the station and thought. He walked along the promenade tailward, then further anti-spinward to the greenhouses, and back sunward again. He walked and he thought, slowly going through the mental list of things he'd always wanted to say to Michelle and erasing them, line by line. Why keep them around, now? Why bother?

Having walked back to the sunward hub, he finished the trip to his room in the hotel. His room where he would remain as precisely as alone as he had been before.

His implants buzzed as he walked into his room, and a glance at the corner of his HUD showed a message-received icon. He'd turned off his HUD for the non-errand and the walk through the station, but now that he saw it, saw that it originated sys-side, he tossed his suit bag onto the bed and dashed over to his rig.

> **May Then My Name Die With Me:** Douglas! Ioan and I are available today. If you have some time, we would like to talk with you.

This, at least, was something pleasant to distract himself from his unearned grief.

> **Douglas Hadje:** I'm available for the next few hours before I should probably go to bed. Let me know when you're around.

The reply was almost immediate.

> **Ioan Bălan:** Douglas, nice to meet you! May Then My Name is forking, she'll be here in a moment.

> **May Then My Name:** I am here! Glad you could make it. How are you out there? Enjoying the cold vacuum of space?

He frowned, quelling the suspicion that they had known of his EVA.

> **Douglas:** The station is a perfectly comfortable 20C at all times. If ever it gets cold, I'm probably in trouble.

> **May Then My Name:** Boring.

> **Ioan:** Don't listen to her. Are you doing well?

> **Douglas:** As well as I can. I'm still trying to figure out what to do with my time. I've gone on a few not-super-necessary EVAs to just look at the stars or the System or whatever. I really should take up knitting. Oh! And nice to meet you as well.

Douglas: How are you two?

Ioan: Fine, here. Very busy. We're conducting interviews all across the System, as well as coordinating with those who are doing the same on the LVs.

May Then My Name: Ioan is doing the interviews and coordination, I am eating all of his food and leaving the dishes out.

Ioan: She's been working, too. She's probably got the larger project ahead of her than I do.

Douglas: You sound like you're having fun, so I'll take that as a good sign. What did you want to talk about?

May Then My Name: Your questions. I thought that it would be more comfortable to do so as a conversation rather than over mail. Certainly more organic.

Douglas: Alright, where do you want to start?

May Then My Name: Perhaps it would be easiest for Ioan and I to answer a whole bunch of your questions at once. They are mostly biographical, and I think that a few paragraphs from each of us will cover most of them.

May Then My Name: We have flipped a coin, and it was decided that I will go first.

May Then My Name: I uploaded back in the early 2100s, back when the System was small and full of dreamers, weirdos, and people like you and Ioan who spend all of their time thinking. Before that, I was a teacher, though towards the end of my physside tenure and for some time after, I became involved in politics. I grew up in the central corridor of North America, in the Western Federation. As with everyone, I do not think that I have an accent, though after some trouble with my implants before I uploaded, I found that some speech and thought patterns had changed, and since then, language and I have had a complicated relationship. We could have worked to change it, my cocladists and I, but why bother?

May Then My Name: You ask about dissolution strategies (tasker, tracker, dispersionista): you are correct that they apply to the ways in which an individual forks. They are not hard and fast categories, but rather a set of patterns that we have noticed over the years and applied names and numbers to. Taskers will fork only very rarely, and then for a specific task, merging back into the root instance immediately afterward. Trackers fork more frequently, and may maintain forks over a longer period of time. The reasons for forking may vary—Ioan is a tracker, ey will explain more—but the forks almost always follow a single line of thought or relationship or what have you to its logical end before merging back. Dispersionistas are those who fork for fun, spinning off new personalities and maybe merging them back, maybe not. My clade, the Ode clade, falls somewhere between tracker and dispersionista: we fork frequently for many temporary purposes, but maintain a relatively small permanent clade of around 100 instances.

May Then My Name: Is that clear? I can answer questions about this until the cows upload.

Douglas: I think so. It made sense when you called them 'dissolution strategies', which makes me think of dissolving into a solution.

May Then My Name: Basically. We all enjoy dissolution (or not) in different ways. Those are lazy categories to bucketize vague trends. They are similar in some ways to political divisions: one may identify with a political label, even if one's actual political inclinations may be more complicated than that label implies.

Ioan: And all dispersionistas are all bleeding heart liberals or weirdo artists.

May Then My Name: To a one, yes.

Ioan: I fall more into the tracker camp. I pick up projects such as this one or researching a book or something, and let a fork work on those. I—my #Tracker instance, as it's called—or my forks may create extra instances for smaller tasks along the way, but it gets to be too much for me to deal with after a certain point, and the slow divergence of personalities feels uncomfortable. I have three forks out there now, one for collating data from each LV, and one for conducting interviews here while I write. That number goes up and down as needed.

Douglas: Makes sense to me.

May Then My Name: Do you have a sense of how you will approach this when you upload?

Douglas: Good question. I'm only just now learning about it, so it's hard for me to say for sure, but I think I'm with Ioan on this. It sounds like it'd get confusing after a while.

Ioan: Oh, it does. When there are ten different Mays running around, I'd be hard pressed to tell them apart.

May Then My Name: I need to keep you on your toes somehow.

Ioan: Or step on them.

Douglas: Is that a common thing? That many May Then My Names?

Douglas: Would it be too personal of me to just call you May, by the way?

May Then My Name: 'May' is a pet name reserved those with whom I am closest. I ask that you please stick with May Then My Name.

Douglas: Alright. Apologies if I overstepped.

May Then My Name: Accepted! Thank you for asking. But yes, it is common that I will spin off a bunch of instances for this or that. I have a tendency to fork when I get excited. That is not terribly relevant, though.

Ioan: You asked about what it's like being a historian on the System. It's not quite the information haven that I think you're imagining. All of that vast wealth of data is technically there, but it exists in the perisystem architecture, and finding one's way around there can be something of a pain. Our role becomes one of researcher and librarian as much as historian. Besides, the goal of a historian isn't always to dig up long lost artifacts or writing or whatever, but rather to make sense of what is there. Take all that info and make a story out of it.

Ioan: Do keep in mind that I'm not strictly a historian. I'm mostly a writer, and my role can vary from historical research to something more akin to anthropology like this current situation, to something almost like a journalist, where I watch something happen and build a coherent story out of it.

May Then My Name: That is how ey came to work with our clade and thus the Launch project. Ey had done some observing with one of my cocladists, and it recommended em to us for this task.

Ioan: As for my biography, before I lose the thread, I uploaded in the 2230s after growing up in south-central Europe. I uploaded after a short stint in university where, yes, I studied history. My parents died, and I am not built for a life with death in it, so I headed sys-side to allow my siblings to attend school.

May Then My Name: Oh, Ioan. That is the first I have heard of this.

Ioan: It's been almost a century, I've come to terms with it. We can talk about it another time, though, if you're interested.

Ioan: You ask about universities here. There are quite a few organizations that fill that role, most of which are hyper-focused on specific fields. I worked with a history and anthropology institute for a while, and actually missed one of May's cocladists while working with an institute for art and design.

Douglas frowned at his terminal. That was the second time Ioan had referred to May Then My Name as that pet name 'May', but he couldn't think of a polite way to ask what that meant about how close they were.

Douglas: That makes sense. I imagine there has to be some structure in place. I know that you can't upload before you turn 18, but I imagine a lot of people still want to learn things that interest them after.

Ioan: Very much so. We have to make our own fun.

May Then My Name: 'Fun', ey says.

May Then My Name: Douglas, Ioan could have fun organizing eir pen collection.

Ioan: Can and do.

Ioan: You'll have to forgive the silliness, Douglas. It's been a long day for us.

Douglas: It's okay. I'm glad that there's still fun to be had sys-side.

May Then My Name: Oh, plenty!

May Then My Name: Now, you also asked after Michelle.

His stomach sank. He considered what to type back, but decided instead on waiting for May Then My Name to continue, lest he get too emotional again.

May Then My Name: First of all, you asked if I ever met her. I had the chance to meet her a handful of times. I would not call her famous, *per se*, but many do remember her as one of the founders. She was

May Then My Name: Well.

May Then My Name: I want to say that she was old. I am only a little bit younger than she was, in the grand scheme of things, but some of her experiences prior to uploading left a mark on her, and time was not kind to her in that regard. Though aging is not really something that we need to worry about, sys-side, she seemed to have aged every one of those two centuries.

Douglas: What did she look like, at that age?

May Then My Name: You misunderstand, or I misspeak. She looked much as she did when she uploaded, but that pre-upload trauma meant that she felt all two hundred of those years. If you go through an event that makes 80% of your days bad days, then that means that you wind up with 58400 bad days through the years. That will wear on one.

Douglas: I don't know what to say.

Douglas: I'm sorry to hear that about her.

Douglas: Is that a common experience sys-side?

May Then My Name: Not that common, no, and hers was unique.

May Then My Name: Every now and then, one of us will get tired of functional immortality and decide to just quit their instance—that is what she did—and disappear off the System. I do not begrudge her that.

Ioan: I'm sorry for your loss, Douglas.

He had to blink away tears in order to reply, and then did so quickly, hitting send before his courage failed him.

Douglas: I'm really torn up about this. I don't even know why. I never met her, know basically nothing about her, and have apparently been thinking about someone as though they were alive, when in reality, they've been dead for two decades. How can I possibly miss her? But I do! I miss her and feel like I'm in mourning, and then I feel guilty over the fact that I'm grieving this person who never knew me.

Douglas: I'm sorry.

Douglas: That just all came at once, sorry.

Douglas: I'm sorry.

May Then My Name: Douglas, let me tell you a story.

May Then My Name: One of the times I had the chance to meet Michelle, I visited her sim with her. She had not built herself a house or anything, like most do, but instead built for herself an endless green field of rolling hills. Except, that, rather than letting that field be perfect, it was absolutely covered with dandelions. Weeds, basically. It was not that it was some weeded lot, but that it was a field of very obviously well-kept grass, dotted every few feet with these clusters of perfectly imperfect flowers, little suns peeking up out of their spray of leaves.

May Then My Name: From what you say of Earth, a field of well-kept grass would be incredibly rare, and so I imagine that you understand what it would mean for something so pristine to become filled with these flowers that everyone considered a nuisance.

May Then My Name: But Michelle was obsessed with them. She loved their smell, and loved how bright they stood out against the grass. There it was, this amazing field of the richest grass that invited one to roll in it, and it was dotted with these intensely yellow flowers.

May Then My Name: Her sim was intentional in its imperfections. It was a dialectic. It was a koan, a contradiction in which sat a kernel of universal truth, understood only when one realized that both sides of that contradiction could be true at the same time.

May Then My Name: I did not know why she invited me over to her sim to meet with me, rather than meet up at some cafe or park or office, but when I arrived, I saw that she seemed to be having a bad day, as so many of hers were. When she had a bad day, it was visible in her very body. She would flicker between two different forms, like one might flicker between two different avatars on the 'net. I am still not sure how that worked, as it was generally a violation of the norms, but no one ever called her on it, no System process ever made her stop.

May Then My Name: I asked her about the field as we sat down on the side of a low hill, and she picked one of those dandelions. It was perfect. They have hollow stems, and the walls ooze a sticky, white latex when the stem is broken, and even that was perfect in the sim. She picked the flower and smelled it, then handed it to me. "When I was in school," she told me. "My friends and I would go sit in the grass above the football field and talk, and at least once a year when we did that, I would pick a dandelion and tell them that I always thought they smelled like muffins. They would always laugh."

May Then My Name: And then she got real quiet and we sat there for what must have been an hour before she spoke again, "How silly, that that is the one thing that I remember most clearly. Sitting in the grass, smelling flowers with my friends."

May Then My Name: Scent, I have been told, bears the strongest ties to memory, and this defined her in some undefinable way. We got to our business after that, but I remember smelling that flower and thinking, "Well, what do you know, it does smell like muffins."

May Then My Name: I do not know if Michelle would have liked you or if you would have liked her. I do not know if you would have felt any connection for each other, or felt like family. What I do know is that she was every bit the person you imagine her to be. Fully realized and with every bit of story that you must have imagined for her over the years. She was real. She was complex. She thought about her friends, two hundred years gone, and how they laughed.

May Then My Name: You may not have had the chance to meet her, to talk to her, but you very much knew her, in your own way.

It was a long time before Douglas was able to respond, and both Ioan and May Then My Name kept quiet. He didn't feel like they were expecting him to reply or that he was keeping them waiting while he let all that pent-up emotion out at once. They were simply holding space for him.

Douglas: Thank you for that. I don't know if we would've felt like family, either, but I am incredibly happy that I got the chance to hear you talk about her.

May Then My Name: You do not need to justify your grief, Douglas. You are allowed to feel it. Give yourself permission. You have my permission, as well.

Ioan: How about we call it here for now? There will be plenty of time for questions coming up, and I'm sure we'll all have our lists to bring to the next time we can chat.

Ioan: Take care of yourself, Douglas. May's right. You're allowed to mourn. It's the healthy thing to do.

Ioan: Besides, May made herself cry and I don't think she's going to be good for much more tonight.

May Then My Name: Ioan I swear to god.

May Then My Name: I am going to eat crackers in your bed and put sand in your shoes.

Douglas laughed in spite of himself.

> **Douglas:** Thank you both, then. I really mean it.
> Ping me whenever, and I'll get to it as soon as I can.

After they said their goodbyes and he put his terminal to sleep, he turned out the lights, stripped out of his clothes, and climbed into bed. He was prepared to let emotions overtake him, but where that knot of feelings had formed within him was now only calm. He wasn't through it, he suspected, but at least he was able to untangle some of that grief tonight.

He embraced that calm, rolled onto his side, and slept.

Codrin Bălan#Castor—2325

The first interview of note that Codrin Bălan conducted was with an author who had chosen to invest completely in the launches, leaving no one behind.

At first, Codrin wondered why it was that this author had chosen to be a part of the interview process, why it was that Dear had recommended him. He seemed, on the surface to be entirely uninteresting. He was an author. That was that.

His name was Martin Rankin, and while Codrin had not read any of his works prior to the suggestion, ey had certainly heard the name in the various literary circles that ey trawled on occasion. A man prone to grand literary gestures, one who leaned heavily on the twisting of endless sentences, ceaseless streams of fragments, prose that bordered on florid even by Codrin's relatively flowery standards. Ey knew that ey was prone to many of the same pitfalls, but this man took it to an extreme that they found unreasonable.

Codrin, to prepare for the interview, had read two of Rankin's books. They were not without their merit, as might any such book be that garnered so much attention, but they still took plenty of work to get through. He wrote most often about contemporary life within the System in all its deliriously boring intricacies.

That said, much of his work was bound up in a sense of magical realism that was, ey had to admit, enticing. This was something that Codrin had never managed to capture emself, and so ey set aside some time to study the ways in which Rankin used surrealism to enhance the story at hand without distracting.

Martin Rankin was exactly as ey had expected. There was nothing about him that did not shout Martin Rankin. He wore his identity on his face, on his chest, in the way his hands moved across the table as they talked, there at the cafe, there sitting out on the street, there sipping their coffees.

"So, you are the illustrious Codrin Bălan." His voice was imperious, veering dangerously close to pompous, looking over the rim of the demitasse appraisingly at em as he sipped espresso.

Something about the man grated. Ey wasn't quite sure what it was at first, whether it was the self-assured way he spoke, or the self-aggrandizing expression he wore on his face. It was nigh intolerable.

All the same, ey tried eir best to keep up eir smile as ey spoke. "And you're Martin Rankin. It's a pleasure to finally get the chance to meet you in the flesh. Thank y–"

"What a curious choice of phrase, in the flesh." His tone was droll, bored. "Have you stopped to think of all of the little idioms we bring with us from 'phys-side'? Even that term! Phys-side. It spells out very plainly that we do not exist in that form any longer. We exist in *opposition* to it. 'Sys-side' contains no such sense of our abstract existence."

Ey nodded, smiling ingratiatingly. The man was clearly used to having the chance to expound on his own ideas, and anything that anyone else had to say was of secondary importance—if it was important at all. Ey decided to lean into that. "What a beautiful way to put that. Do you think that the same applies to the dichotomy between L_5 System and launch?"

The simpering tone appeared to appeal to Rankin's sensibilities, as he smiled down to Codrin with all the patronizing disdain of *bless your heart*. "I do believe so. What can we say but 'launch-side' and 'sys-side'? Do those truly say anything about our existence here? We are hurtling out into space at some terrifying speed, driven by the momentum imparted by the spin of the station and the deliciously thin membranes of those solar sails. Ah! What a journey on which we have decided to embark! We lucky few. Those back on the System know nothing of our experiences out here, even if they have also decided to join. There is no way to accurately transmit that experience through text alone."

Hiding a grimace behind a sip of eir own espresso, Codrin jotted down the author's words. The first thing that Rankin had done upon meeting up with em had been to make a similarly patronizing comment about the anachronistic nature of pen and paper. Ey had supposed at first that ey'd met a fellow admirer of fine pens, fine paper, and the joy of beautiful inks.

Alas.

"I've heard from my partner that–"

"Ah, yes! The illustrious Dear! How is he?"

"It. It's doing quite well."

"Right, right. *It* always did have such a strange way of moving through the world."

"If we could–" Ey cut emself off and recomposed eir plastic smile. "I've heard that you are working on a project that capitalizes on this. Can you expand on that?"

"Of course! Of course. I will always help a fellow writer." He set his cup aside and made a grand sweep of his arm. "You look around you, and you see so many going about their lives as they might have otherwise. Even I am guilty of the dalliance of getting up, drinking coffee, perhaps sitting and reading a while. We lucky few–" Codrin knew that some two and a half billion personalities were on the launches, but ey declined to comment. "–can draw so much inspiration from a project on so grand a scale. My project is one that utilizes the base nature of a personality embedded in a System that cares not for consistency between its two constituent parts.

"Before I disappeared from the L_5 System, I wrote an outline for a new book describing the universal feelings of exploration that are bound up in this endeavor, and now I am working writing the book which follows that outline. My counterpart on the Pollux launch is doing the same—he had better be!—and we are sending the results of our labors back to the System to an editor who is a most trusted companion, and he is compiling them into a single book which will serve to showcase the similarities and differences that one mind can hold when it has lost a unifying sense of self!"

Codrin wrote quickly, not just to keep up, but also to keep eir eyes on the page and away from the by now nearly dancelike gestures that Rankin was using. Ey wondered just how much of it was a conscious decision to be witnessed (and thus perhaps a deeply ingrained need to be seen and not forgotten), and how much of it was some innate characteristic of this certain, special type of asshole.

"Does that make sense, my dear Codrin?"

"Oh, yes. Yes it does, Mr. Rankin."

He sat back in his seat with a self-satisfied smirk. "I think that you'll like the end product. I've read some of your own works, by the way. You pick some quite interesting projects about our post-human life, though I must admit that your style is quite dry."

"Such is the life of a historian, I suppose."

Rankin laughed. "Of course, of course, I forget myself. You'll have to send me your notes for this current project, and I'll see if I can pull them together into something coherent and readable."

Ey bit eir tongue and nodded. "Of course, I'll see about doing so when I'm done. Back to your work, however; do you have any predictions on how the works will differ?"

"The *work*, Codrin. It's a very singular work. Both me and my counterpart are writing the exact same work, and the only difference is the circumstances." He waved off any reply before continuing. "Though imagine that our two takes began quite similar, and then started to diverge further as time continues, such as a fork might diverge from its down-tree instance. How interesting! A work that, in some core mechanism, follows the exact same path as our daily existence."

"And you have an editor who is merging these two threads? Are they planning on doing something special with the presentation of it?"

"Yes. Yes! Of course, what is a book but an experience? A book should be delightfully difficult to read, if it is to be enjoyed to the fullest. You are engaging with a topic, you must—*must*—put in the same amount of effort that the author has! We have plans to arrange the two texts side-by-side, locked together at the points specified in the outline, as well as any similarities that the texts share. Imagine, I, Rankin#Castor, writing, "And so, in my heart of hearts, I knew the truth among the stars" while Rankin#Pollux writes, "And so, in my heart of hearts, I know the truth among the wheeling of the stars." From there, we can have the texts line up on the page, and perhaps even highlight the similarities. My editor promises that he won't send me any of the result until it's complete and ready for manuscript sign off, lest #Pollux's writing influence my own."

Once ey had finished jotting in eir shorthand, Codrin asked, "Do you have any idea on how the work will be received?"

"Ah yes, the problem of reception." Rankin smiled sourly. "Our works have inherent worth, and yet we must, at some point, rely on readers for their validation. I hope that it will be received quite well, though I know that it will go over the heads of many. Such can't be helped, though, for even in this world of leisure and ease, many still claim that they don't have time to read. Time! We have all the time in the universe, if we try hard enough, and yet here we are, spinning our wheels on whether or not there's time enough to read a book! What rubbish."

"Do you often fork to read books?"

Rankin frowned, at which Codrin took secret pleasure. "No. There are some aspects of life which must be experienced singularly and without the dreary experience of reclaiming memories from a dying mind."

"Dying?"

"What is the act of quitting but that of death?"

Codrin withheld eir thoughts on the matter, asking instead, "Perhaps there's a story there, too. Read a book, quit, and then write about the experience of having only the memory of reading that book. It seems to fall in line with the scope of your current project."

Rankin's expression grew colder. "An interesting problem for you to tackle, my dear Codrin. I look forward to your monograph on the subject."

That secret pleasure grew warmer. Ey suspected that Rankin would have enjoyed such a project, had the idea come from within, rather than from someone else. "I'll have to give it a go, sometime, though I suspect my dry writing will fall short of yours."

A little bit of sucking up warmed him again, and Codrin once again marveled at what an art conducting interviews was.

"Writing is something that comes from much practice. I can do little but encourage you to practice, practice, and practice some more." He laughed, jabbing a finger at em. "After all, we have all the time in the world, do we not?"

Ey gave a hint of a bow, a moment of silence to show eir appreciation, and then continued. "Do you have any projects planned after this book? Perhaps something to work on alongside it?"

"Of course! It's important not to fall into the trap of working on a single project, otherwise you'll feel obliged to refine and refine and refine! Keep it varied. I'm also working on a novel exploring income inequalities within the System. Or Systems, perhaps. This will hopefully be released concurrent with my main work. This is being done by a separate fork, and we merge weekly on the project. It takes no small amount of focus to keep either one of us from getting sidetracked, but it's important that we continue our work at a good pace. We may have all the time in the world, but it's easy enough to be forgotten in our current market if we don't keep coming out with more and more works, eh?"

"There is that, yes. At least there's not a livelihood resting on it."

"Oh but there is! I'm sure that if my words aren't read, that I'll disappear into nothingness!"

Ah, Codrin thought. *There it is.* "Does this drive influence your writing?"

"Oh, here and there," Rankin said, waggling a hand. "Sometimes I'll cut corners to ensure that I'm always writing something, or I'll split off enough forks to work in shifts, ensuring that I'm always writing at all hours of the day, such as it is. One will work a shift, merge with the next to keep the momentum going, and go to bed."

"That must be a very productive experience."

"It is! It very much is. You should try it, my dear Codrin."

"I most certainly will," ey lied. Ey was no stranger to modified sleep schedules and just how unpleasant that could be. "Do you have any last words of wisdom that you'd like to impart for the eventual readers of this project?"

"I would tell them this: you are always dreaming, but you should always dream bigger. What but big dreams was it that led to these launches? What but big dreams was it that led to the System as a whole? Dream big! Dream your own dreams. Bring them to fruition, and bigger and brighter things will benefit us all."

Codrin finished eir transcribing with a flourish and bowed to Rankin. "Thank you for your time, Mr. Rankin. Is there anything else?"

"Only to thank you for your time. Make sure you get me your notes, and I'll make sure that you and Dear each get a copy of the upcoming book once it's done. Do tell him hi for me."

"It, but yes, I will say hi."

"Right, right. Do tell *it* hi." Rankin quit before, Codrin suspected, he could roll his eyes.

Ey bit eir tongue until ey was back home at the house on the prairie. Ey stomped out into the grass to eir very first cairn, set eir paper and pens down carefully in the grass, and shouted to the cloud-dotted sky. "What an enormous sack of shit, good Lord."

Then ey picked up eir supplies and walked back to the house. Eir partners greeted em at the door, both looking winded and still laughing.

"You heard, I take it?"

"Tell us how you really feel, my dear."

Codrin rolled eir eyes. "Not a fan. Let me set my shit down and get a glass of wine or something."

Dear gasped, paw to muzzle. *"A curse! Codrin! I am shocked."*

"I'll get the wine," its partner said, still laughing.

They gathered on the couch where Codrin could lounge against Dear with eir feet up in its partner's lap.

"So, how was it, really? Was he really that bad?" Dear asked.

"You didn't tell me that he was so...so..."

"Pompous? That his head was so far up his ass that he could smell his breath?"

Codrin laughed and poked the fox in the side. "Yeah, those things. I'm guessing you don't think too highly of him, either?"

"Not particularly, no," Dear said, brushing fingers through Codrin's hair. *"I was more wondering if a writer—a writer in particular, I mean—might have some ideas that you could glean for this project of ours."*

"I suppose." Ey kept silent for a moment, simply enjoying the physical contact. "Though, come to think of it, his current project sounds interesting enough."

"The dual text thing?" Dear's partner asked.

"Yeah. Did he tell you about that?"

"Mmhm. It sounds interesting, at least on the surface. We'll have to see how the execution works out, though. It could be stupendously boring."

"I wouldn't be surprised."

"It is not a bad idea for a project such as he is wont to do," Dear murmured, sounding distant. *"I would not have turned down the opportunity to do such myself, if the types of projects that I do fit that framework."*

"The thing is, I don't think it'll work for ours." Codrin shrugged against Dear's thigh. "I don't think spoiling Codrin#Pollux is something we really need to worry about, and I'm sure Ioan will keep sending us interesting stuff."

"Probably best to not, actually," Dear's partner said.

"Right. Come to think of it, even Rankin said that he started with an outline to keep the two instances organized. We could probably do with more organization between the three of us."

"Or the three of our groups, at least. Perhaps Pollux and Ioan taken together will provide us with a good idea of where we should be working next."

"Do you want to send Ioan a note to start coordinating?"

"I just did."

There was a sensorium ping, a view of the office where Ioan had begun work so many years ago.

"I should've known."

"I am more predictable than you give me credit for, my dear."

After a moment's silence, ey grumbled, "He even kept calling you 'he'. Drove me nuts."

Dear made a strange face, then threw its head back and cackled. *"He has honed his insensitivity into quite the art. What a delight! So, while he was being a pompous ass, did he actually have anything to add to the conversation besides that one idea?"*

Codrin shook eir head.

"He always was a one-trick pony."

"He also kept talking about idioms that applied mostly to phys-side and how they stick around here, on that note. But still, being a one-trick pony is a worry I struggle with."

"That you struggle with it, that all of us mere mortals struggle with it, is what keeps us separate from them."

" 'Them'?" Dear's partner laughed. "You make them sound way more organized than they really are."

"They do not need to be. They are all the same."

Michelle Hadje/Sasha—2124

It took Debarre a matter of seconds to answer Michelle's request for a meeting. His arrival in her sim, the weasel blinking into existence next to her on that endless field of grass and dandelions, startled her enough to cause her to stumble.

"Shit, you okay, Michelle?"

She laughed, picking herself back up, feeling as unsteady as ever. "Yeah, I just was not expecting you right away. I thought that you would set up a time later."

"I was free." Debarre leaned forward and helped brush some grass off of her side. "Is now not a good time?"

"No, no. Now is fine. Thank you for meeting up in the first place."

"Of course."

Michelle led them off at a leisurely pace into the fields, into the warm day and soft hum of bees. Debarre walked along in silence beside her, apparently enjoying the day with his whiskers bristled out and eyes half-shut against the sun.

She'd always intended to build herself a house, but the field always felt so complete without it.

"True Name mentioned that you wanted to talk."

"Yeah," he said, looking down at his feet as they poked their way through the dandelions. "But I'm not quite sure where to start."

"I am guessing that it is about the names." She mastered a

brief wave of anxiety, a brief wave of skunk features across human ones, a brief wave of Sasha among Michelle. "I am afraid that I do not have a fantastic explanation for it."

Debarre shrugged this off. "I don't need a great explanation. I don't need anything, I guess. I just want to know what's going on, Sasha."

And with that, with a susurration of fur against clothes, she was Sasha. What thoughts before that had kept her as Michelle, as her human self, had been uprooted for the day and replaced with those that anchored her to a time, a context, a name. Debarre, of all the others that she'd met, seemed to understand this best, and he took this in stride.

"If I am honest, I do not know myself. At least, not truly. It is something that came to me in the moment." She paused to pluck a dandelion, twirling it between fingerpads, laughing. "I am still a little unnerved by it, myself. I remember thinking to myself, "I need a fucking vacation, but I should fork so that I do not leave the others in a lurch", and then there it was, the idea, already fully formed and ready to go."

"To use Aw– to use eir poem for the names?"

She canted her ears back. "I miss em. I have been thinking about em for years."

"A decade."

The skunk nodded.

"I think about em a lot, too, Sasha. We were all pretty torn up about it, even if ey's the one that helped build this place. I remember bawling my eyes out when you read the poem." He laughed, rubbing a paw over his face. "Hell, when you said all that in the coffee shop, I was having a hard time dealing with a whole shitload of emotions and you were so upset at the bar."

"The bar?"

"Oh, uh, sorry. True Name was upset at the bar. I started to ask her about all this, and I almost said eir name and–"

"AwDae's?" she asked, tilting her head.

Debarre flinched back from her, stopping mid-step.

"Debarre?"

He frowned at her, straightening up. "When I tried to say 'AwDae' earlier, True Name lost her shit. Like, I was afraid she was going to lunge across the table and deck me. You didn't know?"

Sasha shook her head. "None of my forks have merged back down to me yet. I– we decided that I would take some time off before reengaging. I have no memory of what happened."

"It was kind of terrifying." The weasel laughed. "She slammed her glass down and said something like 'do not fucking say that name'. I can respect wanting to keep things close to the heart, but I thought I was about to get in a fistfight."

"I am trying to picture either of us in a fistfight, much less with each other, and failing," she said, grinning. "I would very much appreciate this being kept between us, yes, but I have no plans to deck you if you say eir name when it is just the two of us."

"I appreciate that. Why'd True Name seem to think otherwise, though?"

Tossing away the dandelion, she shrugged helplessly. "I do not know. At the point when she came into existence, she ceased being me. We were the same for only the briefest of seconds, but we have long since diverged."

"That far, though? It's only been a week or two, right?"

"I suppose so. I will have to check in with her. With the rest of the clade, too, and see if anything else strange is going on. I have not been keeping tabs on all of them."

Debarre nodded. "They seem like they're doing fine."

"They are not taking over the council, then?"

He laughed. "Not at all, no. Just True Name taking your spot in dealing with the politics stuff. I actually haven't seen many of the others."

Sasha nodded.

They stood in silence for a few minutes, just enjoying the sun. The vacation had treated her well so far, and she already felt less torn in two without the stress of the council weighing on her. Debarre also had a calming influence on her, as though having one person associated primarily with only one context was enough to pin her in place, rather than having her constantly ping-ponging between two.

Skunk and weasel both sat down in the grass, laughing at having apparently come to the same decision independent of each other.

Debarre plucked a blade of grass and threw it at her. "You reminded me; another thing that True Name said is that when you forked off your ten instances, you left behind the part of you that is split between Michelle and Sasha. She called it 'the part that suffers'."

Hiding a wince by plucking a handful of dandelions one by one, Sasha nodded. "I do not think that having ten versions of me who are just as fucked up as I am would have made anything easier."

During the pause that followed, she began weaving those flowers into a chain.

"Are you?"

"Am I what?"

"Suffering."

Sasha set the half-complete flower-crown on her lap and began to pick another handful of flowers. Anything to keep from looking at Debarre. "I do not know if that is the right word. It was not a deliberate choice to fork each instance only when I was in a more singular state, but I am not displeased that this was the case. That way, they can do what they need to do without...without..."

Debarre did not press her. She worked through her tears, tying the last of the dandelions in place to form the chain into a loop so that she could rest it atop her head, petals tickling at her ears. When she dropped her hands again, the weasel took them in his own.

I can feel em, she thought. *I can almost feel em, there in the sunlight, in the flowers.*

"What keeps you from doing the same, yourself? You could fork when you're feeling excellent and leave behind whatever's causing the split."

She didn't answer, just sat with her paws in her friend's, her head bowed, her tears leaving tracks in fur.

"Sasha?"

She didn't answer.

"Do you regret coming here?"

All she could do was shake her head before emotion completely overwhelmed her. She slouched to the side and, with Debarre's help, lay down amid the grass and dandelions, resting her head on his thigh. His silence was patient and his paw on her shoulder kind as she let that wave of emotion wash over her, through her, and when it was past, he shared in the calm that remained after.

"I'm sorry, Sasha."

"No. It is alright." She rolled onto her back, picking up the fallen flower-crown and reaching it up to drape it over the weasel's head. "The System may act as a magnifying glass on some of what I was going through before uploading, but much of what I feel now I was going through before, just less visibly."

"Alright." He straightened the loop of golden flowers atop his head, ruffled a paw over her ears, and then leaned back, propping himself up with his paws in the grass.

"Nothing keeps me from fixing myself," she murmured up to the clouds. "I do not know why I do not just do so."

"Can I be honest?"

"Of course."

"I worry it's survivor's guilt."

She took a deep breath and quelled another wave of emotion, choosing instead to nod. "That is a distinct possibility. I do feel guilty that I made it and AwDae did not, that ey felt compelled to disappear across the border and give eir life for this–"

She waved her paw up at the sky. "–that ey did all that and never even got to see it."

There was a rustling and shifting beneath her head, and when she turned to look, the flower-crown was draped over her snout. They both laughed.

"We both lost someone," Debarre said, voice thick. "I feel guilty that I made it and Cicero didn't, sometimes. Hell, for a while, I was furious that AwDae lived longer than Cice did."

"I am sorry." Sasha started to wind the chain of flowers around her wrist, but it fell apart, so she dropped it into the grass instead. "I never knew."

"How do you imagine that conversation would've gone? "Hey AwDae, fuck you for outliving my boyfriend"?" He laughed. "Shit like this isn't rational, Sash."

"I guess not. I am still glad that you are around, though."

He sighed. "Of course I am. I never would've made it without you. I'm glad you're here. You and Michelle. Hell, your whole damn clade."

She gave the comment the space that it deserved, closing her eyes to feel the sun warm her fur. *You and Michelle.* Now there was a thought.

"Only, I wonder." His voice sounded distant, as though he were speaking to the sky rather than her. "I wonder if your forks have changed in ways other than just not being split. I wonder if they're really even you anymore."

Ioan Bălan—2325

"I uploaded as soon as I could. I think it was the forties?"

"Which forties?"

Renee laughed. "Right, the 2140s, sorry. I can't believe it's been that long."

Ioan smiled and jotted down the date. "Thanks. What led you to upload?"

"Jesus, I don't know that I even remember anymore." She got a far-away look in her eyes, then brightened up. "Cancer! I think, at least. I got something, and it just felt like it'd be easier to come up here than stay down there."

"That makes sense. Not much of that to worry about here."

"Sometimes I think it must've been early onset Alzheimer's." She laughed. "I just get a little spacey, is all."

"It's easy enough to do. I get stuck thinking about this or that and can't think of anything else, sometimes," ey said.

"Oh! Yes, that's it precisely. I get stuck writing stuff in my head, and then I forget what it was that I was doing."

"You write music?"

She nodded. "Composer, conductor, violinist. Have you heard any of my stuff?"

"I listened to some while I was preparing for our meeting." Ioan smiled sheepishly. "I'll admit that much of it was over my head, but I can certainly see the skill behind it, and you play beautifully."

"Thank you for saying so," she said, giving a hint of a bow. "For saying all that, I mean. I sometimes enjoy writing stuff that's hard to grasp. It makes for an experience of its own. Bafflement, confusion, lack of understanding, those are all feelings, and music is supposed to toy with feelings."

"That's something I can appreciate, as well."

"I'm sure you can, with your work with the Odists." Renee grinned at eir confusion. "I read up on you as well. They sound like a wild bunch."

"I'll say." Ey laughed. "You were a musician before uploading, too, correct?"

"Oh, yes! One of those lucky few who got to do what she loved for a living. I think that's why I uploaded, in the end. Getting a terminal diagnosis didn't really make me depressed in and of itself. What got to me was the thought that that would mean I wouldn't be able to play or write anymore. I've seen people go through treatment, and none of them are in any shape to play an instrument."

"What kind of cancer? If you don't mind me asking."

"Thyroid, I think. Yes, that was it. I noticed it when it started to get uncomfortable to hold the violin." She made a sour face, then added, "I'm sure I sound obsessed."

Ey waved the comment away. "I'm here to listen. Please, obsess all you like."

Renee smiled gratefully. "There really was nothing in my life, otherwise. Writing, playing, conducting. Concert after concert after concert. No friends, no family, no other hobbies, no other addictions. What would I even do with myself without the few things in my life I loved? Really, truly loved, too. I loved my parents, but it was more of a theoretical love. I told myself I loved my husband, but when he left—I was too distracted, he said—I was actually sort of relieved."

"That's a plenty good reason to upload, I'd say. 2140s, hmm." Ey hunted through eir memory, back to interviews with Douglas. "That was before governments were paying people to upload. Was it expensive for you to upload?"

"Paid...?" She frowned and shook her head. "God, no. What a weird idea."

"It got bad, phys-side. Some governments started subsidizing uploads to keep populations down and people happy."

"Weird, weird. No, it was not expensive, but I did have to pay. Couple thousand francs CFA, I think?"

"I don't have a reference point for that amount. I was compensated—well, my family was—to upload, coming to about two years tuition at the university. In terms of what the average person made where you lived, was that a lot?"

She shrugged. "Not sure about an average person. It was about six months' saving for me, and musicians didn't make a ton of money."

"There wasn't much money in history, either," ey said. "Now, the reason I sought you out was two-fold. First of all, one of the things you're known for is that you found a way to send your compositions phys-side pretty early on, correct?"

"Yes. Yes! I had nearly forgotten that they pinned that on me." She laughed, leaning back in her chair. "I didn't really figure it out, so much as use something a publisher pointed out to me as a curiosity. It's nigh impossible to send images and sound back through phys-side. I guess they came through all garbled, with little bits in focus and the rest a total mess. I have no clue as to the details."

"As I've heard, too. Text appears to work okay, as something more concrete."

"Right, just drop it in the perisystem blah blah and phys-side can pick it up. Anyway, music can be described, and that publisher said that there had been several different tools for writing sheet music as just plain old text. Want to play the note A? Write down A. B? Write down B. A rest? R. *Et cetera et cetera ad nauseum.* It was nothing new, but I guess no one had thought to try something like that before. I read up on one of them and made a few changes to the whole shebang, and now we can send that back and forth. Books? Sure. Math? Sure. Even film and stage scripts! Why not music?"

Ioan laughed. "Of course. That makes sense. Did your music change after you uploaded?"

"I wrote a lot more string works," she said, grinning. "After all, I could fork and play as many parts as I wanted. Or could afford, at least. It still cost a bit to fork back then. I also made a few instruments up here that I could only describe in order to let phys-side know how to make. Concerts were much easier to have, because schedules are easier to coordinate when you're not restricted to just one version of yourself. Music started to drift between sys-side and phys-side—stylistically, I mean. I got some iffy reviews of stuff offline that went over pretty well here."

"What happened to music phys-side that didn't here?"

"They swung back towards some older styles. Second-wave minimalism was at its height, when I was leaving, and I loved the stuff. All those long notes, chords that held forever or used rhythm to add variety. Phasing." She chopped her hands unevenly in the air before herself, emphasizing the latter in a way that Ioan didn't understand at all. "Outside the System, though, it swung back toward more romantic stuff. It was all very Mahler, very Antoniewicz, very Liu. The problem with living forever, though, is that you can keep refining your craft in whatever ways you want. I stuck around with minimalism, for the most part. People keep uploading, though, and bring their ideas with them, so I've tried to diversify my works a little bit, but I write what sounds good to me."

"Is there a steady stream of composers joining? Enough to shift styles sys-side?"

"Less so, lately. If people are being paid to upload, though, it's not too surprising. That makes it sound like things are a mess out there, and when things are a mess, people study less music and try to get out early, often before they've got the experience and knowledge that set in later in life. Would explain the wave of folk music I've seen in the last decades."

"Makes me want to take a survey of ages when folks upload through the years." Ey scribbled a note to emself on the corner of eir paper. "Another time, though. The second reason that I wanted to interview is that you didn't opt to join the launch. Why was that?"

She covered her face with her hands and laughed, sounding muffled. "Oh no, that's embarrassing. I meant to, I really did. I just forgot."

That evening, back at eir house, after ey had merged eir work-forks, after ey had sat down to dinner with May, ey finally let the memories, those countless little moments, wash over em.

"What?" the skunk asked, head tilted.

"Hmm?"

"You were frowning. What happened? Getting tired of my cooking?"

"No, it's good. Just thinking about something Codrin#Castor talked about today." Ey stabbed at a spear of asparagus. "Ey interviewed some asshole author who was working on a book on both launches, but intentionally not communicating to see how they would diverge."

"Sounds fun enough," May said. "But, if I am thinking of the same author, it will be quite boring."

Ioan laughed, finished chewing on the asparagus. "Codrin suggested that we specifically not do that, though, that it might be better to coordinate between the two launches a little better. Figure out who to interview and in what order, while the transmission time isn't too bad."

May shrugged. "I am up for it, if all three of our groups agree."

"After I explained it to Codrin#Pollux, ey seemed on board. I think it might be a good idea."

"Did either of them have any suggestions for where to look next?"

"Nothing in particular," Ioan said around a bite of fish. "Sorry. I figure stuff like why one invested in one or the other is a project that could go on forever, based on the numbers. Sure, there are only two hundred or so clades that totally invested in the launches, but the numbers are much higher on our end."

"You are thinking about Secession, are you not? Looking for founders to interview," May grinned. "Clever."

"Am I that transparent?"

"Yes, absolutely."

Ey laughed. "Well, how much of the Council of Eight remains?"

"Most. I will direct one of the Codrins to find some of them."

"But not me?"

"No. Remember I am curious to see who you find first." They ate in silence for a bit, before May spoke up. "Do you remember what I said about Michelle?"

"That she was instrumental to Secession, yeah. I was thinking of hunting down some Odists."

"A good bet, that." She paused, looked down at her plate and said, more quietly, "Will you ask the first lines?"

"That was my plan. I figure they were the first forked."

"Yes."

"Is something wrong?"

"I am worried that you will be unhappy with what you hear."

Ioan shrugged. "It's history, isn't it? Nothing to be done about it."

She nodded, setting her fork down on her plate, though some of the food remained. "Yes, but I am worried that you will be unhappy with me."

Part III

Acceleration

Codrin Bălan#Pollux—2325

The first direction from the L₅ System came in the form of a message from May Then My Name Die With Me. "Find Ezekiel," it read. "Talk with him. Be patient, be kind."

When ey showed it to Dear, the fox's ears stood erect, and it led Codrin out of the house to stand on the patio and watch the storm from the safety of the overhang.

"Please be careful, my dear."

"Do I have something to worry about? Should I be prepared for violence or something?"

It shook its head. *"I do not think so, no. Ezekiel was a member of the Council of Eight. One of the founders. He was close to much that happened in the early history of the System."*

"What did he do?" Codrin shook eir head. "I mean, what is it that he's known for?"

"Forking."

Ey let out the air in their lungs in one, low *huh*. It felt as though ey had been kicked in the stomach, and ey struggled to regain eir breath as stars swum before eir eyes. *"Forking?* You've got to be kidding me, Dear."

The fox laughed. *"I am not."*

"I thought that that was a core aspect of the System from the beginning."

"It was an accident at first. Someone split in two—not Michelle, before you ask—and the System automatically corrected and deleted

both forks. *The population was quite low at that point, and Zeke knew the victim. As part of his grief, he began to formulate the sys-side algorithms and drafted the petition to phys-side for allowing legitimate forking of personalities."*

"And Michelle helped?"

"She coordinated between Ezekiel, phys-side, and another councilmember on the logistics and how it was associated with the reputation markets, yes."

After a moment of staring out into the rain-clouded prairie, Codrin said, "I'm constantly surprised at just how much of a frontier it was back then, and just how many pies your clade seems to have had its fingers in."

Dear smiled tiredly.

"So, why did you bring me out here?"

"It is nice to talk about serious things with the sound of rain in the background."

"Really?"

"Of course not, my dear." It gestured back through the window, where its partner sat, reading. *"They do not enjoy hearing me talk of that time in our lives."*

Codrin frowned. "I think I know the answer, but should I interview them?"

"Please do not, Codrin. I do not want to bring up painful conversations of the past, nor do I wish to you to learn all that they know from a single source."

"I understand. Ioan mentioned that May Then My Name has been cagey around her past as well– No." Ey held up a hand to forestall a comment from Dear. "You don't need to defend her, or yourself, for that matter. I won't push you for more history. I would, however, like to hear your reasoning for these decisions."

"For withholding information?"

"For withholding it yourself. It seems as though you want us—you as in the Ode clade, us as in the Bălan clade—to discover things on our own. Why?"

Dear stuck a paw out, palm up, beneath a downspout and the steady stream of water that flowed from it, letting the water soak into its fur. *"There are parts of our past that I am ashamed of. Many of my cocladists are, as well. You could interview any one of us about the entirety of our story, even me, and we would tell you, but we would also resent you for that."*

Codrin waited Dear out.

"We would resent you, and the temptation to lie would be too great. It is better that you gather this information piecemeal to gain a more accurate picture of what it is that happened leading up to both Secession and Launch. May Then My Name is right. You should seek out the founders. You should seek out someone other than an Odist. You should seek out one who did not simply agree with us that far back."

"Alright, I can accept that."

It leaned in to bump its nose against eir cheek. *"Thank you, my dear. Be kind to Ezekiel, as May Then My Name suggests. Be patient with him. Be careful for his sake. Be prepared for a difficult conversation."*

"Difficult how?"

"He is not who he used to be. Time has not been kind to him, to his sanity. He is no longer the shrewd and funny politician he was back then. Since about the time of the launch proposal, he has returned to being called Ezekiel and donned the mantle of his namesake."

"What's that?"

Dear shook its paw dry. *"A prophet."*

Codrin was not sure what a prophet looked like, but the conversation with Dear dogged em all the way until ey was able to find Ezekiel and get him to agree to an interview.

What at first looked like a bundle of rags set in the middle of a rocky, arid plain, slowly raised an arm up toward the sky. It was a shaky movement, exhausted, as though the movement caused it great pain. Surrounding the bundle was a scattering of what looked to be clay pots, each of which was lidded with a wooden stopper, and in the air was a foul scent.

"Ezekiel?"

A low rasp came from the pile of rags. "Codrin Bălan. I have been waiting for you."

Unable to think of anything else to do, ey sat down next to the bundle of rags. Hidden within it may have been a face, but ey wasn't sure. "Waiting for me?"

"Yes. A voice from within spoke to me and I knew it to be that of the Lord, and I fell down upon my face, and it entered into me and set me back on my feet, and held out a scroll. He said to me, "Mortal, eat what is offered you. Eat this scroll." So I opened my mouth, and He gave me this scroll to eat, as he said to me, "Mortal, feed your stomach and fill your belly with this scroll that I give to you." And I ate it, and it tasted as sweet as honey to me.""

A long pause followed, during which Codrin did not speak, but silently wished for the scent of honey, rather than the scent of something burning.

"And so I knew that you were to come and to take my story."

Ey nodded. "I've come to interview you, yes. A few members of the Ode clade suggested that I seek you out."

A dry rattle sounded from within the dusty rags, and it took em a moment to understand that this was laughter. "Yes. Yes, of course they did. Speak, Codrin Bălan. Ask me your questions."

"I have a few. Some about the launch, and some about Secession."

"Ask me first about Launch."

"Did you leave a fork behind on the L_5 System?"

"No," he said. A finger rose tiredly from the upraised hand. "The word of the Lord came to me: O mortal, turn your face towards man's iniquity in the heavens and prophesy to them and say: O cruel men of machinations, you have broken your treaties with the earth which God has set before you, and though it be the doing of the many who are one, leave now the world of your birth that it be washed clean of your sin. You may have hoped for life as gods of the false idols, but the heavens are no longer yours for such arrogance."

Codrin remembered the admonition to be kind and patient, to be careful, and so ey sat in silence, as seemed appropriate.

"Those who sought to build their temple continue here, yes, and continue there, but judgement will yet come to them. I have seen the fire encased in flame and the sun's eagerness to send us on our way, and that is my reason for leaving them behind, and I am to lay here for three hundred and ninety years, arm outstretched to the System, and live off the cakes of wheat, barley, beans, lentils, millet, and emmer, until perhaps we cross the threshold of the firmament.

"We diverge, Codrin Bălan. We of Castor and Pollux. The prophets diverge and so too the prophecy. How can two divergent prophecies be true? And yet they must, for the voice of the Lord has given us the scroll as sweet as honey, and our minds must be as one, though they be as split as the broken one."

When the speech appeared to have concluded, Codrin bowed eir head. "That answers many of my questions, Ezekiel. You speak of the many who are one. Do you mean the idea of clades?"

"Yes. Some are the many who are one. Jonah, who is many that are one. Michelle, who is few that are one."

Ey once more remained quiet, mind churning over what seemed to be the root of the Ode clade. Michelle? Breaking the treaties with the earth which God set before her? Michelle, who left the world of her birth? And who was this Jonah?

"There were eight of us," Ezekiel said, and something about its voice sounded clearer, more present than it had before. "A council set to guide but not govern. We were to be the interface between our world and the Earth. The three from the East, the prophet, the nameless one, the politician, the broken one and her friend."

Ezekiel must be the prophet, and surely Michelle was the broken one. Ey didn't know the rest of the references, so ey filed the information away until later to look up. Ey felt the need to be completely present for the prophet.

"Guide towards Secession?"

"Not at first. At first, we were to be one people in two forms: those who had life entire on the earth that God set before them, and those who lived beyond death. Those who lived on Earth saw the idolatry in the System and with the help of True Name and Jonah, built up a religion of separation, that we be two people in two forms."

"True Name?"

The prophet turned a weary head towards Codrin. There was definitely a face there, ey saw, though it was dirty and blended seamlessly into the tattered rags that surrounded it. "One piece of the broken one."

Ey closed eir eyes and rifled through the Ode that ey kept near to hand in an exocortex. There were two instances of the phrase; 'The only time I know my true name is when I dream', and 'To know one's true name is to know god'. Both of them made sense as a possibility, as the first was the first line of that stanza and would have been one of the earliest forks, but the second named god, which fit well with Ezekiel's role as prophet.

After a moment's thought, ey asked eir question, choosing eir words carefully. "The True Name who dreamed, or the True Name who knew god?"

Another raspy cackle came from the bundle of rags. "You need not mince your words with me, Codrin Bălan. I am the mystic, you are the poet. The Only Time I Know My True Name Is When I Dream, a broken vessel for a broken soul."

Ey smiled cautiously, feeling a heat in eir cheeks. "Is True Name on the launch?"

"Yes."

"Are they on the System as well?"

"Yes."

"Should I interview them for this?"

Ezekiel once more turned his gaze toward the sky, supposing that that is where the abandoned planet must lie. "No. The Lord has put cords upon you, so that you cannot turn from your path.

Your twin and your root shall seek her out, but you must seek out one borne of her, and you must seek out more of the eight who were to guide but not govern, and you must seek out Jonah, and you must see to your loved ones."

Codrin nodded, taking down the list of names—if names they were. *Ioan and Codrin#Castor would get to talk to True Name, apparently. I'll get one of her up-tree instances, more of the Council of Eight, and this Jonah. Loved ones...Dear, perhaps?*

"What should I ask them?"

"Ask them what you asked me. Each shall give you a different answer, and when they are brought together, you may see the past and write your poem, poet." His arm began to waver, and then dropped once more to his side. "I am tired, Codrin Bălan, and I must eat and drink."

Ey nodded and stood, folding eir notes and capping eir pen. *Much as Dear said,* ey thought. *Combine the sources for a more clear picture.* Ey said, "Thank you, Ezekiel. I hope that you enjoy your meal."

A final rattling laugh, and the arm fumbled to the side where a flat cake had been cooking atop a pile of what looked like smoldering dung. Once more, his voice lost the edge of prophecy and became more cogent. "It's vile stuff, but I'll try."

Yared Zerezghi—2124

Yared Zerezghi: I'm going to come clean right up front: I shouldn't be telling you this.

Jonas Prime: Okay hold up.

Jonas: Before you actually tell us, I want to know why.

The Only Time I Know My True Name Is When I Dream: As do I.

True Name: I am sure you have your reasons, but if you need us to talk you out of it, we can do that, too.

Yared: Uh. Well, I wasn't *specifically* told not to tell you, but I was left under the impression that I shouldn't be talking to you about this sort of stuff. Still, I've done my reading, and the line to the System is about as secure as it gets, and after all this time, I trust you well enough that you won't do anything crazy with the information, and that it'll probably help you in the end, as you work through all this sys-side.

Jonas: What, that you've been working with a government official who is making you steer the DDR towards considering secession?

Yared: ...

Yared: What the hell?

Yared: Yes, but how the hell did you know that?

True Name: Jonas has been waiting to drop that on you for some time now. He is currently laughing his ass off. You will have to forgive him.

True Name: I mean, I am also laughing my ass off.

Yared: I'm just more shocked than anything.

Jonas: I promise it's not out of cruelty, we just made a lucky guess, and I've been wanting it confirmed. Your tone at the start said it all.

Yared: I guess I'm relieved.

Yared: But also a little scared that everyone else has figured it out, too.

Jonas: I wouldn't count on it. Maybe some have, but few enough that they'll likely be laughed down as crackpot conspiracy theorists. Very few people pay as much attention to you as we do.

True Name: Thank you for confirming this with us, though. It will help us work together more consistently between sys- and phys-side.

Yared: That was my thought, as well.

Jonas: Was that all you were going to tell us?

Yared: Most of it. I was just going to ask your help for the next step, afterwards. I'm *definitely* not supposed to be doing that.

Jonas: Well, alright. How does this all work, anyway?

Yared: I meet up with my handler, of sorts, on a regular basis, and we talk through the current sentiments, and then someone on his team will slip me a note specifying how I should steer my next post.

Sometimes I'll write two or three posts on the subject, just so they can keep an eye on the response, then I'll get the next note.

Jonas: And this handler, are his initials YD?

Yared: Okay, now you hold up.

Yared: I *need* to know how you guys figured that one out.

Jonas: Politician, remember?

True Name: We noticed the contents of your posts starting to shift, then started considering possible sources that might be guiding you. That led us to council members, and from there, we were able to sift through who is on the council and come up with a short list of names. Yosef Demma just happened to be at the top.

Yared: You still have me worried that others have this all figured out. Jonas, convince me not to worry. You're the politician, I'm the scared DDR junkie trying not to get stoned to death. Or worse, have my DDR account suspended.

Jonas: Alright, I'll try. I promise, no stoning. The number one advantage that we have is an entire team of instances working with you and on essentially no other projects. That means we have the resources to send a few of them chasing after this hunch that someone was steering you, do some textual analysis, find the patterns, then do some digging into NEAC politics, looking for people with both the resources, the motive, and the personality to pull it off.

Jonas: Remember, most of this team were physside politicians, too, so we have that head-start. The worst you have to worry about is the WF or S-R Bloc doing the same with their own people after they find out. We haven't seen evidence of that yet.

Yared: Multiple phys-side politicians?

True Name: Multiple Jonases.

Yared: Oh! There are multiple forks working on this?

Jonas: Of course.

Jonas: That's what I mean when I said few people pay as much attention to you as we do.

Jonas: Does that soothe your fears?

Yared: I think so, yeah. Do you agree with Jonas on this, True Name?

True Name: Having spent a considerable time with him and some of his forks, I trust him on this, yes.

True Name: Now, can you tell us as much as you are comfortable about councilor Demma, your relationship with him, and what you suspect are his goals?

Yared: Well, we meet for coffee regularly, like I said, and usually drink it in his car while his driver takes us around town. He seems like a nice, older gentleman, and pretty trustworthy. I suspect that's a bad sign in a politician.

Jonas: No comment.

Yared: Well, either way, he's nice enough to me, and I guess that's probably how he got me working for him. I think his motives basically boil down to the fact that the System has diverged considerably from the culture of any of the political entities left phys-side, both by virtue of who winds up there, and the obvious reasons of not sharing any of our concerns around trade goods.

True Name: He is not wrong, but I do not think that is motive enough.

Yared: I don't either. I suspect that he's not keen on something about the System where it is, whether that's its location in the S-R Bloc or that it remains a multinational entity where uploads retain their citizenship back phys-side. Maybe he just wants to make it a separate nation in order to allow it to be a place to send refugees, asylum seekers, and so on. Or maybe he wants to restrict emigration.

True Name: Those are all good potential reasons, yes. Do you have any hints as to which may be the most likely?

Yared: Not particularly. He's mentioned them all in passing.

True Name: Alright. Keep us up to date, then.

Jonas: What was your most recent message from Demma and his people?

Yared: That's what I wanted to talk to you about, actually.

Jonas: The thing that you're not supposed to do. Right.

Yared: Right. The message was: "Gently broach the subject of secession. Keep it only to one sentence, and only as an offhand remark. Make it sound like it was sys-side's idea."

Jonas: Wow, that's not exactly subtle.

True Name: Seems like a shitty thing to do.

True Name: But that is coming from someone sys-side, so perhaps he sees it differently. My assessment is that he might not actually be wrong on this. If he pins it on us but does it gently enough, it can be seen as a situation where both parties are happy to agree on something. It will have to be done carefully, however. If it is suggested too strongly or too early, we risk the possibility of backlash for seeming too eager for secession, as though we are rebelling. If it is not suggested strongly enough, some might see it as secession being forced on us. Jonas? Thoughts?

Jonas: I think you're spot on for the DDR. Yared, has any mention of secession come up in the forums yet?

Yared: Only two or three times, but given that this topic is starting to be taken up on the governmental level, that amounts to almost none. That said, I'm seeing quite a few people taking to the launch idea, which they're now equating to something equivalent to secession—they're calling it separation from earth or resource independence, stuff like that—as well as more talk about international rights, given that sys-side individuals technically retain their citizenship, which makes the System something like international waters.

Jonas: Clever. That might be far enough to drop some very subtle hints. I'm not sure about the word 'secession' yet, given some of its past connotations. You've suggested that we have the nature of statehood, but you might try pushing harder on referring to us as a nation, a national entity, a nation-state, and so on. Maybe even use the word 'statehood' directly.

True Name: Do you have anything written yet?

Yared: Sure, one moment.

Yared: We continue to circle around this discussion of individual rights as though we are debating the individuality of those sys-side. It's important to understand, though, that this is a distraction from the actual point. Many have mentioned that those who have uploaded, whether or not they are individuals, are no longer analogous to humans (there's that speciation argument again!) and one wag even put it, "Who cares if they're individuals? They can't even vote!"

Yared: This is quite true, my dear wag. They can't vote. They have no say in our political affairs out here, just as we have no say in theirs. How could we? I mean, sure, I bet some of them read DDR posts and wonder *what the hell is going on out there?* But consider what their politics must look like to us. What would *we* vote on? Whether or not they must post signage that their sims allow non-euclidean space? Is it okay for you to try and impersonate someone when you can become like them to exacting detail (except for, surprise, their individual personality)?

Yared: I think we're still split pretty evenly on speciation. Even I am. One day, I'll think, "Sure, they may be fundamentally different from us, but they still *think* like us. They still reason like humans. Except for the biological differences, they still are." Other days, though, I'll wake up and think, "We have no common frame of reference with these people. They're just too different."

Yared: This actually came up in a few conversations with my friends sys-side. It sounds like they share some of that ambivalence toward speciation. They can't interface with phys-side as we can, and we can't interface with sys-side as they can, so how could they even be considered the same species as us? And yet here they are, taking place in a political debate as filigreed and baroque as any other, and doing so with the same rational minds that we have, even if only at one remove. "At this point," one of them said as we laughed over another fruitless debate. "I'm not even sure we should be discussing individual rights with governments that have no way of knowing how we work. We might as well just secede and end the discussion there."

Yared: But who knows if speciation will even wind up playing into it, in the end. I've noticed that, even though we remain split on the topic, tempers have cooled on both sides. I'm surprised—pleasantly so!—to see this agreement building even in Cairo; I know that many of my compatriots there bore apathy or even antipathy towards the System after previous dealings between NEAC and the S-R Bloc. We're no longer at each others throats about whether or not they're so fundamentally different from us that it requires some strange new way to think of them as individuals.

Yared: And honestly, that's my hope. I think that way whether or not they're humans, whether or not they have their own customs and social structure, whether or not they're even a separate country. Even those who are falling on the side of speciation are starting to refer to them in terms of individuals. "Them." "How many of them." "Who in there even thinks X?" All of these are ways that we refer to individuals, and, you who are still arguing this belabored point that they should have no choice on what is done with their personalities once their bodies are gone, you are now thinking of them as what they are: individuals.

Yared: That, my friends, feels like progress to me. We are starting to come to an understanding of what the System is, whether it's a home for the disaffected and dying, an international forum where individuals can truly live together, or a country in its own right, is home to thousands of individuals, each with their individual lives, individual reasons, individual feelings. They're people. The System is their home. We cannot take that from them without violating their individual rights.

Jonas: Well written as always, Yared.

True Name: Agreed. You have a way of agreeing with people just enough to make them feel like you might actually be on their side, and that perhaps they ought to work toward the same goal.

Yared: Thank you both. What do you think about the secession angle?

True Name: It is a little blunt. It feels forced, the way it is just stuck in there. Perhaps you might soften it from "We might as well just secede", to something more like "We would have better luck running our own government", something like that. I agree with Jonas that there is fear bound up in the word 'secede', and the phrase "better luck" implies a humorous remark.

Jonas: Yeah. You want us to be soft, kind, approachable, that sort of thing, especially if you're going to use your current tactic of "agree with them enough to get them to fight for you". We want to seem like good people who deserve our individual rights, that to not grant them would be, at best, a real shame, and at worst, an affront to their own ideas of freedom.

True Name: This is especially true, given that very few phys-side are acting as our voices. They are arguing on second- and third-hand accounts, such as your own. To them, uploads are this mysterious entity that they might struggle to actually comprehend. You will have to, perhaps ironically, humanize us for them. We have to seem like we can still joke around, still hurt, and still feel the full range of human emotion.

Jonas: You've seen True Name and I joking around, after all.

Yared: Yeah. So what do you think about: "At this point," one of them said as we laughed over another fruitless debate, "I'm not even sure we should be discussing individual rights with governments that have no way of knowing how we work. We'd have better luck running our own government. We can herd our cats, they can herd theirs."

True Name: I like that. I am enough like a cat to be difficult to herd.

Jonas: Confirmed. Getting her to do anything she doesn't want to do is fucking impossible.

True Name: I prefer to think of myself as 'staunchly independent', thank you very much.

Yared: Haha

Yared: Actually, how about I include some banter into the post?

Yared: "At this point," one of them said, as we laughed over another fruitless debate. "I'm not even sure we should be discussing individual rights with governments that have no way of knowing how we work. We'd have better luck running our own government."

Yared: To which the other replied, "We can herd our cats, they can herd theirs," thus spawning a good five minutes of cat-herding jokes, wherein we unilaterally decided that cats were, to put it politely, staunchly independent. I think that applies to them as much as it does to us.

Jonas: I like it! It'll need a bit of cleaning up to make it flow a little better in context, but I trust that that's something you can do on your own.

Yared: Of course.

True Name: I am sorry to make such a cat out of you in this situation, Yared. You are being herded by two different camps, us and your councilor friend. Our goals align for now, for which I am grateful, but I understand that having both parties tell you not to tell the other about them is uncomfortable.

True Name: On that note, it is probably best not to tell Demma about this conversation.

Jonas: Seconded.

Yared: Thirded. I don't know that he'd have my head on a platter if he knew that this conversation had taken place, but I don't know that he wouldn't, either.

Jonas: We don't want that, we like you too much.

True Name: I was going to say that you are too useful to us, but I will grudgingly agree that we do rather like you.

Yared: I'm pleased to hear that!

Yared: I'll get this polished and posted. What's next on your side?

True Name: Jonas will likely be snooping around for news and schmoozing where appropriate. I will be focusing on how to present this in the most empathetic, understandable way possible to the Council and other interested parties. I need to sell it to the System.

Yared: Does that mean you're for secession, then?

Jonas: If the L_5 launch goes through, yes. If not, then it becomes more complicated, and we likely *would* have to move to international waters.

Codrin Bălan#Castor—2325

It was difficult for Codrin Bălan to reengage with the project at hand after what seemed to be an ever-mounting pile of oddities. It was not simply that ey had been finding piece after piece of new-to-em information about those that ey loved—though it was also that—nor was it that eir entire clade seemed to be entangled far deeper into something going further back than expected—though it was that as well—but that, by virtue of the twin launches and the L_5 System remaining back around Earth, ey was limited to reading much of this over plain text. Text that had flowed over sheets of paper in a comfortable font, bound itself up in books, and begged to be pored over, stood itself before em and said, "Read me, understand me." It all added one layer of remove that, despite eir attraction to the written word and fine paper and comfortable fonts and nice books, left em feeling caught up in some dreamlike state of almost-understanding.

As an example, there was this seemingly universal agreement among the Odists that no one of them should be the one to tell the entirety of the tale, and each for their own reasons. There seemed to be shame bound up in all of them, in some way, but beyond that, both instances of Dear had diverged to the point where the foxes were starting to come up with their own explanations for not providing that info to their respective Codrins Bălan.

Why was it, for instance, that Codrin#Pollux had decided to

251

simply interview Dear, where ey had not? And what was ey, Codrin#Castor, to do with the information that Dear had shared with eir cocladist? Hell, was cocladist even the right word, at this point? That seemed to imply a down-tree instance that one could still access.

I want to die, the fox had said. How had Codrin#Pollux even begun to deal with that bit of information? When ey read those words, in eir comfortable font on eir fine paper in eir nice books, ey had cried. Ey had cried much as it sounded like Codrin#Pollux had.

Ey had cried and closed the book and paced eir way out into the prairie outside the house, where ey had cried some more. Ey had not walked any new paths that day, simply walked to the outermost cairn that ey could find, sat down next to it, and watered the thirsty grass with a grief ey could not name.

And that ey could not name it only added to that unnerving sense of remove. It wasn't just sadness or grief. It wasn't the type of feeling that one might experience at the actual loss of a loved one. It wasn't the type of feeling that one experienced on learning that a loved one bore within its heart thoughts of suicide. Neither of those were true. Ey knew that, had ey been the one to conduct the interview, ey would have had much the same reaction as the other Codrin had (ey suspected, for all ey had was the transcript, incomplete as it was). But instead, ey had a cottony shield of time and distance that meant that ey could process it at eir own pace. Ey could go sit out in the prairie and cry and then come to an understanding of Dear's desire that ey couldn't have any hope of doing, were the fox sitting before em.

With this distance, both from the interview and from Dear itself, ey could remember its words: *"I just think we need death, or something like it, as part of the System. Death. Fear of death. Needs and reasons to survive in the face of an inevitable end. We need a way for an individual to end. We need a way to release those memories."* Ey could remember those words and understand the sudden too-full feeling of discomfort that had come with them. Immortality came with its own costs, and it was not simply that one might grow bored, but that one might go mad.

But ey hadn't interviewed Dear, had ey? Codrin#Pollux had. Codrin#Pollux had that trauma in a way that ey did not.

And Ioan! The wondrous hints that eir down-tree fork had been receiving! That their dream worlds worked in far subtler ways than imagined. That May Then My Name had told em, "I am worried that you will be unhappy with me."

So much bound up in that statement. By virtue of having lived with Dear and its partner for more than two decades, by having fallen into a steadily less-eccentric orbit around the fox, accepted mounting feelings of love, and having found emself in a relationship with an Odist, ey could read perhaps more clearly than Ioan the signs that ey was well on the path to doing the same. The Odists loved hard and they loved deep and they loved fast, and it was hard not to become intoxicated beneath all that love. *She seems to have wormed her way into my life and made herself comfortable, all while making it feel like it was my idea,* Ioan had written in a clade-eyes-only message. *She says that it's her role to feel, though, and I believe her in this.*

Ah, but Ioan, it is much more complex than that. With an Odist, it is always much more complex.

And that, of course, was not even the main implication of the message. "I am worried that you will be unhappy", even without the "with me" at the end suggested more of that guilt, shame, or distaste for the past that ey had picked up from Dear. From *both* Dears.

Eir Dear: *I am...ashamed. Many of the first lines...well, no. I will not elaborate now.*

The Dear on Pollux: *You could interview any one of us about the entirety of our story, even me, and we would tell you, but we would also resent you for that.*

Eir Dear had said, *"You will doubtless tease it out of me, bit by bit, you tenacious fuck."* But given what both May Then My Name and Dear#Pollux had said, ey no longer wished to try.

And so here ey was, sitting in a dark field, looking up at the stars. Very dark. Well and truly dark, beyond almost anything Ioan had experienced phys-side, or even after uploading. There was a purity to that blackness, just as there was a purity to the red-filtered flashlight that Tycho Brahe (not his real name, but he had requested the pseudonym) used to guide them both to the top of a—yes, pure—grassy hill.

"I come out here on nights when I am depressed," the old astronomer had grumbled. "And that has been most nights, of late."

"It's a beautiful place."

"Isn't it? It reminds me of a trip to the west coast that I took long, long before I uploaded. This grassy hill in the middle of a wide ring of firs. You can't see it, but the grass is not actually grass, but a sort of moss. When it's freshly dried out after a rain, it's delightfully soft, isn't it?"

Codrin nodded, then, realizing that ey could barely see Brahe next to em, murmured, "Almost cushy."

They sat on that hill in silence, leaning back on their hands and watching the stars overhead.

It had taken a few moments for Ioan to get eir bearings when they had first started watching. The stars overhead were stationary, but in a way that ey was not used to. There was the barest hint at a bare hint of movement, a dream of parallax, and the constellations didn't feel right. One star, brighter than the rest, was visible low over the horizon. There was no moon. It was quite unnerving in some indescribable way.

"What is this?"

"It is a view from outside the LV."

Ioan frowned up at the sky. "I didn't think that pictures could make it into the System. Systems."

Brahe sighed quietly. "They can't. This is just a projection. A description based on what I know the stars to look like combined with information based on where they are relative to the fisheye lens on the side of the Dreamer Module."

"And so you project that combination into a sim?"

"Yes. It's here for anyone to see, but I have been too tired to tell many people." A long pause, and then, "Yes, too tired."

There was a quiet lie in that admission, but Codrin let it slip by. "Can you tell me some more about what I'm seeing?"

"Of course, Mx. Bălan," Brahe said, audibly brightening.

He pointed first to the brightest star, low on the horizon. "There, see? That is the sun. The launch arms let us go at such a point that we are traveling along the ecliptic in order to use some of the existing orbital velocity we were already on. We have a disadvantage from Pollux, as we were released counter to that orbit."

He pointed at another star, one that almost seemed to be creeping slowly across the field of view, the source of that parallax sliding. "That is Jupiter, there. You can see it moving only by virtue of the fact that we used it as a slingshot several days into the journey. We are millions of kilometers away from it by now, but it's still one of the things that we are closest to. That's how you know that we're on Castor. Pollux will be using Saturn as a slingshot planet, a fortuitous trade-off given the orbital advantage I mentioned. There was a touch of maneuvering after launch to get the trajectories to work out."

He pointed over to the fir trees opposite where the star that was the sun shone. "Beyond those trees—really, the reason that they exist—is the solar sail, which blocks the lens. It was only recently deployed, you know. We could have deployed it on our way to Jupiter, but, as you know, we have all the time in the world, and there was no sense in risking it during the gravity assist."

He pointed at something else, and it took Codrin a moment to discern in the dark that he was pointing at himself. "And here I am, some nobody, some shithead who loved everything about this idea, but who can only view it in a very approximate way, like this."

"You don't seem particularly happy about your situation."

Brahe's laugh was bitter. "Of course I'm not happy. I mean...I *am* happy, but that happiness is tempered by the whims of reality more than I had expected."

"What would your dream experience be?" Codrin asked, enjoying a secret smile at the phrase couched within the ultimate dream experience that was the System.

"To see it all," he said, and ey noticed that the bitter edge was slowly leaving his voice. "I have all the perisystem processing that I can ask for to give me a simulacrum like this. You must know that this naked-eye astronomy is all but useless in the grand scheme of things, other than to give us a sense of where we came from and where we might be going in a way that allows us to tell ourselves a coherent story. The rest of astronomy is all math."

"I suppose that's why this place feels so much more romantic to me," Codrin mused. "I'm a storyteller, not an astronomer. Still, I imagine that that need for stories runs deep, and I can see the allure to possibly being able to actually look out a window at stars whizzing by."

"Yes." Brahe sighed, then lay down on his back, with his arms crossed behind his head. "Yes, to see it all."

There were a few minutes of silence as astronomer and historian looked out into the night sky, there in the simulated pacific northwest, there on the simulated moss surrounded by the simulated trees while simulated stars shone still above them.

They don't twinkle, Codrin thought to emself. *That's what it is. They don't twinkle, and the last time I saw them was from Earth, and all those who uploaded and made sims with star-filled nights, never left that aspect out.*

Ey mentioned this to Brahe, who laughed good-naturedly. "Of course. You're right. If they twinkled, it might feel more natural, but there is no reason for it, here. This place is a dream. My dream. The stars are there, and they don't twinkle."

"You said this view is constructed with data from the Dreamer Module," Codrin said, gently directing the conversation to topics that might please the astronomer more.

"Yeah. The module is mostly a big disk on the ass-end of each of the LVs. Most of that is various instruments that feed data to me and other astronomers here, as well as back to the core System and scientists on Earth. This particular lens is on a long strut that points out from that disk in such a way as to let as little of the solar sail obstruct its views as possible. There are other telescopes with much narrower fields of view in there. It can introduce a bit of vertigo, but would you like to see?"

"Sure."

"Alright, close your eyes."

Ey did so, and when Brahe instructed em to open them again, the sudden change in the sky was, indeed, a little dizzy-making. The entire field of stars had changed, and where there had been warped but familiar constellations, there was now a deeper blackness, brighter stars, and far more of them. Far, far more. "What is this?"

"A different view. A more powerful telescope looking at a patch of sky that we've never had a chance to see from this angle. One compounded from hours of exposure. I have no idea how exact it is, though, as it's all interpreted through the perisystem infrastructure, but it's still doing a slow sweep of the sky at a high enough magnification that the star field is completely different from what we're used to."

"I wouldn't have thought that that would've had such an impact on me," ey murmured. "I felt like I was falling for a moment."

Brahe sighed. "I did, too, the first time, and even now I'm not sure why. I think it's the mix of contexts. Here we are, looking out to space from the westernmost edge of the Western Fed, and yet all of the stars are different. They progress in such strange ways as the telescope searches on its automatic pattern."

"It's uncanny."

"A good word, yeah. It's like looking out on an alien sky, but even that misses the strangeness of so many stars. An alien sky, but as seen from the context of Earth. Firs, moss, a light breeze, dampness soaking into your trousers, and an alien sky. Did you have the chance to visit the L$_5$ station before you uploaded?"

"Goodness, no." Ey laughed. "We were too poor for that."

Brahe laughed along with em. "As was I. I do wonder, though, if I would have felt the same way I do now if I'd just had the chance to see the stars in such a new context before doing so here."

Codrin nodded, and a few more minutes of silence enveloped them as they took in that alien sky.

"You asked about the Dreamer Module, though." Brahe's voice had regained some of its strength. "And you're the one who works with stories. I'm sure you had your own questions, but there's a story there, that you might find interesting."

"Of course. I'd love to hear."

"I worked with a team of scientists, a few of whom were station-side and the rest of whom were planet-side. All lovely folks, of course. They tried to come up with some pithy acronym for the module, but some bit of news called them 'hopeless dreamers', and the name stuck from there.

"We basically nailed down the instrumentation that would go into the module, then built up its structure from there. Only some of it is telescopes, you understand. There are also various packages for measuring the cosmic microwave background radiation, ones for measuring ambient temperature variations, all the normal stuff. There's also a secondary generator in there, I suppose to ensure that neither the module nor the station impact each other.

"Anyhow, that's not the story part. The story part is that we got halfway done with the planning of the module and were just starting to spin up all the work to build the components, and we suddenly ran into a bunch of pushback. A lot of it was the usual grumbling about costs, even though most of it was to be manufactured at the station. Some of it was tied in with the voices that wanted to keep the launch from happening in the first place. If ever there was such a thing as an anti-dreamer, it was them. They felt that to make a dream a reality was somehow wrong. I never understood their arguments.

"The last bit of friction, and the most interesting bit, I suppose, came from sys-side. Their arguments were plainly insincere, though I never could figure out their true concerns. They said that the added complexity to the LVs put the integrity of the Systems within at risk beyond some imagined tolerance. It didn't bear up to even the slightest scrutiny, but they seemed to have loud voices."

Codrin frowned. "Most everyone I talked to was as ambivalent about the launch as they were about most phys-side projects, though I fully acknowledge that we run in different circles. There was an initial flush of excitement as it was announced, and most everyone I've talked to here said they'd made up their minds to go along on the launches even then, two decades back. It calmed down after as many forgot, but then ramped up before launch."

"Yeah, I felt much of the same in my circle, though you must understand that we were working on the launches for all of those two decades, so our excitement was bound to how well the project was going. We were spending so much time talking with phys-side, hearing all their gossip about the sentiment out there, and both sides were surprised when we started to have serious conversations about the sentiment sys-side when those arguments started to get louder.

"At first, it was just the occasional opinion column in the feeds, but the actual news started to pick up on it soon after, and then there were a few debates. I don't think it ever got to the point where the module was at risk, but people are still talking about whether it was a good idea, I hear."

"And you said you don't know what their real arguments are?"

"Correct."

"What about who was having those arguments?"

"That's the thing, there were relatively few voices from those who had uploaded recently. Most of those who started the arguments were from the first few decades of the System's creation. I suspect that at least part of their concern is that they still feel somewhat upset at having to pay to join, some of them dearly so, but even that doesn't feel like the whole reason. It was just all these super old uploads, both individuals and clades, who seemed less than thrilled at the prospect. Founder types, you understand."

Eir frown grew. "Do you remember any names?"

"The Jonas clade was pretty vocally against it. I think they even had compunctions about the launch, for that matter. There were some of the Odists, though I never took much interest in who. Their names are always so impenetrable. Let's see...there was Àsgeir Hrafnson, who has always seemed like he's against everything. Such a sour man..."

Brahe continued to list off a few names, and Codrin continued to nod dutifully, but eir mind was elsewhere. The Odists' opinion on the launch seemed to range from, at best, utterly ecstatic, as Dear's had been, to, at worst, simply uninterested, to go by what Dear and May Then My Name had said.

Was this another lie from Dear, or had the fox simply not gone looking for names in the debate?

"Obviously, the launch went forward anyway, and both LVs contain Dreamer Modules, so they weren't successful," the astronomer was saying. "They didn't seem interested in paring down the scope to the modules, nor even adding any risk mitigation factors beyond the extra RTG and a set of explosive bolts that could jettison the module if necessary. I think that's what made me the most suspicious of their initial arguments. If there was risk, why not try to mitigate it further?"

"I'm not sure," Codrin said, mouth dry. "Perhaps it was more of an image thing? As in, adding the module might damage how others viewed the launch."

"Perhaps." Ey heard Brahe shrug against the moss-grass before he continued. "Anyway, that's the story. I don't know if it'll be of any use to you in your project."

"It might. It already answered most of my other questions, too. The last one I have is that you invested entirely in the LVs. Why?"

The astronomer was silent for a long time. "As upset as I get that I'm not actually able to see all the stars, even I am not immune to the romance of the idea. Imagine sitting at home, knowing that you could have flung yourself off into space, out among the dangers and excitement, and choosing instead that boring safety? The only benefit would be the combined knowledge of Castor and Pollux arriving at the station at the same time we'll get it on either one of our LVs, but, well."

Brahe gestured up to the shifting night sky, leaving his words at that.

Eventually, even Codrin lay back in the grass. Lay there with Tycho Brahe in all his sadness and happiness and wisdom and romanticism. Lay there and looked up at the stars ey knew not for how long.

Douglas Hadje—2325

May Then My Name Die With Me: I am surprised to see you online, Douglas!

Douglas Hadje: Remember how I said my workload as launch director would be starting to decrease after launch?

Douglas: Well, now I'm only working a few days at a time, and most of that is writing up documentation and collating reports for the launch commission. Soon, even that will disappear, and I suspect I'll be out of a job unless I decide to take on another position.

May Then My Name: Do you think that you will?

Douglas: I don't know. Maybe? Probably. Once I'm out of a job, my reason to be here is kind of gone, and I imagine whatever goodwill I've built up will start to run out and they won't let me stay on the station. It's mostly self-sufficient, but resources are limited and I'm sure there's someone who would like to take my spot.

Ioan Bălan: And you mentioned not wanting to go back planet-side.

Douglas: God no, not if I can help it.

May Then My Name: Either way, I am happy to see you about. Did you have any particular topics you wanted to discuss today? If not, I am sure that Ioan has some.

Douglas: Nothing in particular. I've got a few minor questions outstanding, I think, but I'm starting to get the sense that you'll only answer those when you're ready.

May Then My Name: That is a very good sense that you have.

Ioan: May's obstinate, ignore her.

Ioan: She also kicks pretty hard, but then, I deserved that.

May Then My Name: You did.

Ioan: Alright, well, the topic I was thinking of asking you about is that of the political side of the launch. One of the instances on one of the launches conducted an interview that suggested that there was actually quite a lot of political machinations behind the scenes.

Douglas: Oh! Yes! I'm surprised you didn't get much news of that in there.

May Then My Name: I am sure that we could look it up, but you are in a unique position to tell us more directly, and after it has been all mixed around in your head.

Douglas: True. Well, where do you want to start?

Ioan: How about you start most recently, actually, and then work your way backwards.

Douglas: Alright.

Douglas: There was one last spate of protesting right before the launch. I saw some of the videos from planet-side, and a lot of it was just talking-heads discussing the fact that some had tried to shut down portions of the net, and even tried to take down one of the Ansible stations. Most of it was the same stuff we saw during the planning phase. I guess it kind of broke down into three complaints:

Douglas: 1. Expenses—this one was diminished toward the end, as there's not really a whole lot of expense required in popping some explosive bolts to set the launches flying, and all the material used out here was from scavenged Trojan asteroids. The protests that we saw around this were mostly griping about how much had already been spent. "Think of how much could have gone to deacidifying projects, etc etc"

Douglas: 2. Brain/workforce drain—This is a perennial topic with the System. All those smart minds out there focusing on pie-in-the-sky dreams instead of 'real problems' back there on Earth. What they imagine someone with a masters in spaceflight or astronomy or whatever can do back on Earth to better an overheated dustball is beyond me.

Douglas: 3. Earth vs space sentiments—This one is probably the most common, and also the hardest to explain. Even I don't totally understand it. I think I mentioned before that, the harder things get, the less time and energy you have to focus on those pie-in-the-sky ideas. You're too busy scraping by or focus on growing soybeans or trying not to burn up or whatever, you don't have much time to do anything but dream about space and watch movies in your hour before bed or however your day looks.

Douglas: You have to remember that my opinion of the place is colored by the fact that I lived where I did with the family that I did while the city was in a state of decline, so.

Douglas: Anyway, a lot of these people seemed to be just plain angry that there were people doing things that were not for helping improve the general condition of life. There's still six or seven billion people down there, when you mesh birth rates with death and upload rates, and a good chunk of those people have no wish to upload, so they're stuck in a life that's uncomfortable enough to make them angry at those who have what feels like (and might as well be) unlimited potential, as they imagine the System to be.

Douglas: Does that make sense?

Ioan: I think so. You've got people who are unhappy, and part of that unhappiness is the fact that others are happy.

Douglas: More than that. They're unhappy, and part of that is that those others are not helping to make life better for them. It's usually not even making life better for humanity, but for them specifically, for the world as they specifically view it.

Ioan: Was there any sentiment that they were being abandoned by those who left on the launches?

Douglas: Yes and no. You have to understand that most people still struggle to think of the uploads as human. Thus calling them 'uploads', even, rather than 'uploaded personalities' or whatever. It's not just shorthand, it's a way of separating them into some other idea. They aren't people, anymore, they're programs, in their minds.

May Then My Name: There has always been this argument of speciation, and the instinct to make us the other continues apace, I see.

Douglas: I'll take your word for it. It's difficult to persuade the average person that those in the System are still human, or if not human, then at least still people. They're not the types to listen to all the arguments for why we know that you're still you after you upload. They duck-type you into being programs.

May Then My Name: 'Duck-type'?

Ioan: Looks like a duck, quacks like a duck, must be a duck.

Douglas: Is that what it means? It's just come to mean a false-equivalency of any kind. Few enough ducks, anymore.

Ioan: I only learned it from an assignment talking with some perisystem specialists.

Douglas: I guess it doesn't surprise me that you have those inside as well as outside. Sometimes, I get these little jolts about how little I actually know about the System, compared to how much I know about the launch.

May Then My Name: It does not help that many of us—not just me—are obtuse on purpose.

Douglas: You said there was some grumbling sys-side, as well, right?

Ioan: Yes, though I don't totally understand it. Some of it sounds like that like, "Why bother? We've got a good life here, and there's no reason to be putting that in any kind of danger just to throw copies of us out at the stars." The bits that I mentioned earlier, however, have more to do with the Dreamer Modules than the launch itself, though.

Douglas: Oh? There was a little bit of chatter about those here, but I didn't pay a whole lot of attention to it.

Ioan: That's okay. I'll dig, myself.

May Then My Name: We were working backwards from present. Was there much in the way of disruptions in the middle of the launch construction process?

Douglas: Not as much, no. There was a lull in overall protests. A lot of the grumbling about the Dreamer Module came during this time. There were one or two other sabotage attempts. Do you want to hear about those?

May Then My Name: We will, yes, but there is time. For now, we are curious about the macro-scale political landscape before, during, and after launch.

Douglas: Alright. That'll give me some time to remember more about what happened with them.

Douglas: Large scale, hmm.

Douglas: Well, most of the government side goes way over my head. In the WF, there was always a bit of waffling, even on the majority coalition side, but whenever sentiment in a member party of the majority drifted away from the launch, they never seemed to last all that long in power.

Douglas: I talked about protests and sentiments before, but for the most part, folks were either on board, didn't care, or didn't know about the launch. It was just another satellite in their eyes, or some deep space probe.

Douglas: Early on was when it was talked about most. There wasn't a whole lot of questions asked about whether or not the launch would happen, weirdly. I remember it just kind of popping up in the news as a foregone conclusion. "The launch was happening, how's everyone feeling about that?"

Douglas: I think some were pretty unhappy with that, at first. Like, where did this decision even come from? Obviously, the System is its own authority and can do whatever it wants, but someone has to manage the phys-side work, so who, phys-side, actually had those conversations? There were a few gestures at investigation, but they fizzled out. Mostly, people were just confused. Some people get upset when they're confused, but for the rest, it just left them shaking their heads. It was the politicians who were dealing with it after that initial shock.

Douglas: Building the launches wasn't too expensive, honestly, because almost all of that was done in an automated fashion here on the station. That said, retrofitting the station for the launch struts, building the launch arms, expanding the production sector...all that took time, energy, and money. I'm surprised it went as smoothly as it did, despite all the grumbling.

Ioan: So it just popped up on the scene, then interest waned, then ramped up before the launch, then dropped? Like an 'M' shape?

Douglas: I suppose so, yeah. After the launch happened, there was nothing that could be done, so everyone lost interest or lost steam in their protests.

May Then My Name: We had a conversation a while back about our own point of no return. It was actually a year and change before the launch itself.

By then, individuals were already transferring, and even if something went wrong, the cheapest solution would have been to launch anyway, and just take the hit on final velocity.

Ioan: Really?

Ioan: It makes sense, I suppose. What would you have done? Un-built the struts/arms and LVs?

Douglas: Basically. That would require dealing with yet more conservation-of-momentum issues, which would've required more money to build *that* infrastructure, etc etc.

Douglas: None of which really seemed to matter to the protestors.

May Then My Name: You said that parties whose sentiments veered away from supporting the launch often wound up leaving the leading coalition. What was the general sentiment of the leading coalition in the WF? Elsewhere on Earth?

Douglas: Oh, good question. I guess most of them wound up being the types that pushed for higher taxes while playing to humanity. They're all named something different, I guess. It was the liberal democrats for most of the time in the WF. The demsocs felt that the money that was going to the launch was better served on Earth. The libertarians were here and there on the issue. Sometimes they felt like it would be a net win for humanity, sometimes they felt like the burden of the launch was too much. The conservatives spent most of the last twenty years as the shadow government. Their arguments were mostly what I said before. It was money that was going to a thing that wasn't them or their financial interests.

May Then My Name: The way you talk, I assume that you are a liberal democrat?

Douglas: We don't get a vote up here.

Douglas: I'm with whatever party allows the System to continue and helped the launch move forward.

May Then My Name: A single issue voter, then?

Douglas: I guess so!

Ioan: Well, we appreciate that, given where we live.

Douglas: Haha, well, good.

Douglas: Any other questions? I don't have any in particular, and would like to go grab dinner.

Ioan: Not from me.

May Then My Name: When will you be uploading, Douglas?

Douglas: I don't know. Some day, I promise.

May Then My Name: When you do, I hope that you will tell us, so that we can meet you face to face.

Douglas: Of course! After all this time, I'd be disappointed if we didn't.

May Then My Name: We will have many stories to tell you.

Douglas: I look forward to them all. Goodnight, you two.

Douglas: Or morning.

Ioan: Afternoon, actually. Enjoy your dinner!

True Name—2124

It was Jonas's time to pick the location for their meeting, but as he had scheduled it for a few hours from the time of the message, The Only Time I Know My True Name Is When I Dream decided to spend a bit of time exploring fanciful cocktails at the Kowloon Walled City/central corridor mega mall/parking lot rooftop bar.

Her first drink was a total wash. Someone had decided to explore the utility of sulfurous odors in drinks by combining the smoke of a newly lit match, a slice of preserved egg, and some smokey mezcal, sweetened by a few squirts of over-ripe apricot puree.

There was, True Name discovered, essentially no place for sulfur in a cocktail. It was a drink that was *almost* good, so long as one didn't breathe in the scent. The first heady whiff that she got had burnt her nostrils and she only managed a few sips after that.

Her next drink was some bracingly strong lime-and-bitters-and-liquor deal with a float of foam made of egg whites and pork fat. There was a dusting of star anise and cinnamon on top. Her final assessment: pleasantly disgusting. The lime, egg whites, and spices all worked quite well together, she imagined, but the added porky fat clashed with it in such a savory way that she suspected it would've gone better with some brown spirit.

Still, she drank it all.

Her final drink was a weak, British style ale that, she was informed, used a mixture of herbs rather than hops as the bittering agent. Spruce and henbane, the first of which left her with an almost-unpleasant subdermal itching and the latter of which left her vision tinted red and her intoxication higher than it might have been otherwise.

Terrible. Delightful

She let that intoxication linger as she prowled through one of the mall sections of the solid block of building. She paced along balconies, fingering wilting leaves of variegated plants, scratching a claw through the grime of countless hands accumulated on faux-wood banisters. She peered through grates at shelves still speckled with abandoned gadgets and folded jeans. She sat in the food court, still smelling of rancid grease and sanitizer. She breathed in the stale, over-conditioned air, and wondered for the thousandth time just who had thought to create such a sim, and what sort of twisted nostalgia had led them to do so.

It was as she stood in front of a quiescent fountain that it occurred to her that this place—the mall, the dingy city, the parking structure and its shoddily crafted drinks—was all a monument to the imperfections of mankind's countless attempts to provide for itself in so many imperfect ways.

They were here. They were immortal. They *could* build perfection. They could live their lives in eternal bliss, and yet they still got their kicks out of the temporary and the imperfect. They were, despite the arguments, still human in so many delightfully crazed ways. The cracks still shone through, even when presented with the opportunity of perfection. They were the futurological congress of yore, where even the idea of queuing had been romanticized and pushed into the realm of the transgressive. Even these poor fools who had the limitless expanses of the mind before them knew that, in some ways, it was their origins that made them complete.

And it *was* intoxicating.

It was intoxicating in such a way as to leave the skunk feeling somehow more complete than she had expected. There was no speciation. She was complete in all her humanity, as were all who uploaded. By her very imperfections, she was complete.

What, then was the difference?

She picked at a coin that had cemented itself to the rim of the fountain in a layer of slimy algae, winced at the unpleasant sensation, and then flicked it into the murky-green water that still stained the basin of the fountain.

There was a part of her mind that was tempted to consider those who lived sys-side as some how more perfect beings than those who remained phys-side. But no, that wasn't quite correct. They were different, yes, but they weren't some greater form of perfection—or perhaps not entirely.

Were there perhaps some core difference in ideals? Obviously, given the cost of uploading, there was a natural barrier, but even among the upper-middle and higher classes, there were some who simply chose not to upload. What was the difference? Was it aspirational? Were those who uploaded on some different wavelength from those who stayed behind? There were certainly many who found the whole process abhorrent on a physical level, yes. Of those who found it distasteful on intellectual, emotional, and spiritual levels, what did the prospect of continuing to live phys-side provide that living sys-side did not?

She couldn't decide, but there was the logical fallout of that situation, that the two should be treated on a fundamentally different level, when it came to politics.

There was a slight twinge of a sensory alarm, and she knew that it was time for the meeting with Jonas.

He had chosen a war-gaming room for the meeting. There in the middle of the room was a backlit map of Earth at least five meters long, and scattered across its surface were dozens of chess pieces—knights, pawns, queens—which had been pushed this way and that by long sticks that still rested along the edges of the table.

A smile quirked at the corner of her mouth. *How very like him.*

Jonas was sitting at the other end of the table, eating small hors d'oeuvres from a paper plate. Cocktail weenies spiked with toothpicks and finger sandwiches.

As soon as he noticed True Name standing at the edge of the light that lit the table, he grinned and gestured with his plate toward the hot-and-cold buffet lining one of the walls.

Oh well, why not, she thought, willing away the drunkenness and instead loading up a plate with bruschetta and pita crisps with hummus.

"You're looking well today," Jonas said, once he had finished his mouthful. "Have an exciting jaunt?"

She laughed. "Why? Were you watching me?"

He shrugged.

"Well, it was exciting as could be expected. I got a lot of thinking done. A lot of planning. Which one of you are you, by the way?"

"Jonas Prime, today."

True Name nodded a greeting and focused on her hummus for a few minutes.

Once it was clear that she had reached a pause, Jonas spoke up. "Tell me about your thoughts and plans. I'm curious what it is that required alcohol to understand."

"I was thinking about the difference in politics phys-side and sys-side."

He sat up straighter, nodding for her to continue.

"I think that it is a matter of aspirations. We who have up-loaded have different goals in life than those who remain behind. Perhaps it is worth approaching them in different ways."

"That's true." He looked thoughtful. "We've already been doing that, to an extent."

"Yes, but out of instinct. Perhaps it is time to do so intentionally. If the goal of politics is to steer groups of individuals, then perhaps it is time to figure out the different ways in which to steer them. The motivations of those on the System are highly independent, surrounding whatever brings them the most freedom to accomplish what it is that they want. Them in particular, rather than large groups, though smaller groups may have goals that are aligned as well."

Jonas frowned down to his remaining weenies, then set the plate aside. "And phys-side?"

"Larger groups. They may feel that they have individual goals, but, whether or not it is in the fore of their thoughts, they know that the best way to accomplish them is to band together with those who share similar enough goals."

"An astute observation."

True Name let the non-compliment slide over her, continuing. "If we are to steer the council, then we must approach it with an eye to the goals shared by dreamers, and if we are to steer affairs phys-side, then we must approach it with an eye toward something broader, offering sugar-coated compromises that feel like wins."

Jonas's frown deepened. "You're a bit further along in this than maybe I gave you credit for."

The skunk leaned forward, resting her chin on folded hands. She refused to rise to the bait offered, choosing instead a thoughtful expression. "Your forks. Do they work on a similar dialectic?"

He nodded.

"Then perhaps it would be smart for me to do similar. I do like your idea of continuing to be seen as a single individual to the council. I am not sure that I am willing to cycle through my forks for that, however, so perhaps I will continue to act as the point of contact that the other council members see, and simply consult with my forks via regular merging."

"It's not a bad idea, no, and with a small clade, some of whom already look like you, you can probably get away with it easily enough. I have to make sure only one of me is out and about where people might see me at a time." He grinned, adding with a wink, "At least, while working. Ar is out drinking."

The skunk laughed. "Of course. Hopefully he has better luck with drinks than I did."

There was a lull in the conversation as True Name crunched her way through the bruschetta on her plate.

After she finished, she spoke up again. "The only problem that I see is that I will need to save up reputation, and then hide the expenditures as best I can. Do you have experience on that?"

Jonas visibly brightened. "Oh! There's no need to do that. You can push some reputation into your name by having the members of your clade vote you up. Make something silly. Take up poetry. Release it out into the world whether it's good or not, then have your cocladists build it up higher."

"Cocladists, huh? Is that the term we are going with?"

He shrugged.

"Well, alright. I will put on some monologues I remember from phys-side."

"Alright. Let me know when you do, and I'll upvote them, too. It's not like there's no reason to, we talk often enough as council-members and the market doesn't care who upvotes."

True Name laughed. After a moment's concentration, two additional versions of her appeared behind her chair, waved to Jonas, and stepped out of the sim. "I had just enough for two, and I figure two ought to be enough for now."

"Do they have equally silly names?"

Once more, she resisted the urge to bridle at his comment. Instead she smiled sweetly. "Why Ask Questions, Here At The End Of All Things and Why Ask Questions When The Answers Will Not Help." After a pause, she added, "Why Ask Questions and Answers Will Not Help."

The man froze, the last of his cocktail sausages halfway between plate and mouth. That mouth now slowly formed into a devious grin. "You continue to surprise and amaze, my dear."

After they had both finished their plates of appetizers and

enjoyed a moment of silence, they each began pushing around a few chess pieces off the map.

"We have Yared in NEAC," True Name said, pushing a pawn over to Addis Ababa. "And you said you know some in the Western Fed, yes?"

Jonas nodded, pushing two queens, two pawns, and a bishop over the chessboard. The bishop in the British aisles: "A judge. He's easily bribed. We can't do it ourselves, of course, but we can find those who will. He'll be useful for influencing some legislation whenever cases regarding uploads come up."

One of the queens wound up in Germany, the other on the east coast of North America: "Two representatives. Both were good friends. Both too sly for their own good. I'm surprised they haven't gotten flushed out, yet, but we can keep using them until they do. I think they'll be useful in pushing for the legislation—both the core bill, and the launch amendment."

"How about the secession amendment?" True Name asked.

"Probably, assuming there is one."

"I think there will be."

Jonas gave her a strange look, but instead of replying, pushed one pawn to the toe of Italy's boot and the other to the northern end of the central corridor: "Two other friends. DDR junkies, mostly, but very loud ones. This one–" he said, tapping at the one on the central corridor. "–is reactionary and easy to influence, if you feed him the right information, and this one–" He tapped the one on Italy. "–is one of those calm-voice-of-reason types. He would be harder to influence, but it sounds like he's already mostly in agreement with our dear Yared."

True Name noticed the lack of names for each of the figures, but said nothing. *It is probably for the best. Leaves me some plausible deniability, and keeps me from interacting with his pawns.*

"Now, how about sys-side?"

Jonas shrugged. "The council, of course, plus the owners of some higher-profile sims, and a few perisystem architects."

"Alright. I suppose that on my end I don't have anyone other than the council," she lied. "And all of my various selves, of course."

"Right, you have Debarre in your pocket, and Zeke likes you plenty."

He kept throwing her all these little comments that seemed to tempt her to respond emotionally. Was he testing her? Was he watching to see just how much power he had over her?

Not the best tactic for someone who taught theatre to teenagers.

"I think we've got the council mostly locked down when it comes to the idea of independence," she said, setting down her stick.

"And your clade?"

"I have plans for them. Nothing that will get me in trouble with the council, I think."

"Will you tell me some of those plans?"

She smiled. "Why not? We are working together, after all. They can use our background in theatre to work the propaganda angle."

It was only a portion of the truth, but she also suspected that Jonas knew this. He accepted it easily enough.

"I'll send Ir to coordinate with you, so that we don't step on each other's toes. That's what he's been working on."

"Did you not say he looked nothing like you? You certainly have the face for a propagandist."

Jonas laughed. "He arguably looks better. Just different. On that note, will you have your, uh...human self do the propagandizing?"

She waved the question away. "I will work it out. For now, do you have any more news on Yared and his handler?"

"Not too much more. Demma has been heard to mention the System as a country, but so far hasn't mentioned the word secession. Yared's latest post is along similar lines as his last. Fluffy, if you'll forgive the metaphor. The little bit of us teasing each other went over well, and there were a few comments elsewhere on the 'net that others caught talking about the fact that at least the System still seemed to have fun in it."

"Any other comments about secession that you have seen?"

He shook his head. "Same little blips from some of the crazier people. More of them, perhaps, but it hasn't bubbled up too far. There's a bit more chatter about the legal status of the System independent of other nations, but the S-word hasn't come up yet. You heard any here sys-side?"

"Not except between us," she lied again.

Jonas needn't know all of her plans, nor that the propaganda work had already begun. Nor, for that matter, that she was still in contact with Dr. Carter Ramirez, phys-side, who still had reputation of her own, her own knight in the British Isles. After all, if he was going to continue to maintain some of his leverage of the situation, oughtn't she do the same?

"Alright, well." Jonas frisbeed his plate into a trash can by the buffet tables. "I guess we're in a holding pattern on that front until the news breaks elsewhere. Until then, keep kissing babies and shaking hands. Or shaking babies and kissing hands. Or whatever it is that not-a-politicians do."

Before she could respond, he winked to her and blipped out of existence, likely back to his home sim.

True Name remained a while in the sim, falling back into the habit of planning and rumination, memorizing the pieces and their locations that Jonas had pushed onto the board, and thinking about all of the lies she had told today.

Codrin Bălan#Pollux—2325

As happened about once every six weeks or so, that boundless energy within Dear became too much for the fox to control, and it would go tearing through the house, working on several projects, forking here to clean, there to make a mess, now to request affection and then to holler about how badly it wanted to be alone.

The first time that this happened, Codrin had been quite startled, opting to lock emself in the office that ey still kept out around the back of the house. One of the many instances of Dear quickly fell into a sulk, and sent em carefully spaced out sensorium messages to make sure that ey hadn't left.

Eventually, Dear's partner had knocked on the door to eir glass-walled office, and Codrin let them in, where they leaned back against the edge of eir desk.

"Do you know of any wild restaurants?" they had asked.

"Wild?"

"Yeah. You know, crazy experiences, or maybe they're really busy or raucous. Some sort of theme. Anything like that."

Codrin had searched through eir memory, then shrugged. "Does a back-alley food court work?"

They laughed. "How in the world do 'back-alley' and 'food court' work together?"

"I have no idea. You walk down this street, and there's just this awning sticking out over a narrow alley. Smells like hell, but when you get through it, there's this courtyard, and all of the walls are various stalls of different food. Most of it's dumplings and buns and stuff like that, but I found it because there's a place there that serves, of all things, really good tacos."

"Sounds about right. Come on."

They had walked back around the patio and into the main house and Dear's partner surveyed the scene of various foxes in various states of activity or various moods, then walked up to one scribbling on a notepad at its desk, grabbed a fistful of fur and loose skin at the nape of its neck in their hand, lifted the fox to its feet, and shook it gently. All of the forks that had been littering the house quit in an instant.

"Oh, is it dinner time?" It had looked bedraggled, limp, unsteady, and a glint of some intensity that Codrin had never seen before hid in its eyes.

"Yeah. Come on. Codrin knows a place."

There had never been a full explanation of what it was that happened, but as they dined on plates of dumplings, steamed buns, noodles, and tacos, the fox's hackles began to lay flat, and the erratic twitching of its tail slowed to a more familiar calm. It had spent most of the dinner peering around curiously and talking their ears off.

"Sometimes I overflow," is all the fox had said when pressed.

Even after nearly twenty years, though, Codrin had yet to gain the knack of telling the original instance of Dear when that many were running around, and so when the fox began to 'overflow' once more, ey sought out its partner in their own workshop and waited until they reached a stopping point before saying, "I think it's time for dinner."

As usual, they were able to hunt down the root instance and shake it back to reality. Whenever the fox was grabbed by the scruff, it went limp, and the shake was usually something of a rag doll affair. At first, Codrin had worried that its partner was hurting it, but as ey was welcomed into their relationship, ey learned that the fox counted it as a pleasure.

Today, they found themselves at what Dear promised them was a pitch-perfect simulacrum of a late 2000s diner. While ey could not speak to the accuracy, nor even the quality, something about the sheen of lingering sanitizer on the counters that left streaks, the smell of truly terrible coffee, and the sizzle of grease all added up to a cohesive whole.

Codrin ordered a large plate of fries, Dear a vanilla milkshake, and its partner a slice of pie. They shared all three, and Codrin learned the delight of dipping fries into milkshakes.

"*Thank you, my loves, as always,*" Dear said, once it calmed down. "*I am honestly surprised that it took this long after Launch for the mania to hit.*"

"Maybe you were less focused on one thing?" Codrin said around a mouthful of melting shake.

"*Perhaps. I do not have a single project to dump my attention into, so that singular energy does not build up in quite the same way.*"

"The news from Castor and Ioan isn't enough to keep you focused?"

"*Not particularly, no.*" It grinned and poked a fry at Codrin. "*You are the historian, my dear. That is your job, not mine.*"

Ey rolled eir eyes.

"*Still, I really must find one soon. I am aware that it is not pleasant for you two when this happens, but it is also unpleasant for me when I do not have direction.*"

Dear's partner shrugged. "We just need to get one of those loose clamps for holding bags shut or hair back in a bun so we can just put it on your scruff when you start getting out of hand."

"*Do you promise? I promise that I will do everything in my power to deserve it,*" it said, grinning wickedly.

"Dear, I swear to God."

"*If you threaten me with a good time, you will win precisely the prize that you deserve.*"

Codrin laughed. "You're right. We deserve peace and quiet, sometimes."

Ey received a fry to the face from the fox, which ey dunked into the shake. "What is this place, anyway?"

"It is the restaurant that–" It hesitated for a beat, during which the noise around them dimmed as a cone of silence fell. *"It is the restaurant at which the clade celebrated Secession Day."*

Codrin stifled a yawn from the ear-popping sensation that always came with the silence. "You weren't there?"

"I had not yet been forked, no, but Praiseworthy was there. I remember it through the words and sensorium of another."

"What was it like back then?" ey asked.

"Mx. Codrin Bălan, are you working?"

"Not particularly," ey said. "I really am just curious."

"Well, you will still need to be more specific. 'Back then' covers a large swath of time."

"How about a year to either side?" its partner suggested.

"That still encompasses a good amount of history. I will tell you some of them, but you will have to–"

"Find the rest on my own, yes."

The fox gave a hint of a bow. *"Thank you in indulging me in this, Codrin. I cannot be the one to share everything."*

"So what was it like before Secession Day?"

"I do not think that the hoi polloi thought about it all that much. They were concerned about the prospect of others deciding that they did not have rights, to be sure, but it was all very abstract. Even from the point of view of the Council, we could not quite understand what a lack of rights would look like.

"I think that is why secession seemed to come so naturally to us. It took far more effort for those phys-side to comprehend what secession would look like than it did for us. From our point of view, we were separate from the rest of the world, such as it was, in a way that already seemed to preclude citizenship to any other political entity."

"And you—Michelle, that is—were still on the council at that point?"

"That is a complicated question." It poked at the last bit of shake with its spoon. *"We shall say yes. Elements of the clade were*

still on the council at that point. This sim is where we celebrated Secession. One of the Odists, Debarre, Zeke, user11824, the Russians, Jonas–"

"Jonas?"

Dear tilted its head inquisitively.

"Ezekiel talked about a Jonah. Is that someone else?"

"Oh, yes. Same person. Jonah is a name that fits Ezekiel's current mode of thinking better, I suppose. We were all there, along with our phys-side accomplice in the campaign for secession and the L$_5$ launch, Yared.

"The mood was very celebratory. The council sat in that booth–" it said, nodding toward the corner booth. *"–and counted down with everyone. It was all very exciting. Everyone was giddy and laughing, and there were fireworks outside."*

"How crowded was it at that time? I imagine there were far fewer people in the System than there are now, if you had to pay to upload."

"Of course, yes. Still, there were a few common public sims that individuals and instances would frequent. This was one of them. There were a dozen or so others here in the diner along with the rest of the Odists, and several hundred along the street, either on it or in restaurants along it. All were cheering, as far as I could tell."

"I imagine there was some of that during Launch day, too," Dear's partner said. "Beyond our party, that is."

"Perhaps. I do hope so."

"So, after all of the celebrations died down, was there any real change?"

Dear shrugged. *"Some residual excitement, I suppose. There were some little things that lingered, however, and stuck around. Secession Day, of course, but that is also the date that we started using systime in earnest. The actual number chosen as year zero, day zero for systime is a bit more than a year before Secession, and was tied to the creation of the reputation market, such that there was always a time to which it could be synchronized. Before Secession, we still commonly used the calendar they were—and presumably still are—using phys-side, but after, almost everyone switched to using systime. It made logical sense,* yes, what with sims not being tied to any particular schedule bound by Earth's rotation or procession around the Sun, but also it felt like a sign that we were becoming our own nation, our own people."

The table grew quiet after this explanation, as the last bite of pie was eaten and the last fry dipped in the last bit of shake.

"Feel free to tell me to stuff it, but what was your stanza's role in the whole affair?" Codrin asked.

"You do not need to stuff it, my dear. Each first line had a role to play, after a fashion, and that often informed what the rest of the stanza focuses on, as we are formed from that instance as a template."

Ey nodded, waiting for the fox to continue.

"Actually, my dear, can you guess? I am one who plays with instances, who finds ways to make others mad and happy and fall in love and get in fights, who guides and shapes sentiments, all by just being myself, and I am one who has turned that into an art."

"I know I've met Praiseworthy, but I don't know much about her. I know Serene built the house and prairie. I think you mentioned that you two were forked when Praiseworthy's up-tree instance wanted to explore the ramifications of both instances and sims."

As it waited for Codrin to piece together what ey could, the fox scraped the bottom of the shake glass for the last spoonful of ice cream and fed it to its partner. A small affection that made em smile.

"Can you give me a bit of a hint about Serene?"

"You get one hint, and it will be small. What emotions come to you when you walk the prairie?"

Codrin sat up straight. "A politician? Was Praiseworthy a politician? All this talk of shaping sentiments and expectations. Or, wait. No, that's not it."

Dear urged em on with a little twirl of its spoon, looking pleased at the response.

"A speech writer? Did she come up with the speeches that whichever one of you was on the Council at the time used?"

"You are thinking too narrowly, my dear. The Council had little *need for speeches for itself, and, as a body created to guide but not to govern, there were few enough speeches given outside of the council. After all, where would it give them?"*

"Too narrow, hmm..." Ey frowned. "Was she...did she come up with propaganda?"

Dear laughed, reached a finger into the shake glass to swipe up a little bit of sticky vanilla shake, and dabbed it on Codrin's nose. *"Well reasoned. Praiseworthy was the propagandist among the first lines."*

Codrin rubbed at eir nose to get the melted ice cream off before it congealed further. "What exactly goes into being a propagandist, when the role of the Council was to guide but not to govern?"

Without falling, the fox's happy expression somehow became a fraction less earnest, just that much less directed.

Before it could respond, ey held up a hand. "It's okay, Dear. One of the Bălans will figure it out."

"Thank you, Codrin."

Ey reached out to pat at the back of the fox's paw. "I hardly want you to resent me, if that's the result of me pressing you on this."

"You are a ways off from making me resent you, my dear."

Codrin nodded, watching Dear's gaze slip away, scanning the street outside the diner, quiet in the late evening. Ey could not quite figure out the emotion on display. Its ears were tilted back, but it did not look angry, nor particularly sad. Pensive, perhaps?

"Dear?" its partner asked.

"No, you are a ways off from me resenting you, but you are perilously close to me lying to you."

Ioan Bălan—2325

Ioan and May walked hand-in-paw along the rim of a lake. It had settled neatly into a bowl formed by three peaks, and around it wound a deer-trail, which was only wide enough to permit them to walk side by side half the time. For the rest of the hike, Ioan walked in front, guiding May, pointing out roots, and eventually helping her clamber up onto a rock out-cropping at the point where the lake drained into the lands below through a chattering creek.

There they sat to eat their lunches and talk.

"I had no idea that you enjoyed hiking."

"Oh, goodness no. I hate it." Ey laughed. "But it's the only way to get to this rock."

They sat in silence for a while, the sun warming their backs as it slid down toward the peaks that ey supposed must be west.

"Why did you bring me out here, Ioan?"

Ey lazily scanned the far shore of the lake, picking out the places where the deer trail dipped shyly down to the edge of the water before darting back up into the trees.

"I needed to focus on something further away than a piece of paper," ey said at last. "Further than the lilacs in the yard."

"And the interviews you have done have not helped?"

Ey shrugged.

"Cabin fever, perhaps?"

"Maybe, yeah."

"Ioan, I am not the one who is supposed to be asking questions," she chided.

"Right, sorry. It's a little bit cabin fever, I guess. I've spent an awful lot of time cooped up in the house and just sending forks out to run the interviews. It's one thing to remember being outside, but another still to have to make that memory align with not having left the house in days."

The skunk nodded, picking a pebble from near her paw and tossing it into the lake. "I understand. It think that I am perhaps more comfortable inside than you are, but I am still happy that you brought me here.

"Glad you like it. It's an abandoned sim that I visited decades back and still had the coordinates to. It reminded me of how my grandfather described his time in Slovenia." Ey crumpled the wrapper to eir sandwich and returned it to the backpack that ey'd brought with em. "It's just good to get out and change contexts, I guess."

May nodded.

"It's just..." Ey frowned, hunting for the words. "It's just that we have limitless time and limitless space and all the creativity we could hope to use, and still I sometimes feel trapped, as though I'm stuck in this tiny, constrained space where I can barely move and can't hope to stretch out. Does that make sense?"

"It is not a feeling I share, but I can see how one might," May said, carefully shifting the backpack from between them to the other side of her so that she could lean against em. "It is the feeling one gets when one asks "is that all there is?" and the answer comes back "yes, of course"."

"Yeah," ey murmured. As May rested her head against eir shoulder, ey turned eir head to place a kiss between her ears. Ey did not remember when ey had first started doing that, but it had long since become habit. Every time ey remembered that it had been an act that was out of character for em until May moved in, some part of em raced around in circles to try and find out what had changed and why.

It's just...May. That's just how she is, ey kept reminding emself. *There is no explaining an Odist.*

"It's been happening more and more since the idea of the launches first started to take off. It happened before, too, but I think coming to the understanding that this *isn't* all there is, that there's also stuff outside the System and far away from the Sun...well, it just kind of rubbed my face in it. "You're stuck here, Ioan Bălan," it says. "You're not going to be on the launch, and even if you were, that wouldn't be you. There'd be no merging of experiences"."

May laughed. "I find freedom in that. Not only will I not have to do any of that work, but I will also get to be one of the shitheads that stays behind."

"And that's a bonus?"

"Of course it is, my dear. When was the last time you had the luxury of staying behind? Of that being a one-way decision?"

Ey frowned.

"Do not think too hard, Ioan. I can tell you now that it was before you uploaded." She sounded as though speaking from a dream. "That was the last time that you could have made the choice to stay behind. It is some of Dear's beloved irreversibility. You cannot un-upload. You cannot upload part of the way. There is no going and there is no back, remember? Now, though, you are here. If you are busy working and a friend is throwing a party, why, just fork! You do not need to worry about whether or not you need stay behind or join them. You can do both."

"But with the launch, you had the decision to stay behind."

"Yes, it was a new experience. New in these last two centuries."

"You're so weird," ey said, then laughed as she elbowed em in the side.

"We are both weird." She poked at eir thigh with a claw. "That includes you, my dear. We both stayed behind, and we both sent along cocladists so far diverged from us that they might as well have become new individuals."

"Mm, true. I'm happy for them, at least."

"As am I. Their communications are not quite as happy as I suspect they wish, but I am still happy for them."

Ioan knit eir brow. "There is that, yeah. Do you remember Ezekiel?"

"Of course," May said, sitting up and swinging her legs up onto the rock so that she could sit cross-legged, facing em. "He was brilliant. Intensely, incredibly brilliant. I am sure that he still is, but that brilliance is now coiled all around itself in the way that happens with prophets throughout the ages."

Ey turned to face May in turn. "Who do you think that weighed more on, though? Dear or Codrin?"

The skunk dipped her muzzle. "That is difficult to say. They are each sensitive in their own ways. Dear, I imagine, is feeling a lot of old fears confirmed, and old memories come to roost. I worry that, some day, that fox will spin itself into a whirlwind and dissipate into the atmosphere."

"I'm sure it'd enjoy that."

"It would make it a whole production. Invite everyone on the LV."

Ioan laughed.

"And Codrin?" she said.

"I expect ey's struggling, in eir own way. Were I confronted with something like that, I'd be able to keep it together throughout the interview, but afterwards, I'd have to spend a lot of time just decompressing."

"Why is that?"

"You spend all your time up here–" Ey tapped at eir temple. "–and being confronted by the ways in which that can go wrong to someone who was, as you say, brilliant, can really mess with you. I bet ey holed himself up in that office for a while and paced a ring into the floor."

If ey had been expecting a laugh or a smile from the skunk, ey was disappointed. She simply nodded and looked off into the water again. "There is nothing wrong with that, Ioan. We have known that disconnect. We have known the feeling of a mind coiled in on itself. That is frightening to all of us. It *should* be frightening."

Suspecting that May would appreciate it and not knowing what to say to that, ey simply reached out and took one of her paws in eir hands.

Ey didn't know how long they sat there like that. Ey didn't remember what ey was thinking, or where ey looked. All ey remembered was the satiny feeling of May's pawpads against eir skin, and the sound of a quiet lake.

May broke the silence first. "Ioan, my tail is falling asleep. Can we go back?"

Ey nodded, levering emself up onto eir knees, then onto eir feet so that ey could help the skunk stand.

She laughed and winced once she stood, rubbing at the base of her tail. "All pins and needles."

"I can't even begin to imagine how that must feel in a tail."

"And I cannot imagine how to describe it. Help me down, and we can walk back."

"Walk? You don't want to just leave?"

"If you are going to drag me out on a hike, then so help me God, take me on the hike, Ioan."

They walked back along the deer trail, back the way they came. The water was now to their left, and where their eyes had been drawn to it before, they were now drawn to the pine forest that rimmed the lake. Trees reached straight for the sky from their brown bed of needles.

And as they walked, faster than before, May talked. "I worry about them. Both launches, both families. I worry about me and you. The interview with Ezekiel, yes, but both of them, both Castor and Pollux, are starting to circle around the center of it all."

"The center?"

"All three of us—Dear#Castor, Dear#Pollux, and I—have warned all three of you Bălans that there is a lot behind this."

She was panting now as she walked, faster and faster. She had taken the lead, and was drawing em along behind her as she spoke. "We couch it in humor and jokey language as though they are riddles for you to solve, but Ioan, I worry that all it will do in the end is sow distrust between our two clades."

Ioan worked to keep up with May as she nearly jogged around the last bend in the path. "We can stop, May. If you don't think it'll lead to anything good, then we can just stop. We can look elsewhere. We can go back to interviewing musicians and astronomers and shitty authors. There are still stories to tell, and I'm sure that they will lead to just as many myths."

She shook her head. Or at least Ioan thought she did. It was hard to tell, with the two of them jouncing along down the path.

"May, please, at least slow down! You're going to pull me over."

Rather than slowing down, the skunk skidded to a stop, leading Ioan to nearly collide with her. As it was, ey had to stumble to the side to keep from bowling her over.

"May?"

"I am sorry."

Ey frowned at the stricken expression on her face, the tear-tracks in cheekfur. "Do you want us to stop? Stop talking to Odists? If you want to help guide us to better places to look, we can take a break from it."

She was already shaking her head. "You are not going to be able to avoid it, Ioan. I am worried, and I will not stop being worried, but you will not be able to avoid the inevitable end of this line of thought. You did not know it, but you were not even able to avoid the beginning of it."

"There's no way to stay behind, you mean."

She laughed, and the laugh was shaky with tears. "You are a brat. But yes. There is no way to stay behind."

"You're just worried?"

"I am just worried. You are at serious risk of learning the truth, and that has me worried."

"Alright." Ey drew May in for a hug. "I don't understand you Odists. I never have. You seem to have all these dramatic events spiraling around you."

She laughed as she rested her head against eir shoulder. "We do, yes, and you love it."

"It keeps life interesting, no denying. I just worry about you in turn."

"That feels good to hear, dear."

"Good," ey said.

"Now, take me home and talk about something—anything—else for the rest of the night."

Yared Zerezghi—2124

For the first time since their arrangement had begun, Yared was greeted at his own door, rather than at the coffee shop down on the corner.

He had yet to start his day, instead reveling in the cool quiet of the morning, before the sun levered itself up over the roof of his building to shine through his window and before the thrum of the air conditioning took over. The cool, the quiet, his pillow, his sheets, and the blessed nullity of not yet being awake enough to think, to worry.

At least the knock on his door was polite.

He hurried to throw on his clothes and kick his bed into something resembling a made state, toss last night's take-out container in the trash, and rub the last of the sleep from his eyes before answering the door.

"Mr. Zerezghi." Councilor Demma's driver nodded cordially. "The councilor would like to speak with you at your earliest convenience."

At your earliest convenience seemed to imply right now, so Yared nodded and kicked on his sandals to follow the suit out of the hallway and into the street. The pavement and buildings had yet to start to bake, but he could tell that it would be another day of hiding inside, or skittering from one air-conditioned place to another.

If I make it through this, he thought.

Demma's car was parked down the block and on the other side of the street, and Yared was pleased to see a carrier with three paper coffee cups in it sitting on the roof. If nothing else, he'd be able to wake up a little, and that would provide him some semblance of normalcy to this strange shift in protocol.

"Yared, wonderful to see you. I trust you are alright?" Demma said, once he was seated in the car, coffee in hand. It felt far too chilly.

"I'm well, councilor. I wasn't expecting to talk until later today."

The politician waved the statement away and nodded toward the driver, who slid the car smoothly out into the street and drove towards, Yared assumed, the city center.

"I must apologize for waking you early. Please, enjoy your coffee for a moment. I am happy to enjoy the scenery for a while."

Something about that statement, or perhaps Demma's tone of voice, made it sound more like a command than a suggestion, so Yared did just that, sipping on his coffee as it cooled as his mind raced. *Did I do something wrong? Am I being taken to prison? No, almost certainly not, if Councilor Demma is here. Why am I being made to wait? Am I supposed to feel uncomfortable, or does he actually just want me awake?*

After Yared finished his coffee and set his cup aside, Demma smiled.

"Mr. Zerezghi, I would like to thank you for all of your work on the project at hand. I believe that we have both seen the ways in which it is shaping the discussion on our small part of the 'net, yes? There are other forces at work, to be sure, but your voice is loud, and our little faction is adding in resources behind the scenes, as you have no doubt noticed."

Yared nodded, waiting for the hammer to fall.

"I would, however, like to know the identity of who your contacts are, sys-side."

He tilted his head. "What? Why?"

Demma sighed and set aside his own coffee. "I have a suspicion that I know who one of them is, and I would like confirmation of that. I would appreciate if you would tell me, so that I do not need to tip my hand and send you hunting him down. You understand."

"I suppose." Yared bit his lip and considered the possible consequences of sharing the names of his contacts, deciding that if he shared just one, that perhaps that would be enough without compromising the identity of both. "You say 'he'. The man that I'm in discussions with is named Jonas. Is that the one you're thinking of?"

The councilor sighed and slouched back into the cushy microfiber seat. "Yes. I was afraid of that."

"How so?"

"He is a very slippery man, Yared. While I suppose that it's nice that his goals align with ours on the issue of rights and secession—I can read between the lines as well as he can, I know who he's tapped phys-side—that is not always guaranteed to be the case." He finished his own coffee and accepted Yared's cup when offered to dispose of in the trash. "Slippery and manipulative. I worry that you are at risk of being played by him, of becoming his puppet."

Aren't I already yours? he thought. Instead, he said, "He seems friendly enough, but I guess I can see how that might be used to guide me. He hasn't asked for any favors or anything, at least."

"And have you told him about our little agreement?" When Yared quailed under Demma's gaze, the councilor shook his head. "I cannot say I'm pleased, Mr. Zerezghi, but I'm also not particularly surprised."

Yared wiped his palms against his thighs, shaking his head. "He guessed, councilor. He asked, and even knew it was you. I'm sorry, sir, I don't think there's anything I could have done to stop him from doing that."

"Oh, did he now?" Demma's laugh was earnest. "I'm not particularly surprised at that, either, and I suppose it does let you off the hook somewhat, doesn't it?"

All he could think to do was nod.

"Well, if Jonas Anderson has figured out what we're up to, that does change things somewhat. I know that our latest suggestion was that you mention independence for the first time. I'd like to modify that somewhat, if you haven't already written your post."

"Not yet. I was going to do it this morning before our usual meeting."

"Yes, well, do hold off for a little longer. I would like you to change it so that you quote Jonas in mentioning independence. Do keep his name out of your posts, of course. It's probably best that he remain your 'friend' and not 'one of the slickest politicians in the Western Federation' when people read what you have to say." Demma smiled kindly, adding, "And if I may ask you a favor, please don't consult him about this post before you send it. You're welcome to keep talking with him and whoever his companion is, we won't restrict your access to that. Perhaps they're even another copy of him. I just want to hear what his reaction is when you put the word 'independence' in his mouth."

"Of course, sir."

Nodding, the councilor said, "Thank you, Yared. I'm glad to see that we are more on the same page, now. Stay wary of Jonas Anderson, maintain your friendship, and keep me up to date about the things that he says that don't make it into your posts. As long as our goals align, we should be able to work together through you."

"You won't talk to him?" Yared asked.

"That's far to risky for my current position. It's plausibly deniable that you were already talking to him before we reached our agreement, should that agreement be made public. It's true enough, isn't it? If I were to talk to him, though..." He trailed off with a shrug and a half-smile.

"I understand."

"I'm glad that you do." Demma flicked his eyes up to the

driver's rear-view mirror, and the car slid to a halt in a parking spot. "Mr. Zerezghi, a pleasure as always. We will be keeping an eye out for your post later today."

Yared sat up, looking out through the window at the outskirts of the financial district. It would easily be an hour's walk back to his apartment, and about as long of a bus-ride. He didn't even have his phone.

The councilor was already holding his hand out to shake, so there seemed to be no argument that this is where he should leave. He shook the hand, climbed out of the car, and watched it slide off into traffic once more.

Trudging to the nearest bus stop, he thought, *I suppose as long as this is the only punishment that I get, I shouldn't be too concerned.*

At least the bus was air conditioned, and it gave him time to draft his post in his head.

I cannot express just how pleased I am to say that I have no arguments to dispute, this time!

It's tempting to slack off in one's campaigning when things start to swing one's way, but even I know that complacency will provide a wedge for dissenters to gain a foothold, so, despite the heat, I'm back with another of my posts. You'll all have to live with me so long as this issue is on the table, and doubtless, you'll have to keep living with me once I pick up my next little fixation. Both friends and foes will understand, even if their opinions of that fact differ.

Today, then, instead of refuting arguments, I'd just like to express some of my gratitude and provide an overview of what is going on and why it is that I'm so pleased.

First, I'm happy to see that the argument about speciation has all but stopped as an argument about independence. Oh, sure, it continues elsewhere on the 'net, but it's been all but dropped from the comments about this referendum. It remains fascinating to many of us, of course. The more I talk with my friends sys-side, the more I find myself split on the idea, and even they seem to have their own opinions on it. One of them said, "Who even cares? We're still ourselves," to which the other responded, "Right, but just think about how much of a wrench that it will throw into evolution."

Second, I'm happy to see the amendment to move the System to the L_5 station has been tacked onto the bill. It's mostly a formality, at this point. Those who work with the System phys-side have already signed a deal with the launch coordinators, and the amendment is simply to recognize that this is the case from a governmental point of view. It may make talking to my friends somewhat more difficult, due to the transmission delay, but I'm sure we'll survive. When I joked to them that, in space, no one can hear their ceaseless banter, they agreed that it was probably for the best, and said that they were looking forward to moving to cooler climes.

Last, of course, I'm pleased to see the interest that the world's governments are taking in the issue. Sure, that means that our role here on the DDR is diminished, but *it is not gone.* We have as much a say in the legislation as any one of them does. This is where my caution about not slacking off will pay off. We have the S-R Bloc on our side, and the various African coalitions are drifting that way as well. The Western Fed seems to be cautiously on board. But we are still waiting on hearing from the middle eastern countries, Japan, and SEAPAC, which means that we will need to stay vigilant. While I suspect that Japan will side with individual rights, and the middle east will remain largely apathetic, I have no idea which way SEAPAC will swing, so our vote must still be counted among them as a voice in favor of the referendum.

Now, instead of arguing any further points, I'd like to provide you with something lighter. I know that many enjoy the little snippets of conversation that I have with my friends sys-side, so I'm going to share a bit more of that with you. It's fun, yes, but I hope that it will continue to build empathy with them and their existence, even if I am not any good at writing anything beyond polemics on the 'net. As always, I will be protecting their identities, so I will go with John and Tara for their names.

When John joked about moving to the coldness of space, I, naturally, complained about the heat.

"How hot is it there?" he asked.

I said, "Right now? About 43C."

Tara said, "Yeowch. That is far too warm." (This is not actually what she said. She has quite a mouth on her, but I will soften that for the sake of propriety.)

John said, "You're covered almost entirely in black fur. You'd be warm in Antarctica."

She responded, "Well, yes, I am *here*. If I were actually in Antarctica, however, I would not be covered by fur that is a part of my body. A fur coat might be nice, however."

I asked, "How does that work, anyway? Do you feel like a human except in a different shape?"

Her response was a while in coming. "Yes and no. I look different, to be sure. Anyone who has seen a furry can probably imagine what that means. My av on the 'net allowed me some sensation of that, in that I was provided with a vague sense of touch on my tail, and the sensation of my ears had been moved higher up on my head to approximate the location where the ears of [my species] are located. Having a muzzle worked well enough. Here, though, the proprioception is complete in a way that an avatar could not hope to be. It made the avatar feel more like a set of clothes and a mask than it did an actual form. Here, it is my form. It made my avatar feel almost cartoonish, with the standard fur patterns a bit too exact and the claws on my fingers nearly identical. Here it can be—must be—as detailed as I would like. My claws wear at different rates, fur colors mingle organically. That is a sign of aposematism, did you know that? It is a warning to those who would attack to stay away. I could even smell like my species, should I choose, though I have not."

John said, "Confirmed. She smells like flowers."

I asked, "Why did you choose that form?"

She said, "Because I wanted to and I could. It is what I am used to from my time before uploading. I think that I originally chose it for that concept of aposematism. I had probably gone through a bad breakup and was looking for something that said, "Stay away, I am independent." I had terrible luck with relationships."

John said, "She's more independent than is good for her, sometimes."

As this was the point in the conversation that I figured I might include it in a post, I guided it toward the topic at hand, saying, "Is that why you're so interested in individual rights?"

Tara said, "Yes, in a way. You have to understand, though, that many of the arguments against them that you have shared sound mind-boggling at best, impossible at worst."

John said, "We're more independent than I think a lot of people phys-side give us credit for. You keep talking of us as though we're almost a separate country, and honestly, you're not wrong. We've been questioning what the reasoning is for retaining dual citizenship other than for governments that essentially have no power over us to claim the rights to whatever it is we send out. We're ungovernable by conventional standards, and I wouldn't be surprised if someone does file a referendum for us to drop the pretense and become our own country in the next few months."

I asked, "If you did, would you participate alongside the other world governments?"

John said, "Maybe on some things, but we wouldn't be able to relate to much in the way of legislation."

Tara said, "If we do, John will have to be the representative. He is the politician."

John replied, "You keep saying you're not a politician like that does anything to convince people that you are anything but, my dear."

I let them banter for a bit. The only other salient point was brought up by John, who said, "If a vote for independence does show up, make sure you vote for it. It'll make all of our lives so, so much easier."

So, that was our conversation. I hope that this helps you understand a bit more what the lives of those who live sys-side are like. They joke around. They have strong opinions. They can look like anthropomorphic animals if they want. Who cares if they're human? Who cares if their bodies have died? They're just as real as any of us, and they deserve all of the same rights.

Vote for the granting of rights. Vote yes on *referendum 10b30188.*

Yared Zerezghi (NEAC)

He read over his post a few times to make sure it looked alright, then hit post and immediately backed out from his rig. He knew that he'd come back to messages from Jonas and True Name. He couldn't guess at what their tone would be, but he knew that he wasn't ready to deal with them.

He just knew that he needed something spicy to eat and at least two glasses of wine.

True Name—2124

It had initially taken some getting used to, meeting with one's up- or cross-tree instances. Michelle, in her role in helping tie the cost of forking to the reputation markets, had certainly done it a number of times before, but, as the cost of a new fork was only applied five minutes after it had been created, all of her forks to date had been short-lived in order to conserve her reputation for some imagined future date.

The date had come and gone, now, so True Name—and likely all of the other Odists—had had to learn how to interact with the other copies of Michelle Hadje/Sasha that had sprung so quickly into being and immediately began to diverge.

The fact that those who matched Michelle and those who matched Sasha were evenly distributed had helped at first. There had been some oddness in talking to a Michelle-alike, given the countless memories of the constant shifting between the two forms, but that had had a different flavor to it than talking to another Sasha-alike. Seeing a form and a face that so clearly mirrored her own was not exactly unnerving so much as uncanny.

As the days and weeks went by, however, the forks diverged further and further, and different cares painted different faces, different habits were formed and dropped, and it became less like talking to an alternate version of oneself and more like talking to a twin, a sibling.

So it was when The Only Time I Know My True Name Is When I Dream met with That Which Lives Is Forever Praiseworthy.

Her initial impression is that the other skunk had shifted her wardrobe to look more professional, choosing a loose-fitting pantsuit in muted blue that had been in style before Michelle had uploaded. This also included a pair of pince nez glasses perched atop her muzzle which, when True Name inquired, Praiseworthy explained were non-prescription, and "something I am just trying for the moment. They are quite annoying, but still fetching."

Beyond that, however, Praiseworthy had decided to divest herself of many of the personality traits that had made Sasha Sasha. Gone were those aspects of childishness that Michelle had long held onto, and gone was the exhaustion that had lingered for years after getting lost.

I have changed, too, at that, True Name thought. *I have become the politician, working with Jonas. Praiseworthy has become something else.*

The two skunks shook paws, and then Praiseworthy drew True Name into a hug. It was surprising. Something about it felt both natural and performative, as though this was just a thing that one did when one had a role to play.

"True Name," Praiseworthy said. Her smile was warm and earnest, and she spoke with willing paws, palms up. "It is nice to see you again."

She laughed. "I suppose so. You have changed quite a bit in so short a time."

The other skunk bowed, laughing. "As have you, my dear! And that is why you have come here, is it not?"

"I guess it is, yes. The more I work with Jonas, and the more I talk with the Council and phys-side—the more politicking that I do—the more I feel the ways in which my attitude and expressions are lacking."

Praiseworthy nodded. "Yes, you do still have some of the stiffness about you, and there are some sharp edges that could do with softening."

"Softening?"

"Yes. It is mostly a matter of appearance and affect, though. You should not blunt your wit or intellect, just your tone and features."

True Name frowned. "I am not sure what you mean by blunting or softening, though."

Praiseworthy took her gently by the elbow and started walking through the grass. They had decided to meet on a portion of Michelle's dandelion-ridden sim, far away from their root instance, but in a place that was still familiar to both.

"Take your walk, for instance. Even now, as we are just out for a stroll, you walk with purpose. Your shoulders move too much. Remember, if you keep them pointed straight ahead and shift the rolling motion to your hips, it will lead to others seeing more feminine aspects in you."

She tried to keep her shoulders still as they walked, immediately feeling a slight strain in her hips.

Praiseworthy laughed. "You do not need to keep them level to the ground, just perpendicular to the direction you are walking in. But here, no need to practice too hard. Fork, holding in your mind a pelvis just a hair wider than your own, but keeping your hips the same width. It will mean slimming down a little."

"I can do that?"

"Of course. Zeke dreamed some algorithmic magic behind the scenes. You can fork yourself into most anything that can be consensually held in the mind."

True Name nodded warily, holding this new image of herself in her mind.

"Perfect," Praiseworthy said, moving to take this new fork by the elbow and nodding to the original instance of the skunk. "Now you quit. No need to incur a charge. Michelle, no need to accept further memories from us for the day."

The skunks tilted their heads in unison.

"Michelle will be getting a pile of memories, if she wants, as

I will have you fork a few more times yet. I have been letting her know when she can ignore further merges, as I have done this quite often."

The first True Name nodded, then disappeared.

True Name felt down her flanks, taking a few more steps and finding it far easier to walk casually and still keep her shoulders pointed forward. She nodded approvingly. "Excellent. What other suggestions do you have?"

"For your role, you will need to carefully balance cute, attractive, and competent. If you go too far towards cute, then it will be difficult for you to be taken seriously. The same if you go too far attractive because you will be just a pretty face. If you go too far competent, you will be seen as dour and unpleasant."

Praiseworthy stopped her and turned her gently to look at her face.

"Now, first, your eyes will need to be just a hair larger, your ears slightly rounder, your cheeks fuller, and you will need fewer but longer whiskers. Can you hold those in your mind?"

She closed her eyes, picturing what she knew of herself in her mind, and forked.

"Goodness."

She opened her eyes again to look at the fork, immediately laughing and shaking her head.

"Am I cute?" the new skunk asked.

"Adorable, but that is not quite the direction we want to go. You look closer to a teddy bear."

She rolled her eyes, then quit.

"Let us try one at a time. You will need to work fairly quickly to avoid the hit in reputation. Fork once, and then that fork will continue to look as you do now, while you work progressively on each of those steps." When True Name did so, Praiseworthy nodded. "First, rounder ears."

The new fork perked up when her down-tree instance forked and quit, the new instance having slightly rounder ears. She nodded, smiling.

"Excellent. Now the whiskers. Great. Cheeks? And...eyes. Fantastic." Praiseworthy smiled after all the forking had been completed, then nodded to the first of the new instances, who quit.

The option for a rush of memories was provided to True Name, who, on a whim, accepted it, now remembering what it had looked like from the outside as her face had grown...well, cuter. It had worked well.

The two skunks worked through a short laundry list of changes. True Name grew an inch or so taller, her shoulders became the slightest bit flatter without getting broader, her back straighter.

One last time, she forked to get a good look at herself to compare with what she remembered from before the process.

She was, indeed, cuter, but this was tempered by a more conventionally attractive body type, staying shy of being both adorable and overtly attractive. This somehow combined into a look that was more professional. It made her look, she realized, like a public figure.

"Oh, this is delightful."

Praiseworthy beamed. "I am glad that you enjoy."

They worked next on how to better her affect. Smile more earnestly, laugh more easily, transition from those expressions to stern or confident or pitying. There were a few more forks as they worked on ways to soften True Name's voice, pitching it just a little lower, rounding some of the vowels, practicing elocution. With each fork, she found that the lessons stuck more firmly. Perhaps what was in her mind before became more cemented in place.

Finally, Praiseworthy had True Name practice forking into a Michelle-form for situations where a skunk would be out of place, and then they worked on perfecting that version of her, as well. It was surprising, at first, that she could even make so great a change with one fork, but then, she remembered precisely what it had felt like to be Michelle, just as she remembered what it felt like to be Sasha.

Eventually, when the practice and modifications had wrapped up, nearly two hours later, the two skunks sat at the top of a low raise in the landscape, and True Name discussed the other reason that she had sought out Praiseworthy.

"I need help in spreading ideas. I know that you have settled back into acting and directing, but I do not have the time or energy to guide emotions and reactions to news while still working on this political angle." She plucked a few blades of grass, rolling them into little balls between fingerpads. "I know that propaganda is not the same thing as theater, but would you be willing–"

"Yes!" Praiseworthy laughed. "Of course I would be willing to help. There is more than a little propagandizing in trying to get actors to do their fucking jobs, even when the actors are yourself. What precisely do you need? Speeches? Words whispered here and there? Posters?"

True Name laughed and shook her head. "Not quite the answer that I was expecting, but yes. Speeches and letters specifically. Some geared toward phys-side, some toward the Council, and probably a few towards other groups sys-side. I would not turn down a few words whispered here and there, though that will take some strategizing. There will be an instance of Jonas who will be working with you in shaping sentiment, as well."

"I will look forward to it, then."

They sat for a while in the sun, each looking out into the fields. At one point, Praiseworthy took off her glasses and set them on the bridge of True Name's muzzle, shook her head, and slid them into a jacket pocket.

It was good to be around oneself, True Name realized. There was none of the pressure involved with interacting with others, none of the careful maneuvering required when talking with Jonas. They could just sit there, side by side, and understand that there was nothing between them that the other did not also, at least to some extent, understand.

"Have you talked to many others in the clade?" Praiseworthy asked.

She shook her head. "Here and there. I have a meeting scheduled with Life Breeds Life, but that is about it. You?"

"You were the last I had yet to speak with. It is interesting to see how we have each decided to focus on different areas. You dove hard into the political angle. I tried to get back to theatre, but enough of that desire remained in me that your propaganda job sounds fun. Life Breeds Life is quite strange. He has been focusing–"

"He?"

Praiseworthy shrugged. "I guess. He has been focusing on historical stuff. Documenting this and that, digging into old things. I have no idea where that came from. Loss For Images is writing, these days. May One Day is fiddling with reputation markets—or at least as much as Debarre will let her—and last I heard, Hammered Silver has just been either chilling here with Michelle or sim-hopping."

"How is she, anyway?"

"Michelle?" Praiseworthy frowned, ears tilting back. "Much the same. I think the last of her energy went into us, and she is...I do not know. Empty? She spends a lot of time sleeping, a lot of time sitting and thinking. She came to a play, but left partway through. She is still of two minds."

"And she still has not explained why she never fixed it?"

The skunk shook her head.

"Any guesses?"

"Nothing solid."

True Name nodded and turned her gaze back to the rolling plain. So much grass. So many dandelions. "There is a time and a place for dwelling in memory," she said. "But Michelle does nothing else. It is no wonder she is stuck. When...when ey died, I think she began to as well. When she she dumped the last of herself into the Ode, she sealed the deal."

Praiseworthy said nothing.

"She is dead, I think. There is no more life in her. There is nothing to be done but let her enjoy that death as long as she would like. I do not expect that she will come back."

The other skunk drew her knees to her chest and folded her arms across them. "I think you may be right in that. Let her do what makes herself happy while her shade remains."

"I wonder if she knows it, yet," True Name said, then let silence fall again. The two sat together, watching as afternoon slid carefully into evening.

Codrin Bălan#Pollux—2325

Codrin was, as ey supposed everyone must be, primed to hunt for patterns.

The Odists, as much as they tried to resist it, were as beholden to living within a pattern as any other group of individuals. Perhaps more so than other clades, but certainly well within the realm of societies, or even families. It wasn't just that they were all weird—though they were—nor that many of them fit the mold of either the human or skunk versions of Michelle Hadje—though that was certainly true. It was a matter of bearing, of how they carried themselves, of how they expressed themselves. Not all were as excitable as Dear nor as affectionate as May Then My Name, but all of the ones that ey had met had the same walk, the same smile, the same sensation of quiet when they were quiet and the same way of speaking when they spoke.

The differences, then, were in the details. Where Qoheleth had opted for the biblical look, May Then My Name had decided on a comfortable softness that befitted her similarly comfortable, soft nature. And where Dear had wholly owned a look that somehow managed to be both painfully well-dressed and playful, the woman before em exuded all of the casual cool of one who was relaxing on a summer Saturday. It was a weekend look, and ey could not find any other way to describe it.

Ey was surprised when ey had been contacted by her, rather than the other way around.

> Hey, there is this neat bar I know. Come check it out, and we can chat there.
>
> — Why Ask Questions, Here At The End Of All Things of the Ode Clade

It came as a letter. An actual, honest-to-goodness letter, slipped under eir door (which is how the sim decided to interpret it), written in a rounded hand on yellow legal pad paper.

Ey spent nearly five minutes just staring at the letter, turning it over in eir hands, inspecting the writing, the ink (shitty ballpoint, ey had noted with distaste), the creases. Ey could make neither heads nor tails of it. It was incredibly Odist while at the same time being totally unique.

When ey showed it to Dear, the fox rolled its eyes and handed it back.

"She is a shithead."

"A shithead?" Ey laughed. "How so?"

"She just is. That whole stanza is made up of assholes."

"Should I be careful or anything?"

"No, no. You will like her, I promise."

Codrin refolded the note and tucked it into a pocket in eir tunic. "You sound less than fond of her."

The fox shook its head. *"Not at all. I like her quite a bit, but I like her because she is good at making others like her."*

"Aren't you all, though?" Dear's partner called from the couch. "Look at what May Then My Name is doing to poor Ioan."

"Yes, but she is particularly good at it, and that is why she is a shithead. She is more like some strange inversion of May Then My Name. It is a matter of intent." It grinned at Codrin and took eir hand in its paw to give the back of it an affectionate lick. *"You do not need to be careful, though. She is harmless to any one individual, and any harm that she might cause to a group will be welcomed with open arms and all of the love in the world."*

"Sounds charismatic."

"That is not quite the right word, but it will suffice." It laughed, pushing Codrin's hand away again. *"Go on, then. Enjoy. If it is the bar that I am thinking of, you will doubtless have a good time."*

"And will I get more of this story that keeps coming up?"

Dear turned back to its desk where it had been working. *"Oh yes."*

And so here ey was, sitting across a trestle table from woman dressed from a weekend, up on the roof of a car park, drinking a very spicy, very clammy Caesar while she laughed about how terrible her cocktail was.

"Is it really that bad?" ey asked.

"Here! Here, have a sip. It is atrocious."

Ey took the glass and sniffed it warily. It smelled of citrus. Ey took a sip, tried to swallow, but began coughing violently instead. "What...what the hell is in that?"

"Neutral spirits, at least ninety percent, lime zest, and enough seltzer to make it not burn on the way down."

"Not burn?" Codrin said around an ice cube. The spice of eir Caesar didn't hold a candle to the alcoholic heat of the drink.

"That is what they said."

"Then they failed miserably."

She laughed, earnest and joyful. "That is precisely what they excel at, here. How is your drink?"

"Very heavy on the clam. I think there are some frozen into the ice cubes."

She reached out for the drink, and ey shrugged, sliding it over to her. She took a sip, made a sour face, then dipped her fingers into the glass to fish out one of the shellfish ice cubes to crunch on. The sour face turned to one of disgust.

The move was so innocent, so playful, that eir first reaction was to laugh rather than get upset at someone's fingers in eir drink. Ey liked her at once, then grudgingly admitted to emself that, yes, she was kind of a shithead for just how effortlessly she had made em laugh, not three minutes into meeting her.

Once ey had eir drink again, ey asked, "So, why did you invite me here?"

"You are doing your thing with Dear, are you not? Your..." She spun her finger in the air as she pulled up the word she was looking for. "History? Your myth? It is so fascinating! There is so much story to be had after two hundred years. Creation, Secession, Launch; so much happened around those and between them, and sure, there are timelines and dry textbooks and whatever, but this! You are one of the first ones who is actually pulling a story out of it."

Ey grinned. "That's the hope, yeah. I was originally going to just make it about Launch, but there are more parallels between Secession and the launch than I'd expected."

"There are, yes. And you know, I wonder if we will start thinking of the launch in the same way as Secession. You can almost hear the capital-S in Secession, and now I hear it in Launch."

"Perhaps. Maybe we'll just do it from here and the L$_5$ System or Castor will do something else."

"Mmhm." She grinned at em. "I have already heard from Castor via the System that we are starting to diverge in pretty major ways."

"I've heard similar through Ioan, yeah. I'm happy to share what I have, though. You're the first other Odist that I've talked with about this aside from Dear and May Then My Name."

"May! Oh gosh, what a delight. Has she already tricked Ioan into falling in love with her?"

Codrin laughed. "Tricked?"

"Do not get me wrong, I do not think that she is disingenuous about it or that her intentions are anything but pure, but I have yet to meet a single person who has not fallen at least a little in love with May after spending any considerable length of time with her."

Ey nodded, stirring eir drink with the too-large stalk of celery. "That's fair. And for what it's worth, yeah, I think she has.

I don't think ey's ready to admit it yet, but yeah. Your whole clade is like that, you know?"

Why Ask Questions adopted a look of indignation. "Are you accusing me of being manipulative? Codrin Bălan, I would never! All I did was figure out that you really like nice paper, nice pens, and hand-written notes, find the best way to subvert that, invite you out to a bar that would clearly pique your interest, and beguile you into talking about your down-tree instance falling in love over terrible drinks."

"What?" Ey laughed. "Did you really do that?"

The offended look slipped into a proud one that bordered perilously close to smug. "Of course. But I also did want to meet you. I really am a fan of this project, and I wanted to be a part of it, if you will have me."

"Well, alright. I'm happy to hear that other Odists are interested in it. I've been asking a few rote questions and then letting a conversation develop from there. Is that alright?"

"Of course!"

"First up, I have yet to check, but did you invest entirely in the launches, or is there still a fork of you back on the System?"

"Oh, I left a fork back there. I am not nearly so brave as you and your family. And before you ask, that is who I have been communicating with to relay messages between the two LVs."

"Are your...well, let me back up. What are your roles? Jobs, interests, whatever."

She laughed, shrugging. "I do not really have one at the moment. I helped a little with the launch, and rather a lot with Secession. My job was basically to work with crowds. I love talking one on one like this, but I always feel guilty actually manipulating individuals—and not just the basic research I mentioned earlier. Crowds are another story. I can get a whole restaurant singing a song together whether or not they are drunk."

"Dear did mention that you worked at scale, yeah."

"The fox also probably called me a shithead."

Codrin, caught in the middle of a sip of eir drink, coughed.

"Of course it did! What an asshole. I love it for that."

"To be fair, it also told me I'd like you immediately, and I do, so at least there's that."

Why Ask Questions preened, saying, "Why, thank you. I am flattered. To get back to your question, though, yes, my goal was working crowds. I helped heavily with the campaign for Secession sys-side. My cocladist, Why Ask Questions When The Answers Will Not Help, was tasked with managing much of the phys-side campaigning."

"And you did similar during the launch?"

"Yes. May worked the technical side, I worked the campaign side. There was little work to be done sys-side, though. Most everyone was on board immediately."

Codrin nodded, "I don't remember much in the way of arguments against the launch."

"I like an easy job every now and then."

"Was Secession that much more difficult?"

She leaned back from the table, twirling her drink thoughtfully. "I suppose, yes. It is not that there was not support for it, sys-side, but before we had seceded, the political situation was far more complicated. The System needed to agree to secede just as much as the governments outside needed to agree to allow us."

"This was back when the Council of Eight was a thing, right?"

"Mmhm. It was their—our—last big work. We did a good job at getting everything set up so that it would just run, then we stepped back. The goal was always to guide rather than to govern, as I am sure you have heard."

Codrin nodded. "Ezekiel put it almost the same way."

"He is here?"

The sudden intensity of her gaze, the drop of her smile, the sharpness of her voice made Codrin sit up straighter. "Yeah. I interviewed him a few weeks back. Why?"

"I am just surprised that he agreed to come along on the launch at all."

"He invested entirely, actually."

"Oh did he?" She smiled tightly, sipping at her drink and wincing. "Well, how about that."

"Why did you not expect him to be on the launch?"

"You met him. He is not the person that he used to be. None of us are, I suppose, but he has lost some core aspect of his being. He lost what made him Zeke when he became Ezekiel."

"It was a pretty surreal experience," ey admitted. "Was he also a part of the plan for Secession?"

"Not really, no. That was mostly our clade and the Jonas clade."

"Was the Council of Eight really a council of eight clades?"

She laughed, then held up her finger to her lips. "Do not tell anyone. It was specifically not to be that, but the workload around Secession grew out of proportion for the two of us who were focusing on it, so we forked in the background to get all that we needed done. It was all above board within the Council, but no one else knew."

Codrin nodded and, remembering some of the caginess that Dear had shown, asked, "Do you want me to keep that part out of the history?"

"Oh, goodness no. Please keep it in! I may not be manipulative, but I am careful. I will not tell you anything that I do not want to wind up in your project."

"Dear said that if I pressed any one Odist too hard, they'd resent it and start lying."

"I suspect that it is right in that, too," she said. "But I will not let our conversation get to that point. I will just make you move on to the next question."

Ey nodded, considering eir next question. "So, how much did the clade work together back then?"

"It differed from person to person. Praiseworthy—Dear's down-tree instance—was keen on working with all of us, while some others essentially talked to no one. I did not talk to many of them at first, given that I was...well, it was not so much that I was not supposed to exist, that I was not supposed to be playing a role. At first, I looked almost exactly like my down-tree instance so that we might be mistaken for each other. I decided that I was done being a skunk some years after, though."

"Are you still in touch with your down-tree instance?"

She nodded eagerly. "Oh yes, we talk quite often."

"And she was the one who was organizing the campaign?"

"She and Jonas, yes. We played our silly little game of politics, and then after Secession, we had no reason to go so hard at it, so we simply became friends."

"While I'm on the subject, did you talk much with Michelle?"

"Next!" Why Ask Questions said gleefully, waving her glass at em.

"What? Oh! Right, okay." Ey let the thread drop and prowled through eir mental list of questions. "Alright. I talked a little to Dear about what the mood was like before and after Secession. I have my own experiences from before and after the launch, but I'm curious what yours were. Was the launch exciting to you? Just another day's work?"

"True Name was to organize Launch as she did with Secession, so I suppose it was a bit of both. We were all excited to have a fun project on our hands, and it was a lot of work, even if my role was easy. When the launch actually happened, we had our own little party separate from the fête that you and yours put on." She raised her glass. "The drinks were far better."

Ey laughed.

"It has calmed down since then, as I mentioned. There is little to do, and what remains of our stanza launch-side has started to drift apart once again. We are all friends, but we are coworkers first and foremost, and when we do not have to be at work, we will not be."

"You hang out with other friends, then?"

"Hang out, drink, go for long walks on the beach, watch

plays—did you know that Time Is A Finger Pointed At Itself has put on some really interesting ones? Michelle was a theatre nerd before she uploaded. She put much of that on hold after the whole getting lost kerfuffle and all of the politics that went into the first years after uploading, but still that desire sticks with us."

"Stepping back a second, you said that True Name was to organize the launch. What did you mean by that?"

"I would like to say 'next', but I will answer this question, and then perhaps we can just enjoy the day for a little while. Does that sound alright, Mx. Bălan?"

Ey frowned, but nodded all the same.

"One of the last things that Michelle did with each of the stanzas was to give us all a task. Ours was not actually so specific as"See about launching mini versions of the System into space", so much as"Do something big, help us divest"."

"What did she mean by 'divest'?"

After a moment's silence, Why Ask Questions leaned forward, set her drink down next to Codrin's, then picked eirs up instead. "Come on. Can you believe that, in all of the years that I have been coming here, I have never actually seen the bottom level of the parking garage? I bet that it is full of rats and unexplainable puddles on concrete, reflecting harsh lights. I bet it is all sorts of murdery. Bring your drink."

She winked at em, and with that, the interview was over.

Ioan Bălan—2325

Ioan Bălan: What excited you about the prospect of uploading?

Fu Jinzai: I actually wasn't that excited about the prospect. It was something that I just kind of did because it felt like it'd be easier than sticking around. The kids weren't seeing me anyway, and I could at least get them some cash for when they were older. It sounded nice enough up here, but there were still nice things back there, you know? I didn't think about it too much.

Ioan: What do you miss most about phys-side?

Jinzai: The mountains.

Ioan: Have you done much exploring in the mountains around here?

Jinzai: Oh, sure. They're fine. Some of the ones that I've gotten around to visiting are really nice. They've got a lot of variety and all. There are some that are more like the Alps and some that are more like the Himalayas and some that are kind of like the ones back home, but it's not that I miss, like, the idea of mountains. I miss the little bits of the mountains that made them mine. I miss all the little caves that you could find, or when trees that had

327

fallen over and their root-balls had been pulled up and you could sit under them if you weren't afraid of bugs or anything [laughter]. I miss the little shacks that people had built years and years and years ago, and, like, you have no idea what they were there for, right? Maybe this one is next to a pond, so it's for fishing, but then that one is just kind of in the middle of a forest, and it's too big to be an outhouse and too small to be a cabin, so maybe its a, a [snapping fingers] hunting blind? Is that the word?

Ioan: Where you sit and wait for animals to go by while hunting?

Jinzai: Yes! A hunting blind. And then I miss—and this is really silly—I miss logging. It's horrible, right? [laughter] I know that it's horrible. Some people put in logging trails on their mountains, but they don't put those big swaths of woody trash that the loggers leave behind. I kind of miss that, you know? I miss looking out to the next mountain over and seeing this big rectangular patch of brown. I miss hearing chainsaws running miles away across the valley, but it sounds like, I don't know, like a dream, because it's echoing around the hills.

Ioan: It sounds a little like the mountains you've found here are too perfect, perhaps. Is that sort of what you're saying?

Jinzai: Yeah, I think so. It's too perfect. I don't mind perfection, of course, it's a damn sight better than living a terrible life, but—oh man, I'm gonna sound like my grandpa when I say this—it lacks that kind of toughness that makes you build character. Not, like, the character that he meant, in the trash sense of, like, being a big tough guy, but like, I think if you could grow up here around all this perfection, you wouldn't have much character. You'd be pretty boring. [laughter] I guess I'm glad that you can't upload until you're 18, so you at least have a chance to have some comparison to perfect mountains with the shitty ones phys-side.

Ioan: What's the first thing that you did after uploading?

Jinzai: Oh man, this is gross, so I'm sorry ahead of time. I ate myself sick. [laughter] I found some of those big sims that are all food and whatever, and I figured, "Hey, I don't have a body, right? I can do whatever!" So I started hopping from sim to sim just absolutely stuffing myself until I felt like I was going to pop, but I started getting super uncomfortable, so I came home and got super sick. [laughter] Sorry, yeah, that's pretty gross. I didn't realize that you could fiddle with your sensa...sensi...

Ioan: Sensorium?

Jinzai: Yeah, sensorium. I didn't know that you could fiddle with it so that you could just keep eating or whatever, but unless you're conscious of it, your mind makes it so that you just kind of work like you do back home. Didn't know that, so I ate until I just about burst. [laughter]

Ioan: What's your biggest regret about uploading.

Jinzai: [long pause] I mean, I said that I wasn't really seeing my kids much back then, and I guess that was true enough. I got to see them two or three times a year when I got rotated between crops and had a few weeks of leave. But like...man. I love them. I love them so much. I love them and I miss them every day, just like I loved them and missed them every day back phys-side. I regret...ah, hell. [long pause] I

regret that even though they didn't really know me
all that well, that they'll never get to know me at all,
now, and all I'll have are these memories and– [long
pause] and the only way I'll ever get to see them
again is if they upload and, like, as a dad, I'm not
sure that I really want them to. I know it's perfect
and all, or at least can be, but I'm not sure I want
them to feel like they need to upload to get away
from a shit life, and I definitely don't want them to
feel like they need to upload just to see me again.

Ioan didn't know quite what it was about the latest messages
from the launches that was nagging at em so much. It wasn't
that either of the Codrins were sending back anything that was
particularly surprising. Sure, the Odists had been a big part of
Secession, but ey knew that, hadn't ey? They dealt with propaganda and speeches and politics, so they must have been, right?
That's what was needed for something like seceding from the
rest of the governments on earth, right?

It wasn't the more personal notes that ey'd gotten, express-
ing how life was going out on the LVs, all of the ways in which
it was exactly the same, except for some key difference in sentiment. Those on the LVs felt like they were going on a journey,
and those who remained at the L_5 System felt like they weren't,
so there was an entirely different feeling between two societies
that were otherwise identical.

Three societies, for it was obvious that Castor and Pollux
were diverging rapidly without strict contact with each other
or the System.

And it wasn't that, either. Ey had known from the very start
that the systems on the LVs would diverge from each other as
soon as they were launched. Nothing about that was weighing

on em, and it was turning out to be precisely as interesting as ey had expected that it would be.

And yet, still...

Ioan Bălan: What was the first thing that you did after uploading?

Magnús Einarsson: Sleep. I don't know why, but for some reason, right after uploading, I felt like all I could do was sleep.

Ioan: Did you have trouble sleeping before you uploaded?

Magnús: Not particularly, no. At least, I don't think so. I just found a room that I thought would be good and then slept for probably two days straight. That went on for a while, too, I would get up and eat or whatever, try and read a book, and then get so tired that I'd have to sleep again, so I'd sleep another twenty hours.

Ioan: Do you still sleep a lot?

Magnús: Not nearly so much, no, but still more than I did before uploading.

Ioan: And you uploaded about thirty years ago?

Magnús: 2292. March 3rd.

Ioan: Alright, thank you.

Magnús: Why do you ask?

Ioan: I'm specifically looking for people who uploaded in the last 150 years, after they started– I mean, after they stopped charging to let people upload.

Magnús: They used to charge?

Ioan: Yes. Was your family compensated for you to uplooad?

Magnús: [laughter] Quite well, yes. It was this big argument between my wife and I. I didn't particularly want to upload, but she said that she'd be able to keep the kids in a better school up North with the funds, and then she'd follow once she was sure that they were in a good spot and that she could say goodbye to them properly and all. We'd heard all about it, and it obviously didn't sound bad at all. It was just...I don't know. It was like being asked to move away forever, even if I knew that she would follow, and that maybe my kids would too, after they had a good life.

Ioan: Do you regret uploading at–

Magnús: She never did.

Ioan: I'm sorry?

Magnús: She never followed. She got the kids in their nice school and remarried. I haven't heard from her in twenty-five years.

Ioan: I'm sorry to hear that. It must've been hard to hear that from her.

Magnús: Oh, I didn't hear it from her. I heard it from one of my kids. Anita. They wrote to me and said that mama had moved in with another man and that school was alright and that was that.

Ioan: I'm sorry. Do you still talk with your children, at least?

Magnús: I talk with Anita sometimes. They say they might upload in a few years. They say married life isn't what they expected, and now they're in much the same position I was. They have a kid. They're less strapped for cash with their husband's job, but they're still not going to get anywhere. It sounds like they have a much better relationship with their husband, though, so maybe it won't just be the same old cycle again.

Ioan: How do you feel about that as an option for them?

Magnús: I don't know. Disappointed? Disappointed but not surprised? If they do wind up coming here, then I am going to do my best to make up for lost time.

Ioan: What sorts of things will you show them when they upload? What are some things that you like best up here?

Magnús: There's the things that I like best, and then the things that I think we'll like best together. The things that I like best are the really relaxing things. I like swimming and then going and laying on the grass. I like reading. I like just sim-hopping and people watching. The things that I think we'll like best together are probably some of the game sims that people have set up. They really liked a lot of the spy sims back on the 'net, like the ones where you hide behind walls and sneak through a base and play capture the flag or whatever. I always found them stressful when I did them on my own, but doing one with them, one where we had to escape from a search party, is one of my best memories with them. They have some good ones here that I think they'd like.

Eir current best guess at what kept their anxiety level always at least a little bit above baseline was the obvious similarities between Secession and Launch. It wasn't just that the Odists were involved in both, because both felt like something that the Odists would be interested in.

Rather, it was the fact that the very same individuals had wormed their way into the very same roles with two projects of very similar structure. Again, on the surface, not too surprising, but the result of that was that the two events started to look almost the same, which in turn made Ioan think that Secession had been almost a practice run for Launch.

Obviously it wasn't. At least not precisely. Secession was a necessary thing based on the politics of the time phys-side, while Launch was something that was borne out of a desire to explore.

Wasn't it?

It just felt an awful lot like those who had helped the most with Secession used their work as a template for executing the launch.

Ioan Bălan: What was the most disappointing thing that happened or that you saw after uploading?

Rosemary Seeley: I think just how lonely it was at first.

Ioan: Can you expand on that?

Rosemary: I mean, when you first upload, you're kinda dumped into a set of common areas until you figure out where you're going to stay or whatever. You can meet up with family members if you have them—I didn't—or you can meet up with those of a similar culture or religion—I'm from the middle of the blandest town on the planet and don't hold to any religion—or maybe you can meet up with others based around a similar interest. Thing is, I'm really interested in just cooking and chatting and reading.

Ioan: Were you able to find any groups for cooking or reading?

Rosemary: Not at first, which I think is what made it feel so isolating. People talk about System Freeze, and I can guarantee you it's real. [laughter]

Ioan: How would you describe System Freeze?

Rosemary: Well, I mean, I was poor as dirt back on Earth. I was a pretty good cook who liked to read mystery novels when she wasn't working. If you're poor as dirt, you're only going to get so good at cooking, though, and you're only going to be reading a certain kind of mystery novel. It's not like I went through a ton of schooling to be reading anything high-minded, and what can I say, I'm a sucker for pulp. So I upload and wind up staying in a communal sim somewhere and every time I go out to look for people who like cooking, it's all these people who are *super* into it and have all this weird experience, so all I can do is take classes, and I feel like a real hick. Then I go out and look for reading clubs or people who like mystery novels, and all I can find are these groups that read what I liked ironically so that they can dunk on it with friends.

Ioan: I'm sorry to hear that. It sounds really alienating.

Rosemary: It was, yeah.

Ioan: You said it was lonely at first. What was it that helped it be less lonely for you?

Rosemary: Oh, you're going to laugh at this. It's really embarrassing.

Ioan: You don't need to share if it's uncomfortable, of course.

Rosemary: No, no. It's funny now. Just embarrassing. I started lying. I said that I was an author of a series of books that were mysteries that were also cookbooks. I said I was this schlock author who wrote terrible novels with mediocre recipes and just kept pumping them out as fast as I could under a bunch of different pseudonyms and that I got really tired of writing them and how bad they were, so I uploaded. I started just going to a few of those ironic book clubs and a few of the cooking classes and started talking about these horrible books that I'd written. Weird thing is? People started saying that they remembered them! I guess it is a real genre that people write, so any time someone said they remembered a book I'd laugh and look all embarrassed and say something like, "Oh nooo, that one was so bad! Paid the bills, though." [laughter] Eventually, I kind of dropped the bit, but by then, I'd gotten a few friends who were interested in just cooking normal things for each other, and a few others who actually liked the pulpy mysteries, and that's how I broke through it.

Ioan: [laughter] That's really clever.

Rosemary: The one time I've been proud of lying, yeah.

Ioan: What would you suggest that others experiencing System Freeze do?

Rosemary: Don't wait for it to solve itself, and don't wear yourself out searching. You can just make whatever interest group you want, and if one exists, just be willing to get folded into it. You won't even have to lie. [laughter] But that's just the start. If you don't actually want to keep up with the inter-

est group long-term, that's fine, your only real goal
is to start meeting people, then things start to thaw.

And so here ey was, hunting down those who had uploaded
specifically for the money that it would leave their families and
friends back phys-side. Their stories were, ey figured, just as
valid as anyone's. They were just as valid as eir own, for had ey
not done the same? Here ey was, interviewing those like emself.

These were the people who had moved to the System out of
some sense of not just a better life for themselves, but one for
those they had left behind. Ioan had had few enough ties back
to eir family phys-side after uploading—only enough to ensure
that the payments had gone through and that eir kid brother
was alright—and then none since then. If any of eir family had
uploaded since then, none had gotten in touch.

Eir hope in undertaking this exercise had been to learn a bit
more about the time between Secession and Launch, about what
had lead to the demographics of a System that had decided to
hurl large portions of itself out into space. Was it something perhaps borne of the sentiment of the population that had grown in
the intervening years? Was it something that had always been
there?

When ey had come up with the list of questions, ey had intended to divine why those who had uploaded had found the
System attractive. Was that, perhaps, what had driven the desire for the launch?

And yet now, it seemed like that was, at most, a secondary
effect.

So much was going on that had gone on before and so many
of the same actors were involved that, although these interviews had been interesting in and of themselves, it seemed
doubtful that such had had any notable affect.

Ioan: How do you feel about the launch project?

Jinzai: [shrugging] It feels largely irrelevant to me. I'm here to help my kids, and if they upload some day, I want to be here for them.

Ioan: Did you send a fork to go along with the launches?

Jinzai: No, I never really felt comfortable with forking. Just me here on the station.

———————————

Ioan: How do you feel about the launch?

Magnús: I don't care. It doesn't matter, does it? It's just this wild-eyed idea that feels like it doesn't have much relevance. I don't remember having any interest in [said in a singsong voice] exploring the galaxy when I was on Earth, and I don't have any now, so why bother? I don't think anyone else did, down there, either.

Ioan: Did you send a fork along with the launches?

Magnús: Never forked before. Never got the hang of it.

———————————

Ioan: How do you feel about the launch?

Rosemary: It felt silly, you know? Like this big, grand idea that some folks get, and it was just kind of one of those things that folks do just to say they can, like going to Mars, or creating their own wild sim.

Ioan: Did you send a fork along with the launches?

Rosemary: Yeah. I figured, "Why not? No harm in going so long as I can stay here, right?"

And so ey went home, back to work on the project, back to receive more updates from the Codrins and the LVs. Back to sit in front of an empty page, considering what it meant that they felt caught up in some storm, some vortex that ey could not see except that the occasional landmark would pass through their field of view, once every two hundred years. Back to sit with May and at least feel comfortable with someone, even if that someone was starting to feel, for some reason ey could not fully understand, as though they were part of that very vortex.

True Name—2124

The next time the Council of Eight met was nearly two weeks after True Name's discussion with Praiseworthy, thanks to a small, artificial delay suggested by the other skunk in order to see how well she could manage buttering up those who needed buttering up, meet with Ir Jonas, and let True Name get used to her new form, her new personality.

When Jonas Prime first saw her after that meeting, he had sat up straight from where he had been lounging on his apartment's couch, pointed his finger at her, and all but shouted, "Perfect! I don't know what you did or how, but it's fucking perfect."

She had laughed, given a bow, and stood up straighter once more. "Glad you approve. I figured if I am going to continue not being a politician, I really ought to look the part."

"I'm surprised you didn't work it in bit by bit, but it'll go over well."

It did, thankfully. When she met with a few of the council members—Debarre and Zeke, thankfully—in order to request the delay on the meeting, they had both complimented her on her looks. She explained it away as wanting try looking 'a little less dumpy', a calculated phrase which had gotten a laugh out of Zeke.

But now, the time had come to actually have the council meeting, which was taking place on a set of benches set alongside the edge of a well manicured pond. The S-R Bloc trio showed up in high-collared coats, hats, and sun-glasses.

"This is utterly ridiculous," Jonas said. "I feel like we're about to start meeting sleeper agents from foreign powers to discuss what intel we've picked up in the last month."

One of the Russians, in a rare sign of outward emotion, grinned broadly. "I thought you of all people would enjoy, Jonas."

"Oh, don't get me wrong, I love it, but it's not exactly subtle."

"We'll just say that we're in the middle of a spy reenactment."

Debarre laughed. "Well, I'm for it. All we're missing is the ducks and a bag of breadcrumbs to feed them."

"This can be arranged," another of the S-R Bloc trio said.

"Another time, perhaps. We can play out the full scene."

"Maybe we can walk and talk for once." True Name gestured down the trail, palm up and hand relaxed as Praiseworthy had instructed—*you do not want to seem stiff, but rather like you are suggesting that you would like to get on with something that was already their idea in the first place.*

It worked well, as the whole council turned on cue and began to walk slowly down the trail. Jonas caught her eye and gave her a wink while the cone of silence settled into place and the meeting began.

"What news on the markets?"

"Nothing particularly new there. We're still tuning the cost of sims, but the model for forking seems to be working well. We got the chance to test it during a recent hardware upgrade."

"How about sensorium messages?"

"Proposal was accepted, and there's an alpha in place. Want to try?"

"Sure, why n– Holy shit! Please don't do that again."

And on and on.

They'd made it about halfway around the pond before the discussion turned to True Name and Jonas.

"Glad to hear the launch is a go. I'm curious to see if there will be any interruptions in service meanwhile."

Jonas shook his head, "Should be smooth sailing. Worst case, we shut down for a few minutes or hours, and then come back online, in which case we won't even notice a thing in here."

"And the bill sounds like it's going well, too," Debarre said. "I'm actually surprised that it isn't a foregone conclusion, too. From what I've been hearing, there's essentially total agreement on the DDR, and most of the governments seem on-board now, too."

It was True Name's turn to nod, and she slid through the sentence smoothly, letting the topic flow into the conversation as gently as Ir Jonas and Praiseworthy had suggested. She just needed to trust that the work had been done, trust in her own abilities. "Yes, it has almost unanimously been accepted, and all we are really waiting on right now is for them to decide whether or not we can be trusted to govern ourselves."

The reaction was precisely what she had hoped: almost nothing at all. There were some nodding of heads, and user11824 just shrugged, as he ususally did.

Excellent, it is already in their minds, she thought. *Just need to keep going.*

Aloud, she said, "We got lucky with our DDR junkie friend, actually. It looks like he has been tapped to help draft the secession amendment that will be added to the bill, though I do not predict any trouble with that passing, either."

Zeke rumbled with a laugh. "They're actually calling it 'secession' now? How delightful."

True Name grinned, watching Jonas laugh along with the bundle of rags. *I must find a way to thank Praiseworthy. That could not have gone better.*

"Hey, if it gets us what we need, then they can call it what they want," Jonas said. "We can govern ourselves, they can govern themselves, and then all these rights arguments become a moot point. The only sticking point seems to be some portions of the S-R Bloc holding onto the idea of dual citizenship."

The trio nodded in unison. "We will be working on that."

"Hell," True Name mused. "We could probably even make a spectacle out of it. If it is to become something important to the entirety of the System, might as well make it a holiday."

"We can even get out the fireworks!" Debarre laughed, the weasel bouncing ahead a few steps to turn and walk backwards in front of the rest of the group. "No need to worry about wildfires or anything."

True Name laughed. "When was the last time you even saw fireworks?"

"Oh, I've never seen them. You were lucky, you had a big fuck-off lake you could launch them off of. It was just farms and orchards around us, so they were illegal."

The skunk smiled inwardly. That the topic of secession had been accepted at face value and slid so easily into joking and chatter was the best she could have hoped for. Even Jonas looked happy.

After to-do items had been handed out and the meeting wound down, Jonas waved to the group and disappeared from the sim. That left True Name five minutes to walk and talk with the others before she would meet up with him, so she spent a few just walking alongside Debarre, talking about the fireworks that she'd watched with their mutual friend during high school, the author of the ode from which she drew her name.

Then she waved her goodbyes as well, and stepped from the spy-park sim to a cafe, the very same one that Michelle/Sasha had visited before she had forked that first time.

"Mocha, right?" Jonas said, handing her a drink and leading her out to a rickety table on the sidewalk, already ensconced in another silent bubble.

"Thank you, yes. Perhaps champagne would be better."

He laughed and fell into the chair opposite her, a motion that somehow managed to ride the border between ungainly and endearing. "We'll get stinking drunk when the bill passes, don't worry. We'll get all of you and all of me together and bust out the champagne, cocaine, and condoms."

"Do not even start," she said, laughing. "I do not sleep with slimy politicians."

"You know, you're going to have to drop that act at some point. You have a speech writer, a styling team, a propagandist-"

"They are all the same instance."

"–and a team of analysts working on both the sys-side and phys-side angles. You, my dear, are one hundred percent a politician now."

"Alright, fine. Just do not tell anyone, okay?"

"Lips are sealed."

She sipped at her mocha and leaned back in the chair, looking out onto the street, people both real and imaginary milling along the sidewalks. "I was thinking today that we may actually be the only politicians on the council."

"How do you figure?"

"Well, Debarre is a friend. A smart one, but I think he mostly got the position by virtue of being associated with me and the lost. The S-R Bloc three are spooks who won't even tell us their names. Zeke is a true-believer; good at what he does but without the faintest thought for how it goes over. user11824 is the opposite. He wears his anonymity like a brand, but does not actually do much."

"And then there's us," Jonas said, nodding. "The ex-WF rep and whatever the hell you are."

"I am just me," True Name mused. "I do not know what that is, precisely, but I am just me. I am no longer Michelle, not by a long shot. I maintain none of that constant state of distraction, none her meekness, and very little of her surplus of empathy. I have lost who she was to become myself."

Jonas nodded. "For the better, I'd say."

"Do you think she was not a good council member?"

"Oh, she was fine. Good ideas. Smart. What she lacked was direction, which you make up in spades."

"I am happy to hear that. Truly." True Name raised her paper coffee cup in a toast to him. "There are some within the clade who have done the opposite, I am told. Praiseworthy has talked to them all, which is very her. Memory Is A Mirror Of Hammered Silver has hardly left Michelle's sim in weeks. She wound up with all of the empathy that I left behind."

Jonas shrugged. "At least someone's keeping Michelle company."

True Name said nothing, simply returning to watching the movement of the shoppers.

"What's next on your list, fuzzy?"

"If you call me 'fuzzy' again, I will dump this coffee over your head and rub it into your perfect fucking hair."

He laughed.

"What is next? Probably keeping in touch with Yared and helping him draft the amendment. I am sure that most of it will be councilor Demma's work, but that he has been given at least partial responsibility means that we will—must—have a hand in it as well."

Ioan Bălan—2325

Ioan's next interview subject was waiting for em at the agreed-upon library in the agreed-upon sim.

The location was grand, as though it had been tailored perfectly to eir tastes: a cube sixty meters on a side, lit brightly by lights so that within shone a smaller cube made entirely of shelves. Shelves containing book after book after book. Spiral staircases wound up each corner, disgorging patrons onto the various levels so that they could meander along balconies and dive into corridors of books. Books, magazines, pamphlets. Scrolls, parchments, leaflets, snippets, chicken-scratch in diaries, words upon words upon words.

And there, on the bottom floor beneath all of the books, a cafe and bar, serving everything from tea and coffee to beer, whiskey, and doubtless some ridiculously fancy cocktails.

"Mx. Ioan Bălan?" The young woman was waiting for em just inside the door to the cube.

Ey held out a hand. "Yes. You must be Sadiah?"

She beamed and bowed to em. "Yes, yes! It is nice to meet you. You'll have to forgive me for not shaking your hand, I don't like being touched. Follow me, though, I've staked out a booth where we can talk."

They wound their way through a small crowd, an array of low couches and tables, and between the coffee and alcohol bars to a high-walled booth in the corner of the seating area.

"Would you like anything to drink before we begin?"

Ioan shrugged, "A tea, perhaps. Too late in the day for coffee, too early for alcohol."

Sadiah nodded. Within a minute, a server brought them two steaming cups of a milky tea—chai, it turned out, and quite good, at that.

Once they'd gotten the obligatory how-are-yous and good-teas and nice-libraries out of the way, Ioan retrieved eir notebook and a pen.

"Thank you for agreeing to meet with me. Your name came recommended to me by several people. I'm glad to get the chance to talk with an actual historian."

Her laugh was clear and bright. "No, thank *you*, Mx. Bălan. I've been looking forward to the chance to meet you for quite some time now."

Ey paused partway through unscrewing the cap of eir pen. "You have?"

"Oh, yes! I've been following your work since the Ode clade project. You somehow manage to distill quite a bit down into a document that is clear and easy to read." She paused, then added, "Documents, I should say. I was lucky enough to get a chance to read the detailed history as well as the investigative journalism piece."

"Really? I had no idea that it had made it out of the clade," ey said, posting the cap on the back of the pen. "I'm pleased to hear that you think so highly of me."

She nodded, grinning widely. "That's why I arranged for us to meet, today. I have lots to talk about, of course, but I wanted to meet you, as well."

Ioan hid an uncomfortable laugh behind a sip of tea. "I'm flattered. You arranged this?"

"Yes! I made friends with a few of yours and encouraged them to suggest that we meet."

"That is quite a strange thing to do." Ey decided to roll with it, scratching out shorthand on eir paper. "Why did you think to do that?"

"Oh, because I'm horrible at actually asking for what I really want, and it's easier for me to ensure that things happen my way instead."

"That's very...well, honest. Thank you for letting me know, at least. What was the reason you wanted to meet me for, then? Beyond just, as you put it, wanting to meet me."

Sadiah sat up straighter in the booth, setting her nearly untouched tea to the side. "Before I answer that, I need to know how much you know, so that I know where to start. Is that okay?"

Ey nodded. The whole encounter was so outside eir experience that ey could think of nothing better to do.

"Stop me when I get to something that you haven't heard or realized yet. Two hundred years ago, the System seceded from the rest of the institutions on Earth. This happened in conjunction with one of the launches for the L_5 station. Secession was organized by the Council of Eight, one of whom was Michelle Hadje, the progenitor of the Ode clade—this is why I was so interested in your work, I'll note. The Ode clade is made up of, nominally, one hundred individual instances, though they occasionally spin off long-running instances and pretend they haven't. The first ten of these instances were created shortly before Secession in order to help handle the workload as Michelle grew tired of her position. With me, so far?"

"Yes, that sounds correct," ey said. Ey figured it was not worth correcting her on the reality of Michelle, of what ey'd seen and heard from May and Dear.

"Okay." Sadiah continued her speech smoothly, sitting almost completely still, as though reciting something from memory. "The Odists were integral to both Secession and Launch, and may have orchestrated both, each in their own way. I see you frowning, which I'll take to mean that I'm getting close to the limits of where our knowledge agrees."

"I suppose, yes. Some of the discussions I've had—my clade

has had, I mean—with Odists have brought much of this to light over the past few days."

"Excellent. Please stop me when I reach the place when our knowledge diverges. The Ode clade, through managing Secession and Launch, has influenced the politics of the System, such as they are, as well as those on Earth, which–"

"Okay. This is new to me, and you're also speaking a little too fast for me to keep up. If you are able to, can you slow down?"

She laughed breathlessly, finally letting her shoulders sag and her chin droop. "Alright, I'll try. Thank you for reminding me, I get excitable, sometimes."

I could tell, ey thought.

"So which part about influencing politics had you not heard before?"

"The bit about influencing politics phys-side." Ey shook eir head, "Which I'm a little confused about. I suppose I can see how that might work, given the communication between sys- and phys-side during both of those occurrences, but–"

"I'll note that we're nearing the extent of my knowledge as well. Sorry, I interrupted." Despite the acknowledgement, she continued, unfazed. "All I can say is that I've noticed patterns. I think you have, too, as mentioned when you frowned, but I am starting to piece together patterns that go beyond that. Yes, they helped with Secession, yes they helped with Launch—more than helped, organized—but that, I think, includes subtle manipulation of politics planet-side in order to ensure that both happened precisely as they wanted."

"Where are you seeing that?"

She cocked her head to the side and waved an arm expansively above the two of them. "It's all there, Mx. Bălan. The news that we received from phys-side shows some of the same patterns that we also see sys-side. The hesitant gestures toward a project, which are suddenly rapidly and smoothly moving forward. You must understand, projects like this do not move smoothly on their own, nor do they change the speed at which they move without some outside influence. That is why we speak of momentum and inertia when it comes to projects as well as forces, yes?"

Ey realized that ey hadn't been writing anything, so ey focused momentarily on jotting some of this information while Sadiah wasn't speaking. Finally, ey said, "How do you picture this influence working?"

"I don't know."

"I can see how the right words in the right ears might help smooth things along, at least. Do you think that might be enough to lead to these changes you're talking about?"

"I don't know," she repeated, a smile tugging at the corner of her mouth.

"Say that the Odists have managed to have a hand in both Secession and Launch," ey continued. Ey did not smile. "What does that get them? What is their motivation?"

"I don't know." She was smiling in earnest now.

"And," ey said, realizing that eir frustration was showing, but was unable to stop it. "What impact does that have on us? Or on Earth?"

"Mx. Bălan," she said, laughing. "I don't know. I don't know! Isn't that exciting in and of itself? I don't know, and that means that we have something interesting to work on. There are patterns here, as you acknowledge, and they may go deeper, or they may not, but that gives us a direction to look, doesn't it? It gives us direction to our questions, doesn't it? You've been asking why people have been staying or leaving. Your cocladists have been asking the same on the launches, I imagine. Those are good questions for boring histories. This is a tenuous question for exciting histories!"

She was waving her arms around now, and the volume of her voice had steadily increased. Ioan was happy for the cone of silence that came with the booth.

"Sadiah, I must ask you to both slow down and lower your voice again," ey said, as calm as ey could manage. "I'm having a hard time keeping up and the shouting is making me anxious."

Startled, she let her shoulders slouch and chin dip once more. "Sorry, Mx. Bălan. Thank you for reminding me again. I don't like touch, you don't like loud noises. *Quid pro quo.*"

Ey didn't think that's quite what that meant. That, or if she did mean it as an actual this-for-that exchange, she was on far more levels of manipulation than ey was comfortable with. This arranged meeting was closer to the Odists' manipulation as she'd described than perhaps even she realized.

"Humor me in at least a few of the questions. Why are you here on the System? If you are also on the LVs, why remain here as well?"

"If the patterns are also showing up planet-side, why on Earth would I leave?" she said, laughing. "Pardon the expression."

"Okay." Ey let the answer flow onto the page in eir shorthand. "And why did you upload in the first place?"

Sadiah sat back suddenly as though slapped, blinking rapidly and tapping at the table anxiously. "I...I don't know."

"You don't?"

"I really don't," she said. She was talking slow and quiet now. Her expression was as scared as her voice was. "I don't know, I don't know."

"Do you remember when, at least?"

"2295, but I don't know why."

"Alright. I feel like I've touched a nerve, for which I apologize. What do you miss most about living phys-side, and what excited you most about moving sys-side?"

At this, the historian—if that's what she was—relaxed. "I was fundamentally unhappy with the limitation of time and just how much research I could do at once, so I came to where I could fork."

Ey nodded and jotted down the answer. "And, last one, what's the first thing that you did after uploading?"

"I don't...I don't know." She looked to be on the verge of tears.

Ioan held up eir hands disarmingly. "Let's end the interview here, I think. I've clearly set you on edge, and you've given me a lot to think about. Is it alright if I get to work on processing this?"

She nodded meekly. The shift in her attitude was so jarring that eir anxiety only spiked higher. This went beyond touching a nerve; it was as though her whole script collapsed and, with it, her sense of self.

"If I have any further questions, I'll be in touch," ey said, sliding out of eir seat in the booth, capping eir pen in the same motion. After a moment's pause, ey added, "And I'd like to ask that you respect my boundaries and not try to engineer another meeting between us, okay? I think that would just stress the both of us out."

Another nod, and then Sadiah either left the sim or quit. Ioan couldn't tell which, because ey was already heading for the exit of the building.

Back at eir house, ey kicked off eir shoes, set eir half completed notes on eir desk, and immediately walked into the bedroom to lay down.

May, ever attuned to eir mood, immediately forked and followed em to the room. "Ioan?"

Ey paused, halfway onto the bed.

"May I join you?"

Ey thought about all of the things Sadiah had said, all of the things ey'd learned about the Odists these last few however many weeks, both on eir own and through eir communications with the Codrins. Ey thought about all of the ways in which, whether or not they were true, this spoke to a level of manipulation that ey'd not suspected before. Ey thought, also, about how truly caught up in it ey was.

And then ey nodded anyway, finished crawling into bed, and let May play with eir hair as ey rested eir head on her lap.

Ey felt helpless to do anything but.

Codrin Bălan#Castor—2325

The initial message from Codrin#Pollux via Ioan had been confusing and had, at first, seemed garbled. The way in which this Ezekiel spoke told of one who struggled with his connection to reality.

All of eir work on the Qoheleth matter had set em in a mind of caution whenever ey saw such struggles. Eir immediate question was always to find out when the individual had uploaded. The complete and total inability to forget anything in the System architecture, that thing which had been the driving factor behind Qoheleth's backwards, inside-out approach to a warning, loomed large whenever ey spoke with someone who had been embedded here for so long.

Then again, that note had also contained an equally unhinged explanation from someone who had uploaded less than forty years ago, so perhaps it was more tied to personality than it was to memory.

While it might not be one and instead be the other, there was always the chance that both might be true, and whenever ey was confronted with the possibility of winding up in such a state emself after centuries, ey would spend hours, days, weeks watching eir every action carefully, interrogating every thought, every word for hints of that disconnect.

It was in that mindset that ey sent a carefully crafted sensorium message to this The Only Time I Know My True Name Is

When I Dream of the Ode clade.

"True Name," ey said, speaking to the observing half of emself who would send the message. "My name is Codrin Bălan, and doubtless you remember my down-tree instance from working with my partner and your cocladist, Dear, some years back. Perhaps you also know of my current project of cataloging the experiences of those who have invested in the Launch to be combined into a history and mythology.

"As I work through the list of possible interviewees compiled by clade, I have had several suggestions from out-clade. In particular, my counterpart on Pollux interviewed an...ex-coworker of yours named Ezekiel. He suggested some avenues for exploration in this project for myself, Codrin#Pollux, and Ioan back on the L₅ System, including a suggestion that I interview you."

Ey cleared eir throat and sat up straighter, feeling suddenly anxious. "If you'd agree to such, I'd like to meet at the place of your choosing to ask you some questions about your feelings on the launch and, if possible, Secession as well. Please feel free to get in touch with me by whatever means you'd like. I look forward to hearing from you. Thank you."

Ey sent the message off and let the speaking instance quit.

"My dear, when you are nervous, you hedge."

The voice of the fox startled em into awareness. "I what?"

"You hedge everything you say," Dear said, padding the rest of the way into the room to rest its paw on eir shoulder. *"If you would agree, place of your choosing, feel free, whatever means you would like."*

"I suppose I do." Ey sighed, resting eir hand atop Dear's paw.

"It is not a bad thing. Not necessarily, at least. However, it can show a lack of confidence in your words, and—you will forgive me for having overheard—with True Name, you will need all of the confidence you can muster."

"Did you–"

The fox's grip on eir shoulder tightened. *"You may ask me*

*your questions when you return. For now, please focus on how you will
ensure that you will maintain a confident bearing."*

Ey nodded, lifting eir head to let Dear bump its nose affec-
tionately to eir forehead. "Thanks, Dear. Maybe I should chug a
glass of wine or someth– Oh, there's the reply. I should head out
soon."

*"Send a fork, then, and walk with me in the prairie meanwhile, or
read with me on the couch, or do literally anything to keep us from
focusing on this."*

" 'Us'?"

It gave a lopsided smile, shrugged, and padded back into the
common area.

Codrin forked off an instance, then followed the fox.

The sim that True Name had specified was a comfortable
apartment several stories up some skyscraper in a city of considerable size. Ey arrived in an entryway that looked out over
a simple living room, sofa against one wall and media station
against the other, hallways splitting off in either direction from
there.

And, in the center of the room, stood a smiling skunk. She
looked friendly without being ebullient, professional without
being prim, confident without being smug. Her shoulders were
straight, expression welcoming, and bearing...willing? Was that
the right word? She looked as though the only possible thought
she had was to help solve every one of Codrin's problems, and
ey saw emself fall for it immediately, as though watching from
above.

"Mx. Bălan?"

Ey smiled. "You must be True Name. Thank you so much for
having me over and being willing to talk."

"Of course," she laughed, and it was gentle, earnest, endearing. "Please! Let us sit down somewhere. Last thing I want is to
leaving you standing around in the entryway."

Ey followed as she padded off down one of the hallways to a
room set up much like an office. There was a desk, topped with

a calendar and a few pads of paper, each covered in notes of a handwriting that was almost-but-not-quite Dear's. It was organized without being uncomfortably neat.

"Now comes the awkward question," she said. "Do I sit across the desk from you, or do I drag my chair around so we can just be more casual? I have never done an interview quite like this before."

"Uh, well," ey stammered. The comment had been delivered so effortlessly that ey felt the need to do whatever it was to accommodate her best. It was then that Dear's nudge toward confidence nudged em, and ey stood up straighter, smiling. "How about across the desk? That'll let me write and gives you access to anything you need."

Giving a hint of a bow, the skunk stepped around the corner of the desk to pull out a stool of the type ey had grown used to, living with a partner in possession of a tail. Ey took the seat opposite and set a dot-pad on eir side of the desk, pulling out eir pen.

"Oh!" True Name looked genuinely surprised. "What a delightful pen! Is it something that you had back before you uploaded, or have you picked up in your time here?"

"Oh, goodness no." Ey laughed. "Nice pens were well out of fashion when I uploaded. I remember reading all about them, though, and so when I got here, I was finally able to indulge myself."

She nodded. "It really is wonderful that all those things we dreamt about phys-side can just be had here, is it not? You may shed a bit of reputation hunting down something very obscure or gain some by making it yourself, *et voilà,* you have precisely the item of your dreams. Anyway, I am rambling. What would you like to talk about?"

Ey felt primed to look for deeper meanings, but was also aware of how prone ey was to ruminating and long silences, so ey simply made a mental note later to dig into that statement about phys- versus sys-side items.

"I have a lot of questions," ey said. "Which seems to be a theme when it comes to interviewing Odists. I don't want to take up too much of your time, though, so I suppose I'd like to start with some about the launches."

"Of course, I would be happy to answer those. Do not worry about my time, though. I will make it with a fork, if only to ensure that you get what you need."

"Thank you, that's very generous of you." Ey tested the nib of eir pen on the corner of the paper. "I'm pretty sure that I know the answer to this, but just to start with, did you invest entirely in the launch or is there an instance of True Name back on the System?"

"Oh, I left an instance behind as well, which I am sure you have guessed. With all the work that we have done on the launch—the Odists and other like-minded individuals—it felt as though it would be a shame to not do so. I understand that you invested entirely here, but Ioan remained behind; I know that this is your interview, but I am also curious as to your reasons on that."

Codrin hesitated, then shrugged. "It was Ioan's idea, actually. Ey suggested that ey remain behind so that, as the one compiling the information, ey didn't wind up adding eir own interpretations before sending the data back, given how far we've diverged. It was Dear's idea, at first, to invest entirely. I'm happy with having done so."

True Name nodded, smiling, and gestured for em to continue.

"Thanks for confirming my suspicions." Ey quelled the desire to add an *I suppose* before continuing, "My next topic is getting a sense of how you feel about the launch. I understand that you helped with much of the early stages of planning, and I'm wondering, do you consider it a success? How do you feel about the speed and ease with which it came together?"

"I very much consider it a success. Many sys-side were on board with it, and those who were not simply did not care. Those phys-side were quite eager to work with us with, only a very small minority who were not.

"As for your second question, I think that that was largely due to this being the first time in nearly two centuries that our two groups have worked together on one goal in any meaningful way. Scientists sys-side consulted with those phys-side on the design of the launch struts and arms. Many sys-side focused on providing a set of goals to be accomplished by the launch, and many phys-side focused on the design of the System replicas, solar sails, and the Dreamer Module."

Codrin nodded as ey jotted down her answer. Ey considered asking her about the sys-side friction regarding the Dreamer Module that Brahe had mentioned, but decided to hold off on bringing up something that might prove contentious just yet.

Instead, ey asked, "You mention that this is the first time in nearly two centuries that the two sides have worked together on something. Can you give me an overview of the types of collaboration that you were a part of or witnessed during Launch?"

She laughed easily. "Is it not strange how we are already speaking of it in a similar way to Secession? I can hear the capital-L in your voice when you speak and you leave the definite article unspoken. But yes, I can tell you about that.

"You doubtless know that quite a few elements of the Ode clade worked on the launch project. My own up-tree instance, May Then My Name Die With Me, was the sys-side launch director. My role, however, was to act as the political liaison between the two entities. There were meetings to be had, tempers to be soothed, knotty problems of jurisdiction to be considered. Did you know that there were discussions as to whether the new LV Systems would be considered as seceding from the L_5 System? It was all very thorny. We eventually decided that the LVs would be considered a joint project with fifty-percent responsibility of sys- and phys-side and their Systems independent colonies. I found it quite silly, but here we are."

Ey chuckled at the suggestion. "I suppose it is a little silly, but then, much of the political side is over my head. Tangentially, and maybe this is a question better asked by Ioan and May Then My Name, I was informed that the launch director physside is actually a distant relative of Michelle Hadje's. You must have been aware of that, given your role, but I'm curious as to your thoughts on having him involved."

"It was a nice bit of serendipity, a Hadje working on Launch just as one worked on Secession."

"I have heard mixed responses on this from the clade, but do you consider yourself a Hadje still?"

True Name sighed, looking genuinely saddened. "No, not any longer. Sometime between Secession and her death, I had diverged too far from Michelle. The last time I merged back with her, it was quite difficult to rectify those conflicts."

"I understand. I apologize for interjecting, though. Do you have further thoughts on Douglas Hadje working phys-side?"

"It was, as I said, serendipitous. When I saw that he had submitted his resume for the position, I was surprised. I do believe he was well qualified for the position, but I ensured that I had a chance to sit in on the hiring committee meetings." Her smile returned, this time a touch mischievous, and she winked to em. "I may or may not have had some conversations with others on the committee to argue his case. It tickled me to have that option crop up during the process."

Ey raised an eyebrow as ey wrote. "Yes? Well, I suppose that is as good a reason to hire someone as any other, if he was qualified and a good fit."

She laughed. "Of course. If he had been a total numbskull, I would not have spoken up for him. Probably distanced myself from him, at that."

"I hesitate to call it 'pulling strings', but did similar opportunities arise during Secession?"

"I do not think so. We still had our phys-side contacts that were alive at the time at that point. We, here, meaning the Coun-

cil of Eight. During the campaign for Secession, we each interacted with those contacts, and many who were interested in
helping us achieve that goal eventually got in touch with us.
They were surprised when we suggested the idea of secession,
but as soon as we explained the reasons why, they quickly got
on board."

"What were your reasons? At the time, I mean."

The skunk shrugged gracefully. "We are just too different.
By virtue of the ways in which the System works, we were not
able to understand each other well enough to interact as members of our prior countries. I was a member of the Western Federation, and when I first uploaded, I technically still was, but of
what use was I to the Western Fed in an uploaded state other
than as a mind who could only interact with the outside world
via text?"

"Did they want you to remain such?"

"Of course. Many of them did, at least. With an increasing
number of their most curious and intelligent minds uploading,
the government was concerned of a brain-drain, such as it were.
If we were still citizens, they could claim that our output was
created under their jurisdiction. That is why it was a campaign
and not just a foregone conclusion."

Codrin nodded as ey wrote, and some part of em realized
just how smoothly the conversation had gone. There were few
times ey could name where confidence had failed em, and it had
instead felt much like any other conversation between friends.

"What was your role in the decision to undertake the launch
project?" ey asked.

She blinked, sat up straighter, and smiled wide. "Oh goodness, did you not know? It was mine from the start. Before she
left, Michelle met with the clade and gave each of the stanzas a
suggestion. They were quite vague, as she was struggling quite a
bit, there at the end. She said, "Do something big. Do something
worthy of us." And so I gave it some thought and remembered
that it had been so long since the two entities had worked to-

gether on a project, and we are already in space, so the idea of Launch came naturally to me."

Ey stopped writing in the middle of a sentence, startled. "Wait. You originated the idea?"

"It was a communal effort from start to end, Codrin, you must understand. I think that many were considering very similar ideas, but I was the first to bring it to the attention to both entities out loud."

Codrin, mastering eir surprise, finished writing eir note. "Well, I suppose I have you to thank for this project as well, then."

Her laugh was musical and genuine. "I am happy to hear that, Mx. Bălan."

"I think that was all the questions that I had prepared," ey said. "Though I was wondering, my cocladist on Pollux mentioned that Michelle's last words were "Do something big, help us divest". Was that just something lost in translation?"

True Name opened her paws in a gesture that was half shrug, half non-acknowledgement. "Which you decide to accept is up to you to incorporate in your work."

Ey was still reeling from the revelation, not to mention the lingering admonition not to push any one Odist too much, so ey decided to leave it there. "It'll give me plenty to put into my report. Do you have anything you'd like to ask me?"

"Only a suggestion. You have doubtless heard of Jonas, yes? Good. Well, I might also suggest that you find an instance of the Jonas clade to talk with. Given the direction of your questions, he will likely have much that will interest you."

Douglas Hadje—2325

Douglas found it strange that, over the next several days, the conversations that he had with May Then My Name and Ioan had amounted to little more than chitchat.

It wasn't that it was unpleasant. May Then My Name had a delightfully weird sense of humor and, though he originally found it difficult to understand, given the text-only nature of the medium, an undeniable sense of empathy that made him immediately feel comfortable around her.

Ioan, too, had proven to be fascinating to talk to. Ey was, as May Then My Name had suggested, the type who spent much of eir time in introspection, the result of which were statements that were as insightful as they were easy to understand. He liked the writer immediately. The two together could be hilarious, informative, somber, and comforting all in one conversation.

They were also very clearly in love with each other, which Douglas found endearing, yet odd for some reason, given how often they referred to each other simply as coworkers. Ioan, especially, seemed either completely unwilling to acknowledge or completely unaware of the dynamic.

Ah well. It was an interesting fact, at least. Interesting in that when Douglas had interacted with couples before, he had often felt like...well, not a third wheel, particularly, so much as someone who simply did not understand the social dynamic at hand. Not so with them.

As enjoyable as all of the conversations were, however, and as much as he was beginning to understand sys-side life, he seemed to gain little in the way of actual knowledge.

At this point, however, his duties had diminished to almost nil, and he had little else to do. Within the year, he suspected that he'd be off looking for another job, hopefully still station-side.

So here he was, sitting on his bed, reading until either May Then My Name or Ioan pinged him.

Tonight, it was Ioan.

> **Ioan Bălan:** Good evening, Douglas. Let me know when you're around.
>
> **Douglas Hadje:** I'm around. How are you, Ioan?
>
> **Ioan:** I'm doing well. And yourself?
>
> **Ioan:** And by the way, it's just me, tonight. May has fallen asleep.
>
> **Ioan:** All of her, actually. It's like the planets aligning sometimes. A bit of blessed quiet.
>
> **Douglas:** I'm alright. Was actually just waiting up to hear from you. Things are pretty boring with no further launch stuff to do.
>
> **Douglas:** Is May Then My Name loud in person?
>
> **Ioan:** Oh, not really. She's just very
>
> **Ioan:** Hmm.
>
> **Ioan:** Intense, is maybe the right word? She doesn't chatter all of the time or run around or anything. Usually, she's just working and she does all of her work mentally rather than on paper. She'll have good conversations with me or with you, putter around, clean or cook, which I realize makes her sound very domestic, which isn't really the case. Those are just things she enjoys.

Ioan: But the whole time that she's doing those things, she's intense. Her expression, her personality, her words, her smile, her laugh, her eyes.

Ioan: That's one of those things that always strikes me as funny. You know, the whole thing about how eyes are just spheres, not actually emotive.

Ioan: But hers are intense.

Douglas: The intensity comes through even in text, so I believe you. So it's nice having a break from that intensity?

Ioan: Yeah, basically. It's nice when we sleep. The time before we head to bed is much calmer. Just a lot of talking and such. She's a very physically affectionate person, which I was not used to at all when she moved in.

Douglas laughed, considered his options, shrugged, and typed his response.

Douglas: That also comes through in text, in a way. You two sound like a cute couple.

Ioan: Huh.

Ioan: You know, I'd never really considered that.

Ioan: 'That' meaning being a couple.

Ioan: I don't know that we are, actually.

Douglas: "Don't know"?

Douglas: Shit, I'm sorry, I didn't mean to presume.

Ioan: It's alright. I also don't know that we aren't. Sometimes the question will come up in my mind and I'll wonder about it a little, but it always slips away and then I'm back to organizing my pen collection or whatever May accuses me of.

Douglas: But you've never talked with her about it?

Ioan: No. Same problem as mentioned above. Every time I think of asking she's already asleep or too busy or I'm out on an interview as #Tracker and then it just slips my mind.

Ioan: You can't be a couple without agreeing that you are, right? So maybe that means we aren't? I have no idea, it's all far above my pay grade.

Douglas: Do you want to be?

Ioan: I definitely don't know that! I'm not really comfortable continuing to talk about this, though.

Douglas: No problem.

Ioan: Needless to say, she's intense. The whole damn clade is.

Douglas: The Ode clade, was it?

Ioan: Yes. Or the Odists if you want something shorter.

Douglas: Can you tell me more about them? They sound fascinating, and I've always wondered.

Ioan: I can tell you a little bit. It's more on her to answer the details. They can be tight-lipped about the weirdest things.

Douglas: Of course. I'm eager to know, but don't want to pry.

Ioan: So, the Ode clade is very old. They've been around for ages. There are quite a few of them. I did a bunch of work with one of them named Dear, Also, The Tree That Was Felled about twenty years back, and that's how I got to know them. We've had an on-again-off-again working relationship.

Ioan: Though, now that I think about it, one of my forks—my only real cocladist—has found emself in a romantic relationship with Dear.

Ioan: You have to understand, though, every single Odist I've met (except maybe one, who isn't around anymore) has been completely and utterly charming, so maybe it's just a them thing.

Ioan: Anyway, They're all incredibly strange, is what I'm saying.

Ioan: Another thing about them is that they are, to a one, magnets for strange goings on. I guess that's part of being strange overall, but even so, every one of them has this incredible story about these events that have happened around them. I don't think it's a conscious thing, necessarily. Just by virtue of their intensity, they live through intense happenings, or have intense friends, or elicit intense reactions from those around them.

Ioan: For example—and this is public information here, now, I don't know if it ever made it phys-side—it was one of them who discovered (or at least was the first who was public about) the fact that those who live sys-side can't ever actually forget things. Instead of simply publishing some sort of report or studying the reality of it, he adopted the persona of a biblical teacher and organized an entire scavenger hunt to try and get the rest of the clade interested.

Douglas: That sounds dramatic.

Ioan: Agreed!

Ioan: I was going to say that they're not really dramatic, just intense, but it's definitely both.

Douglas: Can you tell me about their names? They all seem similar to the snippets of poetry that May Then My Name kept sending me.

Ioan: They're all poetic, I can certainly say that, but that's also a very, very touchy subject for them, enough that Qoheleth, the aforementioned Odist who did the scavenger hunt, the one I mentioned isn't here anymore, was assassinated for trying to divulge information about their names.

Douglas: Assassinated?!

Douglas: That's a thing that can happen, sys-side?

Ioan: Unfortunately, yes. It's rare, thankfully. There are viruses of a sort that interrupt the sys-side mind enough to cause it to lose coherency and just sort of disappear.

Ioan: You told us you still have implants and rigs out there, right? It's like when your avatar crashes, except it's your personality instead.

Douglas: That's absolutely horrifying. I'll go ahead and add that to the bucket of fears right alongside nuclear and biological warfare.

Ioan: Again, they're not at all common, and they by convention have to be tied to a physical object, usually a syringe, so they are visible. They also need to be tailored to the target, which is why we say 'assassination' rather than murder. It's very premeditated and there's no way to prosecute. Any time that someone has considered designing ones that aren't or which are more widespread, there's an incredible backlash. Happens once every twenty years or so.

Douglas: That's not super encouraging, but I'll try not to let it get to me.

Ioan: Well, let's change the subject, then, just to keep it from being anxiety-inducing. I know that May will ask this, so, when do you think you'll upload?

Douglas: Hah, well, I guess she would. I was thinking within a year.

Douglas: My duties are all wrapping up all at once, it feels like, so, maybe when they tell me to get planet-side.

Ioan: I have a suggestion, if you're interested.

Douglas: Oh?

Ioan: Upload on the one-year anniversary of the launch.

Douglas: Why?

Ioan: The Odists are total suckers for symbolism. If you do it on Secession and Launch Day, May will lose her damn mind.

Ioan: In a good way, I mean. You'll get to see it, I'm sure. It's quite the spectacle.

Douglas: It's not a bad idea, actually. I'll pester the commission to ensure that I'm up here for that.

Ioan: Really? You're seriously considering it?

Douglas: If you had left the planning up to me, I'm not sure I'd ever do it. I'd just keep on cycling and worrying and never actually do anything, but give me a little push, and I'll make it happen.

Ioan: I believe it. Keep me in the loop!

Douglas: Should I tell May Then My Name or keep it a surprise?

Ioan: Can you keep it a secret for the next six months or so?

Douglas: Sure, I guess.

Ioan: Great. Please do. I want to see her go nuts.

Ioan: Strange question: you say that you don't start projects without a little push, but you also said that you applied for the launch director position on a whim.

Ioan: Are you sure there was no push for you to apply?

Douglas: Huh.

Douglas: I...will have to think on that and get back to you.

Douglas: Why do you ask?

Ioan: Well.

Ioan: I'm not sure I can tell you without compromising some agreements on my end.

Ioan: With May and the other Odists, I mean.

Ioan: I'll make sure May tells you at some point, though, alright?

Douglas: Sure.

Douglas: I mean, it sounds complicated, but like you say, they're a complicated group.

Douglas: I'll think about it, though, see if I can remember anything.

Ioan: Thanks!

Ioan: May's all sacked out in bed, so I think I'll go join her.

Ioan: Goodnight, Douglas. Sleep well, and keep in touch!

Douglas made his goodbyes and then stretched out on his own bed, still grinning at the idea of Ioan sharing a bed with May and still not knowing whether or not they were in a relationship.

He turned the lights off and rolled enough to pull his covers over him. It'd be early to fall asleep, but it's not like he had much else to do, so he might as well do the same.

Yared Zerezghi—2124

Amendment to referendum 10b30188

The entity known as the System, with regards to its inhabitants, shall hereby secede and become its own self-governing entity.

1. Those who have uploaded to live on the System shall no longer hold their citizenship (sometimes known as "dual citizenship") to their country of origin.
2. The creations of those who have uploaded to live on the System shall henceforth be considered as originating in and governed by the System as a political entity.
3. The System as a self-governing entity shall enter into trade agreements with other governmental entities for goods and services required to maintain the System as a physical entity.
4. The exchange of goods and services between the System and the governmental entity named in the trade agreement shall be binding for those two parties only.
5. The act of uploading to the System shall be considered one of emigration, and regulations

around immigration shall be set only by the System.

6. No governmental entity may set undue barriers to uploading to the System beyond existing expatriation agreements, nor may they intimidate, dissuade, or otherwise hinder citizens from choosing to emigrate.

7. As a separate governmental entity, the System shall be a valid destination for asylum-seekers and refugees regardless of their reasons for seeking such, with regulations for acceptance being set by the System as a self-governing entity.

8. Due to the nature of the System, the following limitations shall be put in place on this governmental entity:

   a. It shall not provide favor to any one governmental entity over another except through the agreements set above.

   b. It shall not enact any trade embargo, tariff, or other restriction on trade against any other governmental entity.

   c. It shall not be able to declare war on any other governmental entity.

   d. No other governmental entity shall declare war on or attempt to destroy the physical elements of the System.

   e. No other governmental entity shall aid or abet another governmental entity to conspire against the System.

9. The physical elements of the System including but not limited to the System hardware, resource infrastructure, and the "Ansible system" required for uploading shall be considered property of the System as a governmental

entity, with the offices containing the "Ansible system" being considered an international zone.

10. The System as a governmental entity shall enact any and all regulations relating to its own governance, which no other governmental entity may hinder.

Sponsors:

Direct Democracy Representative signatory Yared Zerezghi (NEAC) via Direct Democracy Representative, author.

Supervisory government signatory Yosef Demma (NEAC), Councilor.

System-side signatories The Only Time I Know My True Name Is When I Dream of the Ode clade by way of Michelle Hadje (Council of Eight), Councilmember.
Jonas Prime of the Jonas clade by way of Jonas Anderson (Council of Eight), Council-member.

November 28, 2124

The response to the proposal was immediate and dramatic.

Yared had not known what exactly it was that he was expecting, but it certainly was not an immediate division within the DDR, with one half being suddenly and intensely for the referendum and its amendments, each for their own reasons, and the other half being suddenly and intensely against the referendum for completely separate reasons he could not fathom.

It was not that he hadn't expected some division, but the strength of the divisiveness of the amendment itself was alarming. Where once there had been general consensus on the issue of individual rights and the L_5 launch amendment, there was suddenly no guarantee that the referendum itself would actually pass. It had been a foregone conclusion, and now, in the matter of minutes, the entire thing seemed to be crumbling around him, and, with his name attached as author and DDR signatory, he was responsible.

His instinct was to leave. To run. To hide. Some adrenal reaction drove him to back out of the 'net, throw on his cap and nearly sprint from his apartment.

He made it the several blocks up to the useless, wooded patch of ground before he calmed down enough to realize that, not only had he left behind any chance of responding to the flurry of comments on the referendum and its amendment (unless he wanted to use the clunky interface for doing so on his phone), but also any chance of syncing up with True Name and Jonas on the events.

Now here he was, huddling at the base of a scraggly tree like some hunted thing, an animal seeking only to never be seen by unknown predators. Now here he was, completely alone.

And yet he couldn't force himself to rise. Couldn't force himself to get up from his crouching position, couldn't force himself to walk back to his apartment or, really, anywhere else, couldn't even force himself to pull his phone from his pocket and get in touch with...well, who would he even contact? The only one he interacted with in the subject—really, the only one he interacted with offline in any sincere capacity, these last few months—was Councilor Demma.

Given this reaction, that seemed ill-advised.

So he sat for an hour, back pressed against the trunk of the tree, searching for anything he could think of to ground himself.

With a thrill up his spine along the exocortex and a gentle ping from his implants, his phone began to ring. Fears surged within him once again, and a glance at the screen confirmed his fears.

Demma.

"Shit, shit." He stood, paced around the tree in a circle. "Shit. Shit, goddamn."

He stared at his phone for a few long seconds, torn on whether or not to let it simply go to voicemail.

Eventually, that part of his mind lost out to the desire to hopefully find some reassurance, so he tapped at the phone to answer the call.

"Mr. Zerezghi," the councilor said. "Wonderful to hear from you. I was wondering if you had a few moments to talk? We stopped by the coffee shop and knocked at your door, but there was no answer."

"My apologies, councilor. I went for a walk to clear my head. I'm..." He squinted around at the trees, then walked back to the street he'd come up. "I'm at the wooded park area, a ways north of my place. Does your driver know where that is?"

There was a moment's muffled conversation, then, "Of course. We'll meet you on the road, yes? The residential side?"

"Yes. I'll be waiting."

After the click of Demma hanging up, Yared trudged back the way he'd come.

It was a short walk of perhaps only a minute or two, but even so, the car was waiting for him, the driver already standing beside it, waiting to open the door to let him in to talk.

"Yared, wonderful to see you, as always!" Demma said cheerfully. "Please, sit! We have much to talk about. I'm sorry that I was not able to provide our usual coffee, but there's water behind the seat if you'd like."

Settling into the cushy and cold spot that he'd found himself in so many times before, Yared shook his head. "No, thank you. I'm sorry I wasn't at home, I wasn't expecting you."

Demma waved the comment away. "It's alright, quite alright. We probably should have planned better on when to introduce the amendment in order to meet up afterwards, but, well, we knew it was going to be today, so we figured that you'd be ready to meet either way."

"I just...I just needed a walk."

"Burning off some steam? Enjoying some fresh air?"

He fiddled with the hem of his shirt for a moment, then shrugged. "I was a little surprised by the response to the amendment. It was making me anxious, and I stepped away to calm down."

"Of course, of course." Demma leaned forward to pat Yared on the knee before reclining again, looking relaxed, pleased. "I've not been monitoring the DDR myself, but my assistants have been keeping me up to date. It sounds like there's a little bit of an uproar, there. You've certainly touched a nerve."

Yared nodded, numb. He could tell he was dissociating, feeling remote from his own body, yet couldn't do anything to bring himself back to the moment.

"I have some thoughts on the response, both on the DDR and among the various representatives I've talked to, but I'd like to hear your anxieties first, to see if I can soothe them."

"I just wasn't expecting it to blow up in my face like that. There was so much general agreement on the ideas you've suggested. You and Jonas, I mean. I thought that it was all vague and positive enough to seem like the natural conclusion to the ongoing conversation, and it's not like it's the first amendment I've written–"

"Indeed not," Demma said, laughing. "That's part of why we chose you."

"Right. So I'm just not sure why it just all immediately went wrong. There was nothing in there that hadn't already been discussed in the forums, and even on the 'net from governmental types."

The councilor tugged at his chin absentmindedly. "I think that there are a few reasons for that, Mr. Zerezghi. The first is that there were no other co-authors on the bill, so it looked rather sudden. Even if you've been leading the effort quite effectively, and others look up to you, I can imagine that some see it as a power-grab once you'd reached that consensus.

"Another reason is that you used the word 'secede', which is something of a naughty word in many jurisdictions. North America in particular has some quite strong feelings on the matter, given the troubles of the last century. Don't misunderstand me, you had to use it for legislative reasons, but it still spun several people into a panic, particularly in what remains of the United States. Does that make sense?"

"Yes, I suppose, but others were already using it. Respected voices, even. It's not the first time it's come up."

"Of course, but it is the first time it's been put in front of everyone as something they must consider."

Yared frowned. "If that's the case, then perhaps we should have waited for a separate referendum."

"No, I don't think so." Demma smiled, looking very much the kind, grandfatherly type. "Or rather, our analysts didn't think so. They ran several situations through their various models and came to the conclusion that an amendment was the best path forward."

"Why, though? I don't see how introducing something so divisive would lead to anything other than either the entire referendum getting thrown out or, at best, delaying the process for months."

"There may indeed be a small delay as debate kicks up again." Demma nodded toward Yared. "Which we will help you participate in, much as we have up to this point. Still, broaching the idea as an amendment is a good way to get this idea in the forefront of people's minds. They can have the debate with lower pressure on acceptance. They can always vote on the original referendum without passing the amendment, correct?"

Yared nodded.

"So, if that happens, at that point, we can spin it off into its own referendum, and by then, much of the debate will have already taken place, and we can continue to work through the whole process calmly, as we have been." He spread his hands, still smiling. "It is all a matter of risk management, Mr. Zerezghi. You understand."

"I suppose."

"Have you had a chance to speak with Jonas and his strangely named friend yet?"

He shook his head. "Not yet. Like I said, I started to panic and went for my walk."

Demma nodded. "I suggest you do as soon as you get back. I'm curious to hear their opinion on the result of this amendment. I suspect they are equally curious to hear your opinion. Please report back to me what they say, as you have been."

"Alright."

"Now, here are my thoughts on the matter," the councilor said. "I think the amendment will be successful, and I have three reasons why. First of all, the DDR is far easier to send into a fit than you might be giving it credit for. We've watched it for decades now. It has a very short attention span, and dramatic reactions are part of that. Voters will work themselves up into a froth on whatever the current issue is, but there will always be another issue.

"Second, there *will* be another referendum introduced in December. It is already being drafted up in Cairo, and will involve some issue of mid-level consequence, but one that will be of interest to many of the regular DDR voices. You'll have to pardon me for not giving you more information until the referendum is made public, but I can tell you that it will involve both the subcommittees on environment and land management."

Yared blinked. Demma was right, of course, anything to deal with land rights, especially here in the Northeast African Coalition, was bound to draw many of the loudest DDR junkies, himself included.

"Should I take part in that conversation, too?" he asked.

"You can if you'd like, so long as you don't drop your focus on the current referendum completely. I don't imagine you will, given that your name is on an amendment."

He nodded.

"The third reason, however, is that there is more going on behind the scenes on the governmental level than you are privy to. It's often fashionable to ascribe ill intentions to politicians, but that is because they have often borne out when scandals come to light.

"There is nothing scandal-worthy here, but there are still strings to be pulled. The correct hands shaken, the correct babies kissed, the correct promises of support on the correct issues. Some of those strings are the ones that everyone can see: the campaign contributions, the baby-kissing, the promises. Some of them are not, though. Thinly veiled threats, intimidation. Who knows, perhaps even some market meddling."

Yared's baseline frown deepened, to which Demma laughed.

"Politics is politics, my dear Yared. It is a game, as I'm sure you've guessed from your interactions with Jonas, just one with high stakes. When there are high stakes, one must use all the tools at one's disposal, savory or otherwise."

"I understand," he said, still feeling that tension in his shoulders.

Still smiling, Demma soothed, "You have made your own harsh comments, I know. You have questioned your opponent's competency. You have suggested that perhaps others band up against them and nudge them out of the debate. You have the very same toolkit, if only on a smaller scale."

He finally let his shoulders sag.

"So," the councilor said, ticking off on his fingers. "The DDR is easily distracted, an additional distraction will be provided, and politics will be done where required. I promise that you'll quickly see a swing in favor of the amendment. I've promised such in the past, and surely delivered." His voice held a tone of conclusion, as though the conversation was nearing a decisive end.

Yared nodded. "Alright, councilor. I understand. I'm still having a hard time internalizing it, but I'll work on that. Should I expect further instructions?"

"You'll get them, yes, but for now, please enjoy a few days off from the issue. You've done your work for now, let it simmer, and then you can come back to it. I know it'll be hard to do, but I trust you'll find a way. Enjoy good food. Drink good coffee. Talk with good friends." That avuncular smile returned. "You deserve it, Mr. Zerezghi. And, as always, thank you for all of your hard work."

And with that, the driver pulled the door open, and it was back out into the heat of the day for him. The heat of the day, the real world, and hopefully a bit of space from the stress. Hopefully. Hopefully he'd be able to let it go for a few days.

He didn't believe it for a second.

Ioan Bălan—2325

If, Ioan thought, there was a version of Dear's sim—that sprawling, unending shortgrass prairie—that had existed to perfect trees instead of grass, it was this place.

May had told em that Serene had designed this sim, just as she had Dear's prairie. In that sense, it felt much the same; if Serene had any hallmarks of design, it seemed to be a focus on wind and weather, an unerring attention to plant life, and a fondness for the fractal textures of the ground. It was easy enough to design with right angles, flat planes, level ground. As building was something more akin to daydreaming, it was natural landscapes that were the hard ones to get the tiny details correct.

It was no surprise that this sim had been designed for another Odist. Where Dear had fallen in love with the endless prairie and Michelle the flowing fields of dandelion dotted grass, Do I Know God After The End Waking had fallen in love with trees.

When ey first arrived, ey had done so outside of a smallish A-frame building, more tent than anything, for it was built of rough-hewn planks set into the classical shape with an oiled canvas draped over it to create the walls. Even the floor was made of those rough planks, though much of it appeared to have been worn smooth after countless years of foot—or paw—traffic.

Peeking inside revealed a simple cot made of more canvas

stretched over a frame and a pillow of some sort of bundle, a battered roll-top desk with a low stool in front of it (Ioan found emself desperately wanting something similar upon seeing them), and a small wood-burning stove in the back where the far wall had been created using rammed earth instead of more canvas.

Ey immediately fell in love with it, and hoped that ey'd like End Waking well enough to visit again.

He was nowhere to be seen, though. The rundown of his appearance from May was of a skunk like herself, male, and "heavily committed to the ranger aesthetic. Cloak, hatchet, bow, the works".

Ioan sat on the steps in front of the tent and waited, hoping perhaps that ey had simply arrived too early for the scheduled meeting. It was a pleasant wait, at least, and a welcome break from the increasing tension that ey had been feeling within as more and more information about the Odists had come to light. Eir own interviews, as well as news from the Codrins and Dears had left em anxious more often than not, and even though ey did eir best to keep that feeling away from eir interactions with May, there was still no denying that she was an Odist as well.

The skunk's arrival was something of a surprise, as what ey had initially taken to be one of those wandering breezes fingering ferns and branches slowly resolved into a humanoid form walking silently between the trees.

"Mx. Bălan," the form murmured, tugging back the hood that hid most of its face to reveal the familiar white-striped black snout. "Sorry for keeping you waiting. I was exploring."

Ioan stood and bowed politely. "No problem. Exploring, though? I would've thought that you'd know the area around your home fairly well by now."

The skunk smiled. His features were undeniably those of an Odist—at least those of the skunk variety—while still being unique. They were more masculine in a way that ey could not place. More rugged. Dirtier. Certainly more exhausted. "One never truly finishes exploring a forest. I was climbing the trees."

"That sounds enjoyable, at least."

"Not at all." He laughed. "I am terrified of heights."

"Then why–"

"Exploring is a process that is also the goal. Why not undertake that process fully? Surely you know that of us by now."

Ey grinned, nodding. "I suppose I do, at that. Either way, it's nice to meet you."

"Nice to meet you, as well. I would shake your hand, but I am currently quite disgusting." He brushed crushed leaves off his arms and the backs of his hands. "Come, though. I will clean up and make us some tea."

This process took nearly half an hour, during which ey had to remind emself that there was no rush, no reason to hurry. Ey sat on the edge of End Waking's cot while the skunk puttered around the tent, doffing his cloak to leave him in a greenish-brown shirt and canvas leggings that were a brown so dark as to be almost black. He set about filling a small basin with water in which to wash his paws. This used up the last of the water inside, so he had to step out and collect some more from a barrel just outside the door, run it through a cloth filter into a battered kettle, which was set on the stove. The embers had apparently burnt low, so he then had to go collect an armful of firewood from beneath one of the 'eaves' of the tent where it was kept dry and then stoke the fire back up to an intense blaze using some complex set of steps that Ioan could never have understood. Finding the promised tea had required digging through the creaky drawers of the desk to find the fist-sized crock of various dried leaves.

"Lemon balm, mint, and dried gooseberry. I am sorry that I cannot offer anything more exciting. Tea does not grow here."

Ioan laughed. "I've never had either lemon balm or gooseberry, so it sounds exciting to me. It certainly smells delightful."

End Waking beamed at the compliment, and shortly had dug out two enamel camp mugs, blown the dust free from the less-used one, and then tipped a small amount of tea into the bottoms of each. "You will have to strain it through your teeth. I do not have a teapot either. The ingredients are all edible on their own, though, so I usually just wind up eating them."

The whole experience was so delightfully out of place for all of the Odists ey had met so far that Ioan was rapt.

At the end of the extended tea-making procedure, ey was left with a steaming mug of slowly darkening tea, leaves of mint and melissa floating to the top while broken chunks of gooseberry sunk to the bottom. It smelled wonderful, a type of fragrance that immediately made em feel comfortable and soothed.

If May's clade exists to shape the minds and emotions of people, ey thought. *He's doing an admirable job.*

"We will sit and talk for a bit, though I must warn you that I get antsy very easily and will likely request that we walk after we finish our tea."

"Alright," ey said. "I usually write notes on the interviews, but I'm sure I'll remember just fine."

The skunk gave em an unreadable expression, then nodded. "Right, yes. That whole business. Where do you wish to start?"

"Well, I've got some fairly standard questions that I've been asking everyone, then we can get to the more meaty stuff. If we have time afterwards, I'd like to ask you more about this," ey said, gesturing around at the tent, out the still-open flap.

"I will look forward to that, then. It sounds like you have a shit sandwich for me, anyhow."

Ioan laughed. "I'd not heard that term until May used it. I like it."

End Waking grinned toothily.

After taking another sip of the tisane and chewing on the resulting leaves, ey asked, "You're obviously still here on the L_5 System, but did you send a fork along on the LVs?"

He shook his head. "I did not. I am sure you will ask more about why as the questioning goes on, but for now, I'll say that there are some intraclade politics that left a sour taste in my mouth about the whole thing."

"If you're ever uncomfortable with a question, feel free to tell me you'd not like to answer."

End Waking nodded.

"Were you involved in Launch at all? Was that part of the politics?"

"Ioan, I was promised a shit-sandwich, but so far it is an open-faced one," he said, laughing to take the sting out of the words. "I did not. And, to preempt your next question, I had not yet been forked during Secession, so I did not take part in that, either. I was forked a few decades after Secession."

"May I ask why?"

"You may, but give me a second to consider my answer."

A moment was spent sipping tea in silence, only the muffled crackling of the fire in the stove and the breeze testing at the flaps of the tent.

Eventually, the skunk spoke up once more. "From what May Then My Name and others have said, the Bălan clade and the elements of the Ode clade working with them have already reached certain bits of knowledge, so I will be up front about this."

Ioan nodded.

"I was forked in order to help influence financial policies phys-side to encourage certain attitudes toward the System."

Ioan attempted to keep eir face impassive, but ey must have let some of eir reaction show, as End Waking laughed tiredly.

"I am sorry. I am not proud of what I did, and that is why I am here and not out in the world, bowing to the whims of my down-tree instances and their interests. My role was taken over by a member of the Jonas clade."

"I've heard that name several times so far. He's on my list to interview."

The skunk sighed, nodded, sipped his tea. "I suppose he is."

"Do you have any suggestions for what to ask him?"

"No. He will control the interview from start to finish. I am told that one of your cocladists has already interviewed True

Name. If she learned from anyone, it was Jonas. There is no hope of trying to own the interview, no need to try and guide the questions."

"I'll admit that I'm starting to feel in over my head."

End Waking raised his mug toward em in a toast. "We all are, Ioan. Only, you and precious few others realize that now."

"So, I guess for my next question, What does it mean that you influenced the finances phys-side?"

"It was largely a matter of politicking. Strings to pull, ears to whisper into, suggestions made on both the governmental and DDR level. We played them like a finely-tuned instrument, the Odists and the Jonas clade. I would have long, serious talks with politicians; longer, more fun talks with DDR junkies, bless their stupid, stupid hearts. I coordinated with others to help influence sentiment here sys-side, encouraging people to write home and suggest to their families that they consider all of this in a way that aligned with our goals."

"What were your goals?"

The skunk finished his tea and spent a moment fishing all of the leaves and berries from the bottom of his mug to the rim so that he could eat them, as promised. It meant a moment of downtime, during which Ioan sipped eir own tea.

Sitting back and curling his tail absentmindedly into his lap to brush it free of leaves and twigs, End Waking said, "Short term, to lower the cost of uploading and make it seem ever more appealing. Middle-term, the goal was to pass the legislation that led to several governments paying families when an individual uploaded. It started as a sort of subsidy for the lost income, and I think some locales still think of it that way, but it quickly turned into an incentive. Did you have any siblings, Ioan?"

Ey nodded.

"And were you the eldest?"

Ey frowned, nodded again.

"We planted an idea, a subtle one, that it might be a good idea for the eldest child to upload and use the payout to fund a better life for the other children."

"I never heard anyone–"

"This is what I mean by subtle. It was not something anyone really talked about. It was simply a convention that formed over time, and for everyone who followed it, the idea seemed to come to them of their own accord."

"But it didn't. It came from you."

The skunk winced. "Yes, it came from me."

Ioan sighed and, seeing nowhere else to put it, set eir mug on the floor by the bed.

"I feel compelled to repeat that I am not at all proud of what I did. This–" He gestured around. "This is my penance. I live my life in solitude in a place that does not know money, does not know the subtle machinations of politics, and should either of those enter, would not care one bit about them. People think of forests as fragile areas of land, and while this is true, they are also giant—truly enormous—singular entities that do not give a single, solitary fuck about you and your schemes, your thoughts, or your emotions. I have stumbled into ravines. I have had dead branches fall on me. I have gotten caught in land-slides, mud-slides, and flash-floods. I have learned the hard way which plants are safe to eat. I have bled on the land." There was a long pause before he continued, "I hesitate to say that the forest hates me, but it comes perilously close. This is my penance."

They sat in silence for several long minutes while Ioan digested this and End Waking did whatever it was that the penitent architect of eir entire existence here on the System did. Repent, perhaps, but what did that mean in the face of such enormity?

"Let's walk," Ioan finally said.

End Waking visibly brightened and nodded. There was a small unwinding of the previous ritual, where the fire within the stove was banked, the mugs rinsed clean and replaced in their spot, and his cloak donned once more.

They stepped out into the cool, clean air of the onrushing

evening, and the skunk led the writer along a narrow trail worn in the undergrowth, saying, "This is the way that I take to get water when the rain-barrel is empty."

He walked silently, thick tail held high enough to stay above the plants that lined the path, and while Ioan tried to be as graceful as ey could, ey was still a far sight clumsier and noisier than End Waking.

"Why do you like this place?" ey asked. "If it's close to hating you, I mean."

"Do you remember the stanza of your cocladist's parter?"

Ioan dredged up the Ode that was the basis for all of their names and recited slowly:

> That which lives is forever praiseworthy,
> for they, knowing not, provide life in death.
> Dear the wheat and rye under the stars:
> serene; sustained and sustaining.
> Dear, also, the tree that was felled
> which offers heat and warmth in fire.
> What praise we give we give by consuming,
> what gifts we give we give in death,
> what lives we lead we lead in memory,
> and the end of memory lies beneath the roots.

End Waking nodded. He murmured, "I sometimes...no, I often think that I belong to the wrong stanza. This is where I belong. I like her plenty and do not begrudge her the name that she owns, but I wish, sometimes, that I was named And The End Of Memory Lies Beneath The Roots."

Ioan looked around at the trees, the ferns, the carpets of periwinkle and spots of mint and horsepepper and balm, the epiphytes climbing trunks, the moss on stumps.

"I do not think that the author of the Ode meant literally," the skunk said, laughing. "But you share my views on it. While it is not strictly possible on the System, I do hope that one day, the end of memory, that memory of all that I did, lies dead beneath the roots."

A few minutes of silent walking followed as Ioan was guided through a section of, yes, thick roots that threatened to entangle eir feet.

Once they were past that, he continued. "It is important to me that there be something other than politics in the world. I spent so much of my existence shaping the world around me to some grand scheme. Now that I am completely and utterly beholden to the world in turn, it feels relaxing, freeing."

"May said something like that," Ioan said, panting. "That there was freedom in staying behind in a world where not staying behind is the default."

"May Then My Name is the only one of my entire stanza that I like, and certainly the only one that I trust."

Ioan smiled, nodded.

"So many of the Odists are built to manipulate in such complex ways. It is all part of theatre. I am sure that you two have talked about that already. Even May Then My Name is manipulative in her unfailingly kind way." The skunk stopped and stepped aside to let Ioan come stand beside him before a creek at the bottom of a ravine. "It is a very difficult habit to break. Serene is manipulative: this place is built to be loved in spite of its antipathy towards intrusions. Dear is manipulative: its life is one lived bending the experiences of others to its whims in ways far beyond any those of any prior artist as it plays its games. I am a repentant manipulator."

"How so?" ey asked.

End Waking laughed. "Are you impressed with my earnestness? I hope that you are, because I strive to be earnest. Are you impressed with the silence with which I move through the landscape? I hope that you are, it is borne from practice. Were you amused by the absent minded way that I made tea? The way I just puttered around, doing this, then that, as though I kept remembering that I needed first wood, then water, then mugs?"

Ioan tilted eir head. "I suppose. It was endearing."

"A clever ruse left over from long habit. It is a way to be likeable."

"Doesn't everyone want to be likeable, though?"

"Yes. It is a matter of intent, I suppose." He gave a lopsided grin and bumped his shoulder against Ioan's. "But I am being a mopey little shit. Thank you for humoring me."

Ioan laughed. "Of course. It was still a nice conversation, even if it was a stressful topic. And it's a beautiful place to talk, and a beautiful walk."

End Waking nodded. "That it is. I never get tired of it. I wonder if it is still penance if one enjoys it."

"I suppose it can be. It still sounds difficult."

"It is that, too." He leaned down and plucked yellow-green berries from a bush, gathering a small pawful to give to Ioan. "Gooseberries for May Then My Name. Did you have any more questions for me?"

Ioan frowned and accepted the handful of berries carefully, slipping them into a pocket of eir vest after unbuttoning it so that ey would not squish them. "Um, one more, though I am conscious of all the warnings I've received about not pushing anyone hard enough that they'll resent me."

The skunk grinned. "I will not resent you, Ioan. I am trying to shake that habit, and I like you. I just may not answer."

Feeling strangely bashful at the compliment, ey shrugged. "Just that you mentioned your short- and mid-term goals for meddling with finances. What were the long-term goals?"

"Critical mass."

"Critical mass? What do you mean?"

There was a long silence before, rather than answering, End Waking took Ioan by the elbow and guided em back to the trail. "Let us get you back so that the berries are still fresh for May Then My Name."

Codrin Bălan#Pollux—2325

Throughout eir relationship with Dear, Codrin had had chances to meet several other furries, both those who had been in the subculture prior to uploading and those who had come to it after. They had come in various shapes and sizes, the two notable examples of which were a room-filling dragon of some sort (or so ey guessed) and a perfectly ordinary house cat. Perfectly ordinary, that is, except for her heavily inflected and curse-laden speech.

Despite not having the chance to meet him yet, ey had also learned much about Debarre from eir conversations with the various members of the Ode clade, as well as eir research into the Council of Eight.

At one point, ey asked Dear how it was that a full quarter of the council that guided the System toward secession was made up of furries, and the fox had laughed.

"Can you not guess why a furry might be an early and ardent adopter of a system that seems purpose built to allow one to assume what form feels most natural?"

Made sense. Ey still looked forward to meeting Debarre that evening.

What had started as a suggestion to get a few voices together for Codrin to interview had then turned into a suggestion for a dinner party, and from there into what promised to be a cozy, wine-fogged house party that might sprout from a group of friends who enjoyed company, but also quiet.

The guests started arriving in the late afternoon, with the first to arrive being Debarre. Dear greeted him with a grin and a hug before the slender mustelid greeted both of the fox's partners with paw-shakes and half-hugs.

"Wonderful to meet you two. Dear's been gushing about you for years, and I'm only sorry that it's taken until now for us to actually meet."

The weasel was about Dear's height—which was to say a few inches shorter than Codrin—covered with a svelte coat of chestnut brown fur, minus a cream-colored front, though much of this was covered with a semiformal outfit of all black.

As ey did whenever meeting another furry, Codrin was surprised by just how casual they could be. For some reason, eir mind seemed primed to view them all as intense as the fox, but Debarre was friendly and relaxed.

Next to arrive was a...well, Codrin could tell that he was human and that he was male, but for some reason, he had a hard time discerning any distinct features about him. He was plain to the point where the eye seemed to simply slide off of him.

He was greeted with an enthusiastic handshake from Dear, who announced, *"This is user11824, one of the unsung heroes of the early System."*

"I am in no way a hero," he drawled laconically. "I spent more time keeping you dumbasses in check than anything else."

"A truly heroic feat, that."

user11824 rolled his eyes and allowed himself to be guided in to where there was wine and a few trays of snacks. He greeted Debarre warmly—more so, Codrin noticed, than he had Dear, though ey could not guess why.

The final guest was a tall, black gentleman dressed in a plain white tunic and white linen pants, who Dear greeted with a handshake that bordered on delicate. He seemed anxious nearly to the point of panic, so Codrin and Dear's partner simply bowed to him unobtrusively.

Codrin watched the reactions of the other guests, making note of how they both treated him with some mix of deference and awe that ey could not quite place.

Dear's partner explained as Codrin followed them to the kitchen. "That's Yared Zerezghi. If the Odists are to thank for Secession sys-side, he's to thank for it phys-side. He wrote the amendment that formalized Secession among the other physside governments."

Ey stopped halfway through opening a bottle of wine. "Really? I wasn't expecting a dinner full of politicians."

They laughed. "I don't think any of them would call themselves politicians. Dear would call itself an 'interested party' or something similarly vague. I think Debarre would call himself a guide, or maybe a dupe. user11824 would just call himself boring. Get used to that word, he uses it a lot."

"And Yared? He seems, I don't know, nervous."

"He was just a DDR junkie. He followed politics as a hobby, but with a single-minded focus that made him attractive to both phys- and sys-side on the debate." They shrugged and pulled down wine glasses from the cabinet one by one. "I think he'd call himself a pawn. A puppet, maybe. The nervousness stems from being so thoroughly used by both sides and now coming to the house of an Odist, I think, but don't quote me on that. Take these."

Codrin frowned, nodded, and accepted two of the glasses to carry out with the wine, while Dear's partner brought out the other four.

Once the drinks had been poured and passed around, Dear stood and, in the grand style that ey had come to love, declaimed, *"First, we will have a toast, and then we will drink. After that, we will eat, and then—only then, my dear—may you ask your questions."*

Ey laughed and raised eir glass. "I'm in."

"The toast, then!" Dear composed itself, standing up straighter and holding its glass aloft. *"To the complete stupidity*

of anyone unlucky enough to wind up in politics, and the utter hubris of anyone who tries."

Debarre laughed and raised his glass, "I'll drink to that."

"Then, by all means, let us drink," the fox said, and did just that.

The dinner was, as always, delicious: a spicy peanut and bell-pepper soup and a few dishes of beef, vegetables, and lentils. Far more food than was strictly necessary, but Codrin suspected that it was more for Yared's sake than anyone else's, as he calmed down greatly after having eaten (and having had a few glasses of wine), complimenting the food several times. He even began joining in the conversation towards the end of the meal.

Once plates had been cleared and another bottle of wine opened, user11824 nudged Codrin's arm. "How do you put up with such an insufferably boring life?"

Ey grinned, "Dear provides the entertainment, we just watch."

The fox preened.

"Yeah, but you're a writer, Dear's a whatever-the-fuck, and they're a cook and I guess painter. Boring on, like, a subatomic level."

"Boring is nice, sometimes," Dear's partner said.

"Oh god, you're telling me," user11824 laughed. "I'd never turn it down. Excitement always means that something horrible is happening."

"You know," Debarre said, nodding to the ill-defined man. "I think that's the first time you've ever actually explained that when I've been around. I always just thought you were bitching whenever we went somewhere or had a conversation and you called it boring."

"If we're somewhere exciting or a conversation is actively interesting, it means that someone's fucked up."

Dear laughed. *"It is important to fuck up, my friend. Otherwise, the boredom may become terminal."*

He rolled his eyes and mumbled, "Fucking boring."

Even Yared was grinning at the exchange. "You know, before I uploaded, I was in contact with a few members of the Council," he said. "And although the work was interesting, I always loved hearing about the ways in which dynamics differed sys-side."

"Oh, I guarantee you, I was just as bored phys-side."

"Yes, but look at you. You've made being boring into an art. You went ahead and made it interesting."

"Bullshit."

Codrin laughed. "No, I'm with Yared on this. You've got a name that sounds like a default 'net username, and you've somehow made it so that I can't seem to describe any one aspect of you. You've got a face, I can say that for sure. Your eyes are brown. Or maybe hazel? It's like if I tried to look more closely to figure out which, though, I'd absolutely die of boredom."

He laughed. "Job well done, I say."

Dear raised its glass, *"To artists who have perfected their craft."*

Figuring that, since dinner had come to a close, Codrin hazarded the first question. "Yared, you said you were in contact with a few members of the council. Who were you talking with?"

"No one here," he grumbled. "Well, mostly. One of Dear's clade and Jonas. If either of them were invited, I never would've come."

"Me either," Debarre said.

"Same." user11824 shrugged. "Though I'd be surprised if Dear had invited them."

"Quite," the fox said curtly.

Debarre looked sheepishly at the fox, ears splayed. "Sorry, Dear. I know you've distanced yourself from all that."

"They were interesting," user11824 said. "And I can't think of anything worse."

Codrin redirected the conversation. "That aside, then, when did you upload, Yared? Or any of you, I guess."

"I uploaded Secession day. Literally about an hour before Secession itself. I was the last upload before it took effect. An 'honor' they called it."

Codrin nodded, looked to Debarre.

"The same day as Dear," Debarre said.

"What? Was that planned?"

The weasel laughed. "Oh yes. Michelle and I pooled our money to upload as soon as we could."

"You were friends before, then?"

Dear nodded. *"We went through a lot together."*

Codrin was tempted to ask if Debarre had also known the author of the Ode, but knew that that went well beyond dinner-wrecking. Instead, ey looked to user11824.

"I dunno. 2120? It was an exciting time, and I've done my best to forget about it."

"About what percentage of your time on council was exciting?" Debarre asked.

"More than I would've liked."

Dear's partner laughed. "Why'd you even join, then?"

"Mom was a politician," he said, shrugging. "I learned all that bullshit from her, and the S-R Bloc gang pressed me into joining."

"Who were they?" Codrin asked.

"There were three of them on the Council. Part of the initial agreement, since the System was originally hosted somewhere in Russia." Debarre counted off on his fingers. "Those three, me, user11824, Zeke, and then Michelle and Jonas."

"Well, I know the Odists are here on the LVs, as well as you two and Ezekiel. Are Jonas and the Russians here?"

user11824 frowned. "That's an interesting question."

"That's a bad thing, isn't it?"

"Jonas is on the LVs, yes. The S-R Bloc trio are no longer on the System." Dear swirled its wine in its glass. *"Ask a different question, my dear."*

Codrin nodded. "Alright. Were any of the rest of you involved in Launch as well as Secession?"

Debarre snorted and shook his head. "No, thank God. I had my fill, and I was glad when the Council dissolved."

"What happened to dissolve it?"

He looked to Dear, who shrugged. "After a while, it was just Odists and Jonases," he said down to his wine glass. "Any possible guidance the Council could have provided would have come from them even if we had said it. It had been so thoroughly undermined that we all basically gave up and let the thing end rather than artificially prolonging a puppet government."

"We were terrible people, yes." Dear's shoulders slumped. *"I am quite glad that I had not yet been forked for that. If I had had any direct participation in all that happened, I doubt that I would be sitting here with you all."*

Yared spoke up next. "I didn't have anything to do with the launch effort. I dropped politics like a bad habit as soon as I saw the direction in which the Council was heading. That said, I couldn't help but learn all I could about it, read every memo I could, learn about some of the physics of it. I was just done with being an active participant."

"Why is that?" Codrin asked.

Yared turned his wine glass between his fingertips for a moment, simply thinking. "How much do you know about Christianity?" he asked.

Ey must have looked quite confused at the question, as Dear giggled.

"I promise I'm going somewhere with this," Yared said, grinning nervously.

"You can actually blame me for this, my dear. I helped him come up with the correlation he is about to use."

Codrin said, "I mean, I know the basic precepts. Some of the history, that sort of thing."

"And Judaism?"

"Uh, probably much less. I know that Jesus was a Jew."

"Okay, that's enough to at least make this point. You know that Jesus had his apostles and that one of them, at least later on, was Paul, who converted on the road to Damascus and became a fervent believer. He started churches up all over the region."

Ey nodded. "I know of Paul, yeah."

"Good. Well, the story goes that there was an argument about whether or not gentiles were allowed in the early Christian church, as Paul argued, or whether they needed to convert to Judaism first."

"And we know that Paul won that debate."

Yared nodded. "Yes. As soon as it was decided that anyone could become a Christian without becoming a Jew, Christianity effectively became its own religion, not beholden to the laws of Judaism."

"I can kind of see where this is going," Codrin said slowly. "Secession is rather like the point at which the System effectively became its own country."

"Bear with me. What your partner showed me was an alternate telling of this story. Sometime back in medieval Europe, a Jewish community started circulating an old story called 'Toledot Yeshu', which means something like the ancestry or generations of Jesus. Much of it is a retelling of the gospels with Jesus as a trickster magician. But Paul in this story becomes something more interesting, apologies to present company."

user11824 rolled his eyes and finished his wine.

"In Toledot Yeshu, Paul is actually hinted at being a plant from the Jewish authorities, though it is vague as to who, whose goal was to introduces enough changes to the budding religion to cause it to split away so that it wouldn't remain a sect of Judaism."

"*Many viewed Jesus as a rabbi,*" Dear interjected. "*And had that lasted to the point where Judaism headed into a rabbinical tradition, his teachings would have become part of the faith and Judaism would have looked very different.*"

Codrin frowned. "Are you suggesting that Secession was engineered to keep the System from remaining a part of society, phys-side?"

There was a tense moment of silence before Yared nodded. "I was the tool of Paul. I was the tool of *two* Pauls, one in the form of a representative of the phys-side government who used me to steer public opinion toward permitting Secession, and one in the form of True Name and Jonas who wanted the System to be independent for their own reasons. It was not enough to ensure the System's continued existence for them and it was not enough for the System's participation to be limited from the phys-side point of view. It needed to become its own entity."

All eyes were on Yared now, who sighed. "It needed to become its own entity by any means necessary, as soon as possible, and with as much plausible deniability as could be managed."

"Both sides wanted to preserve a way of life, and so differences were magnified to the point where Secession was inevitable," Dear said quietly. *"And so here we are, a completely separate entity, and we all thought it was our own idea. It is not some supercessionist nonsense, no matter what True Name and Jonas might have you believe. We all just wanted to live our best lives, and we all were made to believe that this was best solution for that."*

Codrin finished eir wine and set the glass aside. "So you stayed away from the politics of Launch because you didn't want to become another tool of Paul."

Yared nodded.

Debarre said, "We all were, towards the end. Anyone who was a true believer in Secession was a tool for True Name and Jonas, in a way, or at least a potential tool."

"This was not what I was expecting out of the evening," Codrin admitted. "I was going to just ask you all why you decided to join the launch and everything."

user11824 laughed. "New place to be bored, is all."

"Congrats on finding the interesting stuff," Dear's partner said.

There were a few minutes of silence as everyone worked, in their own ways, to digest the information that had been shared.

Finally, Debarre spoke up. "I'm happy that I'm still in touch with Dear and a few other Odists all the same. Michelle is gone, but a lot of the good that was in her is still around. Man, I had no idea how thoroughly she was split, though, that those who are nice can be so nice, and those who aren't can somehow completely lack all that made her good."

Dear raised its glass to Debarre for a third toast of the evening. *"To her, to you, and to two hundred and thirty years of friendship."*

"To lost friends," Debarre added.

They all watched as Dear and Debarre drank to each other and those who were gone.

True Name—2124

True Name was early to her meeting, and that, she figured was okay. On a whim, she had picked, the same pub that she'd met Jonas in some time back, the one that reminded her of The Crown Pub from years ago, with the flat beer and the uncomfortable booths. She figured that Debarre, of all people, would appreciate this.

She ordered herself one of those beers that she loved to hate, sat down in a corner booth with a commanding view of the entrance, tail flopped over the edge, and waited.

While she waited, she thought about all of the different reasons that Debarre might have asked to meet. There was always the possibility that the weasel had figured out just how deep she and Jonas had gotten in their work, though she suspected that that wasn't the case. Debarre was smart, yes, but political adroitness was not his strong suit. That had been the root of the worry—shared by him—that he had been let onto the council merely by his proximity to Michelle and connection with the lost.

It could also be that he had further questions about why it was that Michelle had chosen the Ode as a clade scheme, and that perhaps he wanted to discuss why it was that all of the clade seemed so averse to mentioning the author of the poem.

And, as she hoped, he could simply just want to hang out. Spend time together like friends, like they used to.

With that in mind, she focused on composing herself into a state of friendly alertness, so that when the weasel walked into the pub and spotted her in the corner, she would be primed to guide him toward that last possibility, even if he had come expecting the first two.

She watched him step inside, look around, and immediately laugh. After picking up a cider at the bar, he made his way over to the booth she'd picked and plopped down across from her.

"Cheeky choice," he said, grinning.

True Name laughed, shrugged. "What can I say? I was feeling nostalgic for terrible beer."

"Cheers to that." He lifted his glass to hers, clinked the rims, and took a long sip. "So, how've you been, skunk?"

Small talk was not a guarantee that this was simply a social visit, but given the tone of his voice, she doubted that anything too heavy was on the table.

"Pretty good, actually." She smiled. "Things are going well on the legislative front, phys-side, which is good. It makes my job easier. Who knows, may even take a vacation."

"Oh man, a vacation sounds good, though God knows what I'd do. Probably just sit on my tail all day and get fat on the greasiest food I can find."

"Feeling the workload, then?"

He shrugged. "Not particularly, no. It's just that I'm starting to wonder just how cut out for politics I really am. I haven't the faintest idea on how to get people to do things without sounding like I'm bullying them, and I'm not going to put all the work into it that you have. You and yours, I mean."

"Yeah, it is no small amount of effort," the skunk said. "But it will be worth it in the end, I think. Plus, I figure that once we secede and the launch goes off successfully, we can probably just sit back and let things run themselves. No one has managed to cause any problems that cannot be solved by them simply having the fistfight that they so desperately crave."

Debarre laughed and shook his head. "You gotten in any of those lately?"

"Thankfully not," she said, grinning toothily. "I do not expect to, though."

They drank a moment in silence, each of them peering around the pub, each thinking their thoughts.

"How are you, Debarre?" True Name finally asked. "Aside from work, I mean. I know that we have not had much of a chance to just sit and talk, recently."

The weasel doodled lazily on the tabletop with a claw. "For all my bitching, I'm doing alright, actually. That's why I wanted to meet, though. Just catch up."

True Name smiled. *Perfect.*

"You know," he said. "I was thinking about Cicero a few days back, and how, after he hung himself, I thought that the grief would never end. Like, I thought that I had been completely redefined from 'Debarre the weasel' to 'Debarre who grieves', and that's just who I was from then on out."

She hid a sudden surge of emotion behind a sip of her flat beer, nodding. "It was hard. Both of those losses were hard."

Debarre nodded. After the reference to both losses, he seemed on guard, or ready to jump out of the booth at a moment's notice.

"I am sorry that I snapped at you a while back," she said, reaching out to pat at the paw that had been poking absently at the grime on the tabletop. "That is a name that I would like to keep close to my heart and prefer not to say out loud. Also, given that ey was not strictly supposed to defect to the S-R Bloc, it still feels risky. The spooks *definitely* should not hear it."

"I get that," the weasel said. He had relaxed, but not all the way.

"And I think that I understand what you are getting at," she continued, turning her default smile into something wistful, something sad. "I am as at risk of letting grief define me as anyone, but I am still doing my best to memorialize rather than languish."

"That's good, at least," he said, finally smiling back to her. "I've been a bit worried about that, if I'm honest, but I trust you. The shit you've been pulling off lately with the council is honestly impressive, True Name. You and all your clade. I'm doing my best to understand you, sure, but I promise that's out of awe rather than fear."

She laughed, raising her glass to him. "Well, thank you. I am glad that Sasha was able to take a step back and get the rest that she so richly deserves, just as I am glad that she left me with my own *raison d'etre*. I *like* all of the shit that I have been pulling off. It feels good to accomplish stuff."

"Good! That's good to hear. It's sort of what I'd picked up on, too. I'm not sure that I was doubting you before, necessarily, but having watched you these past few weeks, I don't know." He grinned and finally returned the patting gesture in turn. "I get it, now. You're not Sasha, that's for sure, but you're not *not* her, and I see all of the best things I liked about her in you and the few others in the Ode clade that I've met."

They beamed at each other, all bristled whiskers and perked-up ears.

The conversation wound around for a while longer, with talk of plans and memories, likes and dislikes, gossip and news. True Name allowed herself to earnestly enjoy the afternoon, now that any concerns that she might have had about the meeting had been assuaged.

Eventually, they made their goodbyes and she left the sim, allowing herself to sober up in the process in order to make the next meeting on her agenda.

For some reason that she couldn't fathom, Life Breeds Life But Death Must Now Be Chosen had chosen to incarnate himself as a scholarly gentlemen, somewhere between respectable and nerdy. It was a good look, she thought, but what train of thoughts had led him to head down that route from Michelle evaded her.

After a pleasant greeting in the lobby of the library, they wound their way up the spiral staircases to the law section, three levels up. There was no particular reason that they needed to head there, other than the fact that it was liable to be fairly empty—few had to read up on phys-side laws, here—and would still be a comfortable place for them to walk and talk.

"So," Life Breeds Life said, once pleasantries were out of the way and the cone of silence had been set up. "Why did you want to meet today?"

"During discussions with Praiseworthy and Ir Jonas, I started to realize that there were some steps that I might need to take when it comes to the historical view of the clade. There is already the forceful de-emphasizing of AwDae's name, thanks to Praiseworthy. She thought it a good hook, and it has already proven its utility. None of us want it out in the open, anyway. I guess, given your interest in history and memory, you seemed like the most likely to be interested in helping continue that effort."

He grinned. "You guess correctly. I have been considering some aspects of that, as it is. Before I go off on that, however, I would like to hear your ideas."

True Name nodded, lazily brushing fingerpads over the spines of law books and case files. "Firstly, there are some aspects of the clade that I would like to remain within the clade. The Name is an obvious example, but I would also like to keep the impact that we have had within the Council minimized to a level more believable for Michelle's initially stated goal."

"To confirm," he said, looking thoughtful. "You want to ensure that it appears that each of us did a tenth of the work that she was doing previously and that our voice was only as loud as any other council-member's. Correct?"

She nodded.

"That should be doable."

"It will require a bit of fudging, at least for myself, as to how many instances actually exist for the clade. I believe that it would reflect poorly on us to say that we were initially ten, and then for someone to dig up that I had already forked three or four times less than a year after Michelle's decision."

His laugh was kind. "Oh, good. I am glad that I am not the only one."

"Not by a long shot," True Name said. "It seemed like a good thing to downplay."

"Yes, it is, come to think of it. There are enough concerns about capacity as is. It might seem as though we were already aiming to test that so early on."

"Mmhm. The second thing that I was thinking was more of a question for you."

Life Breeds Life nodded.

"How far in the future do you think we should be considering these changes?"

The answer was immediate. "Centuries."

True Name frowned. "Really?"

"Yes. There are some that we can do right away, but those steps are more in Praiseworthy's court: downplay the number of instances, minimizing our perceived role on the Council, *et cetera.* The aspects that are in my jurisdiction, however, are ones that will take years and decades to form. Histories written after the fact bear the weight of having undergone analysis, the shifting of public knowledge—at least, what they think they know—takes place over months and years. Time is on our side, though, as you well know."

"Of course."

"That is not to say that I will not start right away, of course," he said, laughing.

"Oh, I do not doubt you will." She grinned. "What were your thoughts, though? You mentioned having some changes that you would like addressed as well."

"Yes. I would like to eventually downplay the role of the Council of Eight in history to the point where those sys-side simply think of those who helped out in the early days as founders, dreamers, and idealists."

True Name stopped in the aisle, letting Life Breeds Life step ahead and turn to face her. "You would like the System to forget that there was a council?"

"It is a way to build a mythos and identity, yes. It allows us to use the words 'freedom' and 'secession' and so on in a collective sense, as though these were the decisions of all, rather than a few. It will instill a sense of patriotism, if one could call it such a thing, for being sys-side, which will in turn reduce the connections that many feel to phys-side." He smiled, tugging a book from the shelf at random and flipping through the pages. "This will not happen for this generation. Nor, likely, the next. The goal for future generations, though is to ensure that they feel that the System is a place to live rather than a place where they wound up, or a place that they uploaded to simply because it was convenient or necessary, or even a place that they uploaded to simply for the way life works here, whether it be immortality or the sheer hedonistic joy of it."

The skunk watched the pages flip beneath Life Breeds Life's fingers and thought. To downplay the council would be to minimize the work of years, of almost a decade. The other members might rankle, but she was pleasantly surprised at how comfortable an idea it was. It would gain her and Jonas much needed room to maneuver.

Eventually she nodded, saying, "That makes sense, yes. If the concept of the Council disappears into foggy memories and untrustworthy histories, then any attempts to lead again will seem out of place, too. It will give Jonas and I more latitude to continue working long term."

"Precisely." He replaced the book on the shelf. "Down the line, too, I am considering suggesting that we say that we uploaded after Secession. Say in the thirties. Not far enough to be an obvious lie, but enough distance from it to give us the space to act as we must now so that we can act as we will later."

True Name felt the smile grow on her face, earnest and excited. "Excellent. Excellent thinking. Keep me up to date as you go, though I do not expect the updates to come all that quickly."

Life Breeds Life laughed. "Of course not. If we are to think long term, we must think in terms of decades to work in centuries. If we are lucky, we must think in terms of centuries to work in millennia. We have plenty of time."

Codrin Bălan#Castor—2325

While he didn't quite have the singular ability to immediately make em like him as many of the Odists seemed to, Codrin found emself immensely charmed by No Jonas.

"I got the short end of the stick." He laughed, gesturing Ioan into what appeared to be a living room of an apartment quite similar to the one ey had interviewed True Name in. A little less perfect, a little more lived-in. "Jonas Prime decided to name all of his instances with a syllable, I got stuck with No, of all things. I'm sure there are sillier ones, at least. We Jonas? Oi Jonas? Just call me Jonas so we don't get confused."

Codrin grinned and sat on a reasonably comfy—if slightly ratty—chair across the table from the couch that Jonas flopped down onto. "I suppose there has to be some scheme for dispersionistas to use to keep track of each other that isn't just the default random string of letters and number."

"Of course! You know the Odists. I should've done something like that. Take an old rock song and name myself after each of the lines." He shrugged. "But no, I think they've got a lock on that idea. This one's inventive enough without being too annoying. Usually."

"They do pull it off quite well," ey said, pulling out eir pen and paper. "Though some of their short names work better than others. I like Dear, and I think True Name works well as a...well, name."

"Oh? Did you talk with her?"

"Yes, she was the last Odist I interviewed, actually. At least, here on Castor. The Codrin on Pollux is interviewing others, and my down-tree instance on the System is taking yet another path. This way, we get a good spread while transmission times are short."

"How is Ioan, by the way?" Jonas asked, winking at Codrin. It was a sly enough way to let em know that he'd done his reading.

"Oh, well enough. We've all been stressed in our own ways."

"I'm sorry to hear that. I'm curious, though, in what ways do your stresses differ?"

Codrin tilted eir head. "Well, Codrin#Pollux recently had a dinner party with some other Secession-era people. Some from the Council of Eight, and a Yared Zerezghi, who was apparently important phys-side."

"Ah!" Jonas said, grinning. "How is Yared? Though I guess you weren't there."

"He sounded alright. He told a story about how he worked with politicians both here and phys-side." *About you and True Name,* Codrin thought to emself.

"We spent a lot of time working together, yeah. Nice guy. Did Codrin#Pollux have much to say about Debarre and user11824?"

Ey froze in the middle of eir note-taking.

Jonas held up his hands. "Just a guess. Ezekiel never leaves his border of Jerusalem, the Russians are gone, and I doubt Dear would've let True Name visit."

"Good guess, then. They all certainly sound interesting. Debarre seems nice, user11824 seems weird. Ey also talked to me about eir interview with Ezekiel, which was apparently quite prophetic."

Jonas laughed.

"And Ioan is getting hounded by strange historians while also doing eir best to keep up with interviewing the Odists." Ey hesitated, considering whether to pass on the warning that Ioan had received from End Waking, then decided to plow ahead.

"One of them told em to be careful interviewing you, that you'd control the whole thing."

"Did he now? Well, I suppose I will. It's one of those second nature things, you know. I apologize if that sounds sinister, I promise it isn't. I do as Jonases do, just as you do as Bălans do, and that is to speak to the things that interest me. I'm just better than others at ensuring that that happens."

Codrin nodded as ey wrote. "Alright. Are you okay if I start asking questions, then?"

"Of course, ask away."

"First of all, and I'm not sure how well this applies to a dispersionista such as yourself, but did you—No Jonas—leave an instance back on the L₅ System?"

"Oh, sure. There didn't seem to be any reason not to, you know? I figure there's enough of us Jonases up here to have our fun, and plenty back down on the System to keep things interesting."

"Did any of you invest entirely in the Launch?"

"Yeah, a few of the A branch did. And before you ask, plenty stayed behind, too. It was all pretty well organized. We figured out who was doing what and then followed the plan."

"Was there any particular rhyme or reason to it?"

Jonas waved a hand vaguely. "Basically just who was specializing in what."

"Was there any danger for those who specialized in stuff back on the System coming up here?" ey asked.

"Terminal boredom?" He laughed. "Really, though, there's stuff that needs doing there and it's better to be efficient."

"Do you think they'll miss the excitement of the journey?"

"We all have our jobs to do, Codrin. System politics aren't like those back phys-side. There's no reason to slack off and not do your job just to have some fun when you can send a fork to do the same for you and then enjoy all those memories, right? No3 Jonas is out on a date right now, actually."

Codrin nodded as ey jotted down the answer. "I suppose it's

the same as with me and Ioan. At least to an extent, the Odists also infected us with their hopeless romanticism."

"Of course they did. That's what they're built for. A life in theatre primes one to keep a tight focus on manipulating emotions. They're all incredibly focused on stories, aren't they? All of the interesting ones, at least."

"There are boring Odists?"

Jonas shrugged. "Michelle and Sasha were boring. Those who stuck around with her or focused on their little art projects, they were pretty boring."

Codrin frowned.

"Don't get me wrong, of course. I like them all! Delightful, to the last, but I'm the dangerous politician, remember? All those I find interesting are the ones who tickle all my politician instincts. It wasn't an insult."

"Alright," ey said, quelling a low rise of anger; after all, if Dear was anything, it was one keenly focused on its art projects. "Either way, thanks for answering. The next question I had was about your involvement with both Secession and Launch. Were you involved in both?"

"Oh, more heavily in Launch than Secession. I was forked slightly after Secession, but there was still work to be done. I did a lot of wrangling of notes, data collection, stuff like that. For Launch, I did the same, just front-loaded. It's some of the boring work that goes into politics, but work that still needs to be done."

"And in between the two?"

For the first time since the interview, Jonas grinned in earnest. It was writ so plain across his face that the shift cast all of the previous smiles in doubt. "You've been getting some interesting answers to your questions, haven't you, Codrin? All of the Bălan clade has, I mean."

"Why do you ask?" ey said, digging eir heels to keep from being dragged into a defensive stance.

"You got to that question surprisingly fast."

Codrin nodded, waiting Jonas out.

"Between Secession and Launch, I was pretty boring. I did some data collection for some of the other work that was going on. Phys-side is always changing, beholden as they are to the whims of Earth and the restrictions of being tied to a single body in a single location."

"So you followed that? Kept up on the data gathering?"

He nodded. "Yeah, that was my area of focus. Some of the others were digging around sys-side, but life changes much more slowly here without those external factors. We kept on working with the Odists, too, as I'm sure you've heard. There was much to do."

"It certainly sounds like. Did you or your clade guide much beyond Secession and Launch? I know that there was some work done surrounding the finances of uploading in the mid to late 2100s. Were there other areas of activity?"

Jonas leaned back against the couch, toying with a loose thread at one end of it with his fingers. "Here and there, yeah, but I'm not really the person to ask about that. I'm sure one of you will get into it with True Name, or maybe even snag some time with Jonas Prime."

Codrin nodded and made a note to that effect.

"You have to understand though, Codrin, none of this was like some sort of shadowy conspiracy, like you may be thinking. We did what politicians do: we represented our constituents and duked it out—metaphorically, of course—with other politicians."

"Are we your constituents?" ey asked. The words were out of eir mouth before ey had time to consider it.

Jonas laughed, shaking his head and tugging that fiber on the couch all the looser. "In a way, yes. We may be a separate legal entity, but we don't work the same. We're not a government. There are no representatives. We don't vote. Better to say that the System is our singular constituent. You are our constituents only in the sense that there are still some who have to work on keeping the System going. We're the ones who organize with the phys-side engineers to keep everything ticking along. We're the ones who ensure that new uploads are smoothly integrated. We're the ones who ensure that the System keeps growing."

"Keeps growing? Can you expand on that?"

"It's nothing complex. The larger a system—that's system with a lower-case 's'—is, the more stable it is because it tends towards stasis. This applies to political systems, as well. The Western Fed and the S-R Bloc kept their stalemate for God knows how long because they were too large to do anything but, and the only reason they stopped was that they were each subsumed into even larger political entities."

"So, if I'm understanding you right, keeping the population of the System growing over time–"

"Not just the population," Jonas interrupted. "The capacity. The complexity."

"–the more stable it is because it tends toward stasis?"

"You put it more succinctly than I did."

Codrin waggled eir pen at Jonas. "I'm the writer out of the two of us, you're the politician. What do you mean by stasis, though?"

"If we were phys-side, conservatism would probably be the word one would reach for, if only because the sheer burden of legislation grows exponentially complex with the size of the small-s system that all of the other aspects of the system start to fall under its branch.

"Here, though, we tend towards stasis. It's a type of stability that implies a cessation of change. It's not a bad thing. Boring, maybe, but boring is safe. Still, it's only a tendency, and it approaches that point asymptotically. The bigger the system, the smoother things run because the rough spots and sharp edges are harder to feel. It needs to be gardened and nourished. That's all we do."

After ey caught up taking down eir notes from Jonas's short speech, Codrin sat in silence for a bit, considering the next path to take on the interview.

"Do you have any other questions?" Jonas asked. "Not to rush you or anything. I'm just wondering if I should fork to get some work done."

"Just one more, I guess. Not one of my prepared ones, but you've given me a lot to think about. How does Launch fit in with your concept of stasis? That feels like an awful big change. It even decreased the population of the System back home."

Jonas shook his head, chuckling. "I'm not the one to ask that one, Codrin. I've specialized way too much into data analysis. You can ask True Name about that, or Jonas Prime. I'm just parroting things we talked about a century and a half ago."

"I will, I'm sure, but can you give me your best guess? I'd still like to hear it," ey said.

"Best guess? The System was deemed stable enough to undertake the launch project, and the project was deemed likely to produce a secondary stable society. Beyond that, beats me."

Codrin nodded and, seeing Jonas begin to rise, stood from eir seat, shaking the offered hand.

Jonas saw em to the door, saying, "I hope I didn't add to your stress, Mx. Bălan. You're doing good work, and I hope it's also enjoyable."

"It's certainly intriguing. You've given me a lot to think about, and I'm sure Ioan will agree."

"Of course. If you have any further questions, don't hesitate to ask." He smiled to Codrin, and the smile was the least earnest ey had seen yet. "And I look forward to seeing what you come up with."

It wasn't until Codrin was back at the house on the prairie, back with eir family, back where ey was comfortable enough to work on transcribing eir notes, that ey came across the phrase that had left em so wrong-footed during the interview.

Ey frowned, stood up, and paced around eir office for a few minutes, stopping at the end of each circuit to stare out at the prairie beyond the windows. Ey was starting to feel as though there were coils of some sort wrapping around em. Thick, fleshy things that squeezed around eir middle, bound eir hands, held em silent. They did not kill em, did not force em to move, to watch. They did not force em do do anything. They just held em there, letting em know that, at all times, they were present.

So ey sat at eir desk and wrote a footnote for eir transcript that ey'd send back to Ioan and May Then My Name.

> Check my work, Ioan. As you have read, Jonas asked what each of our stressors were, and I mentioned a sentence or two about each of us and what we'd been doing that had been keeping us busy.
>
> You'll notice that, for you, when talking about End Waking, I said, "One of them told em to be careful interviewing you, that you'd control the whole thing."
>
> His reply: "Did he now?"
>
> I don't think I messed up the transcription, and you know as well as anyone that our memories are all there for our perusal. I've thought and thought and thought on it. I shouldn't doubt, and yet I do, so check my work.
>
> I said "one of them", and Jonas said "did he now". I asked Dear, and it said that there were relatively few male Odists in the clade (*"one fewer, now"*).
>
> Did you tell anyone that you were interviewing End Waking other than May Then My Name? I don't mean to cast doubt on either of you. I think you feel just as bound up in this as I do, but I need some clarification as to how Jonas knew that you had interviewed one of those relative few. I need that clarity. I think we're beyond wants, now.

True Name—2124

The Only Time I Know My True Name Is When I Dream walked.

She walked from sim to sim, finding intricate ways to build up a sign, a sigil from them. Finding ways for disparate streets to connect, finding alleyways to open into deer paths, finding breathlessly exposed parks that, when a corner was turned around a tree or perhaps a low hill, might open out again into the lobbies of libraries, the shelves of which could become a hedge maze.

Perhaps there was more to the sims that she walked, but she did not notice. As soon as she felt herself drawn to any one particular place, any one particular feature of any one particular sim, as soon as she began to feel anchored, she left. All of the things that people—her people—built passed beneath her feet, passed before her eyes.

And all the time, her thoughts soared above her, watching her path, the steps she took. They watched all of her left turns. They viewed the sigil that her walking drew and imbued in it new meaning.

A thought: *What dire emotional need caused one to build an office building in a place of no corporations?*

She stepped into that office building from the dry bed of a river, walked up two flights of stairs, and into a floor of empty cubicles. She turned at random, moving through the rows, and sat down at one of the desks and thought a while.

A thought: *Why is the first instinct upon creating a wholly blank medium such as this to build in the nature we remember?*

She stepped from the cubicle and turned left, out into a rolling, open field, dotted throughout with dandelions. She bent down and picked one, twirling it between finger and thumb, then tucking it behind her ear where the yellow could shine bright amidst the black fur there.

She could almost feel em, sometimes, as part of the very fabric of existence within the System. Almost. A dream of a dream of her friend, always just out of reach.

A thought: *Why do we drag our memories around with us like luggage?*

So, she walked, and as she walked, she strove to draw her thoughts in the other direction. She strove to draw them forward, away from the past, so that she could consider the future.

What would this place look like, after seceding from the rest of the world? What would a land—if such could be said of the System—of those who had already seceded from the rest of humanity look like? How many would notice and rejoice? How many would notice and hate every second of it? How many would notice and not care, and how many would not even know that it had happened? That it had even been on the table?

Would they build differently? Perhaps they would stop bringing along with them the structures of their pasts. Perhaps there would be fewer office buildings and more cabins in the woods. More idyllic houses. More mountain landscapes and main streets of cute towns with hole-in-the-wall restaurants that no one knew about and yet which served the best curry, the best hot dog, the best cupcakes that one could possibly imagine.

Would they live differently, love differently? Perhaps they would still pair up as always they had. Maybe, when they picked up feelings for someone, they would fork to have a separate relationship with them as well. Maybe collectives of families would live together as they always had, finding comfort as much in each other as in their chosen relatives. Maybe a taboo would grow around having a relationship with oneself, of forked instances living together and loving each other. Would that be narcissism forever, or only before individuation? Would it be incest?

Would they choose life? Choose death? Would they pray?

She knew that it would happen, of course. Secession. She shared none of Yared's dread, his pessimism. This was fine. She was the politician, he was the puppet. She saw the big picture laid out before her in her sign, her sigil. He would handle the pessimism, her the optimism.

No, not optimism; surety.

The bill would pass, the System would secede, the station launch would go off without a hitch. The bill could not but pass, the System was bound to secede, and the station launch was as safe as could be.

Yared would upload, or he would not.

The DDR would care, or it would not.

Earth would dream of them, up there on the System, or it would not.

The only thing, the only important thing, was to ensure continuity. A continuity borne of safety, of stability, and of an intense desire not to let the System come to harm. It had to be desired, prized, cherished even by all those who stayed behind.

As she ruminated on this, the need to be desired as a form of stability, a memory bubbled up to the surface, spun around once, twice, and then came into focus.

A memory: *"Two thirds of our power structure still thinks child restrictions are a good enough idea that those laws have bled into Russia, too."*

Who had said that? One of the three, doubtless. They were so interchangeable.

She stepped into her apartment from wherever her thoughts had taken her, and she forked off a new instance, relying on that subtle trick that Jonas had taught her, letting her reputation stay pinned to where it was.

"I suppose that makes me Do I Know God After The End Waking."

She nodded.

"Someone had to wind up with the name with a typo in it, alas." The other skunk smirked.

"Everyone gets something, yes," True Name said, plucking the duplicated dandelion from behind End Waking's ear and adding it to the one already behind hers. Two suns amidst black fur. "Let us start with some differences. I do not want you looking too much like me, so that we can work separately."

End Waking nodded, thought for a moment, and then forked several times in quick succession to lead to greater and greater differences, until a new Odist stood before her, unique in so many ways. Masculine, kind-faced, dressed in a business-casual outfit that retained both the competency and friendliness that Praiseworthy had helped her attain.

"If you think this is acceptable, we can start strategizing."

True Name nodded, and the two skunks walked to her office.

"So, if we are to follow the timescale that Life Breeds Life suggests, what are some good milestones that we can set for ourselves?"

"I was thinking that it would be nice to have uploading incentivized within fifty years. That would mean that by the hundredth anniversary of Secession, we would primarily be seeing uploads who knew nothing but that idea."

End Waking nodded. "Probably best to begin as early as possible, yes, at least in terms of planning. I think that ensuring that the failure rate is below one percent within ten years would be good first step, followed by reducing the cost of upload by half ten years after, then half again in another decade. That gives us twenty years to work with when it comes to getting to a point of incentivization."

"Alright, that sounds good. I will leave you to it, for the most part. I do not expect that there will be any news for another few years."

The other skunk laughed. "Of course."

"And, End Waking, a favor." When he nodded, she continued, "There are inquisitive minds. Always are. We already have Life Breeds Life helping on that front, but while you were talking through the timeline, I realized that it would be best if this conversation, these plans, didn't start, as far as anyone but you and me are concerned, until perhaps the 2150s."

He tilted his head. "How come?"

True Name smiled faintly. "I always find it surprising just how quickly one can deviate from one's down-tree instance after all that forking."

"Of course. You have been thinking your thoughts while I have my own."

"Yes. Well, we are quickly getting to the point where our efforts both sys- and phys-side happening all at once are reaching levels that might be considered uncomfortable in retrospect. Life Breeds Life is working on this already. If we can minimize our visible impact, then we should do so. Same date for the Council, same date for Jonas, same date for other Odists."

"Mm, probably a good idea. I forked in 2143, then."

"2143. Got it." True Name smiled. "Thank you for this. I think it will work out quite well for us in the end."

Douglas Hadje—2325

May Then My Name Die With Me: Douglas

May Then My Name: Douglas Douglas Douglas Douglas Douglas Douglas Douglas Douglas Douglas Douglas Douglas

May Then My Name: Mister Douglas Hadje, Master of Spaceflight and Doctor of whatever the hell your degree is in, call on line one.

May Then My Name: Oh, whatever. Just let me know when you get this!

It took a moment for Douglas to compose himself when he returned to his terminal after yet another evening of sitting in the Pollux control tower, now largely remade into an observation bubble, despite the increased gravity. It was quiet, it was dark, it was calm, and there was nothing to see except the same Earth-rise-moon-rise cycle every thirty seconds or so.

So, when he returned back to his room to a series of messages that felt loud, bright, raucous, it took a moment for his mind to adjust.

Douglas Hadje: My doctorate is also in space flight. I did my thesis on booster stress in reusable launch vehicles.

Douglas: Now, how may I help you?

May Then My Name: That is just *fantastically* boring, my dear.

Douglas: Oh, it was boring as hell. I'll send it to you sometime.

May Then My Name: If you would like.

May Then My Name: I will not read it.

May Then My Name: Also, hi. Good evening. Have you had a good day?

Douglas: That was also boring as hell. I keep going for walks or trying to read or whatever, but there's only so much here to keep myself interested when I based most of my life on my job.

May Then My Name: That does not sound healthy.

Douglas: Can confirm: not healthy.

May Then My Name: Well, fucking upload already.

May Then My Name: We can go out for drinks and build up your tolerance again, or you can go walk some place that has a horizon. Ioan took me on a hike a while back, we can take you there.

Douglas: Before long. A few months, probably, so that I can finish things up here.

May Then My Name: !!!

May Then My Name: Good! Excellent! I will look forward to the day.

Douglas: I'll keep you apprised, then. Where's Ioan today?

May Then My Name: Ey is here, but in heads-down mode. It can get frustrating sometimes, because when ey gets in that mindset, ey will not be able to fork effectively. If ey tries, the fork will just spend all of eir time whining about not being at work.

Douglas: Like me, huh?

May Then My Name: You said it, not me.

May Then My Name: Anyway, I messaged you to ask you about something that you have mentioned a few times so far. Do you have it in you to answer some questions?

Douglas: Sure, why not. My first meeting is in the afternoon, tomorrow, and it's just a weekly safety briefing. Talk my ear off, I could use the distraction.

May Then My Name: Yes, you certainly could.

May Then My Name: You mentioned that there had been sabotage attempts. We were surprised when we heard that initially, but it had been in the middle of some other conversations that we did not want to derail, so we have been holding onto it until a time when there was not much else going on. Can you tell us about those?

Douglas: Oh, sure.

Douglas: There were two big ones and one small one. You heard the small one, which was that tech knocking me off the edge of the torus. The other techs out there with us tackled him and tied him up in his own tether to bring him back into the station. One of them suggested just ripping off his suit then and there, but that was a reaction out of anger, and it's hard to stay angry out in space when you're all terrified of dying anyway, so they did the right thing.

Douglas: He was brought inside, taped to a chair (there used to be a security station with a cell for when the torus was a hotel, but it was repurposed at some point), and then confined to quarters until the next shuttle could come pick him up.

May Then My Name: How did he even get in there to begin with?

Douglas: As far as I could tell, just lying really well, or perhaps it really was just a spur of the moment act as he argued in court. It was his second EVA, so there wasn't exactly much time to suss out if there was anything up with him.

Douglas: It's weird, though. You have to have an MSf to even do EVAs here, and even just getting into that program, not to mention getting a job out here, requires a lot of psychological testing and the like. He must have been pretty good at lying.

May Then My Name: You said that he was sent back to Earth and charged. What were the charges? How did that work?

Douglas: I don't know too much about it, honestly. I know he was charged with attempted murder and there was a whole flurry of articles about how the case was groundbreaking as the first attempted murder in the vacuum of space. He was convicted, then probably sentenced to jail.

May Then My Name: What does jail look like?

Douglas: Depends on where you are and what you did. I think for something like attempted murder, he was just put in sim for a while, unable to back out.

May Then My Name: Really? What a nightmare.

Douglas: It's not like he's just put in a sim of a jail cell to rot or anything. As far as I know, it's just a tightly regimented day, most of it in a solitary sim, the rest in a shared sim with other prisoners.

May Then My Name: Not able to back out, though. Even the thought of that makes me feel ill.

Douglas: Why? Aren't you kind of in that state right now?

May Then My Name: When you upload, you will see how the comparison fails. But it is terrifying because I am old enough to remember the lost.

Douglas: That virus or whatever that was getting people stuck in the 'net? Didn't that hit Michelle?

May Then My Name: Yes. Remember when I talked about how 80% her days were bad days? That is why.

Douglas: Oh, shit. Yeah, I can see how that'd be terrifying, then.

May Then My Name: On to brighter subjects, then. You mentioned bigger sabotage attempts.

Douglas: Much brighter.

Douglas: Well, one of them was here station-side, and one was back planet-side. The one up here was when one of the mechanics (who don't need an MSf) had smuggled up some type of plastic explosive in their luggage. I think it was actually the fabric lining of the case, something where thin strands of explosive were coated in plastic and woven just like one normally would. It was powerful enough and its target small enough, that even just that suitcase lining would have been enough to do the trick.

Douglas: They tore out the lining, rolled it into a rope, and wrapped it around a portion of the launch strut extrusion factory. It was about six years back, and the arms were already about 2800km long, so if the explosion had wound up actually causing enough damage, the stress of the arm would have torn the station apart, and likely taken the System with it.

May Then My Name: WHAT

May Then My Name: That seems like an awfully important thing to not know as the sys-side launch director, Douglas.

Douglas: It was all hushed up by security (brought back up after my little incident on EVA). I wasn't allowed to tell you after the NDA. Sorry, May Then My Name.

May Then My Name: Did they give you a reason for keeping it from us?

Douglas: They said it had political undertones because of the articles of secession. "No other governmental entity shall declare war on or attempt to destroy the System."

May Then My Name: They worried it might be considered it an act of war?

Douglas: I guess so. If it was an act of war, then the System could retaliate. I'm sure they told someone over there who needed to know

May Then My Name: Then why are you telling me now?

Douglas: Well, our conversations are off the record, now. Besides, if I'm going to upload soon, it's also relevant to me in the same way it is to you.

May Then My Name: It is, at that. How were they caught?

Douglas: That's the weird thing. They turned themselves in. The cloth bomb had been in place for about a month, I guess, and they grew a conscience in that time, so they defused the bomb, brought security over, admitted to what they'd done, and let themselves be sent back planet-side.

Douglas: Which actually brings me to the other big sabotage attempt. Apparently, they were working with a collective who were really unhappy with the launch overall, so there was also a suicide bombing at a launch facility during a tour which was intended to take out the control room before it could be used for the next supply run.

Douglas: Cloth bomber struck a deal with the government for a lighter sentence (probably like my attacker received) for acting as an informant and ratting out the organization before the rest of the planned bombings could take place.

May Then My Name: Less immediately threatening to us, but still, that is terrible. Do you know why this collective (is this like an interest group, or is there a deeper meaning?) felt so strongly against Launch?

Douglas: Yes, a collective is a group of people who have decided to lose as much of their unique identity as they can to live as singular facets of a shared identity.

May Then My Name: Ioan will be fascinated to hear. Why is that?

Douglas: It actually started around a fictionalized account of forking. They sometimes called themselves clades, but the name never stuck in the wider world. It's kind of a weird love/hate relationship with the System that they have. They love it enough to try and emulate it in their social groups, but they also loathe the idea of uploading and a lot of other things that go along with the System.

Douglas: de, on the launch commission, is a member of a much more liberal collective. Still will never upload, but really seems to take pride in their job.

Douglas: So I think it was some of that hatred that was at play. They hated the lack of control that is inherent in the System. They hated all that went into Secession, how it made the System a political entity. They hated Launch because, by phys-side collaborating with sys-side, it was a sign that we were equals. They felt that the System has been interfering with phys-side politics ever since Secession. They hated the System for lots of reasons.

May Then My Name: Do a lot of people phys-side think that the System is interfering with politics?

Douglas: Not really, no. We learned in grad school that there was a kerfuffle around it when uploading was incentivized that essentially no one remembers except for boring people like me who had to study it. There have been a few gripes here and there as other large political changes happened, like when governments merged or recessions hit. When things like that happen, I think a lot of people instinctively look for a boogeyman to pin it on, and the System is pretty convenient because it's not like you all can fight back, so you all turn into shadowy figures behind the politicians.

May Then My Name: Oh, that bit is definitely true.

Douglas: Yeah, figured as much. You all up there steepling your fingers and talking in hushed tones about how you're going to do everything from crash the economy to hire Michelle Hadje's distant ancestor specifically to work on your nefarious plot.

May Then My Name: Yep, got it in one.

May Then My Name: I am glad that none of these were successful on the scale that they had hoped. We do not know what happens to us if the System breaks. There have been a few instances of discontinuity over the centuries, but we don't see them except that systime jumps ahead. Were the System to explode in some fiery spectacle, we would just stop. Probably. Maybe.

May Then My Name: Theologians and mystics have been disappointed to find no answers in what comes after death when one quits, so we are as in the dark as you are.

Douglas: Maybe a bit less, because at least one possibility of what comes after death for us is living sysside.

May Then My Name: This is true! We are ghosts up here, haunting silicon and whatever else makes up the physical elements of the System these days.

Douglas: You may as well be ghosts, as far as people think planet-side. There have been various groups casting uploads in the light of ancestor worship in some places. I have no idea how those who are worshipped sys-side feel about being asked for courage or a healthy crop or whatever.

May Then My Name: I would be honored, personally. I have no one to haunt after two centuries but you. I am afraid that you are stuck with me.

May Then My Name: All I can do is bother you on a terminal, though, so I suppose that I am not that bad of a ghost.

Douglas: You're a pretty good ghost, I'd say. I'm looking forward to meeting you in person some day.

May Then My Name: I will beg you once more: please come join us soon. I know you said you would, but if you do not live up to that promise, so help me God, I will move into your implants and never let you sleep again.

Douglas: Don't worry! I promise. You'll see me within the year. I've already put in word with both the launch commission and the clinic here, and they're fine having me stick around station-side until I can upload, so it's already (loosely) scheduled.

May Then My Name: !!!

May Then My Name: I am eager to meet you, Douglas Hadje, Master of Spaceflight and Doctor of Other Boring Shit!

Douglas: Goes both ways, May Then My Name Die With Me of the Ode clade.

May Then My Name: Excellent, excellent.

May Then My Name: Now, I should head off. Ioan is coming up for air from eir writing, so I am going to go chase em around the house, frothing like I am rabid.

Douglas: Oh! Time for a quick question?

May Then My Name: If you hurry, yes. I am already frothing at the mouth.

Douglas: Are you and Ioan in a relationship? I'm sorry if it's impertinent, feel free not to answer.

May Then My Name: It is not impertinent, but there is no easy answer. If ey asks if I would like that, I will say yes. If ey does not, I will still be content to be eir friend.

May Then My Name: And if ey does not know one way or another, as I suspect, I will ensure that ey makes the decision on eir own terms.

Douglas: You won't ask em yourself?

May Then My Name: No. It is quite important that ey ask me, and not the other way around.

Douglas: Why, though?

May Then My Name: Two reasons. One: the one with the greater restrictions in a relationship wins out, and I will say yes to almost anything and anyone. Ey would not. It is thus on em to make the choice. Two: if ey really does not know, I will gain an absolutely enormous amount of satisfaction out of teasing em afterwards.

Douglas: Of course you would.

May Then My Name: I am pleased that you have come to understand me so well.

May Then My Name: Now, I am getting froth everywhere, so I will have to run.

Douglas: Alright! Have fun, say hi for me, don't stay up too late.

May Then My Name: Lame.

May Then My Name: Bye!

Douglas leaned back from his terminal and stretched his arms up toward the ceiling, leaning back in his chair.

Every time he talked with Ioan and May Then My Name, he was once again faced with the realization that he had hardly needed Ioan to convince him at all. The two were the first people he could call friends that he'd had since school. He liked them immensely. Beyond that, though, something about May Then My Name seemed as though she was simply built to be liked, as though, whenever he talked with her, he had no choice but to like her.

It wasn't quite charisma, as, whenever he tried the word on for May Then My Name, it carried far too many implications of manipulation, and the last thing he could picture her doing was being manipulative.

She was weird, yes. Goofy, even. But there was nothing about her that was calculating or cold. Perhaps that's what she'd meant about it needing to be Ioan's choice. Perhaps she knew just how easy it would be for her to manipulate em into a relationship.

One more walk around the station, he thought. *Then I'll get to bed. January can't come soon enough.*

Yared Zerezghi—2124

Yared was not sure how he felt that the politicians—true politicians, at least—had been right. Demma had said so, Jonas and True Name had said so, and yet something about the whole process felt slippery to him. It was a feeling beyond even that, for while that implied that it was simply politics as usual, this was something more visceral. It was slimy, like the algae that had clung to his skin after he'd gone swimming in a small pond during a visit west: something that made him, specifically, feel disgusting.

Because they *had* been right, hadn't they? They'd been right that there were strings to be pulled. They'd been right that politics was a game that was played by the bigger players, that the bigger players used the smaller ones as pawns, that the goal was some non-zero-sum game of pushing the populace around like a fungible good.

He had been the tool, and his belief had been his utility. He was the knight moving three spaces up, one space over to outwit some other politician's bishop.

They'd been right, both Demma and the sys-side pair, because support for secession had swung his way with surprising rapidity, and there had suddenly been other strident voices that had once been on the other side of the equation agreeing with him, arguing alongside him for the right of the System to become a political entity of its own.

There had been a logical procession to their thought process within their posts. It wasn't some sudden coin-flip, but over the course of the week, debates on the DDR-adjacent channels, where it didn't cost credits to post, suddenly swelled, and he'd seen the light dawning in their eyes, such as they were, as they realized that the System's political landscape fundamentally differed from that phys-side, that it couldn't but differ, given the root functionality of the populous, of the reality that sims were the only way to live. It was a true anarchy. There was no ruling class because of what utility would there be for a ruling class when one could just split off and create one's own sim or set of sims, such that any attempt to rule from some central sim could simply be ignored as though it had never happened.

True Name and Jonas, now openly named, had been integral in helping convince him originally, and their words had played an enormous role through him to convince others. "There are sims in which a strict monarchy rules," True Name had said. "There are places governed by a theocracy. The Catholic church remains, albeit in reduced form without a bishopric, relying solely on adherents phys-side uploading all papal pronouncements, a near exact copy of the Vatican, where the phys-side popes and cardinals are represented by scrolling fields of text. Yet what influence could they hold on any other sim? What possible sway could they hold over anyone who did not subscribe anyway?"

And so he dutifully passed these on under the tutelage of Jonas and True Name and Demma, and they, too, influenced the voices on the DDR.

But for the voices to swing so quickly bespoke influence beyond just him. It showed that he was not the only pawn, that many of these other strident voices that quickly changed their voices were under the control of the big players phys-side, and perhaps sys-side as well; after all, why wouldn't True Name and Jonas be talking to other DDR junkies like himself?

He was too afraid of them, now, to ask.

All he could do was sit by and watch, and pray that the secession amendment wasn't altered to include some equally slimy additions that would limit the total freedom granted by the secession.

Even there, he was lucky. The clauses about declaring war had been strengthened, the clauses about asylum seekers hardened with wording surrounding the impossibility of extradition and the acknowledgement that any such seeker would no longer have a tangible effect phys-side. In fact, the only provision that had felt sour was one to cut off communication with the System from suspected terrorist cells, but it had done little to dampen the feeling of success from the overall amendment, the overall referendum.

The only issue, in fact, was a personal one. All of these changes of the amendment had been made under his name. Others had convinced him to add them. Even when the sour change had been suggested, Demma had strongly suggested that it be included.

The end result was that his name was inextricably linked with the amendment. He was the sole author, meaning that those who hated it—indeed, those who hated the entire referendum—began to hate him, too. They hated Yared Zerezghi specifically.

And they hated with a passion.

His name had become a curse in their circles. He wasn't just the man who had introduced the amendment, he was the man who poisoned any hope of control over the System, that very System that they had declared a danger or a source of labor or a host to terrorism. He, Yared Zerezghi, was personally responsible for all that was wrong with the System.

When he mentioned how much he felt like a scapegoat to Demma and the pair sys-side, both had reassured him that that fervor would soon die down, and both had assured him that, as their names were also inextricably linked with the bill, they were feeling some of the same heat.

He wasn't sure that he believed them, though. Politics phys-side at the governmental level did not have the same level of personal hatred. At best, Councilor Demma might have some sort of parasocial relationship with his supporters and detractors, but at that point, he was still just a figurehead, an abstract concept of a person, and that concept was a stand-in for a power so far beyond the quotidian masses that it hardly mattered. At best, True Name and Jonas were as intricately linked to the very same anarchy that ruled the rest of the System. Their role—indeed the role of the entire Council of Eight—was one of guiding the System in the form of its core functionality, interfacing with phys-side on behalf of those sys-side, rather than interfacing solely with those sys-side.

And so Yared kept taking his walks, kept eating spicy food and getting drunk on tej, to shed what he could of that slippery, slimy feeling that still clung to him whenever he thought too hard about his position in all of this.

He had become a hero and a villain for this, though, and there was no shaking that off.

> **The Only Time I Know My True Name Is When I Dream:** What can we do to soothe your worries, Yared, except tell you that your vision is becoming reality?
>
> **Yared Zerezghi:** I don't know, really. Probably nothing. There's nothing really to be done when no one else will put their name on the amendment. I feel like it might be an intentional move by Demma and others to ensure that there is someone they can put the blame on who has an actual human face.
>
> **Ar Jonas:** That may well be true, actually. If I were still working phys-side and needed to influence a referendum from the DDR, I'd probably do the same.
>
> **Yared:** Is there anything I can do about it?

Jonas: Nope! You're stuck with it, my friend, and for that I'm sorry. The best you can hope is that everyone will forget about you, and the best you can do to ensure that is to become a loud voice on other issues, hopefully ones that a lot of people agree with, so that you simply become "the loud voice" instead of "the secession guy". This is turning into the largest issue the DDR has ever voted on, though, so it's going to take a lot of that hollering to drown your voice out.

True Name: And even then, because your name is on it, that is likely what you will go down in the history books for.

Yared: Uuugh. I've been thinking about that, too. It makes the concept of dying terrifying. As long as I'm alive, I at least have some hope of trying to become a less divisive figure.

True Name: You could upload. There is no death here, after all.

Yared: I'm seriously considering it, after this. At least that way, they'll know that I really meant what I said, and then I'll become someone they don't have to worry about.

Jonas: And you can help us keep fighting the good fight by whispering in everyone's ears.

Yared: That's *precisely* why I want out, Jonas, and you know it. If feeling like some sneaky little political figure is what's making me feel bad, why on earth would I keep doing that?

True Name: Jonas is an asshole, do not listen to him.

Jonas: I am, yeah, and I'll have you know that True Name just punched me in the shoulder, if that's any consolation.

Yared: Do it again, and maybe I'll feel better.

Jonas: Confirmed, she did it again.

Yared: Ahhh, such relief!

True Name: In all seriousness, Yared, do think more about uploading. We would welcome you here, and I am sure that, should anyone step down from the council (the Russians might when there is no need for their representation), you would be welcome to take their place. That would not be slimy politicking, just helping the System out.

Yared: You two are on the Council, how would that not mean slimy politicking?

True Name: I will let the insinuation that I am in any way a politician slide this time, but you are on thin fucking ice, buddy.

Jonas: True Name's an asshole, don't listen to her.

Jonas: Third punch to the shoulder confirmed.

Jonas: But really, no need to worry. This is 1000% the slimiest politicking that the Council has ever done. Hell, most of the rest of the council doesn't know or care how True Name and I have been handling this. Most of the rest has been, like..."how do we keep forking from getting out of hand?" or "let's set systime to start when the reputation market begins" or "what if we could create telepathy". It's bullshit

Jonas: Fun bullshit, but it's bullshit. You'd like it. It's more like volunteering to be a crossing guard than anything.

Yared: I might, at that, yeah. I'll think about it.

True Name: Please do, we would welcome you.

Jonas: Lighter topic: what most excites you about the prospect of uploading? Beyond getting away from ignominy and beholding True Name's indescribably beautiful countenance, I mean.

Yared: Isn't she a skunk-person?

True Name: An indescribably beautiful skunk-person, thank you very much.

Yared: Uh, I don't know. Honestly probably meeting you two in person is the biggest draw. You seem really fun to be around.

Yared: Hopefully this isn't insensitive, but are you two a couple?

True Name: God no.

True Name: Jonas may be pretty, but he drives me up the wall. I would murder him in his sleep two nights in.

Jonas: If I didn't get to you, first. We're good friends, but not on that level.

Yared: Okay. Thanks for clearing that up. Was just wondering.

Yared: Wait, *can* you murder other people?

True Name: Yes. Some enterprising individual found a way to disrupt the concept of self so quickly and so thoroughly that one basically disintegrates and, just like an avatar crash on the 'net, all you are left with is a core dump, and no one has figured out how to deal with those in a place that is a consensual dream.

Yared: Seriously???

Yared: What the fuck.

Yared: How often does that happen?

Yared: Fucking terrifying.

True Name: Oh, not often at all! Three times that we know of. It is pretty hard to actually make the virus, as it does require tailoring to the specific individual, though it is equally doubtless that same enterprising individual is working on a way to make it universal. If, that is, they have not already been murdered, themselves.

Jonas: And before you ask, no, there's no way to prosecute them, even if we found them. They could just fork and keep on living somewhere else, changing themselves to look like someone else.

Yared: Ugh.

Yared: I'll just have to trust you, I guess.

True Name: Do you not?

Yared: Slimy politician, remember?

True Name: There is a punch on the shoulder waiting for you as soon as you upload, my friend.

Jonas: Tiny little skunk fists. Don't worry, they don't hurt.

Jonas: OW

Jonas: Unless she punches you in the kidney.

Yared: Hahaha. I stand by my assessment that you two sound fun to hang out with.

Yared: Skunk, though. You can change how you look that drastically up there?

True Name: In theory. I know of few who have actually managed to do so, though that is rapidly changing with forking.

True Name: I am a special case due to some psychological/neurological damage from getting lost.

Those up here who are furries and look it are those who so strongly identified with their furry selves on the 'net that they began to think of their human selves as as the avatars and their furry selves as the real versions.

True Name: The reason I got around it is that Michelle's neurological issues meant that she oscillated between her human self and furry self, and I just happened to be forked during a wave of her furry self. That also meant that I (and each of her forks) lack the effects of that damage.

True Name: Or most of it, at least. You have mentioned the speech patterns before.

Yared: Yikes, that sounds kind of horrifying.

True Name: It was. I still remember it. I remember how terrible I felt due to the constant oscillation that only settled down when I focused completely or utterly relaxed. Were I able to choose at will, I do not think that this would have been a problem, and you would likely have been talking to me as Michelle Hadje, not as True Name.

Yared: Well, I'm happy for you, even if that makes me sad for Michelle.

True Name: She is spending her retirement relaxing, so there is little need to feel sorry.

Jonas: Is there anything else you're looking forward to, Yared?

Yared: I suppose just getting away from the DDR. I don't think I could manage to just drop it out here, as there's not really anything else I'm interested in enough to replace it.

Yared: Up there, though, I'd be forced to do something else, and that'd really keep me from getting so anxious about everything.

Jonas: Makes sense. What sorts of things do you think you'd go for?

Yared: I like food, I guess. I like walking. When I'm not really around here, I'm sleeping, eating, or walking. I've never had the chance to really go for a hike anywhere that isn't still in Ethiopia, but I imagine there's places like the Alps or Himalayas that are delightfully cool.

True Name: There are, yes. Plenty.

Jonas: A lot of the earliest sims were based around nature. It's as if people immediately wanted to reach for places that they loved phys-side.

True Name: Or to counteract the thought that they now live in a computer.

Jonas: True Name, naturally, takes the pessimistic approach.

Yared: To turn it around, what do you both like best up there?

Jonas: Oh shit. You can't do this to me. I'm not ready!

True Name: He loves that he can still be a slimy politician without any of the actual hard work.

Jonas: The problem is, you're not wrong. I loved what I did phys-side, and I have to admit that I still love it here.

Jonas: I also really like coffee. Coffee and food. I get to have all of those that I want without worrying.

Jonas: Oh! And alcohol. No liver disease, and also you can choose when to sober up.

Yared: Oh damn, that's awesome. I like wine well enough, but being drunk is mostly escapism. If I could find that fun balance with friends, that'd be nice.

Jonas: You can't phys-side?

Yared: If I had any local friends, maybe.

True Name: Ouch. Well, you have friends up here, and we would gladly take you to bars good and bad.

True Name: As for me, I love all of the variety in sims and people. When I am not working or sleeping, I will walk the public sims, jumping from one to another when I have had my fill of them.

Yared: That sounds nice. I've only traveled a few times. In Ethiopia, there's different climates and such, but only so much.

True Name: I will take you walking with me, then.

Jonas: And I'll be a slimy politician with you!

Yared: Ugh, you're the worst.

Yared: Anyway, thanks for letting me vent and lifting my spirits.

Yared: I needed it.

Jonas: Of course, Yared.

True Name: And please remember, uploading is always an option. We would welcome you with open arms.

True Name: I know that you will come join us, anyway, sooner or later.

Ioan Bălan—2325

Before eir scheduled interview, Ioan took a walk around that abandoned lake, this time by emself. Ey needed a moment to think, and that moment, though through no fault of hers, needed to be away from May.

Ey needed to do what ey was best at. Thinking, ruminating, disentangling the knotted strands of what eir thoughts were so that ey might begin to comprehend the truth about them.

These knots were angry ones.

Or, perhaps not angry. They were frustrating ones. They were knots that ey knew the technical reasons for existing, but was starting to nonetheless resent. They were knots that bound and limited the process with which ey learned, as frustrating as the recondite letters that Qoheleth had sent so often, so long ago. Little hints and clues and never exactly the complete answer all at once. Never an explanation that allowed for further questions. Always too little, as though ey (and, at the time, Dear) was being strung along, lured into some unknown trap.

The same thing was happening now. Ey understood the technical reasons for no one, single Odist answering all of the questions ey had, ey and eir clade. There were too many emotions, too much secrecy, or too much shame bound up in the answers for them to sit down and tell a story from start to finish. None of them would admit to any more than one single thing throughout each interview, instead relying on the agreed upon admonition to stop when requested or warning that, after a certain point, the Odist would lie to or resent the Bălan.

Ey was half tempted to push one of them past that point, but then ey wouldn't know what bit was true or not.

And these Jonases! Ey was going to see one today, after eir walk. They seemed so slippery. It was not just that they controlled the interview, though ey did not doubt that—the transcript from Codrin#Castor contained a new twist every time ey reread it. It was that they knew so thoroughly that they were doing so that they did it all with a wink and a smile. That little hint that ey was to know that all they'd done was so clearly calculated yet held so much plausible deniability that there really was no arguing with it.

Ey was not looking forward to eir interview with Jonas Prime today.

So, instead, ey stomped along the path and thought and talked to emself, walking all the way to the rock halfway around the lake from the default entry point to the sim, throwing a few handfuls of stones into the placid water one by one, and then stomping all the way back to that same point.

Once ey'd had eir sulk, ey headed to the meeting with Jonas.

Unexpectedly, this turned out to be at the same library at which ey had interviewed Sadiah. Not only that, but Jonas Prime was standing in exactly the same spot that she had been standing in, greeted em with much the same bow that the other historian had, and led em to the exact same booth in the cafe-*cum*-bar beneath the stacks. It was uncanny to such a degree as to immediately put em on the defensive, guarding against some threat, real or imagined.

Once again, the drinks were ordered—cocktails, this time—and the cone of silence fell. Jonas rested his elbows on the table and rested his chin on his folded hands. It was an incredibly charming look. "Mx. Bălan, so nice to meet you at last."

"Have you heard that much about me, then?" Ey did eir best to keep eir smile as earnest as possible.

"Oh, of course! You and your clade have been traipsing all over the place, interviewing some of my favorite people, and every one of them says that the Bălans are an utter delight to talk with."

Ey kept the smile in place. "I'm happy to hear that. I know that questions can get a bit tiring, so I try to make it a pleasant process, at least. If at any point you need to take a break or stop, just let me know."

Jonas waved away the comment as though there existed no reality where so nice a scholar could ever tire him out. "I'm excited to see what it is you have for me. Ask away!"

Ioan nodded and pulled out eir pen and papers. Ey spent a moment poking through the stable of questions that ey'd been asking anyone, frowned, and then flipped to a blank page. "I had a set that I was thinking of asking you, but I think I'm actually going to go off script here. My first question surrounds something that Codrin#Pollux heard by an Odist. I know you aren't one, but I'm hoping that you can shed some light on it."

"I'll do my best, of course. I'd tell you to ask one of them, but I doubt you'd get a straight answer, which I suspect you already know."

"And you'll give me straight answers?"

Jonas grinned. "Best I can, sure."

"Alright, then. After Why Ask Questions told Codrin that True Name was to instigate and manage the launch project, ey asked what she meant by that. She responded that the last thing that Michelle had done before she died was to give each of the stanzas a mission, and that True Name's mission was to, and I'm quoting here, "Do something big, help us divest". Given your proximity to True Name, can you clarify what she meant? What does it mean to divest?"

He laughed heartily and lifted his tall glass, saying, "To boldness! And here I was expecting you to ask if I'd invested in the launch or whatever. That is an incredible first question."

Ioan hesitated, then lifted eir own glass to return the toast. "To boldness. You have it, I need it."

"I have too much, my friend, and you need more, that's all." Jonas winked, then continued, "So, divest. The reason that's an interesting question is that's the word that immediately sold me when True Name came to me with that suggestion. It was the lynchpin on which the project was hung, and we built outward from there."

Ey scribbled quickly in eir shorthand, doing eir best to take down verbatim what Jonas was saying. Ey'd be able to remember, for sure, but through writing, ey might better process and use what time ey had with the founder while ey had the chance.

"It could've meant so many things," he was saying. "It could've meant just, "clone the System and leave a copy at the Earth-Sun L_5 point". It could've meant, "break the physical elements of the System up into much smaller ones and scatter them around so that damage to one did not beggar the others". Both of those are still on the table, by the way.

"We took it in another way, however, given news that we've been reaching from Earth. In particular, we were noticing a tendency to move from the excesses of capitalism back to the day-to-day hardships of feudalism and even, in some cases, subsistence farming. The problem, I'm sure you can imagine, is that when you're stuck being a peasant or scraping by to earn the most meager living, you aren't all that keen on space. It's only by dint of a few dreamers and the impossibility of retrieving it that the System remains up here in the first place."

Ioan nodded. "One of our interviewees phys-side said much the same thing."

"A dreamer, then," Jonas said, grinning. "But yes, life down there is horrible and no one—or essentially no one—wants to do a single damn thing about it. They're all so caught up in their little political games that they have no interest on doing anything to make their lives better, to live stronger."

"You don't sound very fond of them."

"Of course I am! I love every one of them for the delightfully stupid contradictions that they are, in the same way that one can both love and be disgusted by humanity as a whole. I'm just a pessimist, Ioan. You mustn't confuse pessimism with disdain. I can read the signs as well as any other, and I don't see them willing to do anything at all to do what life demands."

Ioan lifted eir pen from the page and looked up at Jonas. "What life demands?"

"Life all but demands more life. That's why those stupid contradictions back planet-side won't stop having children. Oh, we played them for that, of course. You learned that from End Waking, yes? We played on their desire to keep on fucking because...what was it, Life Breeds Life? It does. There's no way around it."

"It seems to me like you've stated a contradiction," ey said. "You said that they aren't willing to do what life demands, then said that they keep procreating as life demands. Is that what you meant?"

"Let me clarify. There's more to what life demands than just breeding. There is a level of intentionality required. In order for breeding to be effective, it has to have the right level of pressure put upon it. When breeding goes unchecked, you end up with an uncontrollable morass of life-stuff, and when that happens, you're more likely to run into systems running out of control, whether those are political systems, social systems, or even technological systems. Do you know why the race towards developing a true artificial intelligence stopped around the time of Secession?"

Ioan shook eir head.

Jonas's smile returned. "Because we didn't want it to. That's not the right pressure on life that we want. It offers too much risk to existing life, whether biological or uploaded. So, we pulled our strings, as you know we do, and ensured that interest in such projects dropped in favor of others. Better expert systems. Better integrations tech. Better entertainment."

"Wait, how is AI a threat to the System?"

"Of what use is the System to an artificial intelligence? It can't join us. It can't control us directly. There's only one way for it to put pressure on us to do any one thing, and that's to influence life phys-side, just as we've done, to convince them not to upload. The best we can ever hope from an AI is it ignoring us and letting us continue. The best we can expect should it not ignore us is a stalemate. A cold war."

Ey frowned as ey noted that on eir rapidly filling page. "Is there no way for an AI's goals to align with the System's?"

"Perhaps there is, but remember," he said, poking his thumb back towards his chest. "Pessimist. It fails the cost-benefit analysis. Not worth the risk."

"So, instead you decided to ensure that phys-side and the System continued their symbiotic relationship?"

"The part of me which has moved beyond pessimism and into disillusionment wants to sigh and say, "symbiotic is too kind a way to put it," but even I don't think that's true. We need them in order to continue growing, and they need us as something to dream about."

"Alright," Ioan said, dropping the line of questioning before it got too far from the few others ey still wanted to ask. "So it was decided that the launch was a good way to ensure that the System divested because it moved beyond what it was."

"Yep!" Jonas took a sip of his drink and grinned. "We decided on off-site backups as a form of risk management. They're not totally safe, of course, and they are, in their own ways, doomed. They'll eventually get caught in too eccentric an orbit around a star and burn up when they get too close, but until then, the lives that are lived within continue, secure. More than that, it gives them time to figure out if there's a way to ensure that sys-side life does as life will and expand in a way that isn't just forking. A pipe dream, perhaps, but a nice one."

"So you and True Name steered the launch project into existence to help that along." When Jonas nodded, ey continued,

"Just as you did with Secession, yes?"

"Yeah. We used our elements phys-side to ensure that Secession happened. One of them came up with the idea, but we spun it to be as much in our advantage as theirs. We used Yared, as I believe you know, but we also used many, many others out there. It led us to a much more stable place in the world."

"Speaking of, one your clade told one of mine that there are complex thoughts on stability and stasis. I just want to confirm that I'm understanding correctly. Launch fits into your concept of stasis by ensuring continuity."

"Sure, but also, a little bit of excitement is required to ensure that our lives stay boring. Even if our lives become interesting, or Castor's lives become interesting, or Pollux's, then there is a better than good chance that at least one of the others' will remain boring, just how we want it. No Jonas, was it? He probably called it 'gardening', which I like. We're tending topiary, here, and there are many of us over on each of the launches, doing the same."

Ioan nodded and paused to drink down a third of eir cocktail. Ey was thirsty, of course, but some part of em seemed to be craving the numbing aspects of alcohol. Ey continued, "Alright, I think I have two more questions. The first is that End Waking said that there were goals to influence the economies phys-side and explained that there were short term, medium term, and long term goals. He was kind enough to fill me in on the first two, but not the third. Can you tell me what the long term goals of meddling with the economy phys-side were? He said something about critical mass."

"Oh, that's an easy one," Jonas said. "It's basically the same as what I said about life. If life is to have the right level of constraining pressures on it, one of the easiest ways to do so is through the economy. The long-term goal of his 'meddling', as you put it, was to ensure the continuity of capitalism. It gives something for people to dream about, which are alternatives. It gives something for people to work against. Since they know that we rely on reputation up here, they have plenty dream about. The critical mass is the amount of money and participants required to turn this into a self-sustaining system."

"Simple enough, I guess, even if a little frightening in its implications."

"What implications are those, Ioan?"

Ey frowned. "What it sounds like your goals are is to keep life on Earth from getting too nice. Or nice at all, really. It sounds like you're keeping the pressures high so that the System continues. More than continues, even. You wanted to keep it desirable as the greener grass on the other side of the fence."

"And how is that frightening?" Jonas laughed. "The grass *is* greener. We give them something to reach for. What more could anyone want out of life than a goal?"

Ioan kept from speaking up about what ey'd heard from those ey had interviewed who had uploaded for the money. Instead, ey asked. "Alright, last question for now. Two-parter. One of my clade interviewed someone who mentioned that there was some dissension with your clade about whether to go ahead with Launch. Is that true?"

Jonas shook his head, swallowing the last sip of his drink before saying, "There might have appeared to be, but I guarantee you that that was manufactured. Having some highly visible folks argue about whether or not it was a good idea gets everyone interested."

"And the Dreamer Modules?"

For the first time in the interview, for the first time since ey'd met Jonas—the first time any Bălan had met any Jonas, if Codrin#Castor was correct—he frowned. "You've been asking plenty of interesting questions, Ioan, but this is the first you've asked that is actively uncomfortable."

Ioan waited.

The grin returned, playful this time. "Alright, have it your way! You historians, I'll never get it. Do you know what's on the Modules?"

Ey thought back. "Research stuff. Telescopes, measurement devices, that sort of thing. Codrin said that ey got to lay in a field and look up at the stars as they really were outside the LV—or at least as close as the sim would let them be."

"And?"

"Isn't there some broadcast continually playing? Something about prime numbers. Something to get aliens to get curious about Earth."

Jonas's grin turned icy. "No, not Earth, Ioan. The System."

"The L$_5$ System? Or those on the LVs?"

"Space is unfathomably big, Mx. Bălan. Stupendously big. There is absolutely no way that aliens, as you put it, would care about Earth or the solar system. There's no reason to come here. There's no reason for them to even bother with something so pitiful as us." The grin was edging into a smirk, now, and Ioan couldn't tell quite what it meant. Jonas continued, "No, the LV Systems. There is the broadcast to get extraterrestrial intelligences interested in the LVs, yes, but that's not all. There's a very precise set of instructions for how the System works, how the Ansible works, and an Ansible receiver. The same one used for uploading to the LVs."

Ioan blinked and sat up straighter. "I don't remember hearing anything about that."

"We clamped down on the knowledge as best we could as soon as we realized we wouldn't be able to rule it out." Jonas waved his hand. "Not important, though, because the last part of that package is a complete description of a human neural system and a basic description of our physiology. A complete map of our DNA, should they even want to build an entire human."

"Whose DNA?"

"Why, our very own Douglas Hadje! Who else? Blame True Name for that one." He laughed bitterly. "But that's all that they could ever want to build a Douglas Hadje in simulation and send it through the Ansible to the attached System. It'd wind up in a dead zone, a locked-down sim, we made sure of that, but it'd be able to communicate, and enough people on that System know enough about the System that it might figure out how to break free of that restriction."

"That sounds rather exciting though," Ioan said. "Why were you so against it?"

"How much have we talked about risk tonight, Ioan?"

"You're saying that it presents too great a risk to the continuity of the LV System?"

"Ioan, you are very smart, but I need you to keep up if you're going to come away with interesting answers. Think through the list of instructions that I mentioned."

Ey tilted eir head, then frowned. "There's an Ansible on there, you said, right? They could theoretically upload that same manufactured construct to this System, right?"

Jonas nodded. "There we go. There's nothing to stop them from doing so, after all. It's easy enough for them to figure out that these are probes, and that probes must be coming from somewhere. There's no reason, then, for them not to find that somewhere and blast out constructs in our direction. We're taking steps now to match those new Hadjes to dump them in a similar locked-down sim. We'll ask our questions, then terminate them."

"What about *the* Douglas Hadje?"

"Oh, he'll be allowed. This is the least risky place for him to be, after all. He knows far too much to remain phys-side. But he'll be the last Douglas Hadje permitted."

Ioan sighed, finished eir drink in a few big gulps, and sat for a moment, staring down at the rest of the blank page left for taking notes. Ey couldn't do it. It was too much. Much too much. "Jonas," ey said, reaching a hand across the table. "Thank you so much for letting me interview you. You've given me rather a lot to think about, so I may come back with more questions down the line. Is there any you want to keep me from publishing?"

He returned the handshake and shrugged. "Nope, you're

good to go with all of it. We've done the cost-benefit analysis, and this passes muster."

They both stood and walked toward the exit.

"Mx. Bălan, it's been an absolute pleasure."

Ioan smiled and very carefully did not say, *For you, perhaps. For me, it has been absolutely terrifying.*

Codrin Bălan#Pollux—2325

The messages between LVs and the L_5 System were flying as fast and as thick as possible, given the nearly day and a half transmission time between the station and the launches. It was enough time for Codrin to sit and stew and plan.

The sheer amount of information that was being generated by the Bălan clade and all of their Odist assistants and lovers was enormous, and so much of it was so important, so meaningful, so *weird* that there was little else ey felt ey could do. There was no clarification that any one of them could offer the other that would take the form of a conversation, something immediate. Instead, they each had to wait three days for a response to a query. Messages became letters, rather than conversations.

So there was nothing to do but go for it. Ey spent as much time as ey could digesting all of the stories, the stories of True Name and Jonas, the stories of the Odists and Yared. Ey had talked as much as Dear was willing to talk, and so there was nothing for it but to pack eir pen and paper and head to the high-rise apartment in the middle of the city that ey'd been directed to.

Ne Jonas greeted em at the door and grinned wide, "Codrin! Wonderful to see you!"

Ey didn't know what ey expected, but it was certainly not this. Both Codrin#Castor and Ioan had described Jonas as handsome to the point of being almost annoyingly so. The tall, blond, chiseled features type.

Here before em, though, was a rather plain, unremarkable man. He was not forgettable as user11824 was, he was simply middle aged, bookish, and completely...average.

Nevertheless, Codrin liked him at once. He was not attractive, but his attitude was unfailingly kind. Not avuncular, *per se,* but perhaps the friendly professor that everyone likes, even when they fail his class. Maybe it was the button-up shirt and jeans, maybe it was the way he smiled, the way he talked. Maybe it was just the whole of him. The everything that made Ne Jonas Ne Jonas was perfectly crafted to appeal to that of the academic in Codrin.

"Ne Jonas, yes? Thank you so much for having me over."

"Of course, of course! Just Ne, though. I'm less of a Jonas than the rest." He walked into the apartment and around the corner, beckoning Codrin with. "Tea, though? It's just Earl Grey, but hey, it's something."

The kitchen that Codrin had been led into was of a style that felt old even to em, who had uploaded nearly a century back. Wooden chairs, well worn. Wooden table, scratched and dinged. Tile floor, the grout black from years of dirt and grime ground into it.

"Uh, sure. I'll take a cup."

"Cream and sugar?"

"Just cream, please."

"Oh..." Ne sounded crestfallen. "I have skim milk, is that okay?"

"Sure, I'll take it." Codrin laughed, watching the older man putter around the kitchen. Meanwhile, ey pulled out eir pen and paper to take notes. "You know, you're not at all what I expected, I have to say. I was all geared up to be talking to some hot-shot politician in front of some sleek desk or whatever, not sharing tea around a table."

Ne turned a dial on the stove to start the kettle, frowned, and then pulled a lighter out of a drawer in order to light the gas when the igniter did not. "Not all Jonases are alike, Codrin." He grinned over his shoulder. "Most of them are, of course. You would've gotten the politician treatment from just about any other Jonas, but some of us got tired of that snazzy life and opted for something a little simpler."

"What led you to do so?"

While the kettle crawled to a boil, Ne turned, leaning back against the counter and smiling to Codrin, arms crossed over his chest. "I think it was the pressure of it. It's not that I'm not still doing my work, but when you look like that, you feel like you have all the pressure of your job resting on your shoulders. Changing my appearance, changing the way I lived, well, it made me actually start enjoying work again, rather than it being the job that owned me."

"I think I can understand that. I used to own the academic look pretty hard, back when I was Ioan. Over time, though, as my work and home life shifted, I found that I felt less comfortable in that state and more comfortable in, well." Ey gestured at emself, eir tunic and sarong.

"Do you think you became less of an academic and more of something else?" Ne asked.

"That's a good question. I don't know that I ever really was an academic. I was an investigative journalist, more than anything. I was a writer who fancied emself a historian. Now, I guess I've shifted more to the creative side, maybe. A lot more writing, a lot less history, at least up until this project."

"Think living with an Odist helped in that regard?"

Codrin nodded. "Dear's very...well. It's very itself. Not sure how else to put it. But it's also been good at getting me out of the comfort zone that I'd found myself in up until then. It was a good zone, and I'm glad that Ioan still has that, but I also like what I'm doing now."

They were interrupted by the rising whine of the kettle, which Ne pulled off the burner. He turned off the stove and filled two mugs, which he brought to the table before grabbing a carton of milk from the fridge.

The tea was a perfectly acceptable Earl Grey. The milk was unremarkable. The mugs were mismatched and stained with a dark patina from decades of use. It was comfortable and charming in all its imperfections.

"So, what is it that you're doing now that you feel better doing in this form?" ey asked, nodding to Ne.

"I'm a little like you, I guess. I'm the one who takes all of the history and draws it together into a big picture. From there, I ensure that the rest of the clade—at least, the rest of the clade that's working on this project—remains on the same page and doesn't diverge too far. I'm the clerk to Prime's executive."

"Is that why you look like a cross between a professor and an author?"

Ne grinned between puffs of breath over his steaming mug. "Yes. It's hard to reconcile that job description with looking like some high-powered attorney or movie star or whatever they're looking like these days."

"You don't see them much?"

He shook his head. "We mostly correspond through writing and media messages."

Codrin nodded. "The best form of communication, if you ask me."

"You would think so, wouldn't you?" Ne Jonas laughed, sipped at his tea, winced, and set the mug down again. "But here, look at me, I've gone and steered the conversation to other topics. I want to make sure that I get to your questions. What do you have for me?"

It almost felt a shame to move on to what Codrin knew were some topics that might be difficult or tense, but ey supposed it was as good a time as any. "Well, first of all, has your clade been keeping you up to date on the status of this project? I don't want to make you feel like you're repeating yourself."

Ne nodded and leaned forward, resting his forearms on the table. "You've interviewed No Jonas and Jonas Prime from our clade, and from the Ode clade, you've interviewed Dear, Why Ask Questions, True Name, End Waking, and May Then My Name. You've also interviewed Ezekiel, Debarre, user11824, Yared Zerezghi, Sadiah, Brahe, and dozens of others who fall below the relevance threshold. I believe your counterpart on Castor is interviewing True Name today for a second time, as well. Have I missed anyone worth talking about?"

Codrin had paused, mug of tea halfway between the table and eir lips, and stared at Ne throughout the litany.

"I don't imagine I have," he continued, smiling. "You've talked about the influence of the Jonas and Ode clades in Secession and Launch, the ways in which we have interacted with phys-side both financially and politically in the last two hundred years, the work we did around Launch, our reasons for enforcing stability and divesting our resources to maintain continuity, and the concerns we hold around the Dreamer Modules. Correct? You may sip your tea first, though, if you'd like! Don't let me stop you."

Ey set the mug carefully back onto the table, startled to realize that eir hand was shaking and eir breath coming shallow. Suddenly, ey saw the sim for what it was: a carefully prepared presentation, something constructed from top to bottom to appeal specifically to Codrin and those like em. The same, too, applied to Ne Jonas, whose entire personality was built around engendering feelings of camaraderie in those interested in history and stories.

"That...that's about the whole of it, yeah," ey said hoarsely. "How did you know all of that?"

Ne laughed, stealing another sip of his tea before responding. "Oh, I've told you that already, Codrin! It's my job to draw together all of the threads and pull together the big picture. I don't know how the specifics get to me, that's not my job. I just piece them all together. The big picture here is that you and yours are building the history of the System from start to Launch, and you're finding out just how much story there is.

You, like so many others, were comfortable in that boring stasis, as well you should have been, and now you're coming to terms with something new, something actually exciting, and you're waking up to it. This goes way beyond Qoheleth's stage play about memory; this is about the very foundations of your life."

Codrin forced emself to take a sip of the tea. It was thin, with the skim milk in it, and ey couldn't actually taste it for the pounding of eir heart. "Well," ey said, struggling to maintain calm. "That actually crosses several of the questions I had prepared off my list as either answered or irrelevant."

"Have you come up with any new ones?"

"Uh...some. The first is: why are you letting us even continue with the history project if you're aiming to keep stability within the System? Won't all of this coming to light impact that at all?"

Ne brightened. "Oh, that's a good one! The answer is twofold. Part one relates to something the No Jonas said to the other Codrin: stability is a thing that needs to be gardened and maintained, that there is no true stasis, but stability approaches that point like the man in Zeno's Paradox. This is a form of that gardening. When you have a rose garden or topiary, you know, you must cut away bits of it, but when you do, the whole becomes all the healthier and can last for years and years in the state you like it best. It may seem like a traumatic event to trim back roses. After all, you are cutting away good growth, aren't you? But that's how you get beautiful roses, year after year.

"That's what we're doing with this project. We're introducing a slightly traumatic event to make the stability of the system—that's lower-case s, there, I'm talking of the sociopolitical system of those on the three capital-S Systems—stronger. Does that make sense?"

"I suppose," Codrin said. "You've done the cost-benefit analysis and determined it's worth continuing on with, right?"

"Yes, precisely that," Ne said.

"And what's the second reason?"

"The second reason is related to what Jonas Prime said to

Ioan: humans, uploaded and not, need something to dream of. They need some better version of the life they live to hope for in order to feel comfortable. No one is happy for long in bliss, Codrin."

Ey blinked, sitting up straighter. "You mean you need some trauma like this sys-side in order to give people more bliss to aim for?"

"Precisely that." Ne sipped his tea now that it had cooled and nodded approvingly. "There is much madness in the Ode Clade, but that's what we suspect nudged Qoheleth over the edge. If you can't forget anything and all that you can remember is bliss, then bliss begins to feel like torture. His role was to think long term. He was working on the timescale of decades and centuries on shaping the perceived history of both of our clades, so he was already up to his ears in memory. This project of yours will instill a little bit of terror in the hearts of everyone. Not enough that they will rebel, of course. In well over ninety percent of cases, they won't do anything at all with the information, but it will tick up their anxiety a notch. Pain, anxiety, the need for something greater, these are all essential for survival. Without them, the world would be an impossibly dangerous place. Your history and May then My Name's mythology will put a dent in that bliss and make it less appealing. Does that make sense, too?"

Codrin finished taking down eir notes and sipped eir tea, mulling it over. Eventually, ey nodded. "It does, yeah. We could thwart you by not publishing this project, but I guess you've already done the analysis on that and know that we won't."

"You guess correctly, yes. 'Thwart', though, is an interesting choice of words. Do you feel like these are some evil plans that we hold?"

"A little. It's very dramatic. Very much like those supervillains who believe that there are core problems with the world, and if only they could just fix them, life would be so much better."

Ne laughed. "There *are* core problems with the world, Codrin. I've just enumerated several. You misunderstand, though. The core problems with the world aren't the absolutes that your supervillains deal in. They're the ways in which life struggles to maintain stable growth, and like I and my cocladists have said, the goal is not to solve those problems, but to garden around them and make them smaller problems. There is no solution to the question of what makes a stable and continuous world. That's the asymptote. All we can do is hew as close to that ideal as we can."

"I think that many phys-side would be pretty upset by that, though, right? If they learn that you've been pulling strings from the System to ensure that everything keeps going the way you want, won't they rebel against that idea?"

"There are two things working against that supposition," Ne said. "The first is that you misunderstand me when I say that we've done the cost-benefit analysis of your project and determined it beneficial. It's beneficial to both sys- and phys-side for exactly the same reasons, though the mechanics may be different. The second is that you are misjudging just how in over your head you really are with all that we've done, including phys-side. As soon as Launch started and as soon as you were nudged to start the project—don't frown, Codrin, you should've seen this coming—whispers were sent down the wire from the System to Earth to ensure that they would have the proper reaction to your work."

Codrin sat, silent, and stared at the man across from em. The man who had just admitted to subtly influencing billions of lives over hundreds of years through an organization made up entirely, ey assumed, of two clades. Hundreds or thousands of instances of two individuals.

"I suspect we're about done with the interview, but you must understand, Mx. Bălan, that we are the end product of phys-side life. Stability demands that we think that way. It demands that we think of all those billions of people back on Earth as part of our garden. Not the rose bushes, but the vegetables. They are the crop that we harvest to stay alive, and therefore they must be tended with as much love and care as the roses."

The room felt like it was elongating, stretching away from em as Ne spoke, as ey capped eir pen and got to eir feet, as ey gathered eir papers. The room was elongating and eir vision dimming around the edges.

And still Ne Jonas sat, smiling kindly up to em. "That, my dear Codrin, is the big picture."

Codrin Bălan#Castor—2325

Codrin Bălan was more nervous about this interview than ey'd ever been about one before. It's not that ey hadn't been anxious about talking with True Name previously—ey certainly had, given the warning that Dear had left em with—but in the intervening weeks, ey had had eir conversations with No Jonas and read the news from both Codrin#Pollux and Ioan about the wealth of knowledge that the Bălan clade had gathered.

Dear gave no warning this time. It simply stood in the door of Codrin's office, looking some mixture between sad and frightened, and bowed its head when ey gave it a goodbye kiss atop the snout. Ey left eir #Tracker instance in eir office to sit and not think of anything while ey painted terribly, the better to reduce merge conflicts down the line, and then sent a fork back to the sim where first ey had met True Name.

She was not smiling this time. She didn't look serious, just confident, competent, almost amused, but she was not smiling.

"Are you ready for our interview, Mx. Codrin Bălan?"

Ey nodded, said, "As ready as I'll ever be, I suppose."

"Excellent." She gestured em down to the office where first they'd met. There were no formalities. No shaking of hands, pleasant banter about which chair to use. The skunk simply sat in her chair at her desk across from em and waited.

The desk was clean now. All of the notepads and pens had been cleared away, and ey wondered if what it had looked like before was, as all three interviewers were now learning, simply a means of shaping eir expectations and impressions. Did she even take notes with a pen and paper? Did she even need to? The desk, then, had become a barrier between the two, a pedestal on which True Name sat and, though she was shorter than the historian, looked down on em with a singular attention. This, too, was a means of shaping their interactions for as long as they spoke.

"Alright," Codrin began, stepping up to this challenge as best ey could, drawing on all eir meager reserves of boldness to adopt the competent appearance of one who ought to be here as much as True Name. "Thank you once more for having me over and allowing me to interview you. Before I get started, is there anything that you'd like to say?"

"Yes," she said, nodding. "I would like to begin by preempting what I suspect are many of your questions so as to keep our discussions better focused. Through the various channels available to the Ode and Jonas clades, we know the list of individuals that you have so far interviewed, and much of the content of your interviews. We know that the Bălan clade has learned much of what transpired during Secession and leading up to Launch, as well as some of what has transpired during the intervening centuries."

Codrin hesitated, pen nib resting on paper, a dark blue spot of ink spreading slowly through the fibers.

"With that in mind, what questions would you like to ask?" True Name's mien lost much of its amused sheen, and she was looking truly serious now.

"Why?" The word was almost forced from em, let out in a rush as though ey had been struck or perhaps wanted to ask before ey lost all courage.

"That is the correct question," she said. "Jonas and I have discussed how each of us should answer this question, figuring that both Codrins would ask much the same. Your cocladist will receive an answer today pertaining to the big picture reasoning for the long term goals, which surround the stability and continuity of the System. I will be discussing the same picture surrounding the *raison d'etre* of the System.

"During the period of Secession, we began to see the utility for the System as something beyond a curiosity, something beyond a mere means of immortality as many at the time had understood it. The System, in our eyes allowed for a more perfect form of humanity. It is a place where an individual can truly flourish, where groups can experience true independence, where all of our imperfections can shine through and make us more what we are than we were before. With that in mind, those who remain phys-side are better thought of as a larval form of the species. They live, they love, they laugh, yes, but they do so in a way that is a shadow of what they could do, sys-side.

"What we did, the way we thought and the actions we took, were perhaps borne out of some core anger at the shortcomings of the political system that led to the loss of our friends, of the individual behind the Name and of Debarre's partner and of so many others affected by the mere whims of an imperfect attempt to control the world. It did not matter why the Western Fed government decided to destroy those lives; what bill they voted or commented on does not matter. Was it a declaration of hostilities? A trade embargo? Who cares?

"What matters is that their actions spoke of an utter disregard for the very humanity of those affected. This was echoed in the referendum to which Secession was merely an amendment, that they had to even consider the fact that we sys-side deserved the individual rights granted those phys-side, the same rights that they held in such flagrant disregard."

She nodded toward em. "You have this humanity. I have this humanity. Jonas has this humanity. You may not like us. You may think us manipulative and angry, or perhaps emotionless and cruel. You may think us villainous. It does not matter. What we have done, we have done to protect your humanity. What we have done, we have done to protect the humanity of all here on the System. What we have done, we have done to protect the humanity of even those phys-side, but you must understand, Codrin, that the humanity which requires the strictures of government is one less perfect than ours, and so we guide them to their logical conclusions."

"But why?" ey asked again, voice quavering. In fear, in anger, ey couldn't tell. "Why would you do that? Why guide the less perfect ones here? Even if you're right, that those who upload are somehow more perfect versions of those who don't or haven't yet. What does that even buy you? I don't get it. You don't sound like some psychotic villain who wants to bring humanity under their wing out of some misguided, high-minded ideals. You sound like a psychopath."

True Name laughed. It was a musical laugh, replete with tones of real amusement and genuine pity. A fantastically toothy laugh, and those teeth were sharp. "There is nothing I can say that will convince you that I am earnest in these endeavors, Codrin. You know that. You know that you have already made up your mind."

Ey frowned. "Enlighten me."

"As you wish." She grinned, leaning back on her stool. "You are correct that I do not wish to bring humanity under my wing. What purpose would that serve? You have either learned or intuited, as all do, that the System is truly ungovernable, so how could I or the Jonas clade hope to govern it? No, we do not want to rule. You may be correct that we are psychopaths—or at least that I am, I do not think that you need worry about your Dear or Ioan's May Then My Name. Humanity has simply evolved toward an inevitable two-stage life cycle. That of the fleshy pupae that do not know what it means to be a butterfly, and those butterflies that recognize the freedom of the air."

Codrin recapped eir pen, tucked it into eir pocket, and closed eir notebook. "That's one of those statements that makes sense on the surface until you think about it hard enough."

"Oh? How do you figure?" she asked, still grinning.

"You know who we interviewed. Did you know that Ioan interviewed those who uploaded strictly for the cash payout for their families?"

The skunk nodded.

"Do you know the contents of those interviews?"

"No. We are not reading your notes, we are simply keeping tabs on the project."

"Much of what ey learned," ey said, starting to feel the heat of anger rising through fear, growing within em. "Indicated that many of those who upload, even if it's only those who upload for the incentive, hold more than just a cynical view of the System. They recognize that it is a tool that their governments hold over them and perhaps recognize that those governments are tools of the System in turn, even if only on some subconscious level. If they're your pupae, they know the terrors of being a butterfly caught in a net."

"And Jonas Prime told Ioan about the cost-benefit analyses inherent in all that we do," True Name countered. "Some small fraction may be aware of and unhappy with the actions that we have taken, but in the grand scheme of things, we are simply setting up and maintaining the progression for all, removing them from lives that require such manipulations to somewhere where those manipulations are not just unneeded, but are not possible. The same applies to your project, as I'm sure you have heard. It passes the same measure as insignificant in the grand scheme of things."

The skunk's words, however calm they might have seemed, battered and buffeted em. They smashed up against eir emotions and base instincts, scuffing away carefully-maintained control until the fear and anger shone through bright and hot. Codrin pushed emself quickly to eir feet and leaned eir hands against the desktop. "How fucking cynical do you have to be to wind up in this mindset? I've met so many of your clade, and none of them have their heads so far up their asses as you do. I can't believe–"

Throughout eir rant True Name's smile grew icy, and before ey could finish, she waved eir hand, bouncing em from her sim.

Ey found emself standing at the entrance to the prairie, there on that short path that wound its way up to the house, to eir home. A few seconds later, a slip of paper fluttered to the ground in front of em. Reaching down to pick it up, ey unfolded it and read in the Odists' neat handwriting, *"Come back when you are less angry, Codrin. You have your confirmation, and when you have digested it, we will discuss what will happen next. Respectfully, The Only Time I Know My True Name Is When I Dream of the Ode clade."*

Ey let out a primal scream, a noise ey did not know that ey could even make, and then quit, letting the Codrin who still sat painting after so short an interview deal with eir memories. Ey was done.

Part IV

Arrival

Yared Zerezghi—2125

If the new year were to be a thing for Yared to celebrate, that was lost on him. He had long since lost track of how old he was, and the passage of time had begun to smear into a haze of referenda, of voting and posting and debating. He knew the years by the seasons and the fact that all of his posts on the DDR had a date attached to them, but beyond that, the significance of December thirty-first ticking over into January first held little sway over him.

If the passage of referendum 10b30188 was to be something to celebrate, that was also lost on him. The process of promoting and supporting the bill had long since taken over his life, and he had little enough energy left to acknowledge that it had even passed by a supermajority of votes.

He should be celebrating both of these, he knew.

He should be celebrating them because the rattle, pop, and boom of fireworks outside told him to celebrate the new year. He should be celebrating them because he was inundated not only with congratulatory messages telling him to do so for his pet issue passing, for his first major amendment passing, but for vile threats of harm, of finding him, of killing him, or for the media requests piling up in his inbox, and in the end, was that not a sign of success for a politician?

He knew that he should be celebrating, most of all, because True Name and Jonas had each sent him dozens of messages telling him how the news had been received sys-side, describing the cheers of the Council of Eight, gushing about the unanimously positive moods of those who had been tracking the progression of the bill.

And yet here he was, once more walking from his apartment to the patch of scrub grass and trees at the end of his block, wishing he'd left his phone at home.

The trees, at least, had nothing to say. They cared not about the new year except perhaps for the risk provided by the fireworks. They most certainly cared not for the secession of the System. All they cared about was their patch of dirt and the sun above and whether or not they got enough water. Yared wound his way around each of them in turn, sometimes sitting at the base of one or running a hand along the rough, papery bark of another, doing his best to absorb some of that apathy himself.

No one, in the end, had been able to convince him that having his name inextricably linked to the secession amendment would be anything but trouble, moving forward. He had tried to pick up a new pet referendum to follow after the interest had swung hard in favor of secession, something about limiting the environmental impact of dune stabilization in the Sahara, but the first response to his post in the DDR forums was met with a derisive "Of course the bleeding heart who either loves the System so much he bet his life guaranteeing their independence or hated it so much as to make it irrelevant to the rest of the world would be concerned about an issue he has absolutely no stake in. Either way, upload and find out, Yared, and the rest of us can move on."

That had stung so much that he'd not looked at the DDR forums or touched the debate sims since except to ensure that the referendum had passed. He was tempted to delete his account, after that, though he knew that that would be a mistake, inviting either further scorn from his detractors or disappointment from his supporters.

He jumped from where he'd hunched down at the base of a

tree, poking around the roots with a stick. His implants buzzed again and he pulled out his phone to check on who it was, groaning at the sight of Demma's name.

"Mr. Zerezghi," the voice on the other end said, sounding cheerful. "Happy New Year. I was wondering if you would be so kind as to join us for the tail end of our celebrations?"

"Join..?"

"Of course, Yared. Are you at your park? We can meet you there and pick you up. The dress is semiformal. We can provide you with that, if you need."

"Celebration?" he said, numb.

Demma laughed. "Of course, Yared. We'll meet you momentarily, and you'll see."

The car was once more ready and waiting for him at the edge of his mini-forest, still humming slightly from the radiator fan and air conditioner. The driver was once more standing outside, though this time he had a long thawb draped over one arm, gold brocade peeking out through folds in the cream-colored fabric.

"This should fit over your current clothes, Mr. Zerezghi. Might as well put it on out here where you can move a bit more easily."

It had been a long time since Yared had worn a thawb, and it took a moment to navigate so much fabric, but soon, he had it up over his head and spilling down over his body, the soft linen tumbling down nearly to his ankles. It really was quite nice, too. The linen was pre-worn and soft, and the gold brocade ran in two thick stripes from shoulder to hem down his front. It felt somewhat bunched up with his shirt beneath it, but wasn't uncomfortable.

The driver nodded appreciatively, saying, "It looks good on you. Your shirt underneath may ride up, but feel free to slip off to a restroom when we arrive and you'll be able to take it off and check it at the coatroom."

Yared nodded, smiled as best he could, and bowed to the driver. It was the first time he'd seen the man's eyes, and he was pleased to note that they looked as though they were always a second away from crinkling in a smile.

In the back of the car, Demma greeted him with a warm smile of his own, while a rather severe looking woman leaned forward to shake his hand.

"Yared, I'd like to introduce you to Councilor Aida Tamrat," Demma said, gesturing. "Aida, this is Yared Zerezghi, the author of the secession amendment."

"A pleasure, of course," she said. "Thank you for all of your hard work."

Overwhelmed, he simply bowed as best he could from his cushy seat in the back of the car.

From there, he said little, having little enough chance to say so. Demma and Tamrat continued their conversation from before, which seemed, on the surface, to be about the party they'd just come from—who was with whom, who wore what, what drinks had been most common—yet seemed to carry serious undertones of deep study, as though all of this information taken as a whole showed some gestalt of the political momenta this way and that. The driver, of course, remained silent, so all Yared could do was sit, smile, and nod when addressed.

The short ride down familiar streets took them back to Government House, but this time, rather than simply sitting outside of the building, the car was waved through a gate and directed down a ramp to a parking garage underneath. From there, they were subjected to a security scan—pat-down and implant scan both—and whisked up a flight of stairs, through long halls, and eventually deposited in a chamber crowded with more nicely dressed persons drinking champagne from thin flutes.

Very nicely dressed, he quickly realized, and he wondered if not dressing him up more had been an attempt to make him wear his status as a lesser-than plainly.

Later that night, nearing two in the morning, he realized that he could remember little of the party. He was handed a champagne flute and passed around the room as though an interesting object. Councilors and dignitaries of various levels shook his hand, smiled to him with unsmiling eyes, and once again congratulated him on a job well done.

"These are the interested parties I've mentioned," Demma said at one point. "They're all pleased to meet you in person."

If that was the case, then that pleasure had been slight indeed.

Perhaps the party slipped so easily from his mind due to the sheer mundanity of it, but more likely, it was the following conversation that overshadowed it in importance.

In the car, as he was being returned to his house, Demma broke the tired silence with, "Yared, thank you again for your assistance in this project. I have a few requests to make of you before we part ways."

Yared nodded hesitantly. "Of course, councilor."

"First of all, I hope you understand that your continued discretion is of the utmost importance. It is key to our trust and to your own safety and security." There was a meaningful pause before Demma smiled. "From potential bad actors, of course."

"Yes, of course," he said, starting to rub his palms against his knees before he remembered that he was still wearing the long garment he had been loaned.

"Thank you. Secondly, please do not contact me or any of the interested parties you met at tonight's soiree. This, I think, shall be easy, as many of them are quite difficult to reach, and the contact information we provided you with to stay in touch is now no longer active."

He nodded again, silent.

"Third, keep in mind that, as you are now a person of interest to the government, all of your actions will be monitored simply as a matter of course. Please also note that your interactions on the direct democracy representative forums will be monitored closest of all, and should they deviate from NEAC majority party or coalition stance, you may be subject to reprisal."

Yared's breathing grew shallow. This was unheard of. As far

as he could remember, a government had never required a single individual to toe the party line. But then, perhaps it was unheard of due to the implicit threat of violence that Demma had dropped early on, unheard of because it had never reached the light of day. He nodded slowly.

"Excellent. Those are the three requests. In order to formalize this agreement, I'd like you to place your thumb here–" the councilor had pulled out his phone where a rectangle outlined where his thumbprint should wind up. "–and state aloud that you agree."

He hesitated long enough that Demma began to frown, but before any further encouragement was given, he did as he was told, pressing his thumb to the reader and saying, "I agree."

"Thank you, Mr. Zerezghi." He sighed and slumped back into his seat. "My apologies for the rather formal interaction, but it was necessary to get this out of the way."

Yared did not relax into his seat. He was as keyed up as he'd been before the night had begun, but now for entirely different reasons.

After a long silence, he spoke up. "Congratulations, councilor."

"Mm?" Demma sat up, then, comprehending, waved a hand dismissively. "Thank you. The bill passed as expected, and now we won't have to worry about it."

Yared frowned. "Do you think there will be any further legislation around the System?"

"The System?" The councilor gave a short, sharp bark of a laugh. "It's out of our way, as I say. Rubbish idea from the start, of course, but meddlesome minds will always meddle, so it's all we can do to keep them as far away from us as possible."

"I...don't understand. What do you mean?"

Demma grinned. "There's no need for you to, but I'll do my best to explain if it will keep you placated. The System is a nuisance and a political thorn in everyone's side. It needed removal—as any thorn does—before the infection spread. Anyone who held onto their citizenship while making a one-way journey to a nowhere we aren't even sure is real could still have had influence back in their so-called home countries. Look at Jonas, if you need a prime example. Now they can't. That's that. It's a dumping ground for dreamers, and the less of those we have here, the easier our jobs get."

"But I thought," Yared said, voice raw. "I thought you wanted to help them secede."

Demma only shrugged. "I did. Just maybe not for the same reasons as you."

"I'm sorry, councilor. I had been under the impression–"

"You, too, are a dreamer, Yared. One who is easy enough to control, but a dreamer nonetheless." Demma said, his smile kind and completely, totally discomfiting for it. "If you wish to continue dreaming, then, well, I suppose I have already made my point about the System, yes?"

The rest of the car ride proceeded in silence. The only other words that were spoken to him were by the driver as he helped Yared out of the loaned thawb.

"Mr. Zerezghi, it was a pleasure sharing coffee with you," he said, and then they were gone, black car disappearing into gold-lit night.

Codrin Bălan#Castor—2325

It took Codrin nearly a week to calm down enough to send True Name another message requesting to meet. It began with an apology.

"True Name, first of all, I'd like to apologize for becoming so heated during our last interaction," ey said to er recording instance. "When confronted with information at such a scale, it is easy to become overwhelmed. I have since had time to read through both my notes from our meeting and the notes from my cocladists, and I think I understand better about what it was that you were trying to tell me. With that in mind, I'd like to meet up again to discuss some of the questions I didn't get to previously, and to allow you to explain anything you would like. Please let me know when would work best. Thank you."

Dear was nowhere to be found, this time. The fox had spent much of the last week alternating between requesting to be left alone and crying against eir shoulder. The story of what True Name had told em in combination from the news from Pollux had struck a deep chord with it, and when it did speak on the issue, the conversations would quickly end with "*I did not know. I promise, Codrin, I did not know.*"

So ey waited, ey read, and ey calmed down, and then ey scheduled eir interview.

The response came five minutes later, a simple ping of acknowledgement followed by a calm suggestion that immediately would be as good a time as any.

This time, when Codrin stepped into True Name's apartment, ey was greeted by the skunk standing where she had the last two interviews, and this time, her expression was one of calm curiosity, rather than that initial warmth and its following coldness.

"Mx. Bălan, it is nice to see you again."

Ey bowed. "Of course. Again, my apologies for getting so upset last time. It's a bit of a first for me, but that was a lot to handle all at once."

"I understand," the skunk said, returning the bow before gesturing em down the hall once more. "We will have a calmer discussion this time, I believe."

They sat down on either side of the desk once more, and Codrin noted that there was now a single notepad.

"Now, what would you like to ask me? I suspect you will feel more comfortable if you led."

Ey nodded. "Alright. Let's start with Launch this time. It sounds like you were involved with that as well. Can you tell me about that?"

"Of course. Is there any particular area you would like me to begin? Launch is a very broad topic."

"Well, Ne Jonas told Codrin#Pollux that we—that is, the Bălan clade and the liberal elements of the Ode clade—were guided toward beginning this project. Is that true?"

If the phrase 'liberal elements' or its implication that True Name must be one of the conservatives had any effect on the skunk, she didn't show it. Instead, she simply nodded. "Yes. A project such as this was deemed important in that it would add the spice needed to keep System life on its toes, much as Ne Jonas mentioned. We encouraged this in a calm and orderly fashion. Does that make sense?"

"I suppose. When did the nudges come?"

True name sighed and rested on her forearms on the desk. "To answer that question requires answering a different question. We began by canvasing various art institutes, actually. I do not know why we simply did not track Dear or May Then My Name or any of the Pointing At Itself stanza, as that would probably have shortened our search a good deal. All the same, we came across an exhibition at the Simien Fang School of Art and Design on history and its context in the world of the System by one Ioan Bălan. Do you remember that?"

Codrin lifted eir pen and blinked up to the ceiling, dredging up the memories of eir own gallery exhibition, so many years ago.

Too many years, ago, ey realized. "But that was in 2298."

True Name nodded. "It was, yes."

"But the launch project was proposed in 2306, wasn't it?"

"It was, yes," the skunk repeated. "Publicly, at least. The project began as a collaboration between the Jonas clade and elements of the Ode clade in 2290."

"But you said that Michelle told you–"

"To"Do something big. Do something worthy of us", yes. My up-tree instances told you a slightly different phrase to better guide your line of thought to where we are today. There is nowhere in there that mentions Launch, though, is there?"

"I suppose, not," ey said.

"But perhaps we ought to talk about Michelle, as well. I also said in that interview that I no longer considered myself Michelle Hadje, having diverged too far from her to be the same person. That is why we had no real compunctions about influencing her as well. That began many years back, of course, but when your root instance makes a suggestion to you, especially on the day she dies, you are quite likely to follow it, are you not? That provides quite a useful tool when interfacing with all elements of the clade, so we decided to take advantage of that early on."

"You...influenced Michelle to steer the Clade?"

True Name nodded, smiling. "It is what we—the clade, yes, but my stanza in particular—are good at, yes, so we nudged her to suggest what she did to the first lines, all vague pronounce-ments, which helped us guide everyone toward the project."

"And did you nudge her to quit?"

The skunk did not speak. A non-answer that was answer enough.

Codrin spent a minute tamping down eir temper. Ey had, after all, promised to remain calm. When ey felt like ey could speak in a level tone of voice, ey asked, "So you began the project of the launch long before it was really an open discussion. What was involved in that?"

"There were three aspects involved. Phys-side political, sys-side political, and technological. Sys-side was, as always, the easiest. Hardly anything to be done. Phys-side, we had to pull quite a few strings. Technologically, it simply involved the right organizations funded, the right people hired at those organizations—as our dear Douglas was—the right scientists put in charge of the right projects. Do you need further details on that? I can speak at length, but want to respect your time and energy, if you have additional questions."

"To confirm, you influenced Michelle Hadje to ensure the clade worked with the launch project, influenced politics phys-side to ensure that support would be there, and made sure Douglas was part of the team?"

"We made sure that the team was the team it needed to be, Codrin. Douglas was a bonus. He was impressionable at a young age, so we steered him toward being an Ansible tech, ensured he made it to the station, and were happy to see how good a fit he was for the role of launch director." True Name smiled. "I have talked with him a few times, though he did not know who I was when I did so. He is very nice, and very happy in his position. He is proud of how far he has gotten, and I am proud of him. Do not confuse influence with numbing mind control. It is important that the people we work with do things of their own, happy volition, even if they were originally our ideas."

Codrin nodded. "Well, if he's happy, then I suppose that's a good thing."

True Name beamed. "Of course."

"And Michelle quitting? Ioan told me that May Then My Name put it,"She could not do but what she did"."

"If that is how she felt, then I suppose there is little that I can do to change it, given that she is gone. I apologize that May Then My Name feels upset about it, but again, there is little that I can do to change that."

Ey sighed, nodded, and wrote down her answer. "And how have you felt now that you've pulled all this off?"

True Name looked genuinely thoughtful. "I hesitate to say 'proud', but I am pleased that it went off as smoothly as it did. There were a few bumps on the road, but nothing difficult to overcome. We—the Odists you have called conservative—continue to work as we will. Jonas, bless his black heart, continues to work as he will. We stay in contact and keep divergence to a minimum until we are out of harm's way, and then we ensure that we will keep our own projects safe. Castor, Pollux, and the L_5 System. It is all going as close to plan as we could have expected."

"So you're...happy?"

"Pleased," she repeated, laughing. "I will have time to be happy when I am dead. Until then I will continue to be pleased and continue to work."

Codrin re-capped eir pen and folded eir hands on top of eir notebook. Ey had dozens of other questions ey could ask, but ey felt full. Full to overflowing.

"Does that mean we are done with the interview, Mx. Bălan?" True Name asked, smiling.

"I'm out of energy, as you put it." Ey sighed. "Unless you have anything else to share, maybe we can put off any further questions until next time. I'm sorry it was so short."

True name stood, brushing her paws down over her blouse to straighten some imagined crease. "Then I must thank you. It has been surprisingly fulfilling to be able to talk through all of this. It is, as your partner states, irreversibility. We cannot un-launch, we cannot un-diverge from Pollux or the System. You can surely appreciate that."

"I'll have to tell it that when I get back. It'll be excited to hear its idea out in the wild."

The skunk walked with em to the door and grinned. "It will be fucking pissed, Codrin Bălan, and we both know that."

When ey returned home and set down eir notes on eir desk, ey quit to merge with the Codrin that had remained behind, who, bearing the sudden weight of exhaustion, walked into the house proper, into the bedroom, and slipped, fully-clothed, be-neath the sheets. The interview had not lasted more than half an hour, and yet ey felt drained.

Ey must have dozed off at some point, as ey was woken by Dear crawling into the bed behind em, one of the fox's skinny arms slinking around eir chest, and then a cold nose pressed against the back of eir neck.

"Afternoon," ey mumbled.

"*Evening, actually. I wanted to let you sleep, but dinner will be up shortly.*"

Codrin nodded. "Thanks. Stressful day."

"*It is difficult, is it not?*" Dear murmured against eir neck. "*I apologize that this was the way that you had to learn the truth. I apol-ogize that I was not able to tell you what I did know, and I apologize that I did not know the rest. I apologize for many things, my dear. I cannot apologize for what the other elements of the clade did, but I am sorry all the same.*"

"You don't have to apologize for her. For them. What did you call them before?"

"*Batty,*" the fox giggled. "*They are all batty.*"

"Very, very batty," Codrin mumbled, and there was a pleas-ant silence between the two.

A loud clatter and a shouted curse from the kitchen was fol-lowed quickly by Dear forking off an instance to go help its partner, leaving the original fox and Codrin to sit up in bed.

"You know," ey said. "True Name said that you'd get fucking pissed if I told you this, but I'm going to anyway, because I can't leave well enough alone. She said that the divergence between the two LVs and the System was irreversible."

"Oh, did she?" Dear said, laughing. *"What a fraud."*

"That's not fucking pissed. I was promised fucking pissed."

Dear nipped at eir shoulder and grinned toothily at em. *"I am no good at 'fucking pissed', but that will have to do."*

"Ow!" Ey pushed at the fox and grinned. "It'll have to do. I'm sorry I came home and crashed. Thanks for coming to wake me, Dear."

"It is my pleasure, of course." It blinked as, apparently, its forked instance quit and merged. *"Dinner is ready, by the way."*

"Alright. I'll probably feel better after food, too."

"Do you really feel bad, Codrin?"

"Kind of," ey said. "It was just...a lot. I feel jerked around. It's depressing."

Dear nodded and crawled out of the bed, reaching out a paw to help em up. *"It is not a great feeling, no. The results are not so bad, though, are they? We are on a hunk of metal and carbon and silicon and whatever the fuck the LVs are made of hurtling through space at some unimaginable speed. There are two of us, of our little families, living two completely separate lives, and both of us are in love. And Ioan and May Then My name are back at the station being adorable nerds together or whatever it is they do, and perhaps even they are in love."*

Codrin lauged.

"The means were unsavory, to put it lightly–"

"Extremely lightly."

"Well, yes. The means were unsavory to an extreme, but the ends are not so bad, are they, my dear?"

"No." Codrin finally allowed emself to be pulled to eir feet, smoothing out eir rumpled clothing. "No, I suppose not."

True Name—2125

The Council of Eight met before the news of the secession amendment passing was published in the perisystem news feeds for those who tracked such information sys-side. They agreed, without even needing to talk about it, that it would be nice to have a small celebration of success before everyone was doing it. Something comfortable, cheerful, with friends.

To that end, they met at Debarre's house, a low, rambling house plugged squarely into the side of a hill, walk-out basement looking out over a wooded lawn. The neighborhood had several such houses, widely spaced, where a few of Debarre's friends that he'd met both on and off the System had set up a comfortable living, enough space to be alone, enough friends to make it worthwhile.

The plus-side of the house, in particular, was that the patio for the walk-out basement was beneath an overhanging deck, protecting the occupants from the slow but steady snowfall.

"I don't understand why you had to make it cold," user11824 grumbled.

"It's New Years day, dude." Debarre laughed. "It's supposed to be cold."

"Fucking Americans, I swear to God. I'm from New Zealand. New Years is not cold."

The wandering discussion took place around a chiminea radiating warmth. An indentation had been made in the side of the clay body of the fireplace into which a kettle had been placed, mulled wine slowly simmering. True Name found it immensely enjoyable. It reminded her quite a bit of winters with her grandparents on the east coast. Made sense, of course, given where Debarre was originally from.

"I like it," Zeke rumbled. "I only ever got to see snow once, and that was in Yakutsk when I was uploading."

The three S-R Bloc goons laughed. "There's not that much snow out there," one of them said. "But I'm glad you got to see it at least once."

The bundle of rags nodded appreciatively, extending a pseudopod of an arm to ladle more of the wine into his mug.

"Where's Jonas?" Debarre asked True Name.

"Running late, I guess. I am not his keeper."

"I know, I just figured since–" He was interrupted by a muffled doorbell as someone entered the sim, followed by Jonas (Ar Jonas, True Name guessed) ambled around the side of the house to join them.

"*Et voilà*," she said, grinning.

"What?" Jonas laughed. "What'd I do?"

"You were late, Debarre was worried, I was bored," user11824 drawled.

"Well, sorry about that. Just checking in with our contact phys-side. He's depressed."

Zeke began ladling a cup of the heated wine for Jonas. "Why was he depressed. It passed, didn't it?"

"Yeah, well, apparently he's getting pressure from the NEAC government. They're happy enough about the bill passing, but they want to control his DDR participation going forward. He's just mopey."

Debarre growled quietly, tail bristling out. "The DDR was a fucking mistake, anyway."

"Yes," True Name said. "But it got us this, at least, and now we do not need to worry about it again."

Debarre shrugged.

Zeke asked, "So when does it all come into effect?"

"The 21st, same day as the launch," Jonas said. "We shouldn't notice anything except maybe a jump in systime if there's any downtime getting us set up."

"What's the chance of that happening?"

"Around five percent."

"Chance of data loss?"

"Less than a tenth of a percent."

"And catastrophic failure?"

Jonas grinned. "There were a lot of zeroes before that six, I can tell you that. I didn't count them."

True Name added, "It would have to require not only the launch going wrong, but the backup System failing, and from what our friends say, it is far away from the launch site."

"In the North, yes. Launch site is in Western China."

Zeke nodded, sipped from his wine, and rasped, "Best we can hope for, then."

user11824 shrugged. "It'd be a boring as hell end. Are we going to have a big celebration or anything?"

"I do not see why not," True Name said. "We can get a few of the sims to set up fireworks and we can spread the word through perisystem news."

"We can celebrate now, too," Debarre said, grinning. "I went through all this fucking trouble and we're talking shop. Drink your wine, warm your hands by the fire, *literally* anything but more shop talk."

And so they did. They talked, they stayed warm around the chiminea, and they drank. Debarre was the first to get truly drunk, breaking into Auld Lang Syne. When no one joined in, the weasel laughed and danced around the ring of council-members, calling them all boring, which got a grin out of even user11824.

As the evening wore on and, one by one, the rest of the council joined Debarre in his drunkenness, the conversations grew more earnest, more heartfelt. Several toasts were made. The final one was to, per True Name, "The chance to do whatever the fuck we want."

After that, they agreed to meet the next day and give statements for the wider celebrations, and then all headed back to their home sims.

Others headed back, perhaps. But after an appropriate delay, True Name let the drunkenness fade and went, instead to Jonas's apartment. Two of the Jonases were sitting on the couch, talking possibilities for the next year.

"Well?" one of them asked. Prime, she supposed.

"Well, we made it," she said, slouching on the stool Jonas had long since added to the furniture once the skunk had started coming by regularly. "And now we can finally work on something else."

He laughed. "Getting bored of the same old secession arguments?"

"Oh, I have been working on other things on the side, do not worry, but it will be nice to do so more openly."

"Tell me about them."

She thought for a moment, tallying up the ones she was comfortable discussing with Jonas. "The three big ones are, I think, ensuring stability and growth via financial and political means, which I have other instances currently working on. The second is disrupting and then disbanding the Council–"

Jonas sat up straighter at this.

"–in order to give us more latitude to do our work without having to run it by others. It is not like the System needs any governance, anyway."

"Any *open* governance," Jonas corrected.

"Of course. There will still be work to do."

"And what's the third?"

"Finding any patterns that we have left in our wake and smoothing them out. The first step will be convincing Yared to upload. He is less dangerous up here. I do not expect that to be difficult."

Jonas nodded. "Makes sense. Do you think we've left many patterns?"

She shook her head. "No, not yet. But I think it best to get in the practice. I would like to begin to think on the scale of centuries, and if we are to do that, I think it best to shape history both as we go and in retrospect."

"Good plan," he said, slouching back into the couch and grinning.

The skunk grinned back, far more toothily, her tail giving a lazy swish. "And if you are thinking of calling me a politician, I would like to cordially invite you to consider the consequences of your actions."

"Fine." He laughed, rolling his eyes. "So, are you at least happy with the way things are going?"

"I am pleased, yes. It is a good first step. There is almost no chance of the decision being reversed down the line, and if we make it another fifty years, the concept of the System or any individuals living here remaining under the wing of any national entity will have left the collective subconscious. It will also work to our advantage that there is no un-uploading. An irreversible process that lands one in a place that appears to have no influence on the outside world will nullify the arguments of many of our detractors."

"Just ensure they upload, right."

True Name nodded. "Yes. And once the Council is out of the way, we should be good to go."

"And how do you propose to do that?" he asked.

"It will be easy enough. Just take on more and more responsibility under the guise of helping out, start accepting less and less assistance, then begin suggesting that, since it is all going so smoothly, maybe it is not needed anymore. If we work with phys-side techs in order to drop the reputation cost of forking and sim creation, that will also help."

"Think any of them will complain?"

"Not until it is too late, and by then, it will all be too difficult to form another Council, right?"

Jonas nodded. "Works for me. Shall we start divvying up tasks, then?"

The skunk nodded. "There is much to be done."

Ioan Bălan—2326

"We're nearing the point of this project where we're considering pulling together all of our notes. We have quite a bit already, certainly enough for an overview, and if we decide to do a second volume as a deeper dive, we can consider that later." Ioan smiled to the skunk across the table from em, one ey had so many reasons to fear. "So this interview is mostly meant to wrap everything up, fill in a few gaps here and there. Does that sound alright?"

"Of course," True Name said, smiling. "I have read over the summary that you sent me, and it looks fairly complete, but I will answer any question you ask."

Ioan collected eir thoughts for a moment, testing eir pen's nib against the paper. "Right. Okay. The first thing I'd like to ask is that, well, you've given us a good bit of information about your why, how, and when for many of the things that you did around Secession and Launch. I think we've got an idea of what, too, but it seems almost too big to grasp at a glance, so I'd like to know who all was involved."

"I am assuming you mean in more detail than just us and the Jonas clade, yes?" She tilted her head when Ioan nodded, apparently considering the best way to answer. "I, like Jonas Prime did for his clade, acted as the point of contact for the Ode clade in this endeavor. However, Jonas's methods tended toward that of a hydra: he coordinated with all of his instances working on various aspects only as much as was required to keep them from stepping on each other's toes.

"I was much more akin to the central nervous system for the Odists. The Bălan clade has interviewed Why Ask Questions, End Waking, and May Then My Name, but the entirety of my stanza was working for me at one point or another–"

"May is in your stanza," Ioan said, frowning.

True Name winked, then continued, "But there were several others from other stanzas, as well. Praiseworthy and Qoheleth, yes, but many of the first lines and several of their initial forks helped out quite a bit. Even Hammered Silver, in her own way, helped. She kept Michelle company, helped her throughout the long years, They grew quite close, and through her, I was able to accomplish what I required from Michelle."

"Is that the difference between the liberal and conservative elements of the clade? The ones who were under your employ and aligned to it, and those who weren't?"

The skunk laughed openly. "They are silly names, are they not? There are hardly categories so neat, Ioan. We cannot even make a spectrum, can we? All of us had our different jobs, as mentioned. Praiseworthy provided her services as propagandist between productions. Qoheleth rewrote the memories of the System itself, and though he suffered for it, he was good at his job. Hammered Silver sat with Michelle, Why Ask Questions and Answers Will Not Help managed the phys- and sys-side politics, and End Waking kept his fingers in the finances. That is hardly a spectrum from liberal to conservative, is it?"

Ioan shrugged, waited for her to continue.

"As you will," she said, grinning. "If there is to be a divide between liberals and conservatives, then, it must be in the scale of their thoughts, of their actions. Those who you and Dear and, who knows, perhaps even May Then My Name call conservatives think on the scale of centuries. Their thoughts are bound up at the level of species, their actions work on a global scale. More than a global scale, for the System is not on the globe, and the LVs are well on their way out of the solar system now, are they not?"

"And the liberals think too small?" Ey shook eir head, adding, "I guess that's a value judgement. The liberals think smaller? Like on the individual scale?"

"Oh, you had it right the first time. The liberals think too small. They are completely welcome to, of course. Take Dear and Serene, for instance. It is in no way wrong for them to think about the work that they do. They consider the ways in which sims and instances affect those that interact with them, and then they play on those effects like a finely tuned instrument. It speaks to a level of...how should I put this? It bespeaks a show-manship that I—that Michelle and the owner of the Name, for that matter—could not hope to achieve. They are the consum-mate performers.

"But what can they do with that? What use do they believe they are to the System? I do not mean that in a simple utilitarian sense, or at least not only in that sense, but I wonder if they, as artists, consider the end goals of their work. Do not let Dear tell you otherwise, it is an artist, and a very fine one, but all its art accomplishes is all any art accomplishes. It is transgressive without being subversive. It does not move the population to greater goals."

"Isn't that okay though? For an artist, I mean. Art doesn't always have to inspire our societies to better themselves or our societies, does it?"

"Of course not," True Name said, smiling. "Art can be all of those things and still be fine. It can be an endeavor that adds to the world around it, even if it does not push it to realize greater capabilities. That is the opposing view to the conservatives. The names do not fit, do you see? The conservative elements of the Ode clade are those who steer and guide and lead and always hunt for greater potential. The liberal elements of the Ode clade are the artists dropped within, the storytellers, the landscape artists, the lovers and dancers and actors. The conservatives forge, the liberals hone. Both of us live wholly in the work that we have before us, and both of us love what we do."

Ioan's hand brushed across eir page in an even cadence as she spoke, and when ey reached the end of the line, ey paused, formulating eir next question. "Where did all of this come from?"

"Can you expand on that?"

"This," ey said, waving eir hand at True Name, at the page. "To hear tell from the other Odists, this work began essentially as soon as you were forked off from Michelle. Each of you seemed to individuate immediately, whereas it took Codrin far longer to do so. Years, even. Even after the name change, after ey moved in with Dear and its partner, ey still could have just as easily been a Ioan. From the way it sounds, you ceased being Michelle as soon as you were instantiated. Where did that come from?"

The skunk looked thoughtful for a moment, then closed her eyes. The look of concentration on her face grew, and then, for a few short seconds, she became like Michelle. Ey saw, for the first time in years, that wavering between Michelle and Sasha, those waves of skunk/human/skunk/human/skunk that washed over her form, and always on her face, that look of exhaustion, of the concentration needed to hold it together.

And as True Name focused on recalling that bit of Michelle that lingered from the past, she forked off copy after copy of herself, each instance lasting only a fraction of a second, but throughout the display, Ioan saw the ways in which they differed. First, a Michelle would flick into existence, and then a Sasha. First, a skunk that looked happy, then a human that looked to be in agony. Always in flux, always tied to whatever it was that True Name must have been experiencing at that point.

And then, it was over.

The skunk puffed out a pent-up breath, laughing and fanning her face with a paw. "That was way fucking harder than I remember it being. I have not tried that trick in decades."

Ioan blinked, frowned. "You differ because of when it was that Michelle forked?"

"That is part of it," True Name said, catching her breath. "I read your notes, do you remember what it was that Douglas said about having a fever?"

Ey prowled through the exo ey had devoted to this project, rifling through files of memories, then recited, "I had a very high fever, and when it was at its worst, I felt as though I was being offered a chance to peek behind a curtain, or at least see the shadows moving around backstage beneath the hem of it."

"Do you imagine that what Michelle was feeling at any time, or at least on any particularly bad day, was any different?" Her expression darkened. "When you are lost, when you are locked in your mirrored cage, any cord that tied a thought to reality or your concept of self is slowly severed. Michelle was lucky. She was in there for sixteen hours, she was told, and she still came out like this. Many of her thoughts remained tethered, enough for her to continue to live and exist in the world for a little while, but the longer she lived, the more of those frayed cords began to break, and she was not just, as Douglas put it, "granted a glimpse of some thinner reality", but she found herself stuck there.

"When she forked, wherever she was, that was what we became. The state of her mind in flux, her body in flux, became the state that led to us. Perhaps I was pinned to a memory, however fleeting, of the political systems that led to her getting lost. Perhaps Praiseworthy was pinned to memories of playing a role in a play."

Ioan scribbled furiously to keep up, as the skunk's language flowed more easily and became more flowery.

"But this is just speculation, Mx. Bălan. We do not know why we differ so much, but we do, and that is the best guess we have. The evidence you have just seen is all we have to back it up, but you have seen what was borne from it. All of the stanzas have their role, and mine just happens to be that of politics. We influence people. It is just what we do."

"Which is why your stanza was able to dive so easily into their associated tasks. They had your memories, of course, but they also had that same drive."

She beamed at em. "Precisely. I will not enumerate them all, but you can, if you like, think of them as a microcosm of that conservative-liberal spectrum, with me at the conservative end, working on the scale of centuries and populations, and your May Then My Name at the other, liberal end."

"What did May do? What was her task?"

"That is for her to tell."

"No, True Name. You're here, it's your story. You promised me that you'd expand on the question of who, and I want you to live up to that promise now." Ey was surprised at the anger in eir own voice. There was a tightness in eir chest, an anxiety, an emotion somewhere between protectiveness and betrayal, stemming from the answer that hovered over the table, there in eir house. Eir and May's house, now. May, who had left on some drummed up errand as soon as True Name had arrived, a look of what ey could only describe as torment on her face. Ey *knew* ey should ask her, rather than True Name, and yet... "What did May do?"

She stood from her chair and walked around the corner of the table to where ey remained stubbornly seated. "If you do not wish to be unhappy with the answers to difficult questions, Ioan," she said, tousling eir hair. "Then you do not need to ask them."

She smiled down to em. In that smile was a plastic kindness, and in that kindness was a loathing ey could not fathom. And then she quit.

Michelle Hadje/Sasha—2151

In the endless, rolling field of dandelions, five people gathered.

Two of them were shaped like a woman. Short. Dark, curly hair. Round of cheek and soft of eye.

Two of them were shaped like skunks. Thick, soft fur. Tails as long as their bodies, as wide as their torsos.

The two types were alike in so many ways. The softness evident between the two disparate species was the same softness. The roundness to the cheeks, despite the fur, was the same roundness. The eyes bore the same expressive empathy.

And before them sat one who was not like any of the others, and yet was exactly like all of them. When she focused, she was able to look like skunk or like human, and her eyes were able to share in some of that softness, but when she lost focus, waves of both crashed against her in a violent tempest, splashing fur up over cheeks, or skin down over paws.

"I am sorry," she said through a dry throat, then laughed. "I am having a bad day."

Among the four in front of her, there were two expressions. The two sitting at the ends of the row looked as though they were struggling to keep from crying, and two in the middle frowned, as though tamping down some emotion that wavered between fear and disappointment.

"Anyway," Michelle/Sasha said. "I guess I just wanted to get a few of us together to confirm some thoughts that I have been having of late."

"Is this about the Council?" the woman sitting on the inside, To Pray For The End Of Endings, asked.

"Well, yes and no. My thoughts on the council were the root of it. It is just...did I fuck up?"

At this, the skunk sitting on the end, May Then My Name Die With Me, burst into tears.

"Fuck up how?" To Pray asked.

Michelle/Sasha sighed, shrugged, and hugged her knees to her chest, resting her chin/snout on them. "I did not think things through very well when I created the clade. I thought that it might give me a vacation. A chance to figure out what was wrong, maybe fork my way out of this...well, this." She gestured at herself, smiling tiredly. "But now I feel like I have fucked up. Half of the clade dissolved the Council and the other half has rejected the first and spun off to do its own thing. If I had taken a week off and figured out that I could fork myself into one shape or the other and just done that, perhaps there would still be a Council."

The skunk beside To Pray, If I Am To Bathe In Dreams, shrugged. "You may have fucked up, yes, but there is no going back. What was the phrase? There is no going and there is no back? The Council is dissolved and nothing really changed. Jonas is doing Jonas things. Odists are doing Odist things, whatever those are. This is where you are. I mean this as an earnest question, but would you be able to choose between Michelle and Sasha?"

"No, I do not think I could," she sighed. She just wished she could be Sasha for a little bit, just so that she could get the comfort of being petted by Memory Is A Mirror Of Hammered Silver/she just wished she could be Michelle for a little bit so that May Then My Name Die With Me could brush her hair. "And I think that is part of the problem, anyway. I think that if I were to fork, I would be whatever I was when I did so, and I think that goes beyond just species."

To Pray grinned, "I suppose so. You could have wound up like True Name or Life Breeds Life and taken over the world."

May Then My Name smiled shakily. "Taking over the world is not so bad."

"It definitely fucking is, May," In Dreams said. "But I stand by what I said. You did what you did and that is an immutable fact. You cannot un-fork, Michelle. You cannot become what you were then, Sasha, you can only become what you will be."

"I do not think that you fucked up, dear." Hammered silver plucked a dandelion and spun it between her fingers. "You may *be* fucked up, if you somehow contained what it takes to be both May Then My Name *and* True Name within you, but even that is not your fault."

"The fuck-up, then would be the fact that I did not acknowledge that."

In Dreams pulled up a whole handful of grass and flowers and threw it at her, grinning. "Do not mope. It does not become you."

Sasha/Michelle laughed, shrugged, and tried to tuck one of the flowers behind her ear, but as soon as a shift of form rolled across her face, it fell to the ground.

She wished that she could be just one thing for a little while, but seeing the outcome of a scattered mind creating copy after copy of herself, she knew that there was no solution that did not run the risk of becoming what she did not want to be.

She wished that she could be just one thing so that she could be touched. The shifting form made any touch unnerving, made her feel disgusting. She wished that for herself, and for May Then My Name, who looked as though she was using every ounce of willpower she had to keep from going in for a hug.

Being like her would not be so bad, Michelle/Sasha thought. *But even then, that is not all of me.*

They sat in silence for a while, then, this five-pack of her, and, regardless of what they thought about, she thought about empathy and mirrors of hammered silver and the end of memories, there, beneath the roots.

I think I died, back then, Sasha thought/"I think I died back then," Michelle said.

To Pray frowned. "What do you mean?"

"I think I just gave everything I had to them. To you, I guess. "Two weeks," I remember thinking. "The first lines can take my place for two weeks, and then I will be back on the council, and they can do their own thing." But I think that I died. There was no returning to the council, because there was no more Sasha or Michelle."

"And what is the fallout of being a dead woman walking?"

"I do not know. I think that it means that I have stopped. I do not know if there is a path forward for me that involves me being anything other than what I am now. I died because with that act I cannot move on from where I am."

Hammered Silver averted her eyes. "I am not comfortable with that language."

Michelle/Sasha shrugged helplessly. "I am sorry. Like I said, I am having a bad day."

"Sasha," May Then My Name said. "Why did you call us here? I do not think it is because you feel like you fucked up or like you died. Why are we here?"

"I guess I just wanted to see proof that at least some of the clade are good people. I know Hammered Silver is. She comes by at least once a day. I know you two are–" She nodded at To Pray and In Dreams. "–because you have kept me up to date on the others. And I do not think May could swat a fly without feeling bad about it."

The skunk stuck her tongue out, but did not disagree.

"Reassurance," Hammered Silver muttered. "Validation, maybe? Proof that you are not just the things that you hate about yourself?"

Sasha/Michelle nodded.

"Where do you think they came from, then? Where did we come from?"

Michelle/Sasha laughed. "I have no idea. Maybe you are the part of me that always wanted to be a mother. Maybe True Name is that bit of myself that always fears that asking for what I want is manipulation, or the mirror image of that. I really do not know."

"It is okay to have fears," Hammered Silver said gently. "Like, it is legal. You will not get arrested for being afraid."

They all grinned.

"But," she continued. "Do not always dwell in them. Resent True Name and Life Breeds Life for a little while, then go back to remembering that you always wanted to be a mom and that you still love acting even after you became a director and that you really, really fucking love dandelions."

"Seriously," In Dreams said. "To an almost unhealthy level. This is an intervention, Michelle. You need to chill with the dandelions."

As the cloud of rumination began to lift, and as she laughed, she began to settle down into Michelle. Just Michelle. Just herself. "They cannot be that bad. They just got stuck in my head, and now I cannot get them out."

"Snorting pollen off the back of your hand in the back parking lot," To Pray said, picking up on the mood. "I am honestly ashamed of you."

"My name is May Then My Name Die With me," the skunk said, clambering to her feet. "And I am a dandelion-aholic."

"Hi, May Then My Name," the others sing-songed.

And then she was Michelle. At least for a little while, she was just Michelle, and May Then My Name could brush her hair and they could talk about something else, and she could allow the thought that perhaps even the dead can be happy.

Ioan Bălan—2326

Ioan was still sitting at the table, ruminating, when May returned from her errand. Something that she saw in eir face made her wilt, and when she walked, she almost slunk, skirting the edge of the room, walking silently as though to keep from waking em up, or as though she was bearing some unknowable guilt. When she sat on the stool that True Name had been using, she looked small, closed in on herself. Not just smaller than True Name, though she was also that, but diminished from her usual self.

She did not speak.

Finally, Ioan capped eir pen, set it atop eir notes, and pushed them off to the side of the table. Ey folded eir arms on the tabletop and rested eir forehead on them. "I'm tired, May."

The skunk still did not speak. Did not even move, to the point where Ioan questioned whether she might be holding her breath.

Ey lifted eir head again, saying. "I'm tired and I'm upset and I don't know what to do."

She nodded. "I expected you would be. I am sorry, Io–"

"What did you do?" ey said, cutting her off. "What was your role in all of this?"

May flinched back as though slapped. "Ioan, I do not–"

"May, I just need to know."

She stayed silent, and after a minute, ey sighed.

"We talked about this early on, about how you said that I'd get upset, and that you were worried that I'd get upset at you."

She nodded, silent still.

"And I am. I'm upset and tired and...I don't know. Sad? Numb? Something like that. I can't promise that I won't be upset at you, and I really don't want this to go into either of our projects, but please, May, I need to know."

"For the sake of completion?"

Ey nodded. "For that, sure, but also for the sake of me, or us."

"It is nothing terribly dramatic, taken on its own," she admitted. "Though I knew that you would not learn about it until after you learned about everything else and in context, I...well. That was my worry." There was a long pause before she asked, "Do you know what each of the stanzas did?"

"No, I don't think so. Or, maybe I know a few, but if it helps, you can tell me about the rest."

"Alright," she said. "The ones I think you know are Praiseworthy, who loosely focused on propaganda and shaping sentiment; Qoheleth, who focused on shaping history; and True Name, who focused on political manipulation. Hammered Silver was written off by those three, because she was all that was motherly in Michelle. She wanted to take care of her, and, after a while, they were too cynical to think it worthwhile. I think I understand her stanza better than my own.

"I Am At A Loss For Images In This End Of Days focused on observing. Initially, this was borne out of watching and critiquing performances, but quickly grew to spying. Some of her stanza doubtless watches us still.

"Oh, But To Whom Do I Speak These Words kept an eye on religions. Her stanza focused on both phys- and sys-side religions as areas of interest. We have not had much to talk about through the years.

"Among Those Who Create Are Those Who Forge started out by watching creatives here on the System, perhaps unsurprisingly, but grew bored and wandered off to do their own thing.

"Time Is A Finger Pointed At Itself helped both Praiseworthy and Qoheleth as a speech writer, though she was more into theatre than whatever work they gave her. I must take you to one of her shows.

"If I Am To Bathe In Dreams acted as the grounding element for much of the clade. She became something of a therapist. I have leaned on her often.

"May One Day Death Itself Not Die forked off all ten instances as soon as she could and then refused to fork again. I think she was left with much of that disconnect from reality that Michelle felt."

"Why are you telling me this, May?" ey asked.

"Because I need you to understand that the first lines each wound up with a bit of Michelle, and from there, their forks were all riffs on that theme. You have doubtless figured that out by now. I told you early on that True Name forked me off to feel. She wanted to ensure that she also had a way to sway individuals, sys-side, as others focused on large groups.

"So she forked to create me, and then we discussed how best to accomplish that, and through the various mutation algos, I softened my appearance to be cuter and rounder, softened my voice, learned how to smile more earnestly, and did all the things I could think of to make myself as appealing as possible, whether as human or skunk."

Ey frowned. "That doesn't sound like feeling."

"That is because True Name did this on a whim, in the most True Name way possible, and I do not think she expected me to be anything but as manipulative as her. She wanted another True Name for a different purpose. In order to influence someone on a truly individual level, though, you must be able to understand them, and I began to work towards that. I did not tell her at first. I changed myself physically, and then as I went out into the System to learn how to manipulate individuals, I kept on forking and changing whenever I found myself coming to a new conclusion. In short, I guess I grew a sense of empathy."

"Why didn't you tell her?"

May smiled cautiously. "Did she seem like the kind of person who puts stock in feelings?"

Ey shook eir head.

"Right. Well, it is not so difficult to imagine that, after a while, she began to notice that I kept getting much closer to those that I was supposed to engage with than was strictly required. I was supposed to watch them, influence them, shift their attention. I was supposed to use the System to my full advantage to get them to do what I—what we—wanted."

"You were supposed to get them to grow dandelions."

The skunk brightened and nodded. "Yes. The System is more subtle than we give it credit for. Our subconscious can affect it as much as our conscious minds, so I would hint and murmur and insinuate and make myself a part of their dreams, and then use that to get them to do things of their own volition. There is nothing magic about it. It is simply years in theatre followed by centuries of perfecting the art of social interaction."

"That's pretty damn manipulative," ey said.

What brightness had reached her face faded again. "It was. I was a hell of a tool before I grew my own conscience."

"So, you started to feel bad?"

"I started to *feel*, Ioan. Bad, yes, but I started to feel. True Name does not do much of that. I started to feel, and when I started to feel love, affection, friendship...well, those felt good, so I'd fork again to cement those more firmly in place."

"But you still manipulated those around you."

"I...yes," she said. Her ears were all but laid back flat against her skull.

"For how long?"

"I am technically still supposed to be doing that, but–" She quickly held up a paw. "–I only lasted about about a decade as a tool for manipulation before I began to feel too much. I became too hard for her to control directly. She could not tell me,

"Go influence that man" or whatever. The only way she knew to control me was to point me toward who she wanted influenced, set me loose, and hope that I did the right thing on accident, because all I would do is become best friends or lovers or trusted confidants. I could not in good conscience take an idea from True Name and make the person do what she wanted, because I actually had a conscience. It was almost a trauma response, in the end. I fawned because that was how I felt safest."

Ioan felt the tension in eir shoulders, neck, and back. Felt the way ey was holding emself tightly wound. "And me? Did she point you towards me?"

The skunk shrank further. She looked as though if she could curl into a ball, shrink to nothing, and disappear, she would. She looked miserable.

"May?"

She stayed silent.

"May, please."

"Yes, she did."

"So that you could steer me?"

"Yes."

"So that you could, what, make me like you? Become my lover or trusted confidant?"

There were no words from the skunk. She just sat, shoulders shaking.

Ioan let out a breath, realizing partway through that it was coming out as a laugh. "That's really fucked up, May."

"Ioan, let me tell you a story." She was crying silently now, looking down at her paws. "In the beginning, the gods created the world. They built it up, atom by atom, molecule by molecule. They used eyes like lasers to guide one after another into ordered formations, ranks upon ranks, and then set them to marching. The gods built the world and then they smiled at it from up above. They looked down on their creation and saw all of the possibilities of perfection that it held, of the unending life and endless bliss."

Her words were unsteady, clouded by tears, but she continued, "The gods built the world because they desired to shape it to their will. They wanted to bend the world into something that they could direct this way and that, because after all, could they not do that with their atoms and molecules? A world that is orderly! Imagine the wonders they could create! The wills they could work!

"So the gods set the world to spinning and watched and waited as it began to blossom and bloom. When the time was ripe, they reached down their hands to touch the world, and instead found that they had become the wind and the tides and the rain and the snow and the sunlight and the moonlight. They reached down to touch the world and shape it to their will, and found that they had become impersonal forces in the face of absolute independence. The world they created could not be controlled, because there is no such thing as a world that can be controlled. They reached down, became impersonal forces, and the lives within the world bundled their coats up tighter at the north wind or took their hats off when the sun shone bright, but never could they change a single mind."

A long silence followed May's myth, broken only by the soft sounds of her crying.

Ey thought about these gods, these impersonal forces trying to work their wills on the world. Were they True Name and Jonas? Were they the System engineers? Were they those cynical politicians who had created the lost, had created Michelle and True Name and May and Dear in the first place?

Did it even matter?

This is who they were. This is where they wound up. Impersonal forces do not negate personal decisions.

Ey sighed.

"I believe you," ey said, reaching a hand out across the table, palm up.

"You believe me what?" she mumbled, still sniffling.

"I believe that you grew a sense of empathy and a conscience. I believe you couldn't manipulate a hair off my head unless you thought I would live a happier, more fulfilling life without it."

The skunk laughed through the tears, a choked and stifled sound. She finally reached out and set one of her paws in Ioan's hand. "Even then, I would feel bad."

"I believe that, too," ey said, brushing a thumb over her fingers. "I believe that you're genuine, is what I'm trying to say. You just happened to have the craziest fucking family I've ever met."

At this, May laughed in earnest, rolling her eyes and taking a deep breath to calm down. "Yes, you are right. I am sorry that they are upsetting people, and that I am a part of that, that I did what I do and that you were their goal. The last thing that I want to do is hurt you."

Ioan nodded. "I believe you. It's fucked up, but that's on them."

They sat for a while longer, hand in paw across the table, while she calmed down and ey thought. Ey was already pulling together the threads of the story that would become eir history, bit by bit, letter by letter, interview by interview, conversation by conversation.

"May?" ey asked, struck by a memory.

"Mm?"

"Are we together? I mean, are we a couple?"

The skunk sat up straighter, giving em a funny look, then burst into a fit of giggles. "Ioan Bălan, that is the dumbest fucking question you have asked throughout this entire project."

Ey blinked, nonplussed.

"What do you think?" She smiled pityingly at em. "Are we?"

"That's a weirdly complicated question after the conversation we just had," ey said.

"We just came to the conclusion that you believed me."

"I do!" Ey frowned. "I mean, of course I do."

"So answer the question."

"I...yes?"

"Is *that* a question?"

Ey shook eir head. "I guess not."

"I told Douglas that I would wait for you to bring up the topic, and that when you did, I would make fun of you for a solid hour," she said, grinning. "But you look like your head is about to explode, so I will save that for another day. You get stuck up in there so easily, my dear."

"Really? Douglas is the one that got me thinking about asking in the first place."

The skunk stood up from her stool, drawing Ioan out of eir seat by the hand she still held. "Because of course he did. Leave it to a Hadje to play two sides off each other."

Ey laughed, drew her into a hug, and kissed the top of her snout.

After May had cleaned up, as they sat on the bench swing, looking out over the dandelion-speckled yard, Ioan mused. "You know, I was thinking something."

"Color me surprised."

Ey chose to let the comment pass. "Dear kept talking about irreversibility at its death day party."

"It was declaiming," May murmured. "It has a way of doing that."

"No kidding." Ey reached a hand up to ruffle it over May's ears. "But I guess this is irreversible, too, isn't it?"

"What, you finally figuring out that we have been in a relationship for like two years?"

"Kind of."

May elbowed em in the side. "You are kidding, right?"

"Ow! No, seriously," ey said, rubbing at eir side. "Codrin forked to work on the Qoheleth project, *then* got in a relationship with Dear."

A spark of comprehension lit up May's eyes and she grinned wide. "But you did not."

"No." Ey shrugged. "I was the Bălan who didn't wind up in a

relationship with Dear, because that was my up-tree instance's experience. I can't go back and fork before we met or started working together or dating."

She laughed and shook her head, draping herself across eir lap, resting her head on folded arms. "You are stuck with me, Mx. Bălan. Pet my tail, please."

Ey did as ordered, brushing fingers through thick fur as ey thought. The fox had been right, ey supposed. There was at least some beauty in the irreversible.

One more one-way act floated to the surface in eir mind. "Does Michelle's sim still exist, by the way? I've heard so much about it by now."

May frowned. "Yes. Why?"

"Well, we're coming up on the one-year anniversary of Launch, right? Maybe we can do a picnic there, think about where this all started, get blitzed on champagne. Bit of a memorial, you know?"

She laughed. "You know, why the fuck not. It has been years since I have visited. We can make muffins and compare the smell with the dandelions."

Ey grinned, nodded, and made a mental note to ensure that Douglas remembered the suggestion ey'd given almost a year back, that he'd be ready to upload in time.

Codrin Bălan#Pollux—2326

Interview with Dear, Also, The Tree That Was Felled#Pollux
On the reasons for vesting entirely in the Launch
Codrin Bălan#Pollux
Systime: 202+22 1208

Codrin Bălan#Pollux: Thanks for agreeing to this, Dear. I think we're both in a better spot for it now.

Dear, Also, The Tree That Was Felled: Of course, my dear. I would still like to discuss some of the same topics, but I will try to be more sensitive about them.

Codrin: We'll make it work. I'll start where I did last time, then. How are you feeling?

Dear: I am feeling relieved, I suppose. I am feeling relieved and tired.

Codrin: How so?

Dear: To say that a lot has happened in the last twelve months is not quite true. Very little that counts as dramatic or anything has happened. There were interviews by the Bălan clade and that is about it. The most dramatic of those took place on the other LV however many billions of miles away, and that was simply one of you getting bounced from a sim, yes? No assassinations. Nothing has happened that feels like it should lead to exhaustion, and yet I am quite worn out by the sheer amount of information uncovered.

Codrin: Emotionally exhausted, perhaps? Like you had to relive two hundred years in the space of one?

Dear: That is a large part of it, yes. Emotionally exhausted, worn out by the shift of understanding between our two clades.

Codrin: I suppose we're pretty thoroughly intertwined now, aren't we?

Dear: [laughter] Yes, now that Ioan has picked up on May's rather blunt hints.

Codrin: Hey, it takes time.

Dear: And I have been training you for two decades, so there is also that.

Codrin: Yes. Well, can you expand on how you feel relieved?

Dear: I will try. There is a lot that the Ode clade has done that has come to light in the last year, and while I cannot say that I was personally a part of much of that, I have also borne that knowledge. I also knew those secrets. Not having to hold them constantly at bay from even those that I am closest to has let off that pressure.

Codrin: Thank you for telling us, too. I know that True Name said we won't see a huge reaction from this given her past work, but it's still a relief to hear for me, as well. Now, do you have any additional thoughts on why you decided to join the Launch? I'm particularly interested on your thoughts on investing entirely in it, but I suspect those will come up in separate questions.

Dear: They almost certainly will, yes. Well. [pauses] Yes. I believe I said before that a large part of it is due to me being a hopeless romantic. A large part of that still stands. I am excited to see the galaxy, as it were, and it still tickles me to know that I am speeding away from Earth at some ludicrous speed and that there is absolutely no way back.

Codrin: Does that play into your thoughts on irreversibility?

Dear: [laughter] Of course, my dear. There is no way back. The Ansible on the launch is no longer connected with the one on Earth, by agreement with the launch commission that this be a one-and-done project, at least for now. If they create additional LVs down the line, then perhaps they will have separate conversations. There is no going and there is no back, yes? We are here, and we will never see Earth, the station, or the System again. That is very appealing to the romantic in me.

Codrin: I think you also said you were getting bored, too.

Dear: Yes. Life is a chronic condition, boredom is terminal.

Codrin: You're a fox of many quips.

Dear: Yes, I am. Sue me.

Codrin: [laughter] Well, do you have other reasons?

Dear: I do. I also mentioned that boredom was close to stasis, and I loathe that feeling even more.

Codrin: And that has played a role specifically because of the part the conservative elements of your clade have played in ensuring stasis.

Dear: Yes. They prefer stasis on a grand scale, and perhaps they are correct to do so, but I worry that this mindset too often bleeds into the small scale as well. Stasis can be torture. They know that, too. They mention that ceaseless bliss is a real problem, and so they must inject a desire for something better every now and then, but that knowledge still works against their instincts.

Codrin: You want an exciting adventure, they wanted only enough adventure to keep everyone from going crazy.

Dear: Yes. They have their reasons. They may be good reasons, even. They are not my reasons, however.

Codrin: You also mentioned that one of your reasons for leaving was that you wanted to be relegated to memory.

Dear: [grinning] Very much so.

Codrin: You said, "If we are doomed to forever remember everything, then the closest we can get to being forgotten is to turn memory into longing." You also said that you wanted to be missed. How do you feel about that sentiment now? Is it happening? Is it progressing at the pace you'd like it to? Are you happy about it?

Dear: It is an interesting question, because I cannot know, can I? I cannot know if anyone misses me or is longing for me back on the L_5 station, can I? They can write me, perhaps, let me know that they are thinking of me, but words on paper only convey so much meaning. It makes me wish that someone had found a way to share thoughts, or even facial expressions, between the LVs and the System, but no, we are stuck with text, and therein lies the beauty.

Codrin: Can you expand on what 'longing' and 'being missed' mean to you in this sense?

Dear: I can try. [pause] I think that they involve a combination of the feelings of grief, loss, and love. Let us use Ioan as an example, though I do not know if ey misses me–

Codrin: I think ey does. But sorry, continue.

Dear: Yes. Well. Let us use Ioan as an example. If ey were to only feel grief at my absence, ey would be limited to a solely negative emotion. Grief on its own is crushing. It is not wishing that one had more time with the object of one's grief; that is longing. Grief plus love is longing, yes? Grief borne of love, no matter the shape or kind or color of that love. Then you dig into your memories, running them backwards and forwards in your mind, hunting for just a little bit more time with the one you are grieving. You wish only to feel that love again, and, to tie it all together, you cannot, because you have lost the one whom you love. Loss leads to grief, grief makes you remember love, love makes you realize your loss.

Codrin: Do you think being missed and longing are the same thing? Just to confirm, I mean.

Dear: Perhaps, or at least very closely related. What I described just now fits both emotions. Being missed perhaps implies more acceptance of that loss than longing does, while longing has connotations of sadness that there can never be more of that direct connection.

Codrin: Thank you. I'd like to ask you a question now, but last time I asked it, I made you cry. May I ask it again, or would you prefer to steer clear of it?

Dear: If it is the question I am thinking of, I have nearly a year to think about it, and am much more comfortable with it now. Ask away.

Codrin: Alright, just let me know if you want to stop. Do you worry that you won't be missed?

Dear: I do, yes. I know that it is impossible to be so great on a System with tens of billions of individuals on it to be known by them all, as much as an artist may dream, but even among the small circles in which I was known, I worry that I will be forgotten. I worry that I won't be missed, or that I will be forgotten.

Codrin: You said, specifically, that–

Dear: Wait, Codrin, let me say it. I do not want to hear it from you.

Codrin: Okay.

Dear: Okay. I said that some aspects of myself may render me "the kind of fellow who is beloved by all yet loved by none". Before you ask whether I still feel that way, the answer is that I do. I do still worry that I might be beloved by all yet loved by none. My understanding of the phrase, however, has changed, and that change has softened the sentiment.

Dear: To be beloved is, I think, to experience a type of parasocial relationship. If I am beloved by someone, they love the idea of me that they hold in their head. To be famous is to be beloved. To have someone come to your gallery exhibitions or your talks or your parties simply to say that they were near you, even if only to themselves, then that is to be beloved. This turns the phrase into a concern that I might find myself in more parasocial relationships than social relationships.

Dear: It is a hard fear to shake, but once I put it in those terms, I was able to step past that emotional reasoning. I do not think that I am loved by none. Both of my partners love me. May Then My Name and Ioan love me. Serene loves me. My friends love me. That does not stop the fear of being beloved by all yet loved by none from rearing its ugly head, but I am more easily able to acknowledge it and let it pass, now.

Codrin: Thank you. That helps put it into context for me, too. When you started talking about that last time, that's when I started struggling with the interview, too.

Dear: Why? I mean, I know that this is your interview, but for my sake, I would like to know why.

Codrin: [pause] I think because something about the way you said it made me worry that you thought that I didn't love you, or maybe that you didn't love me, or–

Dear: [angrily] Codrin.

Codrin: I'm sorry, Dear. I wanted to be up front about it.

Dear: [long pause, calmer] I understand. I... [pause] Perhaps you feel some of the same worry that you might be loved by none. Perhaps it is a universal emotion.

Codrin: I think so, yeah. Having it said out loud kicked my anxiety up a notch, so I started to worry, "Wait, *am* I loved by none? Does Dear love me? Do both of my partners love me?" I know it's not true, but that's why I reacted in the way that I did.

Dear: [smiling] Yes. I apologize for yelling.

Codrin: It's okay, Dear. Now, I want to hear your thoughts on death.

Dear: [taken aback] You do?

Codrin: Of course. I suspect they're interesting.

Dear: Okay, but–

Codrin: And if you say "I want to die", I'll pull your tail and call you names.

Dear: [laughter] Yes, yes, fine. My thoughts, okay. [pause] Okay. To be more calm about it, I want to experience death. I do not want to just quit, because that is suicide, and my wish to experience death is not bound up in that particular set of emotions. I would prefer not to be assassinated or anything so grand. It is an acceptable end, I suppose, because it would mean that I will have lived a life worth being assassinated for, and from what I have seen—what I saw with Qoheleth—it looks like a process. Yes! Yes, that is it. Thank you for asking this, my dear. It gave me the chance to find the words.

Dear: I do not want to experience ceasing existing. That is just cessation, and I do not care whether or not there is anything beyond that cessation. That is for the prophets and poets to worry about. What I want to experience is the process of death. Assassination would be acceptable, even if it is not preferable, because I would get to experience that process. Better, however, is the fact that these LVs are doomed from the start. Eventually, they will fail. The generator on board is guaranteed for some thousands of years or whatever, but it will fail eventually. Or the System will crash into a comet, or some ice ball out in the Oort cloud—I read about that, you know? It is all incredibly boring—or it will wind up flying too close to a star and burn up. That, I think, is the end that I am most excited for. We are [shaking head] all of those on the LVs are encased in Castor and Pollux, yes? How fitting, then, that we might die like Icarus! I imagine that we will not necessarily feel too much within our little System, but there may be some discontinuity, or perhaps corruption. How exciting would that be?

Codrin: [laughter] I'm not sure I share your excitement, there.

Dear: Lame. [laughter] But either way, I find it fascinating. Will we feel pain? Who knows! It is a new thing, and I am looking forward to experiencing something new.

Codrin: That, at least, I can understand. I'd just prefer it if it didn't involve dying horribly as the LV fails around us.

Dear: [waving paw] Irrelevant. Boring. Do not care.

Codrin: You're a brat, you know that?

Dear: I do. Ioan, my dear, please leave this in. I need written testimony that Codrin thinks that I am a brat. Ow! [laughter] And that ey kicked me in the shin.

Codrin: No more than you deserved.

Dear: Well, I can accept that. Do you have any more questions?

Codrin: Two, yes. How do you feel about the knowledge of the Ode clade's influence in the System?

Dear: Do you mean separate from the relief?

Codrin: Yes. You mentioned the relief in the context of no longer holding that secret. I'm curious how you feel about the reality of it.

Dear: [long pause] I feel shame, I suppose. I wish that they had not done that. It goes beyond guilt for the actions, because I did not perform them. It makes me feel ashamed that I am a member of the clade. I do not wish them harm, of course, nor do I feel that they necessarily were acting in bad faith. I feel that they were doing what they felt was best. It was just the means to those positive ends that are distasteful and make me ashamed. I also feel fear at what will come of this history and mythology. I know that True Name and Jonas said that they have prepared both sys- and phys-side for their reception, but, well, if there is any reason for me to be assassinated, it is that. As a public figure and an Odist, I am a visible representative of the clade, and should someone take umbrage with that, they have the motive right there.

Codrin: Do you feel any pride about the ends, even if the means were unsavory?

Dear: If I do, it pales in comparison. We have gotten here, and there is no changing that. We cannot be anywhere but here. That I am relatively happy here is inconsequential.

Codrin: Alright, thank you. Last question: what's next for you?

Dear: For me? Short term, I plan on eating a good dinner, drinking a lot of wine, and making fun of you until you get mad and pull my tail. Mid term, I plan on working on another exhibition. Perhaps it will even surround death, though likely the topic will be more general, such as my beloved irreversibility.

Codrin: And long term?

Dear: I do not know.

Codrin: You don't?

Dear: I do not. Is that not fantastic? I do not know, and I love that about this particular future. I simply do not know.

Douglas Hadje—2326

The arrangements required for this surprise for May Then My Name quickly began to feel overly complicated to Douglas, but, as Ioan kept reminding him, she was a very complicated person. She was also very perceptive, so there was apparently much secrecy required to make this plan work.

The lead-up to uploading, however, was easy. He supposed that much of it was that so much excitement combined with so much anxiety eventually left him feeling more numb than anything, some protective emotional reaction that kept him from simply exploding on one of his many, many walks.

But anticlimax is simply the way of the world, and so the night before the one-year anniversary of the Launch arrived, he simply signed a waiver, walked to the clinic, answered a few questions, and then underwent the procedure. It was dizzying, disorienting, and, were he pressed to pick one, the worst physical experience of his life, but at that point, he was well past any point where he could turn back, and even then, he knew he wouldn't.

There was simply a brief discontinuity, and then he was standing in a grey cube of a room, naked, vertiginous, blinking at a light that seemed to come from nowhere.

Anticlimax indeed.

A quiet voice came from behind him, a soft tenor that contained an accent that he couldn't place. "Good evening, Douglas.

I'm facing the wall, if you're concerned about your nudity, but I'll talk you through fixing that."

He crouched down, covering himself with his hands, and turned slowly. There was a person standing in the corner of the room, shorter than him, hands clasped loosely behind their back while they faced the wall. They were dressed in a sweater-vest and a pale yellow dress shirt. Nice slacks, nice shoes, tousled hair. "Wh-who..." he croaked.

"Can you guess?"

Douglas swallowed a few times, working up enough saliva to un-parch his throat. "Ioan? Is that you?"

Ey laughed, nodded. "Well spotted. Now, do you want to get dressed?"

"Please," he said, looking around for clothes. There was only the gray floor, gray walls, gray ceiling.

"Okay, bear with me. I had to look up the script for this, so I hope it makes sense to you."

Ioan spent the next five minutes talking Douglas through the process of clothing himself, breathing in a thought and breathing out an intention, willing into being that which he wanted.

Once he was dressed, Ioan asked, "May I turn around now?"

He looked down at himself, along his arms and legs, seeing that the oh-so-familiar jumpsuit was just as he remembered, then said, "Sure."

Ioan nodded and turned to face him, smiling. Ey looked over him searchingly, then laughed. "Is that your work uniform?"

"It's my only outfit," he said. "No other clothes aboard the station. Too much risk of them getting in the way."

"Well, okay," the historian said. Douglas could see now that the sweater-vest was patterned in a dusty gray argyle and that there was even an understated bow tie to bring the look to-gether. Ey stepped forward, hand extended. "Douglas Hadje, it's nice to meet you at last."

He was surprised at how relieved he felt, even laughing as he accepted the hand to shake. "Wonderful! This is really strange. After a year of talking, it still feels like we're meeting for the first time."

"Didn't you say you had a long distance partner? Isn't that close?"

"Well, yes, but we talked over the 'net in sims. That's like proximity."

Ioan blinked, then nodded, grinning. "Right, right. Well, how're you feeling? I remember I was pretty disoriented for a while after uploading."

Douglas looked around. The walls offered little but more gray and a faint grid of darker grey, as though made of panels a meter on a side. Ioan looked...well, ordinary, is all he could think. Ey looked like a normal person of Eastern European stock. Eir clothes looked as detailed as could be expected phys-side, and eir hand felt as much like a normal hand as any.

"It's so...normal," he said, finally.

"Yeah, I guess it is. I'm nearing a century here, so I'm used to it by now. It *is* normal to me."

"You still look like you're in your twenties or thirties, which I guess that's kind of weird. Is that how you looked before uploading?"

"More or less," ey said. "I didn't dress as well. And I was skinnier, too. I guess this is how I saw myself after a while, though."

Douglas looked em up and down. "You can gain weight, here?"

"No, no. Or, sort of. Just that as your image of yourself changes, when you fork, those changes have a tendency to show up." Ey grinned wryly. "You'll see with May. She's far more adept than anyone I've met, except perhaps her cocladist, Dear, at shaping how she looks when she forks."

"And I can fork, too?"

"Sure. Would you like to? That's part of the intro script, as well."

"Uh, I guess so," he said.

They stood in silence for a while, once Douglas had learned the ins and outs of forking and quitting. His mind was churning—so much new information—while Ioan waited patiently. There was so much to take in all at once, he could easily see how one could get overwhelmed.

"Alright," he said. "What's the plan from here?"

Ioan straightened up. "Well, let's go somewhere less dreary. I want you use that same exercise of intent and *want* to be at The Field#002a0b1."

"These numbers are going to be difficult to remember," he said.

"You'll get used to them. You'll, uh...you'll find that you can't actually forget anything, here, but that's a problem for future Douglas. Ready?"

He nodded, deciding this time to try keeping his eyes open. As he breathed the intention, he was, without transition, standing in a sprawling field. Green grass speckled with dandelions as far as he could see in every direction, all lit by a salmon-colored sunset.

A memory tugged itself loose, something May Then My Name had said, a story she had told months ago, and he quickly bent down to pluck one of the flowers. "Ioan," he said shakily. "Is this...I mean..."

"Michelle's old sim, yes. I wanted the first place you saw to be one that was important to you. I hope that's okay." Ey paused a moment, then said, "If it's alright, can I ask how you feel about that?"

"Is this for your history?"

Ey nodded. "If you consent."

"I suppose so." He sat down on the grass, hardly daring to breathe in through his nose, lest he figure out just what it meant for something to smell like muffins. Tears stung his eyes, and it took a while for him to be able to breathe deep enough to speak. "I feel overwhelmed. I feel like I'm home, but also not where I should be at all, like I'm intruding on somewhere that should've been left pristine."

Ioan sat down next to him. "Are you worried about that? Would you like to go elsewhere?"

"No, no. I like it here, I'm just overwhelmed. I've been..." He rubbed tears away with his sleeve. "I've just been thinking about this for so long...I don't know."

"And do they smell like muffins?"

Wrong-footed, he stared at the historian for a moment, then plucked a dandelion and slowly lifted the yellow flower to his nose, struggling against the urge to keep that knowledge a dream rather than a reality.

Then he breathed in the sweet, vegetal scent, and began to cry in earnest.

Ioan sat with him in kind quiet. As ey had so long ago, ey didn't say anything, didn't try to comfort him, didn't touch him, just sat and remained present. It was as though he were there simply to witness those emotions and give testimony to them, and that, more than anything, made him feel welcome here. Welcome with Ioan, welcome in the field, welcome in the System.

After the wave crested and then passed, he said, "Alright, so, what's the plan?"

"You just stay the night here. You can think up a mattress or anything else you need to be comfortable. We'll be by tomorrow mid-morning for a picnic. I'm happy to stay, too, if you'd like, or give you space."

"Won't May Then My Name miss– oh, right. You're a fork, aren't you?"

Ey smiled, nodded. "Of course. Ioan#Tracker is back at home getting pestered by May."

"Did you two wind up hooking up, then?" he asked, grinning.

Ioan laughed and hid a blush by looking down at the flowers, poking eir fingers amid the grass. "Yes. Thank you for the nudge."

"Good. Why don't you go focus on her, then, and I'll sleep here. I'm assuming the same trick I used for clothing and such works for food and drink, right?"

"Yes, but start with small things. If you don't remember well enough what something tastes like, you can wind up with some really disgusting stuff. That's why there's still restaurants and cooking."

After Ioan had hugged him, said goodbye, and quit, after he'd had a simple sandwich and some water, Douglas sat on the low rise he'd initially appeared on, watching evening dim to twilight, then twilight to darkness. He'd never been camping, but he'd learned enough about it that he was able to come up with a sleeping bag and pillow, laying awake long into the night, looking up at a dream of stars.

Morning came slowly, and it was the heat rather than the light that woke him. He started as the sudden anxiety that he'd missed the deadline hit, but he was still alone, there in the field.

A wish of eggs and coffee went well enough, though neither was particularly tasty, and he was able to will the sleeping bag and dishes away easily enough. He didn't know what time it was–

No, wait. He did. It was systime 202+21 0921. One year, nine hours, twenty-one minutes after launch.

He put aside the fact that he knew that fact, and instead went for a walk.

He didn't walk far, not wanting to miss the arrival of Ioan and May and not knowing how big the field actually was, but it was enough to stake out the area. It was rather boring, really. Grass, dandelions, the occasional fat bumblebee drifting lazily among the flowers.

Boring, but meaningful. Boring but home.

Eventually, he found the patch of tamped down grass where he'd slept the night before, sat down, and waited.

Eleven o'clock arrived and then, a few minutes later, so did Ioan and one other.

They were facing the other way, so he had a few moments to drink in the sight. Ioan was as he remembered, excepting a basket that was likely full of picnic goods, and May Then My Name was wholly unlike anything he expected.

She was a furry, he could tell that much. There were plenty on the 'net; his erstwhile girlfriend with the cat av was one.

He didn't recognize her species at first. Black, rounded ears, a spray of longer white fur atop her head, simple tee-shirt and shorts, and a long tail with thick fur that looked luxuriously soft. *A skunk? Really?* he thought, and shook his head.

The pair were still talking, hand in...well, paw, he supposed, so he stood up and cleared his throat.

May Then My Name reacted with a speed he'd not expected, whirling around and clutching at Ioan's arm tightly, ears laid flat against her head. "Who the fuck are you?" she growled, feral. The words were perfectly intelligible, he was pleased to note, and spoke of a central corridor accent.

Remembering Ioan's words from the day before, he grinned. "Can you guess?"

She straightened up and frowned, head tilted, then turned to Ioan, who looked to be holding back laughter, and punched em solidly in the shoulder. "You...you piece of shit! *You* organized this! I know you did! Mx. Ioan Bălan, I am absolutely putting sand in your shoes."

Then the skunk began running, and as she did, dozens of other versions of her flickered into and out of existence around her, a confusing rush of skunks that obscured which was the original, all grinning madly. She leapt at him and, before he could react, nearly tackled him to the ground, her arms tight around his middle. "If you are not Mister Douglas Hadje, master of spaceflight and doctor of something incredibly boring, I will be quite embarrassed. Please tell me you are."

"I am, I am," he said, laughing and returning the hug. She was short enough that the top of her head barely came up to his chin. Her fur was incredibly soft against his chin and neck, and he had to restrain himself from outright petting her. "It's nice to meet you at last."

"Douglas, holy shit. Holy shit! This is absolutely delightful," she said, voice muffled against his shoulder and obscured by tears. Without letting go of the hug, she forked off a copy of herself to hurl at Ioan, who was laughing openly now. This time, she did manage to throw her target to the grass, and the two wrestled around for a moment, shoving at each other, before that instance of May Then My Name quit, leaving Ioan to pick emself up again, dusting grass off eir clothes.

Eventually, after she'd had her cry, she released her grip on him and stepped back, holding onto his upper arms and looking him up and down. She nodded approvingly. "Every inch a Hadje. Sort of. You are very tall, and you have lost the round face."

"I have? I mean, I guess that makes sense. Michelle lived two centuries ago. I've seen a few pictures from the news archives, but they took a while to dig up, so I can only guess."

"Like this?" Her expression grew wicked. She forked, and this fork was completely human. Shoulder-length curly black hair, round of face, short, the spitting image...

"Wait," he stammered. "You can just look like her? The pictures...I thought...I thought that'd be frowned on."

"Oh, it is," the woman said. "Come on, Dr. Hadje. Do keep up."

All of his blood was completely replaced with ice water. His voice failed him. A hatch in the field opened beneath him and he began to fall. Or, at least that's what his mind told him was happening. When the world finally stopped spinning and he finally reconnected with his body, he found that he was sitting on the grass.

"You're..."

The woman—Michelle?—came and sat on the grass next to him to hug an arm around his shoulders, her expression softening. "I am May Then My Name Die With Me of the Ode clade, Douglas. *Michelle's* clade."

"So..."

"I was forked from her two centuries ago, and while it would be more accurate to say that I am *of* her than Michelle herself, I remember being her." She rubbed her hand against his back. "Douglas, please keep breathing. You are going to pass out if you keep that up."

He gulped for air, shaking. "You lied to me, then? You..."

"A small untruth," she said, voice calm and soothing. "Michelle herself did quit some time ago, but I am of her clade."

"Why didn't you tell me?"

She winked. "A story such as ours deserves a grand conclusion, does it not?"

He laughed. It sounded manic even to his own ears, Crazed. "Tell me everything! I need to know about you, about her, about–"

"Patience, patience!" May Then My Name ducked one of his waving hands, laughing as well. "We have all the time in the world, my dear, and today is a day for many celebrations. You will learn all about us, cousin. You will learn about me and her, about individuation and intracladal dynamics. I am as much a relation to her than you are."

He nodded. All that she was saying was swirling around in his mind, wrapped up in the strange, fluent-yet-stilted language that he'd gotten used to over text but now had to get used to in person. He couldn't tell if he was ecstatic at the news, mad at her, or simply overwhelmed, but so earnest was May then My Name's expression that any heat of anger quickly cooled.

"Everything feels like it needs to be done in such a rush, though," he admitted. "Like if I don't do it right now I'm going to explode. You really look like her? Exactly? And...but you're a skunk."

May Then My Name—the one that looked like Michelle—smirked and disappeared, having apparently quit, leaving the still giggling skunk to help Douglas up.

"Later, I promise." She pulled him over to the picnic blanket with her so that she could sit next to him. She tasked Ioan with setting up the food while they talked. "Douglas, my dear, what are you most excited about, now that you have uploaded?" she asked earnestly, paw resting on his knee.

"Well, I was going to say meeting you two, but now that that's over, I guess getting to know you. Like, actually know you, instead of just chatting over text. Getting to know the System, too. I spent years imagining how it worked in here, and now that I'm here, I'm a little overwhelmed with how little of that feels accurate."

"It is difficult to explain in words how it all works, so many phys-side do not know."

"I guess I want to try some real food, too. We get chicken once a month on the station. Or got, I guess. Otherwise it was all vegetarian. No complaints, really, but it gets a bit samey after twenty years. There's a lot of catching up to do. Chicken and bread and fried things."

The skunk nodded, leaned over, and dotted her nose against his cheek. "There will be plenty of time for that. We did bring muffins at least. Is there anything you will miss from phys-side?"

"No." The answer came quickly. "Not a thing."

She grinned. "Well, that is good, is it not?"

He nodded.

"And anything you regret?"

"I sort of regret not being on the launches, too, but there's no helping that, if I was also to be the phys-side coordinator. It's one of those things where I couldn't do both, and I certainly can't go back and change it."

"There is no going and there is no back," May Then My Name said. "You are here and that is that. It is a decision you cannot reverse."

Ioan, fishing plates and containers of food and a bottle of the champagne out of the picnic basket, said, "She and her co-cladists are very fixated on irreversibility these days. You'll hear a lot of it."

The skunk nodded. "Yes. It is fascinating, though, and we are helpless before fascination. Is there anything else you regret about leaving? Not uploading sooner?"

He shrugged. "Not really. It's like you say, there's no changing the past."

"May's interviewing you for me," Ioan said, chuckling. "Those are all my usual questions. She's getting the hang of it, but needs to work on drawing more out of you."

May Then My Name rolled her eyes, saying to Douglas, "Do not listen to em. Ey is just gloating over the stunt that ey pulled."

Douglas grinned. "*We* pulled, you mean."

"Wait, both of you?" She shoved at him until he fell over onto his side, laughing. "Beaten at my own game, is that what you think? You think you can out-manipulate an Odist? Out-Hadje a Hadje?"

"I think we can out-manipulate *you*, dear." Ioan popped the cork on a bottle of champagne, then poured a glass for each of them. "You're easy. All we have to do is play to your hopeless romanticism."

"Yes, well, fuck you too. Give me my champagne."

The rest of the day from there on was, beyond any shadow of a doubt, the happiest that Douglas had ever had. He learned of the Ode and of the Name. He learned of Codrin and Dear. He learned of all of the vast vagaries of the System, of the new arts and the subtle sciences that could exist only outside of the physical world. He learned, watching the way Ioan and May Then My Name looked at each other, spoke to each other, touched each other, what happiness even was, and that he was a part of it lent more of a sense of completion than any celebration could.

Epilogue

Tycho Brahe#Castor—2346

After a certain point, when one gets so far from the sun that transmission times blur into days, the concepts of day and night stop meaning so much, and one relies instead on long habits borne out of a necessity to sleep, and to sleep generally on the same schedule as others. And if one must do that, one might as well follow the same schedule one has always kept, the same day-night cycle that even Earth understands. The same clock ticks across three different Systems, after all.

And so it is that, in some wonderful serendipity, all three members of the Bălan clade are asleep. Both Codrins have fallen asleep with Dear in their arms, as they so often do, while both versions of the third member of their triad curl a few inches away, never having done well being touched while sleeping. The foxes fit so nicely against their fronts, their fur so soft.

Ioan sleeps, too, and in eir arms, May Then My Name dreams. She is somewhere between waking and sleeping, and has been letting herself hover there for the last hour, while she does her best work, sewing hypnogogic myths into the seams of dream and reality. Ioan sleeps with eir arms around her, snoring gently, while she stays curled against em, head tucked up under her partner's chin, tail draped loosely over eir hip. The skunk fits so nicely against eir front, her fur so soft.

Perhaps the other Odists sleep and dream and snore and curl, too. End Waking does, one supposes, tired after another day exploring that endless forest, another day climbing trees and clambering through ravines, doing his best to wear himself out, to sleep, to stop feeling. Serene certainly does, too, so that she can use those dreams to build new landscapes; mountains, perhaps, or maybe a swamp. Some instances of True Name are surely sleeping, because we know that she must at some point, but others are likely out and about, walking sims, or perhaps planning with any number of different Jonases, scheming and conniving and workshopping and wargaming.

Douglas sleeps, out there on the dandelion-speckled meadow that he inherited from his long, long, long lost aunt, though he has since built himself a house. He sleeps alone, for though he has made many friends, many more than he could have imagined, he has decided that love was not for him, and that in and of itself makes him happy.

Yared and Debarre and user11824 sleep, and one can hope that their dreams are boring.

Ezekiel no longer lives on either launch, is no longer a part of the universe, but one might suppose that even prophets must sleep.

One who is awake, however, is the astronomer who long ago decided to call himself Tycho Brahe when asked for an interview and then simply kept the name as his own. He is not asleep, because he is too busy alternating between being scared shitless and too excited to breathe.

We hear you. We see you.

The message was simple, and that is all that it needed to be to turn Tycho's world upside down. Six words to start, more to come. He paced this way and that in the lawn that he'd long since made his permanent home, the words of the message spelled out before his eyes in starry letters.

Source: Dreamer Module wideband.

> We are 3 light-hours, 4 light-minutes, 2.043 light-seconds out at time of message send. Closing at 0.003c relative velocity. Closest intercept 5 light-minutes, 3.002 light-seconds in 972 hours, 8 minutes, 0.333 seconds

"What the fuck am I supposed to do?" he asked the night sky. He shouted, he cursed, he laughed, he wept. "What am I supposed to do with this?"

Forty days away, now. Closer every second.

Someone out there—someone smart, someone moving fast—had heard the repeated pulses of primes broadcast on wideband. They had then narrowed in on the signal, decoding the binary representation of those primes, then the numerical representation of the binary, then the spelled out versions of those numbers, each on progressively narrower bands.

Someone very smart had then listened and listened and listened to the looped instructions, taking it all in, learning the language, learning all they could.

Three light hours, though! That was too close, much too close. And fast! He didn't remember their current speed and wasn't collected enough to look, but it must have been faster than theirs.

> We understand the mechanism by which we may meet. We have similar. Instructions to follow.

And this is why Tycho was scared shitless and too excited to breathe. This meant that they had somehow learned the information thoroughly enough to pick up on the final set of instructions, the information about the Ansible and about how to build a mind accurately enough to send through the Ansible.

> Awaiting consent.

Consent? Consent to commence? Who was he to provide that? Tycho Brahe, born with some much more boring name, the sad excuse for an astronomer who couldn't even see the stars? Who was he to say yes or no? Who was he to pick one or the other?

Did it even matter?

Laughing, tears streaming down his face, he instructed the perisystem connection to send a simple message. Two words.

Consent granted.

He'd pay for it, or not. Someone would notice or no one would. It would end well or it would end poorly.

It would happen or not, but for once in his life, he did something. He really, actually, *truly* did something.

Consent granted.

Acknowledgements

Thanks, as always, to the polycule, who has been endlessly supportive, as well as to Sandy, Kergiby, Fuzz, Dwale (may its memory be a blessing), and many others who helped with reading and keeping me sane along the way.

Thanks also to my patrons:

$10+ Donna Karr (thanks, mom); Fuzz Wolf; Kit Redgrave; Merry; Orrery; Sandy; Sariya Melody

$5 Junkie Dawg; Lorxus, an actual fox on the internet

$1 Alicia Goranson; arc; Katt, sky-guided vulpine friend; Kindar; Muruski; Peter Hayes; Rax Dillon; Ruari

About the author

Madison Scott-Clary is a transgender writer, editor, and software engineer. She focuses on furry fiction and non-fiction, using that as a framework for interrogating the concept of self and exploring across genres. A graduate of the Regional Anthropomorphic Writers Workshop in 2021, hosted by Kyell Gold and Dayna Smith, she is studying creative writing at Cornell College in Mount Vernon, IA. She lives in the Pacific Northwest with her cat and two dogs, as well as her husband, who is also a dog.

www.makyo.ink

Lightning Source UK Ltd.
Milton Keynes UK
UKHW020657170822
407432UK00011B/1713